# *LOVE, SEX, AND MURDER*

"Outstanding . . .               f
caffeine. . . . A g
can almost talk wi
and computer de             variety of
restaurants and mansions described with gusto. . . .
Entertainment law and the Hollywood power
game here fall under the lens of a graphic intel-
ligence. . . . Cameron [is] a first-class commercial novelist."
### —*Kirkus Reviews*

"Amazing book. I read it straight through the
night. I had to know how it ended before I could
sleep."
### —Joely Fisher, star of ABC's *Ellen*

"Not since *Looking for Mr. Goodbar* has the life
of a single woman been so chillingly portrayed."
### —Rona Barrett

"Experience erotic intercourse as you've never
known possible!"
### —Victoria Principal

*more . . .*

"A gripper... [a] richly researched legal thriller ... [with] a strong heroine who puts most female lawyers on film or television deep in the shade."
—*The Hollywood Reporter*

"Sue Grafton, look out! Here comes America's next great mystery novelist. Sue Cameron has written a gripping contemporary thriller packed with suspenseful, unexpected twists, hot sex, and eyebrow-raising Hollywood gossip. I couldn't put it down."
—Ed Margulies, co-editor of *Movieline* magazine; co-author of *Bad Movies We Love*

"Murder ... sensuality ... I love them both ... and Sue Cameron's LOVE, SEX, AND MURDER thrilled me again and again."
—Kim Novak

"Really has it all—love, sex, murder, cybernetics, Hollywood settings. Truly enjoyable ... and the heroine is wonderful."
—*Ellenville Press*

"Great book ... a real page-turner! The shocking ending captures the Washington, D.C. that few people know."
—Lynda Carter and Robert Altman

# LOVE, SEX, AND MURDER

Published by
WARNER BOOKS

Also by Sue Cameron

*Honey Dust*

Published by
WARNER BOOKS

# SUE CAMERON

# LOVE, SEX, AND MURDER

**WARNER BOOKS**

A Time Warner Company

This book is a work of fiction. Certain real locations, products and public figures are mentioned, but all other characters and the events and dialogue described in the book are totally imaginary.

WARNER BOOKS EDITION

Copyright © 1996 by Lurk, Inc.
All rights reserved.

Cover design by Diane Luger and Elaine Groh
Cover photo by Herman Estevez

Warner Books, Inc.
1271 Avenue of the Americas
New York, NY 10020

Visit our Web site at
http://warnerbooks.com

W A Time Warner Company

Printed in the United States of America

Originally published in hardcover by Warner Books.
First Printed in Paperback: September, 1997

10 9 8 7 6 5 4 3 2 1

This book is dedicated to Dr. Stan Ziegler and
Helen Kushnick—
Heroes . . . friends.

# Acknowledgments

I would like to thank the following people for being so supportive of my work: Larry Kirshbaum, Maureen Egen, Susan Sandler, and Debbie Stier of Warner Books, with a special thanks to Ana Crespo at Warner for helping me every time I needed it; to Jackie De Shannon and Marlo Thomas for their beautiful parties in my honor; to Dick Grant and Dick Taylor for their loyalty and brilliant PR efforts; to my media compatriots Jeannie Williams, Ed Margulies, Charlotte Hays, Mitchell Fink, Seth Baker, Helen Gurley Brown, Ann S. Moore, Jeanette Walls, and Cindy Adams; to all those wonderful segment producers and hosts who have made my talk show experiences so great; to Victoria Principal for her gift of the great title; to Norma Jean Almodovar for her "fowl" inspiration; to Lynn Graham and her generosity; to Stanton Optical for inventing computer glasses so I could work without getting headaches; to the Peninsula Hotel of Beverly Hills for sheltering me and pampering me after each draft of this book; to Connie Armijo for distracting me daily with her phone conversations; and to my special friends who are so famous that I don't need to name-drop here, and my dear ones who are famous only to me . . . I love you.

A number of lawyers helped me on this book and I'd like to thank Marcy Cox for her research on DNA cases, Linda

De Metrick and James Campbell for painstakingly helping me with every legal scene, David Colden for his comments, and the Honorable Judith Abrams for her general advice throughout.

And most of all, to Susan Shore.

# *Prologue*

The screams from her bad dream woke Nikki up. She grabbed the sides of her bed and started to cry, wishing she could be in bed with Mommy. It was her favorite place to be. Mommy was so beautiful and loved to play with her. Nikki loved the fluffiness and softness of the satin sheets and comforter. It was taking a long time for Connie, her governess, to come in. Her crying escalated to sobs. The darkness in the corner scared her. Monsters were coming out of it any second to get her. She had to escape.

She was sorry now that she had pushed to get rid of her bed with the railings. Right now, she didn't want to be a "grown-up." It was a long drop to the floor for a six-year-old. She crept to the side of the bed, took a deep breath, and jumped. The thud was muffled by the thick yellow carpet. Nikki cried automatically, but stopped herself when she realized she was okay.

She ran as fast as she could to her mother's room, down the long corridor of brocade-padded walls and gold sconces. The door to Lauren Laverty's room was slightly ajar. Even at age six Nikki knew what fame was. She saw Mommy's face on the movie screen a zillion stories high. She knew people wanted to take her picture because she belonged to Mommy and that she could never go anywhere without a lot of people around her. Everybody commented on how much she looked like a baby Lauren.

"Mommy?" the little voice said.

There was no answer.

"Mommy, wake up!" shouted the little girl at the lump in the darkness.

Nikki approached the bed and pulled on the emerald green satin comforter. As it fell on the floor she looked up and just started screaming, louder than she had ever screamed before. The screams echoed inside her head until the pain almost obliterated her vision.

Connie arrived, took one look, and, stifling her own screams, grabbed Nikki to her, covering the child's eyes with her robe. She wondered how long Nikki had been staring at the nude body of her mother, each limb tied to a post of the bed with a black cord, black spike-heeled feet at the headboard, with the final cord tightened on her twisted neck at the bottom of the bed.

# Chapter 1

No! No!" screamed Nikki. Her body was paralyzed. She couldn't breathe. Desperately she tried to move her hands to her throat to remove the cord.

Nikki's choking woke Meredith up yet again and she started toward Nikki's room.

Nikki's sobs were louder now, agonizing.

"I'm here, I'm here, baby," cooed Meredith to the terrified child, noticing the sheet was twisted around her right forearm.

"He was there again. The bad man. My arms, my legs, I can't move them. They won't work."

"Yes they will. Look," said Meredith, picking up Nikki's little foot. "See, it can go anywhere it wants. So can your arm. Want to play patty-cake?"

Even as a little girl Nikki knew her mother didn't like Meredith. When Lauren said the name she sort of spat it with the emphasis on the "th," which she took pleasure in drawing out. "Meredithththth," Nikki could remember, watching Lauren concentrate on painting a toe. Nikki was about the height of her mother's raised foot then and the dark shocking pink polish was memorable. "You can keep her presents, but we don't play with her, dear," said Lauren.

That's all Lauren ever said. "We don't play with her."

And now the six-year-old had been whisked away in the night from the only life she had known, and Meredith was her only playmate.

Meredith Easterly was married to an unassuming, rather remote dentist, Dr. Bill Malone. With the money she had earned modeling in her early years, she bought a thirteen-acre ranch in Carmel, California. She was smart, invested well, and never needed Bill's money, although he contributed equally. Meredith was a beautiful blonde with aquiline features and great bones. She was smarter than Lauren Laverty, realizing that the fuss of Hollywood, even though she could have had it, was not for her.

"C'mon, Nik-Nik, you come with me," said Meredith. "I'm going to take you to a very special place. Would you like to meet some little babies to play with?"

The child wouldn't speak. Nikki had only been at the house a few days since the murder, and she was still in shock. "We're going to walk over here to this pen. See all the wood tied together? That's how we keep our animal babies from running away. I want you to meet some special friends."

Meredith took Nikki's hand and opened the gate. She could feel the child start to bolt back outside as the furry little llamas came toward her.

"Here Nikki, listen to my sound. Here's how I talk to them," explained Meredith.

"Hummmmmmmmmmmmm," Meredith sang softly. "Hmmmmmmmmmmmmmmm."

"Did you hear it? Did you hear how I do it like a little scale? I start out low, then I go high and I end low again. Do it with me. Are you ready?"

Nikki was looking at her with some interest. At least Meredith was succeeding in distracting her.

"Hmmmmmmmmmm."

Meredith heard a faint hum coming out of Nikki.

"Good girl! That's how you say hello. Now look. Here's Sweet Pea, she's coming up to you. Stay still. Don't be afraid. She loves you. She's going to come up and sniff and tickle your face. It's so sweet. That's why we named her Sweet Pea."

Meredith had deliberately taken her to the gentlest llama of all and Sweet Pea didn't disappoint her.

Nikki giggled, she actually giggled with delight when she was nuzzled.

Thank God, thought Meredith, who was terrified at the prospect of raising a child. Meredith felt that Lauren never took care of Nikki in an organized fashion. Nikki needed routine, something she could count on. It would help to make her feel safe, and Meredith was determined to do a perfect job.

The main house of the ranch was two stories high in the big living room, which was the center of the house. In the middle of the living room was a big round stone fireplace with chairs all around made of leather and carved logs. Meredith and Bill's bedroom was on one side of the house. Nikki was much too young to be put in the loft bedroom above the living room, so they put her into a converted den nearby.

"Nikki, c'mon, this is it," said Meredith's soothing voice in Nikki's ear. "Time for our morning rounds. Your cocoa's waiting, and don't forget to dress warmly. It's a cold morning."

Meredith waited for the little girl down by the fireplace. Soon she saw her, all wrapped up in a little red snowsuit.

"Sit by me here and we'll drink together," said Meredith. "Doesn't the fire feel good?"

Nikki nodded.

From the moment Nikki arrived Meredith was determined to have her days start off happily, and she did it the same way every morning, figuring that routine would make Nikki feel more secure.

"Today's a very important morning because Pocahontas's leg bandages come off," explained Meredith. "Would you like to help me with it?"

"Will it hurt?"

"No, it will be fine. How about it?"

"Okay."

Meredith took Nikki's cup and her own and put them in the kitchen. "Look at you, how warm and toasty you are. I'd better get a big jacket. It looks really cold this morning. See the frost melting off the porch?"

Meredith took Nikki's hand and stepped out into the morning air. "Ahh, breathe in, sweetie. Just smell those trees and the beautiful air. Let's walk by and say hello to Hunka Hunka first." Nikki had been afraid of the large horse at first and Meredith wanted her to see him every morning to get her used to him. She noticed that Nikki was always a little bit afraid. She planned to have her get comfortable with the animals first, feel really good about being among the trees and the earth, and then get her used to humans. After what Nikki had seen in Los Angeles, Meredith knew she had her work cut out for her.

"Hunka," called Meredith.

Nikki hid her head against Meredith's leg.

"Oh, sweetie, he's a cute little guy. Take a look at him. He's your friend, see. He looks like he's smiling at you."

Meredith was relieved when Nikki lifted her head and

glanced at the horse. "Good girl! He likes you! Now let's go say good morning to everyone, give them their food, and head off for our walk."

Nikki put her hand in Meredith's and seemed happier.

The path they followed went all over the property, and sometimes they would stop to collect pine cones. Every morning they would end up in Meredith's favorite place. Cut out of the forest was a little glen with a stone bench that Meredith had made. Standing guard over the forest was a three-foot-tall wooden statue of St. Francis. Nikki ran over to him and touched his robe.

Meredith placed her hand on his head. "Good morning, Father. We ask you to bless this day in your way, as we bless it in ours. We give thanks for your goodness and we're so glad that Pocahontas is feeling better. Thank you for letting us be with your creatures and we love all that you've made of our world. We want every day to be as happy as it can be and we love you very much. Okay Nikki, are you ready?"

The little girl nodded.

"All together now . . . Our father who art in heaven . . ."

As time went by Nikki did begin to make friends with the animals. She came alive each morning and became more communicative and able to show some feelings by hugging these loving creatures, something that was not easy for her with humans, and Meredith noticed how important the St. Francis ritual was to her. Meredith hoped that Nikki would always start every day with a moment of prayer for the rest of her life.

But no matter how capable Meredith was of creating a lovely daytime for her, night was a different story. It was a nightmare for both of them.

Nikki hated the dark and she hated going to sleep. She soon learned that any cry would bring Meredith running.

"My stomach hurts," Nikki whimpered.

"Where, baby?" asked Meredith's soothing voice.

"All over. Can we play Pick-Up Sticks or something? I don't want to sleep."

"Why don't I read you a story. I'll get in bed with you. Just cuddle next to me and dream along with the words."

"No, I don't want to dream!" shouted Nikki.

Meredith realized at once that she had chosen the wrong word. There were very few nights that Nikki didn't waken her with nightmares.

"I promise you that tonight if you just think about the fairy princess, you will have beautiful dreams, okay? You're my little fairy princess, you know."

Nikki huddled next to Meredith as she began to read. In a few minutes Meredith could tell by her breathing that she had fallen asleep. Looking at this little girl brought tears to her eyes. How on earth was she going to help her? No one could erase the memories, and Meredith was exhausting herself trying. She needed sleep and she needed help.

"Wake up," said Meredith, poking Bill one morning at three-thirty.

He stirred and opened his eyes.

"I can't take this."

"What?" he said groggily.

"You sleep through every night like a baby. You leave early and go to work and come home, where I have dinner on the table. You spend about ten minutes with Nikki and then she goes to sleep. I, on the other hand, am killing myself hourly to make sure she's okay. I can't do this alone. You are absolutely no help whatsoever."

"I didn't marry you to raise other people's children, particularly a bastard child of your sex-crazed sister."

Meredith slapped him right across the cheek, something she had never done before.

"How dare you speak that way? Nikki would have no

family at all without us, and Lauren didn't plan to have herself murdered."

Meredith turned to see if the door was shut because she didn't want Nikki to hear.

"And keep your voice down," she whispered.

"You're the one who hated Lauren, don't tell me all of a sudden you're heartbroken," Bill shot back at her.

"I hated who she became, I didn't want her dead, for God's sake. And that child is adorable. It's hard work, very hard work, but she has brought some joy into this house for me." Meredith paused and looked at Bill for three or four long seconds.

"I need Nikki, Bill. I'm lonely. You've been shutting me out for a long time. I kept hoping it was just a phase for you, but you're still doing it. We just never talked about it. We're at a crossroads here and I hope you decide to join the family and become a little less self-involved. Perhaps if you spent time with us together you'd feel more a part of things."

"That may be," Bill retorted, "but I also think you need help from someone other than me. I'll try to make some changes, but you keep blowing off that Mark Ferguson. He was Lauren's fiancé and he loved her. He's Nikki's executor. The two of you should be partners on this. You shouldn't just cut him out of her life. Why don't you like him?"

"I don't know. I just don't want anyone who was a part of Lauren's Hollywood life involved with Nikki now. I think it would be a disaster. She needs to be totally away from that environment."

"She is away from it, but I think there might be some legal issues here as well as the fact that you need to establish some sort of relationship with him. He's going to be in Nikki's life until she comes of age, anyway."

"All right, I'll think about it, but don't take the focus off your shortcomings by discussing me," said Meredith.

Bill paused for a moment, thinking, and said, "Am I behaving like a jerk?"

"Yes, you are," said Meredith more gently. "I think it happens frequently to new fathers. They forget they're part of the family. Why don't you join us on our walk this morning?"

"Okay," said Bill. "I'm a jerk. I'll do it."

"Good. As soon as you get that down I'll teach you night patrol!"

It took Meredith a week, but she finally called Mark and invited him to Carmel for lunch. That way it would be a short visit with time limitations and he could go back to Los Angeles on the four P.M. plane. She debated whether or not she should have him at the house. His presence there might confuse Nikki. She decided to have him meet her at the Pine Inn, where they could have a little lunch in the Courtyard Restaurant with Nikki. Nikki had been there before on a Sunday with Bill and her and she thought it would be a comfortable place.

"Where's Nikki?" asked Mark, rising to greet Meredith on the patio.

"She's coming. I asked Bill to bring her here in about half an hour so we could talk."

"I miss her so much," said Mark. "This is very hard for me."

"It's hard for all of us. None of us asked for this to happen."

"I don't mean to be so pushy, Meredith, but you sound bitter."

"I always told Lauren that Hollywood would end up hurting her."

"But we've got to let go of that now and concentrate on Nikki. How is she? How are the nightmares?" asked Mark.

"Things are still the same," said Meredith.

"Have you given any more consideration to my suggestion of sending her to a child therapist?"

"Yes, I'm going to meet with a couple of them this coming week. I think we need help, you're right."

"Is she still waking up at night?"

"Yes, and I feel so sorry for her," replied Meredith.

"Lauren used to have nightmares, too. She would wake up in a sweat . . ."

Meredith heard the sadness in his voice. Mark Ferguson was so much more than an attorney to Lauren. He had loved her so much. He may have been in more pain than anyone over Lauren's murder, even though Meredith knew Lauren had refused to set a wedding date. She was almost sorry for him now, as she looked across the table.

"Lauren used to tell me about a movie she had seen as a child called *The Mystery of the 13th Guest,*" Mark recounted. "It was about a man who gave a dinner party and the thirteenth guest didn't show up. As each guest was called to the phone for one reason or another, the guest would fall dead after listening to what was said on the other end. The host had white hair and penetrating black eyes, and he would never move, just sit there in a high-backed chair staring out after each death. It was the face of that man, just staring out, not moving, that woke Lauren up every night. I tried so hard to fix it for her but I just couldn't."

"Mark . . ."

"I know, I'm sorry," said Mark. "Switching the subject back to Nikki, maybe I could come up soon for a weekend."

"I'm not sure," said Meredith. "You know I'm trying to keep the people Nikki knew in Hollywood away from her so she can rid herself of the memories."

"Maybe that's not such a good idea with me. You know how much we love each other," said Mark, trying to keep the edge off his voice.

"I do know that, but I want to try this for a little longer. Why don't we see how it goes with the therapist and get his or her input."

"All right. I'm glad you're seeing different people to make a choice. My instinct would be to pick a woman."

"Mine, too," said Meredith. "Oh, look. Here she is now!"

Nikki squealed with delight when she saw Mark and ran right to him.

"Oh my little darling," said Mark as he hugged her close.

Meredith felt Bill's elbow in her ribs. She refused to look at him.

"May I take her for a walk?" asked Mark. "Please?"

"Of course," answered Bill. "Walk down Ocean to the beach. She loves that."

Watching Mark and Nikki walk off hand in hand, Meredith started to cry.

"What's that about?" asked Bill.

"I just feel so sorry for everybody. We have such huge responsibilities here. My God."

After the visit with Mark, Meredith allowed him to talk to Nikki on the phone occasionally, and Nikki seemed to respond well. The nightmares continued, but in Meredith's opinion they weren't related to Mark's phone calls. She also tried to get Nikki involved in things inside the house as well as out. Meredith loved cooking and baking, which she thought Nikki would enjoy.

"The trick to these cookies is to add Raisinettes to the batter instead of chocolate chips," explained Meredith to Nikki, who was standing on a stool trying to mix the batter.

"You know how much you love chocolate, Nikki? Well just picture chocolate-covered raisins instead. You get a double treat with every cookie. Here we go. You just pour this bag into the bowl."

Nikki looked at her and giggled. She put a finger in the batter and started to taste, then looked back to get Meredith's permission.

"Go for it, sweetie, and while you're there, get some for me, too."

Nikki stuck her forefinger in the batter and touched it to Meredith's mouth. Meredith then put her finger in the batter and gave some to Nikki.

"Oh boy, isn't that good?"

"Yes," said Nikki enthusiastically.

"Now watch me take just a teaspoonful of batter and drop it on the cookie sheet and then you do the same thing. They'll be ready for your tea party in about twelve minutes."

When Meredith realized early on that Nikki was more comfortable in small spaces, she asked Bill to build her a one-room dollhouse out of leftover wood so she could go inside and play. It almost looked like a little Swiss chalet with eaves and molding, a split front door so Nikki could look out the front while still feeling enclosed. Meredith sewed lace curtains for the windows and bought dolls as big as she could get so Nikki could pretend they were her friends.

Inside there was a table set up with real china for tea. Along one wall was a stove and sink, and on the opposite wall was a little bed; Meredith had papered that wall in little roses. She knew it made Nikki feel better to be in there after one of her difficult nights, which were becoming more frequent, so much so that it really was time to call in a professional.

Meredith decided to make another batch of cookies for Bill. She wanted to whip it up quickly with an electric mixer rather than use the simple "Nikki method" of stirring it with a wooden spoon and counting the strokes. She reached way back in the drawer where the cord should be, smashing around some utensils. She found the beaters, but no cord. Frustrated, she started to tear the kitchen apart, and after a minute or two realized that her behavior was excessive. What was upsetting her so much about Nikki? she thought to herself. Was it that she was stuck now being a parent?

Was she upset that her sister died? Of course she was sad about Lauren, but she had to admit that there was a peculiar feeling of gratefulness . . . not for her sister's death, but because it proved Meredith was right about leaving Hollywood herself. That it was insanity to live that life. She was glad Nikki was with her. She was confident that Nikki would have a better life being raised in Carmel. She would have better values, be less troubled eventually. Maybe things do work out for the best.

Dr. Carol Stanley was in her late thirties. She was a tiny woman with a mass of brown curly hair, deep brown eyes that were automatically sympathetic, and a smile the size of Cleveland. Her office was on Dolores, a side street off of Ocean Avenue, the main drag of Carmel. It was a residential area with quaint, almost Hansel-and-Gretel-looking houses. Dr. Stanley's office was in the guest house behind her home.

"My house, my house, it looks like my dollhouse!" exclaimed Nikki when she saw Dr. Stanley's office.

Meredith was delighted. "Dr. Stanley is a very nice lady who is going to be our friend. We can talk to her about things that are bothering us, or we can just come here and play. You do whatever you want," said Meredith, using the words that Dr. Stanley had suggested.

Inside Dr. Stanley's guest house it looked like a child's playland. It was furnished with big comfortable pillows instead of hard, imposing chairs. Dolls, toys, crayons, finger paints, hand puppets, all in bright primary colors, were scattered throughout the room.

"Hi, Nikki, it's so nice to meet you," said Dr. Stanley. "Call me Carol. Is it okay if you meet some of my friends and Meredith waits outside? I want us to play together. She doesn't mind."

"Okay," said Nikki, excited by all the new things.

Dr. Stanley told Meredith to be back in an hour.

"Who's this?" asked Nikki, holding up a doll with long blond hair and a white dress.

"That's Missy."

"She looks like my Mommy," said Nikki as she put her down and went over to the crayons.

Dr. Stanley was amazed that Nikki had brought up Lauren so quickly, but she didn't push it.

"Would you like to draw something?"

"You too," said Nikki.

"Okay," said Dr. Stanley. She sat down to play with Nikki and then gently draw her into conversation.

"Do you like where you live, Nikki?"

"I have a pretty room, but I don't like it at night."

"Why not?"

"Bad people are there."

"Who are they?"

"They want to hurt me. Look at my sky. Bad night."

Nikki showed her a crude picture of a house surrounded by black.

After an hour she left Nikki inside and met with Meredith in the waiting room.

"She's such a sweet child. It's tragic that her head is filled with evil at this age. It's going to take time. I can help her, but she must grow to trust me. It's obvious that there's a dark side to her, and it's too early to tell whether it was there before the murder and intensified by it, or was created because of the murder. For most of the session she was adorable. She's a sunny little girl, the kind any mother would want to have. But we're going to have to help her overcome what's going on inside. You're doing what's best for her. Just keep being positive and showing her fun things. Make sure you talk to her school and make the teacher aware of who she is, and that no one should ever bring up the subject of Lauren Laverty."

"I've already done that, and they say she has a good time there and talks readily with people. She's very friendly," said Meredith.

"This really will be the beginning of her trying to understand what has happened to her. It will happen slowly, and obviously I'll be very gentle, but in order for her to be able to deal with life and grow up to be a healthy adult, she's going to have to start the process now."

"I understand," said Meredith, "but it makes me nervous."

"This is a difficult situation, but it will turn out all right, you'll see." Dr. Stanley took Meredith's hand and squeezed it with confidence.

Despite the sessions with Dr. Stanley, the nightmares didn't stop. As the months went by it was easier for Meredith to sleep in Nikki's room. That way they would both get at least some sleep. The school reported to Meredith that Nikki was beginning to have problems communicating. If asked a direct question she would become indecisive, start to fidget, and stammer slightly. Dr. Stanley said that it would go away in time, after they conquered the nightmares.

"Not dead! Not dead! No!" screamed Nikki into the night.

She was now in the second grade and Meredith had long since returned to sleeping in her own room. For a while the nightmares abated. They didn't occur at all for a few months, then they'd come back only sporadically. But Meredith had never heard her say those words before.

She ran into the room where Nikki was crying hysterically.

Nikki was doubled over in the fetal position, saying over and over again, "The bad man is hurting me, the bad man is hurting me . . . dead like Mommy."

"No, he's not, darling. It's just a dream," said Meredith soothingly as she covered Nikki's body with her own.

"Yes he is. The man who hurt Mommy," wailed Nikki. "Help me!"

"Don't worry, I'll stay right here. Nobody's going to hurt you ever, I promise," said Meredith, trying to keep the vengeance out of her voice.

Meredith slept with her for the rest of the night, her heart breaking over Nikki's pain.

"I expected this," said Dr. Stanley calmly over the phone. "It's a natural progression. It does get worse before it gets better. You need to be prepared for that. I will get through to her. Remember, the nightmares went away for a long time. We are making progress. But she will always be damaged by the murder; she has to learn to live with it and not be afraid. That takes time. As she matures it will get easier and easier."

It had been six months since Mark had come for a visit. It didn't break Meredith's heart that he was such a hotshot Hollywood lawyer that he didn't have a lot of free time. An occasional weekend was fine for her. Nikki seemed to like being around him, but it brought up so many questions about Lauren, and Meredith didn't think that was good. Dr. Stanley said it was all right though, so she went along with it.

Despite her mixed feelings toward him, she understood what Lauren saw in him. Mark was six-foot-two with an athletic build, black hair, and impeccable taste in clothes. He had very thick eyebrows and thick lips that Meredith had to admit were sexy. He was only one of Lauren's many romantic attachments, and she knew that it drove him crazy. Even when they got engaged Meredith knew they would never get married. But Mark remained loyal to the end, and he loved Nikki with all his heart.

Mark's presence made Meredith wonder about Nikki's father, but Lauren would never tell anyone who it was, yet another problem that Lauren created. Meredith realized her resentment was showing and she stopped it. She wanted

Nikki to have a good time, and Mark was only going to be around for two days.

Nikki loved showing Mark around the property. She took him on the morning walk, showed him her favorite flowers, the drawings in her room, and introduced him to all the animals.

"You've done a great job with her, Meredith," he said when Nikki was out of the room. "She's so happy and well-adjusted. I'm very grateful to you."

"We are in a good period again. The doctor explained to me that the good periods will keep getting longer and the bad ones will decrease. That seems to be happening, thank God. I hated seeing her so tortured. And I must say, she loves being around you. I've never seen her as animated as she was today at the Tuck Box. She loves that little restaurant, but today she was beaming because of you. She loves to show you everything."

"Obviously I love being with her and wish I could come up more. It's hard on me, though. Isn't it hard for you to see her every day? She looks so much like Lauren."

"It's harder for you, I'm sure," answered Meredith.

Nikki was back. "Uncle Mark, come look at my doll-house. I want you to have tea."

Mark smiled at Meredith and took Nikki's hand. The setting for the little house was idyllic, surrounded by trees with its own little flower garden in front.

It was impossible for him to fit into the house. He crawled on his hands and knees to get through the door, and he would have to remain in that position, since he could not stand up.

Nikki was chattering away, introducing him to her dolls and "pouring" tea. Mark was elated to see her have a good time. He would have stayed in that uncomfortable position forever if it gave her pleasure.

He looked around the house at the craftsmanship and told

himself he must compliment Meredith and Bill on the beautiful job. His eyes wandered over to the little bed and the teddy bears and rabbits on it. For a flash of a second he thought he saw something odd. Not wanting to alarm Nikki, he crawled as far to the right as he could. He had spotted a doll's arm with an electric cord around the wrist just peeking out from under the stuffed toys. He gently moved the toys and had to contain his horror as he saw a blond doll tied to the bed exactly the way Lauren had been tied when she was murdered. He knew not to change his tone of voice, even though his body was chilled.

"Nikki, dear," he said very calmly. "You didn't introduce me to her. Who's this?"

"That's Mommy. I made her dead," said Nikki matter-of-factly as she placed napkins on the table.

Within thirty minutes Dr. Stanley was face-to-face with Meredith and Mark in her living room.

"Thank you, Doctor," said Mark. "We appreciate your seeing us on a Sunday."

"Considering the circumstances, it's the least I can do."

"We're so worried about Nikki," continued Mark.

"I understand, but as I have told Meredith all along, these things happen in phases. I'm sure you're aware that some children blame themselves for their parents' divorces even though they had nothing to do with it."

"Yes, I know that," said Mark.

"Well, take it one step further. Children blame themselves for all tragedies that happen to their parents. It's normal, considering what Nikki has gone through, that she would feel responsible. More than the nightmares, more than her own fear of being killed, the guilt of feeling responsible will be the hardest thing of all to get rid of. I'm convinced that we are nearly through the first two phases. The nightmares have almost stopped. From time to time they will come back, but very briefly, and I can work on it with her. It will end, for the most part. But the guilt is a different matter. I will continue to work with her throughout her teens if necessary. But this murder was so horrible and so public, it will never be out of her life. I'm not saying she won't be capable of having a happy life, but you will see in various choices she makes that she'll never totally be free of it."

# Chapter 2

"When do I get to the good stuff? I'm sick of divorces. This is not what I went to law school for," said twenty-five-year-old Nikki Easterly, striding into Mark Ferguson's office.

"That's true," Mark responded. "After all, you've been out of law school for over a year. You should be in front of the Supreme Court."

Mark paused and looked at the girl in front of him. It still pained him. She looked exactly like her mother, five six, alluring, strawberry blond. Spunky, with just a few freckles on her nose. Lauren Laverty had played up the sexiness more and covered the freckles for the camera, but their essence was the same.

"I plan on it, just like it happened for you, Uncle Mark."

"Please, Nikki, it's just Mark in the office."

"I know that. We're behind closed doors."

"Well since we are, I can't tell you how happy I am that

you came to work here. In fact, I think it's the best thing that has ever happened to me."

It was no use for Mark to argue with Nikki. It never had been. The time they spent together through the years had led to this point now. It shouldn't have surprised him that she wanted to become a lawyer. She was bright and she had a strong drive for justice, but he needed to break her in just like every new lawyer.

"Let's get back to the subject at hand. Carly Singleton is one of our biggest clients. Her series profits give us over $200,000 a year in legal fees," said Mark.

"I understand that, but she's an idiot," said Nikki.

Mark sighed and sank into his burgundy leather chair.

"Nikki . . ."

"I know what you're going to say, Mark. I'm supposed to be part of a team. You've been telling me that for over a year, but I can't help it. I have problems with idiots. And more so women who are idiots over men. Carly is a gorgeous, successful fifty-five-year-old. Why is she surprised that her teenybop surfboard-salesman husband has pictures of her and wants her to buy them so he doesn't sell them to the tabloids? What is she doing getting compromised like that? Where is her self-esteem? It's appalling."

"Are you through?"

"For the moment, but I'd really like to work on something more meaningful."

"Meaningful usually means less money," said Mark.

"Oh, come on, Uncle Mark, you may have your flashy Hollywood cases, but you're a first-rate appeals lawyer. Wouldn't you rather be working on something like the Valaderez murders? You loved that case. Getting innocent people off is the thrill, not sitting at Jimmy's. You know it as well as I do. We both know that's why I came to work here."

"You're right, kid, but that's the frosting. A law firm needs bread and butter to keep going. No matter how talented you are, you need to pay your dues and do the routine stuff. Think of this as grad school. I had to do it. Everyone has to do it."

"And how long did Roland serve in grad school?"

"What makes you think he's graduated?" asked Mark. He knew that there was immediate bad blood between his youngest partner and his newest lawyer.

"That's not funny," said Nikki. "I know he's a partner, and I guess he earned it, but his attitude toward women is unbearable. He looks at me like fertilizer."

"You'll learn to fight it. Wait until you get before Judge Hoffman. He's doing Carly's case. It's going to be very unfortunate. Now just get ready for the surfer's deposition. It's going to be a beaut. Hopefully we can scare him so much in here that we never get to Hoffman. Make sure Karl Johansson never knows what hit him."

Nikki was back in her office.

"Bev, can you pull all the clippings for me on Carly Singleton and Karl Johansson? I want to study them tonight at home. Also the videotape of their *Entertainment Tonight* stuff and *Lifestyles of the Rich and Famous.*"

"It's already on your desk," said Beverly, fixing her with the all-knowing stare that she was famous for.

Nikki knew what it meant. Beverly Piontak was a godsend to her. She was more than a legal secretary. She had known and adored Lauren, and was like Mark's sister. Beverly really ran the office, and it didn't take her long to realize that Mark assigned Beverly to her to be her guardian angel. Although born to wealthy Upper East Side Jewish parents, Beverly had chosen to teach school in Harlem and was a tough cookie. But inside she was a pussycat, a great nurturer. Her work was her life. Nikki even wondered if Beverly even went home at night. Fiftyish with salt-and-pepper hair, she had shrewd eyes that saw everything.

Nikki smiled thankfully at her and went into her office. Century City in Los Angeles was a special city development on land formerly owned by 20th Century Fox. The buildings, restaurants, theaters, and hotels were very modern. It was unique architecturally because there were connecting walkways or bridges above all the streets so you didn't have to take your car or fight traffic on foot if you needed to get to another building or street. It was like working at a New Age space station.

The offices of Ferguson, Miller, Rothberg and Schwartz were the epitome of elegance. They were on the twenty-seventh floor of a forty-floor building. Former president Ronald Reagan had offices on the fortieth floor. There was a private elevator for his use and the use of his guests. Ferguson, Miller had half of the twenty-seventh, not because they had hundreds of lawyers, but because the partners' offices and the conference room were so big. However, a firm of eighty lawyers was nothing to sneeze at. There was also a private dining room and kitchen with a chef who was there for every lunch. If no partners or associates were eating that day, he cooked for the secretaries. Mark Ferguson wanted a happy company.

Nikki's office was not one of the palatial ones. Those were reserved for the partners. But even her smaller one was impressive. It was an outside office in the middle of the row of offices. One wall was glass overlooking the Los Angeles Country Club. One wall was covered with filing cabinets. She had a brown leather couch and a glass coffee table, and her large wood desk. Her law school diploma was on the wall, as well as a Cézanne print of a blue mountain that she had always loved. It was simply a workspace, not a showplace.

Ferguson, Miller, Rothberg and Schwartz was a full-service law firm. It had departments for wills, litigation, real estate law, contracts, whatever a client needed. Once you were a client you never needed to go outside the firm for anything. Miller, a former U.S. senator from California, brought in corporate business, not necessarily related to the entertainment industry. Rothberg and Schwartz were general service lawyers. A man named Alvin Marantz was "of counsel," but he lived in a different city and Nikki knew nothing about him. They had many entertainment and private-sector clients, all quite wealthy. The firm had an excellent reputation for quality work, but it was Mark Ferguson's reputation that held the place together. He was a premier appellate lawyer. A master of trials. The tougher the case, the more he liked it. He would get calls from all over the country when people wanted to appeal a ruling. This was what attracted Nikki to the firm, and she had her Aunt Meredith to thank for it, whether Mark liked it or not.

As soon as Nikki graduated from law school and agreed to work for Mark, he rented an apartment for her in the Shoreham Towers, a beautiful condominium high above the Sunset Strip, one with a great security system and doormen. The condos had two views: the more expensive ones faced the city, Nikki's faced the hills. It was the least expensive unit in the building. Nikki was not unhappy with the hill view; at least the green reminded her of home, which to her was Carmel, not Hollywood. She would have liked more space, however. The apartment was one big room with a bathroom, closet, and a kitchen nook that was partitioned off from the main area. Mark saw to it that the kitchen was fully stocked with food and had new appliances when she moved in. He had the place painted a soft celadon green and put in matching carpet. Nikki liked that part. It was peaceful and didn't make things seem so cramped.

Mark rented furniture for her, too. A sleek gray leather couch that pulled out into a bed, a cherrywood coffee table and matching end tables, a reading chair and floor lamp, a secretary desk that closed up like the couch to save space, and a wall unit with a TV, VCR, fax, and space for books. The decor was in good taste: minimal, not luxurious. Mark also made it very clear that after the first month Nikki was to assume all payments for rent, furniture, electricity, phone, and groceries. She was on her own financially, but she was hardly hurting. Her mother had left her a trust fund and Mark's clever management of the principal through the years had made it grow handsomely. Nikki didn't really care about money. She cared about work. And she cared about people who needed help: they were like the animals she grew up with.

Hanging up her clothes right away, and putting the dirty ones aside in a hamper for the cleaners, Nikki put on some powder blue sweats and got to work. She put the pile of tapes next to the VCR and the file folders on the table next to the black leather chair. She couldn't believe that Mark had picked out for her a reclining chair like old folks used. When she first saw it she laughed out loud at him.

"You'll soon thank me," he said.

He was right, as corny as it was. The chair was incredibly comfortable when she pulled the footrest out. It was a great place for studying. Nikki loved to cook, thanks to those many lessons from Meredith, and dinner was on her mind. Cooking gave her time to think and create: she was sorry that tonight she didn't have time. She put a potato in the microwave for dinner, and carefully prepared it for herself. Meredith's ingrained standards meant that even Nikki's baked potato had to be perfect. She could do anything she wanted with it. She could use butter, dill weed, and Parmesan cheese, or she could change the cheese to cheddar. She could just put fresh salsa in it, or she could go whole hog with butter, sour cream, and chives. Nikki was annoyed that time frequently forced her to use the microwave. If you baked a potato in the oven you could get the outside crispy and the inside fluffy. The microwave just created fluffiness.

Well, fluffiness will have to do tonight, thought Nikki. At least the butter and dill weed would amuse her.

She decided to watch tapes while she ate. The apartment wasn't big enough for a dining room table. The only eating place was the counter that formed a partition between the kitchen and the big room. Because she was going to view tapes she got a tray table and set it up in front of the couch.

Karl Johansson's smiling face appeared before her, his thick blond hair windswept by the gusts coming up from the Aegean surrounding the private yacht. It wasn't that private, though, for Robin Leach then appeared on camera. Nikki was watching a segment of *Lifestyles of the Rich and Famous*. Wrapped around Karl was Carly Singleton, wearing a purple bikini, oblivious to the possibility that her wig might blow off. They were smiling at each other as she ran her hands over his ample chest. Leach was doing a voice-over about the happy couple. It was easy to see why she was attracted to Karl; he was gorgeous, thought Nikki. But you don't marry that kind, she thought to herself. You just sleep with them. Nikki laughed at herself out loud.

She switched tapes and started watching the *Entertainment Tonight* coverage. It was of the big Christmas party that producer Cruger Fowler gave at Spago for the cast of Carly's show, the nighttime serial *Evolution*. It was number one in the ratings and there was even talk about it going to two episodes a week. That would increase Carly's salary to $250,000 a week, a fact that Karl did not ignore. In his lawsuit he claimed that his advice and nurturing work services furthered Carly's career and he was entitled to half her income, not only for the two years they were married, but for all future *Evolution* earnings. The show probably had a good five years or more to run, so the cost to Carly would be sizable.

Nikki knew that early on in Carly and Karl's relationship Mark warned Carly about getting involved, and Carly ignored him. When Carly announced she was getting married, Mark drew up a prenuptial agreement without even asking her. When he presented it to her she practically threw it in his face. Eventually Carly relented and had Karl sign it, but now he was suing to reverse it.

Nikki looked back at the tape. Karl was dancing with Kathleen Turner and winking at the camera. Nikki hated him and was furious at Carly for being so stupid. She felt that anyone could have seen through Karl. He was such an obvious, cheap hustler. No one of any repute in Los Angeles would represent him, so his lawyer of record was not a heavy-weight. Nikki felt that all she had to do was put him on the stand and he would destroy himself. The jury would see to it.

Nikki watched the rest of the tapes while eating Ben and Jerry's Chocolate Fudge Brownie ice cream. She was more convinced than ever after seeing everything, including some interviews with Karl, that he would self-destruct.

She took off her sweats and put on loose boxer shorts and a T-shirt. She hated the annoying but necessary process of moving the coffee table and opening up the bed.

As she lay awake she dreamed of the day when she would once again have her own bedroom as she did in Carmel. When she was a young teenager she moved from the small den to the entire upstairs loft, which Meredith had enclosed for her. Each night she would climb the stairs to the high-ceilinged room with beams and big windows. It was a large rectangular room, almost like a dance studio. There was room for her king-size brass bed, a library area with brick shelves for all her books, and the old piano that belonged to Meredith. Nikki loved to try to play and compose, and soon Meredith was giving her lessons. Nikki loved to compose: it helped her think and calmed her down. Nikki had been so busy her first year in Los Angeles that she never even thought about playing. But she thought about it tonight, and resolved to get an electronic keyboard. She could plug in earphones and play away without disturbing her neighbors.

"Research, research, research," said Mark as he paced before Nikki. "It's all well and good that Karl is despicable, but you can never trust a jury. You must always have that surprise up your sleeve. Throw everyone off with the unexpected. That's the way you always win. Find the one thing that no one knows about and spring it. It never fails. I want you to always remember that, Nikki. If you don't learn anything else from me, learn what I'm telling you today. It will take you through life."

Nikki was impressed by his insistence on this point and touched by his caring. He was the only Hollywood part of her family that she ever knew or would know. It was at times like this that she missed her mother and wondered what she really was like. The horror of it all was still terribly painful but she was more practiced now at putting it out of her mind. Carol Stanley taught her that. Practice, practice . . . each time it comes up . . . let it go. It's not your fault. Carol's words echoed in her head, and Nikki had practiced as hard as she could. But sometimes practice doesn't make perfect.

Mark was talking.

She switched her attention back to him.

"I'm going to call in Hayden Chou. I believe I introduced you to him when you first came here. Do you remember?"

"I think so," said Nikki. She had a vague recollection of occasionally seeing a young Chinese-American going in and out of a far office.

"He's the best," continued Mark.

"The best what?" asked Nikki.

"Hayden's a lawyer who became a special investigator with amazing computer skills. He's been my secret weapon for years and now he will be yours."

Mark went back to his desk and buzzed his secretary, Penny Bruskoff.

"Would you ask Hayden to come in, please?"

"Hello Mark," said Hayden, nodding to Nikki as he passed her.

"Hayden, you've met Nikki Easterly before, haven't you?"

Hayden smiled at Nikki and really studied her face.

He wasn't going to give just a casual "Oh, yes, how are you" unless it was true. He extended his hand and said warmly, "We've only actually seen each other but never been formally introduced. It's very nice to meet you."

Hayden was wearing a light gray glen plaid sports jacket with light gray pants and cordovan loafers. Even though Nikki was sitting down looking up at him, which would have made him look tall anyway, he seemed taller than most people of Asian descent. She stood up to shake his hand and he was indeed six feet to her five feet six.

Nikki had seen the movie *The Last Emperor* ten times because of its beauty and her fascination with China and Eastern religions, but, more important, because she thought John Lone was one of the most gorgeous men she had ever seen. Hayden could have been his twin. Nikki thought of the scenes in Europe with Lone, so dashing in three-piece suits and tuxedos—the epitome of elegance and taste. He looked just like an Ivy League graduate and so did Hayden. He was casual about it and very comfortable with himself.

"Where did you go to school?" slipped out of Nikki's mouth.

"Princeton, for undergrad and law," he answered politely. "And then Yale's School of Criminal Science."

"I'm sorry," said Nikki. "I'm very happy to meet you, too. I don't know why I've started interviewing you already. Forgive me."

They both sat down.

"You're a lawyer, that's all," he said easily and then laughed.

Mark explained Carly's case to Hayden and what it needed. He understood completely and was ready to get started.

"Nikki's taking the lead on this one so I want you to work together. It's about time she sees the other side of the law. You know what I mean, Hayden."

"Yes, sir, it will be my pleasure."

Hayden turned to Nikki and said, "Are you ready to go on a hunt? I'll pick you up at seven-thirty. Shoreham Towers, right?"

He was good, thought Nikki.

Roland Bixby closed his door quickly, hoping that Hayden wouldn't notice. He was very disturbed. Why was Nikki Easterly suddenly getting the Hayden treatment from Mark? Her work in the office had been good. He had to concede that she was a bright lawyer, although young in the trade. He was furious when Mark gave her Carly. Carly should have been his. He'd endured enough lunches with her, he thought, to be rewarded by Mark. He was a partner after all, and had been for the past five years. He didn't want any new partners, not for a long time. He was the Golden Boy.

He was approaching thirty-six and in his opinion was starting the prime of his killer-lawyer phase. He had done everything right. He had concentrated on making himself into the perfect man, the perfect lawyer. He was embarrassed about having gone to Southwestern Law School. It was a decent school in Los Angeles, but it was far from Ivy League. It was for people who couldn't get into USC or UCLA or Stanford. It galled him that Nikki graduated from Boalt, the law school at Berkeley. Even though it was a public school, everyone knew the brightest kids went there, and

Nikki could have afforded USC or Stanford if that was where she had wanted to go.

Roland didn't have any inheritance. His name wasn't even Roland. He changed it from Roy when he went to get a job at thirteen bagging groceries in Gardena, very much a lower-middle-class suburb of Los Angeles that was half Hispanic. His father worked in an aerospace factory on an assembly line. His mother was a teacher, and that made all the difference. She instilled in him the desire to succeed, but he knew he needed money to really make it the way he wanted it, and he knew he was smart.

He was a voracious reader of the classics and learned manners from Henry James novels. He learned style by watching old Cary Grant and David Niven movies late at night. He knew his mother was watching him study. She didn't bother him when he changed his name. He was the only kid at the market who wore pressed white shirts and ties, black or khaki slacks. He had only two white shirts and two pairs of slacks and he was responsible for washing and pressing them, a task he did happily. He had never owned a pair of jeans. He was fastidious about everything. His hair never changed according to fads. He was blessed with rich-looking chocolate brown hair that he wore like Peter O'Toole in *Lawrence of Arabia*: the sweep in the front from the part to his ear was one length, and the rest was cut properly short. It was very European and very "royal."

While he got a scholarship to Cal State Long Beach, thanks to his good grades and his mother's connections, he wanted to ensure the rest of his career. In college he had managed to earn enough money for two sport coats to add to his wardrobe, a navy blue blazer and a black and white delicate shadow plaid. If you didn't see him every day, you would think he was a millionaire, the way he looked, walked, and carried himself. People were attracted to him because of his air of sophistication. He had his act down.

Women were drawn to him, thinking he was their knight in shining armor, but he wasn't interested. Women weren't the people in the world who had the money. It was the men. That's what he'd concentrate on, or at least that's how he rationalized his desires originally. He'd get his own personal scholarship to law school. No need to panic.

Nikki was wrapped in a towel, her hair soaking wet, when her doorbell rang. It could only be one person, she thought. No one from the outside could get into the building because of security, and there was only one person inside the building who felt comfortable enough to show up unannounced.

"Hi Joely."

"Babe!" Joely almost yelled as she gave Nikki a high five and breezed into the apartment.

"Gym time again?" asked Nikki, who was always teasing Joely about her obsessiveness over her body.

"No, I was pouring tea at the Regent Beverly Wilshire," she answered flatly, standing there in a leotard and tights with a towel around her neck.

"Well, it's working," Nikki deadpanned as she looked Joely up and down. Joely was drop-dead divine. She was five eight, weighed 110, and had naturally curly blond hair, hazel eyes, perfect nose, and a rosebud mouth. She was hysterically funny and had what Nikki called "The Body of Death"—38-23-36. At twenty-three she was two years younger than Nikki, but much wiser in the ways of the world.

"More research and baked potatoes tonight, babe? Gonna have a hot one?"

"Very funny," said Nikki, drying her hair. She had liked Joely Graham from the moment they met. She was very different from anyone she had ever liked. Joely was sweet and silly. She was on earth to have a good time.

"I'm going out," replied Nikki, "but it's business."

"Naturally."

Joely sat down on the couch, her feet on the coffee table.

"Did I tell you I've nominated you to be an honorary nun? I think you qualify. I've known you over a year and I've never seen you with anything—man, woman, goat. You never go to my parties or out clubbing with me . . . well, there was that one time at Nicky Blair's . . ."

"And that was enough! I've never seen such a clientele. It was straight out of a movie . . . guys in shiny suits and women who look like—"

"Okay, okay, but we're not all bad," said Joely. She knew Nikki was aware that she took money from time to time for her efforts, but she wasn't official. It was her choice. She belonged to no one.

"So what's up, babe?"

"I can't tell you."

"Ah ha! One of those cases."

"Maybe," said Nikki, putting on a black pants suit, a white silk blouse accented by a red, white, and black silk scarf. "Actually you might be able to help. You know this is confidential. I have to be able to trust you."

"Honey, the information my brain has inside is worth a fortune. Just the names from the As to the Cs could get me offed. I know how to keep my mouth shut."

"Do you know Karl Johansson?"

"The Blond Bumshell?"

Nikki's ears perked up. "Then you *do* know him, don't you!"

"Sure, all the girls do. He's quite a number. Was available for both guys or girls. A high price, too."

"I love this," squealed Nikki. "You're not leaving this apartment until you tell me everything."

By the time Nikki met Hayden at the bar at Le Dôme she was ready for bear. Le Dôme was the perfect spot. Hayden did not suggest it by accident. It used to be one of those Hollywood nightclubs in the 1940s with gambling in the back. Today it was a very chic restaurant frequented by major show business figures. At lunch it was deal-making heaven—all the regulars had their own tables almost assigned like in a business cafeteria. By night it turned even hipper, particularly the bar, peppered by characters you never really wanted to know unless you were in Joely's business, or the business of nailing others with information.

The white stucco building looked Greco-Roman, with all glass walls facing both the Sunset Strip as well as the city in the back of the restaurant. The plush carpet was dark, dark green, the tables glass with purple velvet chairs. The bar took up the center of the restaurant and was round like a wheel with the chairs all around the perimeter. If you were a people addict this was your place. There was always something for everyone.

"You look great, Nikki," said Hayden.

"Thanks. I hope that means I look like I don't belong here."

"Point well taken," said Hayden. "You'll make it through."

"It won't be that bad, will it?"

"I just hate these phonies. They're all dressed up in designer labels and they don't have any money in the bank," Hayden went on. "I'd rather hang out with hardened criminals, in a way. At least they're not pretending to be something they're not."

He took a sip of his drink.

"Club soda," he said. "Work."

"I'll have a Coke," said Nikki.

"It's better if you don't. People mistake my club soda for vodka tonic. They need to think you're drinking with them. A Coke is too recognizable. Will you settle for a ginger ale? They'll think it's scotch and soda."

"My my, all these little tricks."

"Well, Mark told me to show you the ropes. See that couple at the table under the arch?" Hayden nodded toward a man in a baggy black silk suit with his hair in a ponytail and a statuesque brunette in a red scoopneck dress.

"Of course."

"Well, he's a so-called producer who came from France three years ago. He had a lot of money and bought his way into some independent deals. Hired a press agent to get him in all the columns. He bought his women the same way. Had six of them living in his house at one time, gave parties with cocaine in silver bowls on the coffee table. Got the girls hooked and then used them for prostitutes. He gave up the party girl operation when his producing career got going, but he still gives those girls small parts in his movies. Now when he parties it's more for his productions. The cocaine has moved to the back room. I found a picture of him with Karl in the files at the *Times*. It was when Karl first arrived in L.A. It won't be that hard to prove that Karl is a bad character, but we also must come up with evidence that he deliberately deceived Carly. When the girl goes to the ladies' room I want you to follow her. Strike up a conversation, get in Karl's name. I'll take Meurice."

Forty-five minutes later the girl made her move and Nikki was on her heels. She even went into the stall next to her. Much to Nikki's surprise, the toilet in the stall was a French one with paper seat covers that revolved from a machine behind the toilet. You never had to touch paper to cover the seat. She was so fascinated by this that she almost forgot to come out when the girl was washing her hands.

"Isn't that toilet amazing?" asked Nikki.

"You must be very new here," the brunette said, fumbling around in her purse. "You don't mind, do you? You look okay."

Nikki wondered what she wasn't supposed to mind.

The brunette took a rocket-shaped clear plastic vial out of her purse. The bottom half of the cylinder had white powder in it. The top half contained some sort of release switch. Nikki watched as the girl took two hits in each nostril.

"Don't you just hate it when the guy you're supposed to meet is late?" said Nikki, trying to ignore what was going on and keep her in the ladies' room.

"I sure do. Most guys here are pigs. But they're pigs with money so it's more bearable."

"Well I'm furious. He came on so strong and he's really cute. I'm going to tell off that Karl Johansson if he ever shows up," said Nikki forcefully.

"You've gotta be kidding. He's flake number one. He hit up Meurice for a thousand bucks to get some girl an abortion and never paid him back. Stay away from him."

"Who was the girl?" asked Nikki, a little too quickly. She realized that if the brunette had not been stoned she would never have talked. Nikki was a little clumsy in her new role of detective.

"Sharon somebody. I can't remember. Gotta go now. See ya."

Nikki was ecstatic at her discovery. This coupled with the information from Joely could make a very ugly picture for Karl.

"No luck with Meurice. He's cagey," Hayden reported.

"The girl was a snap," said Nikki, smiling as she told him what she learned.

"What was her name?" asked Hayden.

"Oh. I didn't get it," said Nikki somewhat dejectedly.

"Right," said Hayden. "Lesson number one. Introduce yourself with a fake name and get theirs. They might be using a fake, too, but it's unlikely at this level. I could have run her name through the computer."

"I'm really sorry. I'll do a more complete job next time."

"Try to get any details you can—hometown, follow them to their car and get a license, anything."

"Got it," said Nikki. "You really love that computer, don't you? I haven't really gotten into them."

"I'm married to it. I have a mainframe almost as big as the FBI's. There's very little I can't access or find from my own files. It's not only my hobby but my life."

"Music and cooking are mine," added Nikki. "And speaking of food, my friend Joely told me to order spaghetti here. I don't know why. It sounds like a very ordinary thing to do."

"It's still a little early for Nicky's so I'll have Eddie get us a table," said Hayden.

Nikki watched him approach Eddie. Hayden was very handsome with beautiful thick hair. She wondered for a second about whether she might be attracted to him, but she gave it up quickly. Her attractions never seemed to pan out. Those things made her feel uncomfortable and she didn't care to know why. There were more important things in life.

"Well, now that I see the spaghetti I understand. This must be Hollywood spaghetti," said Nikki, eyeing the noodles in a white cream sauce with vodka and fresh beluga caviar on top. She loved how the caviar bubbles, smothered in the vodka sauce, burst in her mouth. "I don't care who comes to this restaurant for whatever reasons, I'll probably be the only one who'll come for the food."

"Food doesn't mean anything to me except as something to keep me alive," said Hayden.

Nicky Blair's, next door to Le Dôme, was also wall-to-wall people, but was truly bizarre. Nicky was having a costume party, but only the hookers were in costumes. The customers were trying to "win" them. One girl was dressed like a spider with webs painted on her skin. When she turned around it was obvious that the paint was all she was wearing. Another one had on a fluffy white cat suit with whiskers and fur ears. But it was a topless cat with a thong up her rear. She had glitter on her face, shiny white eyelids, and a tail, of course.

"I really don't care for this place," Nikki whispered.

"Remember, we're on a job, not socializing here by choice," said Hayden. "Nicky's crowd makes Le Dôme seem like the palace at Monaco. These women are really obvious hookers, and the men have very close ties to the Mob," explained Hayden, "but it's worse than usual with all these costumes. I bet these women have worn this stuff to bed a few times."

"No kidding," said Nikki.

"Try not to look like you're sniffing the air and getting a bad odor, okay," chided Hayden as they went to the bar and he ordered their usuals.

Suddenly a hand was on Nikki's back.

"Babe!" Joely cried.

Nikki introduced Joely to Hayden, who looked uncomfortable.

"Don't worry," whispered Joely. "I'm cool," and then she pinched his thigh and laughed.

"Did you ever know a girl named Sharon who was friendly with Meurice?" asked Nikki.

"Not offhand, but I'll check it out for you. Do you want to meet my date? He's a real live one."

"What do you mean?" asked Nikki.

"Help her out, Hayden, will ya?" Joely said, grabbing both of their arms and leading them to her table.

Nikki and Hayden were face-to-face with Ted Chapman, one of the hottest young movie stars, and David Sonnenstein, the producer of Chapman's huge hit car racing movie that was number one at the box office.

"Hang here everybody, I'll be back in five." Joely disappeared.

"Are you hungry?" asked Chapman, looking at Nikki with divine eyes.

"No, thanks. We ate at Le Dôme."

"Wise move. You don't come to Nicky's to eat, although the food can be good here," continued Ted. He paused and looked at her more closely.

Nikki knew what was coming and braced herself.

"You're Lauren Laverty's daughter, aren't you?"

"Yes," said Nikki, always uncomfortable when this came up.

"She was my dad's favorite. I think she was great, too," said Ted.

Hayden noticed Nikki shifting in her seat slightly and tried to break into the conversation, but Ted was too fast.

"It's really terrible what happened to her."

Nikki winced.

"I'm sorry. That was very stupid of me. It must have been awful for you."

"Had you been around in my mother's time you probably would have made a movie together. That would have really been something," said Nikki, trying to smooth over the situation.

Joely caught Nikki's eye and waved her over to the ladies' room, leaving Hayden to fend for himself. When Nikki got back she was smiling and placed a piece of paper in his hand. On it was written "Sharon Stanton, Batavia, Illinois."

"Sorry everyone but we have to go now," said Hayden, rising and taking Nikki's elbow. "It was nice meeting all of you."

Once Nikki and Hayden were in the car he said, "Now you're going to see technology at work. I'm taking you to my lab."

After half an hour she found herself at the east end of Sunset Boulevard heading to Chinatown. Soon he had stopped the car on Broadway in front of the Empress Pavilion, an upscale modern shopping center with all Chinese shops and restaurants. It stood out against the smaller, older Chinese shops that had been around for decades.

"This is a totally unlikely place for an office," said Nikki.

"True, but where else can I draw no attention to myself. I blend in. No one looks at me. I have total autonomy. And besides, I have everything I need here if I have to stay overnight."

Hayden took a special elevator key and let her in. They went to the third floor to a door marked CHINA EXPORTERS, LTD. and went in. He locked the door behind her and turned on the lights.

"My God, this place looks like the Pentagon or something!" exclaimed Nikki, looking at all the computers, database recorders, monitors, and missing the cot in the corner. "What's this thing?"

"It's a database and switcher, similar to what Compu-Serve or American Online uses. It has as much information or more, and I can hook into any existing database with it. Only a few government machines are bigger," said Hayden proudly.

"How did you get it?"

"Never mind. That's of no consequence," he said, almost with a little bow. "Now watch this."

He sat down and typed in what looked like hieroglyphics to Nikki. She knew about computers from law school and wasn't totally illiterate, but this was a lot bigger than the Macintosh Plus she remembered. She could make out "Sharon Stanton—Ill."

The machine started clicking fast, throwing up charts and codes. All the while Hayden pressed the necessary keys.

"Batavia isn't that big a town. We're lucky. I'm calling for birth certificates, driver's records, high school records, police files, the works. Then we check L.A. if we have to. We should be home free soon if we're lucky," he said excitedly.

Nikki's heart raced. This was all new to her and she loved it.

# Chapter 3

Joely Graham didn't think of herself as a call girl. She loved sex and needed money, so what was the harm? She was performing a service and was being compensated. Everybody was happy. She loved her condominium, her Ferrari, her Armanis, and her bank account. And she was independent. No madam for her. She wasn't going to get caught. She just accepted presents. She paid her taxes, too. Any cash or checks she received went into her corporation for her "image consulting" business. All her records were complete for Uncle Sam.

She didn't think that way growing up in Texas. There she was a little angel. Everyone told her she was perfect. She was the little blond princess, the cheerleader—and she hated every minute of it. She smiled throughout her childhood; it was part of her job. After all, a perfect person should always be perfect. She had been plotting her escape since she was thirteen, when she was asked by a local modeling agency if she wanted to work. She saved all her money from extra jobs after school. She studied the Miss America Pageant, seeing it as a ticket out. It was either that or saving for a one-way bus ticket and living expenses for six months in Los Angeles. She'd try both.

Joely would watch TV shows hour after hour and imitate speech patterns to get rid of her twang. She learned to sew clothes, meticulously copying designer outfits from pictures in magazines at her modeling agency. She spent almost every waking hour trying to better herself and prepare for her trip to Hollywood.

At fifteen her agency entered Joely in the Miss Seabrook Pageant. Seabrook was a little town near the Gulf. Her grandparents lived there, so the agency used their address and got her in. Every day after school she was coached and fluffed. Soon she was more at home on a runway than a regular floor. There were times when she just stood still, surrounded by adults discussing her hair, teeth, eyes, clothes, walk, posture, diction, as if she weren't there. She hated her life, but she was positive this was the way out.

The education she received going through the first stupid little pageant would serve her for the rest of her life. She saw mothers and daughters sleeping with judges. Money exchanging hands for good lighting. More favors for clothes, positioning in the contest on the runway, rubber falsies, fake eyelashes, fake everything. She was stunned. She saw smart girls playing dumb and ditzy—the men fell like a ton of bricks. It was a lesson and a technique she decided she would use. She came in second and won $100. First place went to the daughter of the mother who spent her time on her knees in the judges' area.

By the time she was eighteen she had been in twenty-three contests, winning nineteen, and placing second in four. She was a master at playing one piece on the piano, Van Cliburn reincarnated, as long as she never played anything except Mozart's Piano Concerto in C Major. Her prize money was accruing safely at the bank.

She knew it was nearing time for her escape. She had paid her dues and worked hard. She felt strongly that the Miss Texas Pageant was the ticket out. She believed her life depended on it.

All her energies were directed toward the Miss Texas Pageant. Winning Miss Houston was crucial, and she did it. Six weeks later was the end of the rainbow. Win Miss Texas, and she was on to Miss America. She had her coterie of professional sponsors and advisors now. Her clothes were made especially for her, with the tab picked up by her sponsors, a dress shop chain and the largest beauty supply store in all of Texas. They hired "interviewers" to rehearse her by the hour with different questions. They videotaped each hairstyle and gown . . . how it would look sitting, walking, turning. They did color tests with backgrounds, shoes, jewelry. Nothing was left to chance. They paid for a masseuse to be with her every day for two weeks prior to and including the event.

Joely did not expect Sherry Dee "Blonde Flip" Davis to show up with a new turned-up nose and breasts that could nurse Des Moines. Six weeks ago she was an also-ran. A terrific singer, Sherry Dee always gave Joely a run for her money, but she never placed higher than third. One look at Sherry Dee and Joely knew that tonight she was going to have to pull out all the stops. She shared a motel room with Miss Tyler and she didn't want her to see what she was up to. She snuck into the bathroom and stuffed her bosom with Kleenex. This was an old trick, one that she had never needed before. On top of her natural 38D chest, it should even out with Sherry Dee. But as soon as the contest parade began, Joely was blown away by Sherry Dee's new wardrobe. Joely was resplendent in her powder blue chiffon strapless gown with the sweetheart neck. She had won every competition with it. Right from the start that dress said,

"Here is your little angel." It worked every time. Sherry Dee had a new dress. It was similar to Joely's, probably deliberately she thought, but was white chiffon instead of blue, with little gold angels on the shoulders and a plunging neckline. It was a cross between a virgin and hooker, and Joely could see the judges go wild. She was unprepared for Sherry Dee's wardrobe. Usually the contestant who won Miss Texas would then spend the big bucks for Miss America. She knew their talent was equal so it would be a battle of wardrobe and personality. Thank God the swimsuits were regulation!

There was one act in between Sherry Dee's song and Joely's piano piece. If Joely heard "You Light Up My Life" one more time she was going to throw up. She tried to tune Sherry Dee out while she was waiting. It was much easier to concentrate during the baton twirler. From the applause Joely could tell Sherry did well. She put it out of her mind and played her piece over and over again with fingers on imaginary keys while she waited.

Then her moment came. The stagehands wheeled out the piano during a commercial and then she was introduced. She sat down, adjusted the bench, took a breath and attacked the keys like a winner. Her fingers were flying, her confidence soaring, and then she hit the high note, the crucial topping in the first half of her piece. It was flat. More than flat—it was as if the string inside the piano were almost lifeless. It so startled her, the judges, and the audience that she stopped temporarily. The second that she stopped felt like an hour to her. In that instant she knew that someone had tampered with her piano. She could either stop her piece, blow the competition, and wait until it was fixed, or she could continue like a trouper. She chose trouper and tried to avoid that note, or play it very softly throughout her number. The extra pressure was too much. It made her hesitant, she was rattled, her fingers were sweating and she finished as best she could.

She didn't have to look for Sherry Dee to know the expression on her face. Joely came in second to the mammaries. She and Sherry Dee locked eyes as that crown was placed on her head. Joely knew at that moment that she was capable of murder.

As soon as the live TV show was over Joely ran off the stage, out the door, and into the freezing February cold. She huddled against a studio wall, wailing. The pain was excruciating. Everything she'd worked for her whole life was in the toilet. She wanted to die.

She heard his voice softly at first, as if it were coming from a fog. It was saying, "Don't worry, you're the one who's the real winner," over and over again. She turned and saw a curly-haired man in his late twenties, with sandy hair, blue eyes, dimples, and an adorable smile.

"I'm Rob Sobel. I was one of the judges and I voted for you," he said.

"Thanks," said Joely, sniffing, "but it wasn't enough to help me."

"Why don't you let me be the judge of that?"

Joely just looked at him.

"I live in Los Angeles and I'm a personal manager. I have a couple of clients on sitcoms," he continued.

"You mean you're some kind of agent?" asked Joely.

"Sort of. I take care of the whole career though, not just booking jobs."

Joely didn't quite understand the difference, but she thought he was cute in his tuxedo.

"I want you to consider something," he said. "I think you have a special quality that will do well in Hollywood. I'd like to help you. I want you to think about coming out there. You can stay in my apartment until you get settled. I have two bedrooms. I can drive you to appointments. I think you stand a real shot. You're gorgeous. Here's my card. Please don't be too upset about tonight. Sherry may be going to Atlantic City, but you can go to Hollywood." He took her hand and kissed it. "I hope to see you."

Joely's mind was made up before he was out of her sight. It was where she wanted to go anyway, and he seemed so nice. He would protect her, help her, and she had her own money. It was a win-win situation.

"Just where do you think you're going?" yelled Joely's mother that Sunday morning.

"Hollywood."

"Like hell you are."

"You can't stop me, Mama. I'm eighteen and I can do what I want."

Joely looked around at the faded slipcovers on the furniture, the TV that needed replacing years ago. She couldn't end up like this.

"I'm sorry. I love you, but I'm leaving, and I'd like to leave knowing you wish me the best. You've seen how hard I worked."

"Well, I worked, too. Where do you think our money came from?"

"You, Mama. But I thought you did it for me. I have to go now."

Mrs. Graham softened a bit. She approached Joely, already holding her suitcase.

"You be an angel now, remember that."

"I will, Mama, I will," said Joely, hugging her mother goodbye.

He was at the bus station to meet her. He took her to his apartment on South Rexford Drive in Beverly Hills. To Joely it was a palace.

To Rob it was the best he could do in his quest to go north of Sunset, the choicest area in the city.

The apartment was very modern with all-white walls,

navy blue overstuffed furniture, and large mirrors on the wall. It looked very elegant and very sexy. Joely was a little concerned. Also, when he met her at the station he was shorter than she remembered. Cute, but short.

"Here's the guest room," he said, pointing Joely to a den with a navy blue and white checked pullout couch. "I've made room in the closet for your clothes and you have your own bathroom right over here."

Joely's eyes grew larger as she looked at the bathroom. It was all mirrored so everywhere she looked she saw herself reflected. The shower/tub had a clear glass door trimmed in chrome and all the fixtures were gleaming chrome. The effect was dazzling.

Rob was pleased by her reaction. He knew it wouldn't take long for things to progress.

That night he took her for a drive in his leased Cadillac and showed her the beautiful houses in Bel Air, the Sunset Strip, and 20th Century Fox. He could get on that lot because he had a client in a show there. What he needed was a really major star to attach himself to. That way he could become *big* time. He'd force himself onto her deals as executive producer, push his way onto magazine covers with her, and ride her for all she was worth. He was hoping that Joely might be his ticket, and he knew that she didn't have a clue. He would just see to it that she did everything he told her to—and he knew she would.

Joely had been sleeping in the guest room for a week when she heard him come in. She opened her eyes and looked at the clock. It was one-ten A.M. Each night when she went to bed she had deliberately been wearing pink baby doll pajamas, but he never tried anything. "It's about time," Joely thought. She was very confident about her bedroom capabilities. She had had a very good time in high school and thought nothing about sleeping with anyone who interested her. It was for her own amusement. She had no interest in whatever people were saying. It was her life and she was happy with herself. She was very curious to see what Rob's technique would be. After all, he was a big Hollywood manager and certainly had ample opportunity to develop it.

"Now," he said, slipping off his shorts and climbing under the covers with her. "God, I love that nightie."

"I've been wearing it since junior high. Is it okay for here or do I look silly, like some farm girl or something," said Joely in her most coquettish voice.

"It's perfect," he said, lifting the baby doll off over her head and climbing on top of her.

She puffed out her lips a little bit in anticipation of his kisses, but he didn't notice. Instead she felt his fingers pressing between her legs, but they weren't stroking or teasing, they were pushing them open, almost crudely. Joely shut her eyes to go along with it, giving him every chance to do what he wanted to do, but in seconds the fingers gave way to his organ plunging in and out without even caring whether she was ready or not. She decided she could handle anything and she thought of Marc Friedland, the center for the basketball team, and what his tongue did to her; she got very wet instantly. She heard Rob groan, and chuckled to herself because the idiot thought her excitement was for him.

Within a minute or two it was all over. He was rolling off of her and ready for sleep, totally oblivious to her. She was shocked that Rob, the first Hollywood man she went to bed with, was so inept.

The next night it happened again the same way. Then again the night after that. Each time it happened she hardly felt anything—it was over in a minute. In her mind she called him the "Two-Minute Man." It was fine with her. She didn't want him that much, he was a means to an end, and it was great that it didn't take up too much of her time. But she had to discover why she couldn't feel him. She needed to touch him, to look at him. If she made any attempt in either direction, especially if she tried to put her mouth on him, he would turn away instantly. She couldn't figure it out, but she was determined, and what Joely wanted, she got.

He started sending her out on general interviews with casting directors. There were several in town who knew that Rob had a good eye and they would give him a shot.

Joely needed to get her SAG card and some acting lessons. With her looks he felt she could fake it because she was so poised from the pageant training. The first few times she had to read for a casting director Rob saw to it that she didn't do cold readings. That was much too dangerous for Joely so Rob saw to it that she was given the script overnight and he set up an appointment with an acting coach to get her through it. It was a surprisingly easy technique because Joely was a fast learner.

Joely quickly realized that there were four kinds of casting directors: gay guys, straight male letches, straight unhappy women—usually failed actresses who were furious that they themselves weren't beautiful enough to make it and subsequently wanted to kill Joely—and gay women who were much too nice to her. The gay guys were easy for Joely to take. She had fun with them. The other guys she could flirt with, tease them, ask them for their advice for the "poor little newcomer," and know just how far to go. Usually they were friends of Rob's and it was okay. And then there was that nice Lori Openden at NBC. She was pretty in her own right, delighted with her job, and fair to everyone. Joely liked her. But Rhonda Kramer she despised.

Rhonda was someone to whom another casting director sent her. It was not set up by Rob. One day after a good reading with someone casting a TV movie, Joely was sent to Rhonda to read for a nighttime soap. She didn't have the script pages of the particular audition scene overnight so she ran to the studio to get them and have time to study them. Rhonda herself opened the door to the office because it was lunchtime and her secretary was out. Rhonda was about forty, overweight, with curly dark hair just beginning to show some gray, glasses, a nose that had been done too many times, and capped teeth, a reminder of her lost dream of being an actress. Joely sensed that Rhonda hated her on sight.

"Here, take these and come back in fifteen minutes," said Rhonda.

"Thank you, but don't you start again at two?" asked Joely, hoping to get more time.

"Yes, but for you I'll be ready in fifteen minutes."

She walked back into her office.

Joely was going to stay in the waiting room to study but she decided against it. The vibes were too bad there. She walked outside and found a tree by the commissary. It was a foolish place to try to study because everyone was walking by for lunch. But Joely began to enjoy herself.

"Want me to run lines with you?" said the voice with the French accent.

Joely looked up and saw a foreign-looking man with his dark hair pulled into a ponytail. He was slick, but she thought he must be important to be on the lot.

"Can you act?" asked Joely.

"No, but I can read aloud."

"That'll do. I have only five minutes left before I have to read for this bitch."

"I'm Meurice Castel. Let's hurry and I'll take you to lunch here after your reading, okay?"

"Okay," said Joely, liking his accent.

Five minutes later she was knocking on Rhonda's door.

"Come in."

Joely was led into a room with industrial brown carpet,

some worn furniture, and a desk with nicks in it. She had been to enough readings to know that studios spent no money on casting offices. Everything was temporary. Rhonda was sitting in front of a window at the peak of the sun. She was backlit and Joely could barely see her. She knew instinctively that Rhonda had placed her desk there deliberately when she first moved in.

Rhonda never looked up. She was reading the trades.

"Tell me about yourself," she said, her eyes never leaving the paper.

"Well, I'm from Texas and—"

"Get rid of that accent," interrupted Rhonda.

"I thought I had," said Joely, dropping the cutesy act.

Rhonda put down the paper and looked at her.

"Really?" said Rhonda. "Go."

"Go where?"

"Read. Let's do it."

Without missing a breath, Rhonda began saying the opening line without giving Joely a chance to get into it at all. Rhonda's line readings were flat and monotone, and she deliberately kept changing the pace—coming in late or early to throw Joely off. The whole thing was over in two minutes. Rhonda put down the script, picked up *Variety*, and waved Joely out without a word.

Joely slammed the door so hard the building shook.

Meurice was waiting outside for her. He started laughing at her exit.

"It's not funny!" snapped Joely. "What kind of pig would treat someone that way?"

"An unimportant pig," said Meurice. "Don't pay attention to the women in this town. Only the men. Remember that."

Joely would remember that, and Meurice too. She thought he had a funny look on his face when she said she was staying with Rob. Meurice gave her his number and said he would expect her call.

When she got home and told Rob about her lunch with Meurice he was furious.

"How dare you go out to lunch with someone and not tell me? I'm here to protect you. If you go off doing crazy things like that there's no telling what would happen. You're mine," he screamed as he pulled books off the shelf and started throwing them. "Do you hear me? Do you get it?"

His face turned beet red. He stamped his feet. More and more Joely thought he looked like a spoiled child. Since she was still basically alone in Hollywood, she needed him. Sex would pacify him, but he totally bored her. She had had enough of this nonsense: it was time to find out his problem.

She got her answer that night. To hold him off a little bit and make the sex last longer, she grabbed his penis so quickly that he couldn't move. He jumped and tried to get away, but Joely held on like a vise. Then Joely knew why. As she ran her hand up and down the shaft she was shocked to find that his penis was oddly shaped. The tip and bottom were a normal thickness but right in the middle it was thinner by at least an inch. Unfortunately for her and whatever other women he slept with, this failing on a most crucial part of his anatomy made him a loser, and he knew it. That's probably why he screamed so much and tried to throw his weight around. He was so dumb and arrogant that he never bothered to investigate other ways to satisfy a woman.

Several weeks later, when Joely saw all the cocaine he was using, she knew she would have to plan an escape. He would never be able to get her where she wanted to go. Plus his obsessiveness was strangling her. She could have car keys only when she had an interview, and sometimes he would drive her. He went with her to the market, to department stores, he followed her everywhere. There was no way she could pack and leave. She was afraid that if she called a cab he might trace her. She would simply have to wait until he had an important appointment without her. Left alone in

the apartment, she would have to leave on foot carrying her
luggage, but it wasn't too far to the bus stop. What bus
should she get on? Where could she go? Then she remembered Meurice and his offer. He would help her. The trick
was to get to a phone without Rob. No matter what, she
would pull it off. She had to.

It didn't take long.

Meurice's house was a huge Victorian mansion in Bel Air,
a suburb of Los Angeles where many movie stars lived.
From the outside it looked very grand, but when Joely went
in she noticed that it looked used, almost dilapidated. The
crushed velvet on the chairs was worn, the hardwood floors
were scratched. It looked like the aftermath of a thousand
parties.

"Come in, Joely darling," said Meurice, his ponytail
curled over his shoulder just so, resting on a white silk shirt.
"Welcome to my home," he said proudly.

Joely was glad to be there. She was glad to be anywhere
other than Rob's apartment.

"I'll show you to your room," he said graciously. "On
your right is the screening room, past that is the billiards
room. We all stay upstairs."

"We all?"

"Oh yes. You're not alone here. I have many friends who
come and go. You'll like them I'm sure."

"I don't mean to impose. I just needed a place to go for a
little while until I know what I'm doing. I hope I'm not . . ."
Joely fumbled.

"Nonsense," said Meurice. "I wanted you here. That's
why I gave you my number. This will be a good place for
you. You'll see. I have a feeling you'll be right at home."

Joely's room was covered in dark green flocked wallpaper
with a matching bedspread on the four-poster. Even though

it was meant to be elegant, again it was too worn-down to make it. She was grateful nonetheless.

"Make yourself at home. Take a swim. Relax. Dinner will be at nine tonight with cocktails at eight. I look forward to having you at my party."

Joely unpacked her things and put them away. She took a long shower and reflected on things. Rob would be wild by now. He had no idea where she was, but when he found out it wouldn't be good. She hoped Meurice would be ready for him.

She could barely hear the knock at her door above the sounds of her hair dryer.

"Hi, I'm Erin Evanson."

Joely recognized her name from the tabloids. She was a twenty-year-old beauty who had been with some lesser-known rock stars, and then with Sabre, the world-famous maniac lead singer whose group was also called Sabre. Joely remembered their fights, how she ended up in court suing him for battery and winning. She had wondered what happened to her and now she was at her door!

"Can I come in?"

"Of course."

"You're new here and I just wanted to make you feel less lonely. I've been here for six months now and I like it. It's a safe house and if you're smart you can make great contacts and not get into too much trouble," she explained.

"Trouble? What kind of trouble?" asked Joely.

"Oh, you know . . . the fun kind."

"I see," said Joely, only seeing partially.

"Guess who's coming tonight! Stephen Ball."

"You're kidding! He's gorgeous. He's one of my favorite actors," said Joely excitedly.

"And he lives up to his name, too," said Erin. "Well, I

gotta go. But I'll see you tonight. You know, Meurice said you were nice and you really are."

She's sweet, thought Joely.

Precisely at eight Joely descended the stairs wearing a short red taffeta cocktail dress. She was surprised how her pageant wardrobe worked so well in Hollywood. She had dyed satin heels to match the dress and a fake ruby and diamond earrings and necklace set. Her blond hair, even lighter now since she added platinum streaks just before she left Texas, was up-swept and secured with a "diamond" hair clasp. Five young ladies surrounded Meurice at the bar. She immediately recognized Erin, and was introduced to the others, who all seemed to be the same age and very good-looking, though fairly in-distinguishable.

The doorbell rang and in came four men. Introductions were made; Joely didn't recognize any of them or their names. The standard uniform seemed to be leather and turtlenecks, lots of gold jewelry, black slacks, and boots.

A waiter appeared with some cheese and crackers on a tray, which no one ate except Joely. She saw Meurice put out some lines of coke on the bar: the communal sniff sounded like a vacuum cleaner convention.

"C'mon, try it, Joely," urged Meurice.

Joely hesitated. "I don't know. I've seen what it can do."

"Yeah, but have you *felt* it?" asked Meurice. "Get with it."

Joely felt some guy's hand on her back pushing her to-ward the bar. What the hell, she thought. I am in Hollywood. Maybe I'd better . . .

"Do a two and two," Erin said and then demonstrated that it meant two hits of cocaine in each nostril.

Joely did it.

"I don't feel anything," she said.

"You will," said Erin.

Five minutes later Joely said, "Wow," almost to herself.

She felt her body begin to race and get very happy. She felt a sense of confidence, well-being, and she began to talk to everybody. She felt great and she wanted more. She was doing a line when Stephen Ball walked in.

Ball was the son of a well-known director who was instantly a star in his first film directed by his father. Ball legitimately had the talent, and his stardom was deserved. He had lots of thick black hair, a nose that was in a couple of fights but that only made him more appealing, and a body that showed he worked out . . . and those white, white teeth.

"Well, Meurice," said Stephen. "Who's the new one?

"Hi, darlin', I'm Stephen," he said as he shook Joely's hand. A jolt went through her body as their eyes met.

Meurice was pleased. He motioned to Erin.

"Stephen," said Erin, kissing him full on the mouth. "Isn't Joely sweet?"

"She certainly is."

Forty-five minutes later Joely had enough cocaine to totally kill her appetite. She wasn't familiar enough with the drug to know that that was what it did, she just knew she wasn't hungry . . . at least not for food.

"Why don't you let Stephen and me show you the rest of the house?" asked Erin. "There are so many rooms you haven't seen."

Joely was more than ready. She had never felt so good and they both were so nice to her, two of the greatest people she had ever met.

They passed through the corridor of bedrooms upstairs where Joely's was, and then crossed a second-floor lanai leading to a room over the pool house.

"Where are we?" asked Joely.

"Oh, this is a very special room," answered Erin.

"It's my favorite place in the house," added Stephen.

The room was very dark with black velour walls and carpet. There were pink spotlights carefully placed in the ceiling to highlight a couch area that was as big as a playpen, a little kitchen and music area, and then something that looked to Joely like a fluffy floor. On the coffee table by the couch a bowl of cocaine was placed as well as a small vial of pills.

"Help yourself," said Erin, popping one in her mouth and then in Stephen's. "This just helps you float with the cocaine. It's like a tranquilizer only a little stronger. First a pill and then another hit."

Joely was having too good a time to think. She happily took the pill.

Erin put on Rick James and Teena Marie singing "Fire and Desire." "Over here, guys."

Stephen led Joely to the fluffy floor. It turned out to be a featherbed mattress built into the floor. You just sank into it and luxuriated on the satin cover. Stephen lay down next to Erin and put Joely on the other side. Erin was taking off her clothes.

"Kiss me," said Stephen as he pulled Joely's face to his, rubbing cocaine that was on his finger on her lips. "You won't be able to get enough of me."

He was right. Joely's lips were a little numb so she kept kissing him harder and harder.

Erin was taking Stephen's clothes off.

Joely was going wild over his body, it was so toned, and covered with just the right amount of hair. She felt Erin's hands unzipping her dress and pushing it over her head. She liked the feel of it.

Joely was on top of Stephen now, licking his nipples, but Erin wasn't by his side. Joely still felt her on top of her, kissing her back and trailing her tongue around in circles. Joely had never been this excited. Erin slid off her just as she was really getting into it. Joely felt a trail of wetness on her back. She saw Erin's face coming toward hers and Stephen's, and suddenly Erin's tongue was on hers as they both went inside Stephen's mouth.

Stephen was writhing in delight, wanting so much more.

Erin gently pulled Joely's mouth away from Stephen's and devoured it with her own. She flipped Joely onto her back, grabbed her hands, pulling them above her head, and started to head down toward Joely's wet V. As her mouth traveled down, her hands found Joely's nipples and tickled them, at times pinching them as Joely moaned. Erin went even lower as Joely spread her legs.

Joely screamed as she felt Erin's tongue. No man had ever felt like this. Erin's strokes were quick and light and she knew just when to go inside and be harder. She was lightly rubbing her mouth on Joely's private lips, making her beg.

Stephen saw Erin rise up on her legs, her divinely round rear end edging up toward the ceiling. He moved in behind her, his giant erection looking madly for a home, and he entered her from the rear.

Joely felt the rhythm of Erin's tongue change. It became more intense and was pushing in and out. She felt Erin's whole body start to rock back and forth and she figured out what was happening. As Erin came, Joely held herself back even though she was as ready as could be. She knew there was more.

As Erin lay down Joely looked at Stephen and grabbed that strong shaft. That was more like it, thought Joely silently, laughing at Rob. She pushed Stephen down.

"Wait," he said gruffly.

Joely watched him rub cocaine on the head of his penis. "Now, baby girl!"

Joely jumped on top. His size was incredible. Her breath was taken away. Closing her eyes she was crazed over this fabulous roller coaster when she felt Erin kissing her mouth and caressing her nipples again. It was a pleasure explosion inside and out. Joely had never crossed over the moon before and now she didn't want to come back.

*  *  *

When Joely awoke sometime around one P.M. she was back in her bedroom, without a clue how she got there. Her nose was stuffed up and her eyes watery. As she got up to go to the bathroom she noticed an envelope that had been slipped under her door. Puzzled, she picked it up. What if it were a note from Stephen? she thought, suddenly getting excited all over again. Inside were five $100 bills and a note from Meurice, "You are a delight to have as a houseguest. This is just to show you how much you are appreciated."

Joely dropped everything on the floor. How dare anyone think that she was that kind of girl? She felt dirty and furiously ran to the shower. The hot water was cleansing and healing, covering her with absolution. She was a good girl, a beauty queen, an actress. She needed an agent, not a pimp, unless they were one and the same. That thought actually produced a laugh out loud in the shower. She felt better as she got out and dried herself off. She blew her nose, brushed her teeth, and walked back into the bedroom with a towel around her.

The $500 was staring up at her. She knew she desperately needed the money. She thought back to the contestants and mothers who prostituted themselves for nothing on many occasions, just the hope of a win. Joely now had guaranteed payment at something she loved. It wouldn't hurt her acting career, she thought. She didn't want to be a waitress. She liked it in Bel Air. She picked up the money and changed the course of her life forever.

Roland knew luck had nothing to do with his lifestyle. It was hard work. He was standing in his walnut-paneled dressing room in the house on Mapleton in Holmby Hills next door to the Spelling mansion, deciding between the Nicole Miller tie or the Hugo Boss. Cruger used to tell him he looked a lot like the Boss model. It had been a while since he heard that and he would have to do something about it. He never wanted Cruger to lose interest. After all, he could be replaced with a younger version. Tonight was his thirty-seventh birthday and he wanted to be the prettiest. In his crowd that would be easy because most of them were Cruger's friends and they were in their fifties. He looked over at the silver-framed picture shot the night that they met, sixteen years ago. That wasn't luck either.

He knew in his senior year that he had only three months to secure a scholarship for law school. He had put in all the applications and was waiting. He did everything he was supposed to. But that wasn't enough for Roland. He couldn't take any chances.

When he drove to Numbers, a hot bar on the Sunset Strip for men, he was wearing a navy blue blazer, white shirt, striped tie, gray slacks, and cordovan loafers. He looked right off the cover of *GQ*. Most men with money were attracted to that type. He didn't care if his quarry was married either; that might even be better, less hassle.

He could feel the eyes on him as he walked from the entrance to the bar. He didn't mind being "fresh meat." He found it amusing. That's why he didn't frequent any bar too long. It was never good to be old news. He spotted Larry, a model and former trick of his, at the other end. They nodded to each other. He liked Larry. Larry had some money from his print work, but it wasn't anything for Roland's future.

"Hi guy. You look good tonight," said Larry.

"Thanks," said Roland, flashing his best Peter O'Toole smile.

"I just stopped by for a drink on the way home. I'm having a little dinner party tonight. Why don't you come?"

Roland thought it over. In a second he decided that Larry moved in good enough circles and perhaps it might be a valuable dinner.

"I'd love it," said Roland.

"Come over in about forty-five minutes. You remember where I live, don't you," said Larry in mock seduction.

"Cute," Roland said in mock sarcasm as he waved him out.

Larry lived in "Boys Town," an area below the Sunset Strip filled with little two-bedroom one-story houses with only one bath, maybe two if you were lucky. But it was a good area, well kept up by the "boys" and a very respectable place to buy a first home. This was a neighborhood way above anything Roland came from, yet he had already turned his nose up at it. He would be North of Sunset or North of Nothing.

It was a nice crowd of guys, some in advertising, a few actors, a shop owner. At twenty-one he was the youngest of the bunch. He was having a pleasant evening, but he didn't feel it was going to lead to anything, until Cruger Delafield Grozbach Fowler IV walked in. Cruger was in his early forties and was president of the television division for Warner Brothers. He was a wunderkind, and the catch of a lifetime. Roland knew that he was just the right age. He was a little concerned that there were some models there, but he was just as good-looking *and* he was getting an education. Cruger would have to be impressed with that, he would just have to.

They ended up sitting together at dinner. Roland positioned himself just behind him in the buffet line and struck up a conversation.

"I wonder if there's any cream in the chicken sauce," said Roland.

"I certainly hope so," said Cruger. "It's bad for me, but then maybe I like things that are bad," he added, eyes shining.

"I certainly hope so," said Roland mimicking him.

Cruger laughed approvingly.

"I'm impressed. Fresh carrots and asparagus, and not just Uncle Ben's rice, but an Indian basmati. Very good," said Roland as if he were a food critic.

"Do you like dinner parties?" asked Cruger.

"I do when they're done well. It has to be the right mix of guests, excellent food, and a superb presentation." Roland knew what a perfectionist Cruger was from articles he had read. He was sure he was saying all the right things.

Cruger seemed very interested and Roland continued talking. Roland noticed that Cruger was a little overweight and that his sandy hair was thinning. He was decent-looking enough, thought Roland, and probably was more gorgeous behind his desk in that fancy office.

Roland could sense that others at the party saw the connection that was being made. Cruger was smiling freely and telling story after story just to Roland. Roland was determined not to go home with him that night. That would be bad business and bad form. Make him want it, thought Roland. Make him desperate. I'm the marrying kind. I don't lie down unless I have a ring.

And so the courtship began. Roland never let Cruger pick him up. They either met at a restaurant or at Cruger's house, a beautiful English Tudor in the flats of Beverly Hills, an area between Santa Monica and Sunset boasting gorgeous homes. It was one of the finest areas in the city, but it was south of Sunset, although the only acceptable area to be in if you did live south of Sunset. Roland made a mental note about moving north.

The presents started early. First it was a sweater from Carroll's in Beverly Hills. Then it escalated to a Cartier watch. After Roland began spending weekends at Cruger's house they'd go shopping on a Saturday and Cruger would buy him three complete outfits at Ralph Lauren's Polo store on Rodeo Drive. By fall, Roland's entire law school tuition was paid in advance and he had moved into the house permanently. He was driving a BMW convertible, having turned down the Mercedes because he didn't want to look flashy at law school. He had very little spare time because law school studies were time-consuming and Cruger took up all the rest. Cruger was very much a demanding "husband," with Roland suddenly in charge of the house, the parties, and the staff. Everything had better be run correctly.

Roland took his eyes off the picture and returned to reality. Now, as he was turning thirty-seven, and he and Cruger had been together for almost sixteen years, he was running the mansion in Holmby Hills, the Palm Springs getaway, and the co-op in New York. He had the staff cracking so he was free to concentrate on winning cases.

Life was easier for Cruger, too. He had given up administrative corporate work a few years ago to open an independent production company supplying television shows to networks. Currently he had three shows in the top ten. One of them was *Evolution,* starring Carly Singleton, and that's why it angered Roland even more that Mark gave Carly to Nikki. No one had a better in than Roland. Mark knew that. Years ago Cruger saw to it that Mark hired him. He had proved that he was worth the money. He was so good he could work for any firm or start his own. Maybe that's what Mark wanted, maybe this was his way of pushing him out. Well, he was not an idiot. He didn't want the pressure of his own firm. He liked being a partner and having his home life. But if he could talk Cruger into going to Weisberg, Wilson, he might even get a bigger partnership percentage, and Mark would go crazy.

Weisberg, Wilson were his biggest competitors. They had offices across the street from Mark's in Century City, and they had two floors compared to Mark's one. Mark's line was always that he wanted to give more personal service, so he didn't want to expand beyond what he currently had. That was partly true, but Weisberg constantly called Mark's operation boutique, which galled Mark. The companies' billings were approximately the same, with the same balance of big-name clients, but Roland knew that for Weisberg, Wilson the

AT&T-size operation was a big sell. They had offices in New York and London as well, while Mark preferred to travel to New York himself to do business. A former partner in Weisberg went to Universal Studios as president two years ago, also a useful relationship for the law firm.

Regarding his own salability in the marketplace, Roland knew he had good clients, but Cruger was the ace. His billings were enormous, and he held Roland's future in his hands. Roland realized that he had really better take care of business in all aspects before he made any fast moves. Getting to Weisberg wouldn't be hard; after all, Wilson was on his knees to Roland in the shower at the gym—that way his wife would never find out.

He walked downstairs to inspect things before the guests came and, more importantly, before Cruger did. The house was a Waldo Fernandez stone mansion on a hill overlooking the city. The most gorgeous spot was a circular side room with a veranda and a large picture window. There was a huge mirrored bar at one end, French doors leading out to the veranda at the other, with the large picture window in between. Opposite the picture window was a fireplace. The fresh flowers, a minimalist arrangement from Kensington Gardens, were on the coffee table. Nuts were in silver dishes. On the bar was Petrossian caviar in a crystal dish sitting on ice surrounded by toast points. No onions, eggs, or sour cream were in sight. Roland knew that Cruger felt that the only civilized way to eat caviar was just with a little lemon. Roland adjusted the lighting a bit before going into the living room.

The living room was a larger version of the den, with an even bigger picture window, a piano grandly in front, a walk-in fireplace, and the pièce de résistance, a small double-sided stairway leading from the front hall down to the living room. The area from the front door leading to the living room and den was a raised foyer, very effective for showing art. What made the house unique was that all the furniture was molded out of stone and covered in down pillows. Even the coffee tables were stone. The colors, or noncolors, were all beige and gray . . . natural stone tones, including the floors, which were slate. Some people thought the house was cold, but Roland loved it because of that. It was cold and hard and strong, just like Roland.

The flowers were placed correctly on the two coffee tables in the two conversation area groupings in the living room. Mendelssohn's Trio No. 1 in D Minor was playing. On one coffee table there were more silver dishes with nuts, on the other there was goose liver pâté with toast rounds. Roland had planned a lot of hors d'oeuvres for tonight and he didn't want too many things on tables. He preferred that hors d'oeuvres be passed.

"That's perfect," said Roland as he surveyed the dining room's Villeroy and Boch china, Baccarat stemware, and flower arrangements low enough to allow conversation. At each guest's place was a small blue Tiffany box with a silver key chain inside as a party favor.

"Well done, Chang," said Roland, entering the kitchen.

The houseman bowed, as did his two cooks and three waiters.

"Let's review it one last time," said Roland as he paced before the six-foot granite island in the middle of the kitchen. "You start with baby pizzas, plain cheese and one with prosciutto, followed by the fresh shrimp. Wait ten minutes and then bring the spinach empanadas, and then start all over again with the pizza. The salad is Boston lettuce, only slightly chopped, with tiny bits of grapefruit and thinly sliced avocado with a honey mustard dressing and toasted pine nuts on top. We follow with boeuf roulade, rice pilaf, and fresh broccoli. Make sure you pass the rosemary bread, and wait a good twenty minutes after you've cleared the main course to bring the flourless chocolate cake with crème

anglaise and fresh raspberries. I think that's it. Except for
the after-dinner drinks, which you already know about."

"Yes, sir. Everything is taken care of."

Roland wished the rest of his life could be taken care of
as easily as the food. A forced calm overtook him as the
doorbell signaled the first arrival.

"Nikki, you're going to love it," said Mark.

"I'm not very comfortable at parties," she said sheepishly.

"But this is our annual Christmas party. You were away
last year, you're starting your second year with us and I want
you to go as my date. You're in your office so much, I think
it's important for you to mingle with everybody. I know
you're not a snob, but in this town if somebody comes from
a famous background and they're aloof or shy, it's misinter-
preted."

Nikki didn't know whether to be hurt or angry, so she
didn't speak.

"This is all part of the law business. It's not just being
good in court or keeping a client happy, or posting huge
billings. It's about being part of the community, being involved with people, going to the right restaurants, the right
charity dinners, volunteering with certain organizations."

"I know you're right," said Nikki. "There's a part of me
that really wants to try it, to get out there, and another side
of me just wants to devote myself to the actual law and to
making people's lives better."

"It all goes together, Nikki," Mark explained gently.

"It does, but I have a hard time, for instance, having to
work on divorce cases or contract disputes. Who cares if
some of these spoiled Hollywood people need someone to
clean up after them? I want to do something important."

"That's good, Nikki, but I also want you to meet Alvin
Marantz."

"You mean there's a person attached to the letterhead?"

"Yes."

"I've been wondering about that."

"Well, Alvin and I were in law school together. He and his wife, Sarah, live in San Francisco, and he specializes in corporate finance. They're very special people to me. If it weren't for them I don't know how I would have handled your mother's death. They took care of me like family. That's why I always keep him on the letterhead. He's my best friend and an expert in his field."

"C'mon, we're going for a walk," said Mark, getting up and ushering her out of his office.

"Why? It's eleven-thirty in the morning," said Nikki.

"Well, didn't you and Meredith walk every morning?" asked Mark. "Let's go."

They rode the elevator downstairs and Nikki followed Mark as he walked across the bridge to the shopping center. They stopped in front of a man dressed up like a gondolier serving hot cappuccino from his copper machine.

"Two café mochas," said Mark.

They walked along holding their white plastic mugs and sat down on a bench under one of the few trees in the outdoor mall.

"Nikki, I used to feel just like you. When I started I was given the grunt work. As the years went by and I got more important clients, I realized that the work is all the same. Everybody is important, no matter what the case is."

"Mark, you're not going to lecture me about people, I hope, because I'd rather be working for some innocent person who doesn't have any money who's been screwed over."

Mark laughed. She was sounding like Lauren now, but he didn't want to mention it. Instead he said, "Everybody gets screwed over, honey. That's why the law is important. But in Hollywood we do play on a higher level. Maybe they're screwed over for ten million instead of a hundred dollars. The good news here, aside from the money we make, is that our high profile can give us the opportunity to do something really meaningful once in a while, even take on a case for nothing if we think it's important. That's why you have to see the balance of things and gain respect for all of it."

"So when can I get a case that's really meaningful?" said Nikki.

"I hear you, but while Carly's divorce may not be meaningful to you, it's very meaningful to her. You just keep doing the good work. I'll find a little case for you down the road, some do-gooder thing that will keep you happy. Just please take in everything that I've said and go buy yourself an Armani cocktail suit as my Christmas present to you and wear it to the party. We're taking over the Garden Room of the Bel Air Hotel."

"Oh, God," said Nikki.

"No, oh good," said Mark pinching her cheek the way he did when she was little.

She squeezed his hand and they walked back to the office arm in arm.

That nerve left her as she was preparing to walk into the Christmas party with him. It was a fairy-tale setting with tiny white twinkle lights in all the trees around the hotel. There were swans swimming in two ponds at the entrance. Multicolored Christmas lights were around every door and along the windows.

"How many people did you say would be here?" asked Nikki nervously.

"Well, our firm and spouses make about a hundred and sixty, plus clients and friends. I think it's about four hundred," answered Mark.

Nikki swallowed hard and began to fidget with her hair.

"Your hair looks perfect," said Mark.

"It's just this one spot here. It keeps curling," said Nikki, pulling on a forelock.

"That's the same piece you pulled on whenever I visited you in Carmel. It looked great then, and it looks great now. Relax, you'll have a great time. The only photographer in there is one I've hired. There are some newspaper columnists there, Mary Hart from *Entertainment Tonight*, and Connie Chung and Maury Povich. You'll recognize a lot of people."

When Mark and Nikki walked in, a spotlight hit them at the door and the orchestra started playing "Jingle Bells." Nikki was mortified but plastered a smile on her face. Mark waved to everyone, and soon they were engulfed in greetings. The crunch of people made Nikki very nervous.

Hayden rushed to her side.

"Would you like to come with me to get a drink?" he asked, eager to rescue her.

"Would I ever!" said Nikki gratefully, walking by a sea of tables each decorated with its own Christmas tree, lights, ornaments, and miniature presents.

"How many of these have you been to?" asked Nikki.

"This is my fourth, and I've always had a great time. See, over there is Barry Diller talking to Bette Midler. Bette's really nice, so's Paulette Wilde. She's really not a bitch at all, she's just crafty. She's Roland's client."

"Seeing all of this in one room is a bit overwhelming, but I suppose this is my baptism of sorts. I'd better jump in the water. Introduce me to Bette, if you would when we get close. I really like her work."

"I'd love to, and then I'd better get you back to Mark for a little while. I wouldn't want him to feel deprived, although it will be hard for me to lose you, even temporarily."

Nikki thought Hayden was really sweet. It was something about his voice. He wasn't doing a sleazy come-on number. It was genuine, and she was a little embarrassed by it.

By two A.M. when Mark dropped her off at the Shoreham Towers, she felt confident and happy.

"Everyone was wonderful to me tonight. I had a chance to get to know two of our tax department lawyers, the litigation specialist, Maggie in real estate, the political guys, it was really something. You're right, it's not enough just nodding to people in halls. I feel better, Uncle Mark, and it's all because of you."

"I love you, Nikki. You are the most special person in my life, and Lauren would be so proud of us right now."

Nikki was startled for a second, and then said, "I heard some people whispering her name a few times tonight as I went by them. It really bothers me."

"That's always going to happen," said Mark gently.

"I wish it wouldn't," said Nikki adamantly.

"Maybe one day you'll think differently and be able to attach the memory to something positive."

"Yeah, right," said Nikki dejectedly.

"You never know," said Mark, kissing her on the cheek. "Now focus on the good time you had and have sweet dreams."

Dreams, thought Nikki. That word is not my friend.

# Chapter 4

"At the most this will take two days, Carly," Nikki explained in the back of Carly's limo. Hayden, Grant Taylor, who was Carly's press agent, and two bodyguards rounded out the passengers.

"How many reporters do you think there'll be?" asked Carly as she checked for the umpteenth time her mascara in her mirror.

"Tons. You'll be on every newscast and on the cover of every paper around the world. I just hope we have enough bodyguards," said Grant.

"The fact that I have to see that venomous swine really galls me," continued Carly. "I want to smack him."

"Please don't," Nikki jumped in. "In fact, I'd like to suggest that when you get out of the car you look a little bereaved and betrayed, not angry and put upon."

Carly flashed her dark eyes at Nikki. "I certainly hope this annulment plan works. It seems to me a divorce would be so much easier."

"You hate him, right? He's a pig, right? You don't want to pay him another dime, right? Mark and I would never let you down. Okay?"

Carly got it and changed the subject. "Should I say anything to the press?"

"I would prefer that you didn't," answered Nikki. "I would like Grant just to say that you'll have a statement when the case is resolved."

The limo pulled up to the courthouse in downtown Los Angeles, the scene of the trials of the Manson clan, Sirhan Sirhan, and O.J. Simpson. The car was enveloped by photographers and TV news crews.

"Here we go," said Hayden.

Nikki and Hayden flanked Carly, with the two bodyguards on either side of them. Grant got out first and took the barrage of lights and questions.

Nikki watched Carly make her entrance, looking positively funereal with her head bowed slightly and a handkerchief clutched in one hand. It was Emmy time, she thought.

They raced through the screams as fast as they could. Nikki felt stifled and claustrophobic. She had never been crushed by a crowd before.

A reporter broke through the barrier in the hallway and shouted, "What's it like for Lauren Laverty's daughter to return to Hollywood?"

Nikki froze. She was totally taken aback. In that instant she realized that it would truly be impossible for her to ever be a normal person. She would always be the daughter of a murdered star, always fodder for the press. Even in the middle of all the Carly Singleton clamor, she was a visible target herself. To her dismay she realized she should never forget that.

She turned toward the reporter, knowing she shouldn't answer the question, and recognized that choking sensation in the back of her throat that happened when she tried to speak as a child if someone asked her an important question in school or she found herself in an awkward situation. It hadn't happened very much as she got older. She had no problems in law school or moot court, so she was stunned when it came back in this situation, because she was excited and confident as she approached the courthouse. But that was before someone mentioned Lauren.

Hayden saw her discomfort and put his hand on her hand behind Carly's back and squeezed it.

Nikki felt a little better, and was surprised how she responded to his touch.

"When's the last time they painted this place?" asked Carly under her breath as they were seated at the plaintiff's table.

Nikki caught herself before she made a crack.

"Don't turn around, Carly," whispered Nikki. "He's here and he's walking to his table," referring to Karl Johansson. "Remember, don't look at him yet. I'll tell you when. Please."

Hayden, who stuck around in the hall, reported that Johansson came in later than Carly because he was busy making statements to the press about how he was deprived, how hard he worked on Carly's career, and how she took advantage of him.

"Keep staring ahead, Carly," urged Nikki.

Nikki looked at Johansson. He had on a gray silk suit, a white shirt, and a red and gray tie. His blond hair was short, instead of the longer style he wore with Carly. He looked much more businesslike now, Nikki thought.

"All rise," said the bailiff. "This court is now in session. The Honorable Joseph Hoffman presiding."

Hoffman was a large man, balding, with salt-and-pepper fringe. He had a slightly purple nose and looked like he'd rather be at the bar after a round of golf.

Nikki sat down when the judge did and thought she noticed a slight look of disdain as he looked at her. She hoped it was her imagination.

"Is plaintiff ready?" asked Hoffman.

"Yes, Your Honor," answered Nikki, standing up.

"Defense?"

"Yes, Your Honor," answered Billy Kraines, Johansson's attorney.

Nikki remembered Hayden's caution, that Kraines was a real ambulance chaser and would do anything for a buck.

"Call your first witness, Miss Easterly. It is 'Miss,' isn't it? You can't be a 'Mrs.' yet."

Nikki felt the back of her neck turning red with anger. Next he was going to call her "little lady"! He would never treat a man that way, she thought. It took everything she had to ignore him and start her case.

"We call Carly Singleton."

When Carly rose the room stirred. She wore a charcoal gray Donna Karan suit with gray and black heels, pearls, and a gray and black silk blouse. She wore her false eyelashes, but the rest of her makeup was toned down.

After asking the background questions of how they met and how long they were married, which Nikki asked just to allow Carly to feel comfortable on the stand, she began the good stuff.

"Did you ever hire a detective to investigate Mr. Johansson?"

"Objection! Immaterial, Your Honor."

"Objection overruled."

Nikki looked over and saw Kraines start to confer with Johansson. She waited until the rest of the courtroom returned their attention to Carly, and the judge saw it as well before nodding to Carly to respond.

"Yes I did," said Carly.

"Please tell us the circumstances."

"Well, it was about three months after we were married. I just had a feeling, call it an actress's intuition, that something just wasn't ringing true. I could never get any information on Karl's family. He never wanted to talk about it. He started asking for an increase in his allowance—uh, I mean salary. I just wasn't feeling right about things."

Nikki had made her way over to Johansson's side of the courtroom during Carly's testimony. She was positioned directly in front of Johansson when she asked, "And what did you find out?"

"That he had two ex-wives in Denmark, that Karl Johansson is not his real name. He is really someone named Varde Alborg and he was convicted of check forging and spent time in prison at Odense."

A cry rang up from the spectators as reporters attempted to rush through the door to get to phones.

"Order! Order in the court!" yelled Judge Hoffman, banging his gavel. "I will not have this turn into some sort of circus. If anyone makes a sudden move I'll remove everyone. Sit back down!"

Nikki caught Carly glancing at Karl for the first time. Carly was trying to hide a smirk of triumph.

The reporters returned to their seats.

"No more questions, Your Honor."

"Mr. Kraines," said the judge.

Kraines had to break away from an animated conversation with Karl.

"Mrs. Johansson," he began snidely, emphasizing her married name, "did you and Karl have long talks during your courtship?"

"Yes, why?"

"I'm the one who asks the questions, Mrs. Johansson."

Carly sat up even straighter.

"Did the talks sometimes go into the night?"

"Sometimes."

"Isn't it true that a couple in love confides in each other?"

"Some couples, not this one apparently," she shot back.

"Are you sure that Mr. Johansson never spoke of any part of his background to you at any time?"

"Positive."

"Are you sure that perhaps he told you about his family and his homeland and you forgot it because you were so busy memorizing scripts?"

"He never told me anything."

"Did you ever see any mail come to him from overseas and talk about it?"

"I told you, no. What I learned from the detective was new to me."

Defeated, Kraines said, "No further questions."

Nikki then called the detective to the stand, who corroborated everything Carly had said.

Kraines tried to get the detective to admit he was hired before the marriage, but that simply wasn't the truth.

Nikki could see that Kraines was surprised by her tactics. She knew he was going to put Karl on the stand to testify how much he helped Carly in her business, how he was invaluable to her career and therefore he earned more money than what was in the prenup. It would have been a good case if Nikki and Hayden hadn't been so thorough in their research.

"We have one more witness, Your Honor. We call Dr. Mort Rosenbaum to the stand."

Nikki looked at Karl Johansson and smiled. She saw Johansson turn absolutely white with rage. "You can't!" he screamed, rising to his feet.

"Counselor, control your client," said Hoffman.

Kraines was totally perplexed by now. Nikki saw Karl wave off Kraines's questions and put down his head.

"Your Honor, may I have a five-minute recess to confer with my client?" asked Kraines.

"Five minutes and no more," said Judge Hoffman.

As the five minutes went by Nikki sat smugly in her chair. She could imagine what Kraines was going through.

"Your Honor." Kraines was standing now. "I'd like to go on record that Dr. Rosenbaum is a hostile witness."

Dr. Rosenbaum just stared straight ahead with a look on his face that said he'd rather be anywhere else but in the witness stand.

"Dr. Rosenbaum, what is your specialty?"

"I'm a urologist."

"Is there one particular procedure that you do more than others, Doctor?"

"Yes. I do approximately twenty-five operations a week called a penile enhancement."

"Would you explain what that is?"

Hoffman's attention was riveted to the stand and you couldn't hear a sound in the courtroom except for breathing.

"Many men are unhappy with the size of their penis when it is at rest. They wish to look 'bigger' in that state. It makes them feel better. I have invented a process whereby I cut two tendons to relax the penis and lengthen it and then I take fat from another part of the body and shoot it into the organ to make it fuller. This process enlarges it permanently."

"Objection," said Kraines. "What is the relevance here?"

"I'm coming to that, Your Honor," said Nikki, choosing her words deliberately.

"Hurry."

"What does this operation cost, Doctor?"

"Five thousand dollars."

"Do you know Karl Johansson?"

"Yes, he was a patient."

"And what did you treat Mr. Johansson for?"

"Objection, violation of doctor-patient privilege," said Kraines.

"Your Honor, I have a subpoena for Dr. Rosenbaum's records signed by District Court Justice Marlborough. I can have them here in thirty minutes or Dr. Rosenbaum can answer the question now."

Judge Hoffman looked at Dr. Rosenbaum. The information was going to be brought forth in any case. "Answer the question, please."

"He had the enlargement process approximately two years ago."

Hoffman glared at the spectators, daring them to make a move.

"That would be six months before he met Carly Singleton," said Nikki.

"Objection, the doctor has no idea when Miss Singleton and Mr. Johansson met."

"Objection sustained."

"I have no further questions."

"Your Honor, at this time I feel it is appropriate to ask that you grant an immediate annulment on the grounds of misrepresentation and fraud. We also ask that you set aside the prenuptial agreement."

Hoffman paused for a second, shaking his head at what had just transpired in his courtroom. "So granted."

A whoop went up from the spectators as Carly waved to them. The look that she gave Karl Johansson was beyond description.

The press was waiting on the stairs outside for her statement.

"I feel that today I have scored a victory for all the women who have ever been lied to by men, and I put men on notice. We will all be hiring detectives *before* marriage in the future, should any one of us ever decide to take that step again. Frankly, I hope I never do. I just want to devote myself to my art. Thank you."

"Can you imagine what the tabloids are going to do with this?" asked Carly when they were safely in the car.

"Well, it's just something that can't be prevented," answered Nikki seriously.

"Prevented? I think it's hysterical. I love how that pig and his phony prick will be raked over the coals. It's divine and I'll be hotter than ever. You're the best, Nikki Easterly. Mark was right. Drive home slowly, driver, I'd like to give the photographers time to beat me there," said Carly, leaning her head against the velvet pillow.

The news had reached the law firm before Nikki and Hayden did. When they walked in a cake was waiting in the conference room. "Good work," said Mark. "You two make a wonderful team, don't you think so, Roland?"

"Good money was earned, a client satisfied, and now we'll see how the publicity will turn out, won't we," he sniffed.

As people filed out and went back to work, Nikki stayed to talk to Mark. She shut the door.

"I need to ask you something."

"You look troubled. What is it? You should be happy right now," said Mark.

"What seems to be the problem with people? First the judge treats me like a little girl, and Roland resents everything I say and do."

"Nikki, it's just part of the deal. The legal business is tough, and it's been a man's business for a long time. It doesn't have anything to do with you personally. I think unconsciously or in some cases consciously, the good old boys try to keep their club exclusive. They feel they are being invaded."

"And how do you feel, Uncle Mark?"

"I love you. I'm prejudiced."

"C'mon, really."

"I'm probably better about it, but I could improve. Sometimes I look around the firm and I realize that we have hardly any women lawyers at all compared to the number of men we employ. The world is changing, but it's changing slowly."

"Well it's not changing fast enough for me. Your boys had better start expanding the clubhouse, I'm going to see to it that you get some new members," said Nikki as she pinched his cheek and went back to her office.

"To Joely," said Nikki and Hayden in unison as they raised their glasses to her. "We owe it all to you. Leading us to Sharon was the key to Karl's past. Bravo!" They were seated in the corner window table at Spago. It was the only place to go after Nikki had been on the evening news with Carly. Barbara Lazaroff, co-owner of the restaurant with her chef-husband, Wolfgang Puck, was thrilled to meet Nikki.

"Your mother was so beautiful," she gushed. "I bet you wish she were here today to see your triumph."

Nikki looked at her, once again slightly stunned by the reference to her mother, but she knew Barbara meant it nicely. "Thanks. Now tell me, how many people have told you that you have the most beautiful hair they've ever seen?"

Barbara laughed and modeled it. Her waist-length hair was thick and black with the sides swooped up behind her head and reams hanging down her back. It was dramatic and gorgeous, as was she. She waved and went off to another table.

A special "Jewish pizza" was delivered. Nikki looked puzzled.

"This is Wolf's trademark. Remember lox and bagels?" explained Joely. "Well this is the Hollywood version. It's smoked salmon and cream cheese on pizza dough with fresh dill."

"Amazing," said Nikki, crunching on it happily. But she had peace for only a moment.

"Excuse me, my name is Frank Ronnell and I book *The*

*Tonight Show.* I think you'd make a wonderful guest, Ms. Easterly. Jay was crazy about your mother as a little boy and everybody's talking about you from the news tonight. Here's my card. I hope you'll call me."

He looked at Joely. "Help me out here, okay?" He winked at her and left.

"It's sort of fun sitting here with you at Spago and seeing how many people know you," said Hayden with a big smile.

"What's funnier are the ones who are avoiding me. Now that's the real story," said Joely, emitting a huge laugh.

They both were trying to keep things light because they saw Nikki's face while Frank was talking to her. She wasn't laughing at anything.

"Now I see what my aunt was protecting me from, why she wanted me to practice law in Washington. This city is going to be difficult."

"Well, yes and no," explained Hayden. "It might be harder for you emotionally because you have to face some reality here, but as far as business and profile are concerned, this is a city of images and fame, and you've already got both just because of whose daughter you are. That could be cultivated and used wisely."

She was only half listening.

"I really do look like her, don't I?"

Hayden thought Nikki asked it as if she were noticing it for the first time, but then she was almost as old as Lauren was when she was murdered so Lauren's face at this age was the one that was frozen in everyone's minds.

"Yes, but you both are beautiful. You should be proud."

"It didn't seem to matter much growing up. Nobody mentioned it so I tried not to think about it. My aunt never did— it was as if Hollywood didn't exist. Being here now I feel like a mysterious half of my life is suddenly right in front of my face. Do you know that I've not seen any of my mother's movies since I was six? I don't really know anything about her. I stopped asking right after . . ."

Nikki's voice had trailed off. Her face looked haunted. Joely and Hayden just let the silence take over for a moment.

It was broken by the waiter's voice, "Compliments of Wolf and Barbara," as plates of food were served.

Nikki looked down and saw grilled salmon with lime ginger sauce over mashed potatoes with carrot flowers. Joely had Chilean sea bass and Hayden was given seared ahi tuna with pommes frites.

"Doesn't anybody order in this restaurant?" asked Nikki incredulously, her mood breaking.

"Not when you're celebrating something," answered Joely. "Wolf and Barbara love to do this. They're the best. It's one of the reasons why I'm so glad we live in the Shoreham Towers."

Joely provided distraction for the rest of the dinner with pleasant gossip about everyone in the room.

"See that guy over there?" asked Joely. "He doesn't know I know his computer code name. We have fabulous sex on CompuServe."

"I didn't know you were into computers," said Hayden excitedly. "Do you know about my mainframe?"

"You can show me it any day, cutie," said Joely.

"Hold it, hold it, you two. What do you mean, sex? What are you talking about?" asked Nikki.

"I'll show you when we go home. I'm totally hooked on it."

"I've never played in that area," said Hayden. "I love doing my research and sleuthing work so much I don't have time for that."

"I'm totally lost here," said Nikki.

"Not for long," said Joely.

When dinner was over they went to the parking lot to wait for Hayden's car.

"I know we could walk home," said Joely, looking up the hill, "but up is a lot harder than down."

"I'll drive you the two blocks; c'mon, get in."

"I want to walk by myself," said Nikki. "It will only take five minutes. I just feel like it. You two go ahead."

"Okay," said Joely. "We'll wait for you at the top."

Hayden wished Nikki had chosen to join them.

The man couldn't believe that she was going to walk by herself. He had been standing in the cold, damp earth behind the Dumpster in the Spago parking lot for three hours. Finally this opportunity made it worth it. He saw the car pull away and he let her get about a half a block ahead of him. He was glad his work boots had rubber soles. He was sure she wouldn't hear his footsteps on the sidewalk.

# Chapter 5

Hot 'n' Ready: Do you want to play tonight?
The Master: Don't ask too many questions.
HR: I don't submit easily.
TM: Perfect. How ready are you?
HR: Why don't you find out?
TM: You got it.
HR: Where are you from?
TM: Your imagination.

He just loved the start of these adventures. He knew if he went into CompuServe at about nine P.M. his time they would be waiting for him. Every time he typed "GO CB" and went into the Adult Band he opened up his world. He could be anything he wanted and do anything he wanted. He wasn't restricted by society or morals. He had a special room in his house with a lock on the door so he wouldn't be disturbed. Before he started he went to his bedroom and took off all his clothes. He placed his business attire on a standing valet to air out before putting it away. He put his socks, shorts, and undershirt in the hamper. He put shoe trees in his shoes and put them in their proper place in the closet. Nude, standing in the closet, he pushed open the secret door leading to the computer room. He loved the feel of the cold leather on his buttocks as he sat in front of the computer. He had a color screen, one of those two-page monitors that cost $6,000. It was worth it.

HR: What do you look like?
TM: I'm 6'2. Strong body, big and skilled. And you?
HR: I look like Victoria Principal.
TM: What are your measurements?
HR: 36-26-37.
TM: Hmmmm. What are you wearing right now?
HR: White satin pajama tops and no bottoms.

I've got a good one tonight, he thought, as he felt himself get slightly excited.

TM: I do whatever I want to you, whenever I want.
HR: I can handle anything, can you?
TM: Let's just see about that, shall we? Lie down.
HR: Make me.
TM: Grabbing your hands and tying one to a post on the four-poster. Tying your feet. Stroke yourself with your left hand slowly. I want to see you move.
HR: I'm getting so wet my hand is slipping.
TM: I'm very hard now. Tickle my tip with your tongue.
HR: I love it. I'm going down the shaft now, too. Up and down.
TM: I'm untying you. Sit up. I want to fuck your face.
HR: I want it all. I can take it all. Go deep.
TM: Ahhhhhh. More.

HR: Do it, honey.

TM: Turning you over on all fours now, my hand getting your wetness from you and rubbing it on your anal part, my thumb going in and out.

HR: Give me more than your thumb. I want your big, hard cock.

TM: Shoving it, grabbing your hips, pulling them to me.

HR: Screaming.

TM: Not enough, you're going to get more. I'm turning you over now on your back. Your legs are up in the air over your head. I'm holding myself just over your come button. You're begging me to touch it, to go inside.

HR: Please! Please! I'm throbbing.

TM: NOW. I'm pushing deep. My shoulders are keeping your legs up as I go way inside. You're loving it . . . you want it. NOW for me . . . now . . .

He grabbed one of the towels that he kept by the computer as he came. He didn't want to soil the equipment. As soon as he was finished he disconnected from the computer. He was done now and didn't care about her at all. She had served her purpose. The screen turned black.

"No way did I see what I just saw," said Nikki, turning red.

"Oh yes you did," said Joely. "Sometimes I'm Hot 'n' Ready, sometimes I'm Satin Cutie, I just name myself whatever I'm in the mood for. Macintosh is really easy to use, I bet even you could do it. You saw what I did. I just turned it on, went into CompuServe, got on the CB Adult Band and gave myself a name. Sometimes I get so hooked I stay up all night with it. Sometimes I pretend I'm a man and I get the chicks hot because I know exactly what they want. It's hilarious. When a guy's a dud, I drop him and go on to the next."

"This is just mind-boggling that people are doing this all over the country," said Nikki.

"How about all over the world," added Joely. "You've got to get a Mac."

"That I don't disagree with, it's helpful for business and files. Beverly has one. I've been working up to having her order one for me. She and Hayden can teach me."

"Get a Powerbook so you can take it home as well. It's more useful for you."

"Soon, soon," said Nikki. "But it's for work, not play. That is definitely not for me."

"Fine," said Joely. "Have Hayden show you how to get into the law forums, or political rooms, or food, whatever interests you. You'll enjoy it. Perhaps you can even swap recipes."

"You're teasing me again, aren't you?"

"Not me," said Joely, grinning. "I know when to give up."

# Chapter 6

"Does the name Greggie Alcott mean anything to you?" asked Mark when Nikki was seated in his office.

Nikki looked at Mark admiringly. He was so handsome in his three-piece navy blue suit. His silver hair was full and wavy at fifty-five. Thoughts of her mother crept into her head as she looked at Mark. He must have been devastating in his thirties. No wonder Lauren was engaged to him. His voice brought her thoughts back to the present.

"Nikki?"

"No, I've never heard of her."

"She was a girl who was murdered, part of a call girl ring. It was hushed up very quickly. They found the killer immediately and it was over. Open and shut."

"Why are you telling me this?"

"Frankly I owe a favor to a friend of mine. He wants me to see the mother of the boy convicted in the murder. She claims her son didn't do it," said Mark.

"Really?" Nikki exclaimed.

"Calm down, the case is a loser. The boy's fingerprints were there, he had sex with her. It's a disaster. But I don't want to let down my friend. I don't have time for this myself, and I'd ordinarily toss it to another firm. But you've done good work, and this is just the kind of bleeding-heart case you've been looking for. We made a lot of money off Carly's divorce, so here's your reward. Think of this case as a little present from me, deal with it, enjoy working for no money, and then get rid of it. And don't let it interfere with your other cases. I'm not going to transfer any of them away from you. I want you to be a well-rounded lawyer. You're just going to have to make time to take on this extra case."

"Oh, Mark, thank you! I won't let you down, and I'll work around the clock if I have to to get everything done."

"Uh huh," responded Mark almost condescendingly. But he was happy Nikki was happy. Now everybody would be happy. The law business was full of favors.

Nikki went rushing down the hall to tell Hayden her good news.

"Greggie Alcott, let me see, that rings a bell somewhere," said Hayden. "Let's run it through the computer."

He entered the name in some section that Nikki didn't understand and waited for the information to come up.

"Oh, yes. This case had a lot of rumors attached to it, but nothing came of it."

"What do you mean?"

"Well, when Greggie was killed it was thought at first that it was just another hooker. But the police discovered a set of keys in a hidden drawer next to her bed and they led to a safe-deposit box in Century City. In the box was a black book containing the list of her clients and their sexual, ah, how should I say this? . . . proclivities."

"Really?" said Nikki.

"Supposedly there were names of stars, studio heads, agents, lawyers, directors—you name it. She worked for someone named Madame Ana. Everyone was afraid they'd be implicated. But it died down almost as fast as it happened. Most of the attention was centered on executives from Atlas Studios, but as soon as the murderer was found, Ana just went quietly out of the business and everyone kept their mouths shut and went on to other things. I think one guy quietly resigned from Atlas. I can't tell you what a flash in the pan it was. No one has mentioned anything about it in years. It's as if it never happened."

"My appointment with Mrs. Marleaux, the boy's mother, is tomorrow morning at ten A.M. Since Mark gave this case to me, I'm asking you to join me on it."

Hayden was flattered, and delighted at the chance to work more closely with Nikki, but he also had a full load of his own work.

"I'd love to help you as much as I can, but I'm a little strapped for time. Why don't you and I get all the information out of the computer that we can this afternoon, and I'll meet with you and Mrs. Marleaux tomorrow. I'm sure you can handle it from there. I'd be surprised if it went anywhere. Everybody knew then that the kid was guilty."

Nikki began to wonder about the "gift" from Mark. No one seemed to be too impressed or as interested as she. Well, throwaway or not, she was going to give it her all.

Nikki and Hayden first used the office computer to check into the newspaper accounts.

"Wow, look at Greggie," said Nikki. "She was so gorgeous. My God, she looked like Miss Teenage America!"

"All of Ana's Girls looked like that, or so I've been told," explained Hayden. "Ana was a smart girl from a lower-middle-class family who went to Europe and got started there. She was an entrepreneur and wanted to be her own boss. She eventually built a large business. But it never made the papers until this murder."

Nikki was mesmerized by the story.

"I remember hearing that Greggie was one of her top girls, but she was a problem. She had a big mouth. Ana was discreet and wanted her girls to be the same. Greggie was a loose cannon who knew too much. One day she was found dead and an unemployed kid who used to be a messenger boy from Atlas Studios was convicted. Ana quit her business and went into real estate. She's very wealthy and proper now."

"Your information is amazing. I can't believe the whole case died," said Nikki.

"My information is not what was necessarily released to the press. The murder was just a little blip in Hollywood and nobody talked about it."

"I'll read what we have tonight. I know how much you love your computer, but I'm a little old-fashioned. After the meeting tomorrow I'm going to the big public library in downtown L.A."

"Did you order your Mac?"

"Yes, I did," answered Nikki reluctantly. "It will be here by Friday."

"Good, you'll be proficient by Saturday. I'll see to it."

By ten A.M. Nikki and Hayden knew as much as they could know considering the short lead time they had. They had a lot of questions, but they wanted to hear from Mrs. Marleaux.

Jeanne Marleaux was a slight woman, five feet tall with sad, soft brown eyes. Her hair was graying rapidly and she looked older than her fifty-two years. Her faded green print dress just hung on her as if she were a hanger. She spoke haltingly because her English was only fair.

"I thank you. I am not trouble. I must help my son, Guy. Something is wrong here in America. It has been so, yes? I not want my son to come here but he loves movies. So happy he is when he get job at Atlas movie studios. He meet the stars. He know famous movie men in big offices. His work is good. He never get in trouble. He tell me things about people . . . things that don't sound good to me. I think they are not very nice people but he defend them, you understand?"

Nikki's mind flashed to the comment Hayden made about one Atlas executive resigning quietly. She thought it was interesting that Guy was an Atlas employee. Maybe it wasn't by chance. She would have to check it.

"My son is innocent. He is an angel. He would never hurt anyone. I have been trying for five years to get enough money together to come here and try to help. I know that your firm is good for appealing. That is what he needs."

"Mrs. Marleaux, all mothers think their children are innocent," Hayden said. "How do you explain away the fact that semen and hair samples belonging to your son were at the murder scene?"

Mrs. Marleaux started to cry and her voice rose in hysteria. "I don't know! I don't know! I don't understand these things. I only know he is innocent. He told me so and I believe him. You must help us. I just know there is something wrong here. He is a good boy."

"Mrs. Marleaux, have you ever heard about DNA?" asked Hayden.

"DNA? What is this?"

"It is a complicated chemical thing, but we all have it in our bodies and each person's is different, like fingerprints. No two people are the same. DNA is left at crime scenes and only recently have tests been invented to check it. It might be a long shot, but if your son's DNA doesn't match the samples at the crime scene, he would be innocent and we could move for a new trial and we'd win."

"Oh my God, oh my God. Could you do it? Please!"

Nikki looked at Hayden imploringly.

"We will start asking some questions and get back to you in a week. It would be difficult, expensive work," explained Hayden. "If we felt there was a shot we'd have to file an appeal to allow the DNA testing. It's a relatively new process and courts are reluctant. We don't know how long it would take or how high we would have to appeal."

Mrs. Marleaux was sobbing by now.

"We'll do it!" said Nikki, knowing she might have to kick in some of her own money on the case, but what was her inheritance for? It had been her dream to work like this on cases where she could make a difference.

Hayden sighed, for he knew Nikki would never let up.

As soon as Mrs. Marleaux left the office she was on him. "Tell me more about DNA," said Nikki.

"It's a controversial subject. Each state has different rulings, police like it, defense attorneys don't, particularly if their client is guilty. Lawyers have had more success ruling it in if it exonerates their client. The big problem comes when there's a match and then the defense lawyers try to discredit the testing. Many judges won't even allow DNA results as testimony. Frankly it's a mess," explained Hayden.

"Okay, that's your lawyer-hat talking. I know you're not a scientist, but you have a mechanical mind, always looking for new inventions. What does that part of you think?"

"I think DNA's a real winner. It's going to take quite a long time for it to be totally accepted and for all the states to come to a consensus. Perhaps a federal ruling will have to come about, but scientifically it's terrific. I think it's a good idea for this case; in fact, it's probably the only idea we could come up with."

"Did you say we?" asked Nikki.

"Let's give it a shot, shall we?"

\* \* \*

Roland Bixby hoped that he wasn't walking by the door too often. He knew something unusual was going on and once again he was being kept out of the loop. He went back to his office leaving the door open just enough to see who was walking down the hall when the meeting was over. He didn't recognize the woman, and was struck by the fact that she certainly didn't look like a typical client of the firm's.

His tailbone began to tingle. That was a bad sign. It was his body's alarm system and had never failed him. Rather than take drastic measures right away he thought he would be straightforward for the moment. He'd make sure that he ran into Mark today and simply ask him if there was a new case. Depending upon the answer he would go from there.

Roland looked at his watch. It was twelve-fifteen P.M. Mark had a standing reservation at The Grill in Beverly Hills every Tuesday. Roland pressed the intercom.

"Marge, would you call Miss Lansing's office and ask her to meet me at The Grill today instead of La Scala?"

Nikki enjoyed the drive from Century City to downtown L.A. The farther east one went, the older-looking the city became. It was like traveling into another world. Downtown looked like an Eastern city with old architectural masterpiece buildings. The public library was already preserved as a historical site. It had ceilings that were three stories high with carvings and moldings all around. The floors were brown marble; as Nikki walked across she felt the footsteps that had gone before her. She was more comfortable in a traditional atmosphere. She liked the feel of paper in her hands, the index cards, the books. She couldn't get the old newspapers, though. For that she would have to read microfilm. By now she knew there wasn't that much on Greggie or the case, because it was all dispatched so quickly, but there certainly had to be something on Atlas Studios.

There was almost an entire file drawer on the studio.

Nikki was excited and exhausted at the prospect. She decided to take twenty-five cards at a time, get the books or news files involved, and then read them. She soon discovered that many items were cross-referenced and duplicated, and basically the information was in ten similar books about the history of Hollywood, plus two biographies on the founder, Borice Kagan.

Kagan and his cousin Alfred founded the studio in the 1950s as an independent upstart. They discovered a champion swimmer with a great body and put him in some B action-adventures. Much to their shock, the movies were huge hits and they started to be competitive with Warner Brothers, MGM, and the like. The Kagans began building a library of action heroes and by the late 1970s their holdings were very valuable. There were pictures of the cousins with presidents, world leaders, and stars of the time. Nikki was very impressed. A picture of them with Konrad Adenauer, the chancellor of Germany, was on the screen. She was surprised these successful Jewish men would pose for such a picture, but Adenauer was holding the MightyMan costume and smiling. She clicked to the next picture and froze. It was of her mother, Lauren Laverty, being held by MightyMan. Lauren's tantalizing smile lit up the picture. Her manelike blond hair was flying in the wind. Nikki looked at the date on the photo. It was January 1975, two months before her mother was murdered.

Nikki snapped it off the machine and went back to the clippings. She forced herself to concentrate on the research.

The Kagans apparently received a multimillion-dollar offer from the Kinney Corporation, which owned a lot of theaters. Kinney bought them and then created a takeover situation with Warner Brothers, which was cash-poor. Atlas was absorbed into Warner until 1987, when two up-and-coming young agents went to Europe and got financing from

Franc International to buy back the name Atlas Studios and get the rights to their heroes. The young upstarts wanted to redo the action franchise movies with new stars of the day. They were betting that a whole new generation would love them much the way the Superman franchise was reincarnated. The agents quit their jobs and became the new heads of Atlas Studios in the U.S. They remained in charge until 1992, one year after Guy Marleaux went to jail, noted Nikki.

She realized that while it was good for her to know all the background of Atlas, the critical period was between 1987 and today. She needed to know more about the duo that headed the studio during those years, as well as Franc International, before she could even get into the Ana-Greggie-Marleaux connection. Between the articles in *Vanity Fair*, *People*, and the gossip columns, it was easy to form a fast picture.

David Solomon was born in the Bronx in 1956. His father owned a neighborhood deli and his mother worked the cash register there. Even as a little boy David hated his surroundings. He longed for the big cars and shiny suits. His mother trained him behind the cash register. He loved the feel of money between his fingers and developed a keen knowledge of figures and math. He was short for his age, so he became tough and scrappy to scare away kids. He had a mass of black curly hair on his head as well as on his body. Instead of being embarrassed, he used it. He was the school bully *and* he was smart. At eighteen he left home to be a roadie for a rock group—anything to be in show business and near the flash. When the group started having hit records their gigs got larger, as did his responsibility. Their manager was not very bright, and the booking agent from Premier Talent began to depend more and more on "the kid."

Despite his growing love for leftover groupies and new drugs, David never let that interfere with his job. Nine months later when the tour ended, David was offered a job as an agent-trainee at William Morris, the oldest agency and the most respected in the business. He grabbed it. By the time he was twenty-eight years old he was running the music division and was second in command of the movie-packaging area.

Joel Bronson joined the agency just as David was given second position in the movie area. Joel was perfect. He was a graduate of Harvard and the Harvard Business School. He wore crisp navy blue pin-striped suits, Bally loafers, bright white shirts, and foulard ties. His manners and speech were impeccable. At six two, he was quite good-looking, almost as good-looking as Warren Beatty, some of the magazines said. He had beautiful blue eyes, large white teeth, and a great build, the result of dedicated workouts. According to *Vanity Fair*, Solomon and Bronson were almost instant buddies. Bronson gave Solomon class, and Solomon's financial mind as well as sense of fun were a perfect blend with Bronson's education.

Their coup in buying back Atlas and setting themselves up as studio heads without anyone in Hollywood getting wind of it was one of the most startling events of the 1980s. When they turned out to be creatively astute, too, it was the success story of the decade.

Nikki learned that their guardian angel was Phillipe Gascon, chairman of the board of Franc International, a holding company in France involved in everything from cable television to electronic importing to real estate. No one had ever been able to get a complete financial analysis of the company. Nikki learned through further research that Gascon's daughter was at Harvard and brought Bronson home to dinner on a number of occasions. The dinner was in France, of course, and Bronson made a permanent lifetime contact.

By this time her eyes were crossing and her brain felt like mush. The facts had been absorbed, notes taken. She looked at her watch and realized she had been there for six hours.

Already, she realized, her other cases would be neglected, at least until she had something to eat and a nap.

Suddenly she was famished and she thought of Phillipe's—funny . . . the same name as the Franc International man, she laughed to herself. Phillipe's was an old French dip sandwich place that had been in Los Angeles since the 1920s. She parked in their lot and went in. She loved the sawdust on the floor and the waitresses who looked like they were characters from *Five Easy Pieces*. They all wore brown uniforms with white collars and cuffs and little white hats and white aprons. As she stood in line at the counter she was approached by a flame-red bouffant. "What's your order, honey?"

"I'll have the roast beef, double dipped, cut in half. A side order of cole slaw, lemonade, and chocolate cream pie for dessert."

The waitress smiled. She liked the decisive young lady. "Be right back."

In a second Nikki's order was placed before her on a tray.

The seating was all together at long tables, or booths in the back room with high walls, or a counter facing the street. Nikki chose the counter. As she bit into the sandwich she was thoroughly satisfied. Her teeth going through the crisp crust and then hitting the moist roast beef was perfection. She had remembered to put on just the right amount of sweet and hot mustard, which set off the dish to perfection.

She didn't notice him as he sat three seats down from her at the counter. She didn't see him stare at her every bite as he gripped the counter in rage. She was enraptured with her sandwich and the view of the train station. Nikki thought its tall Spanish arches and tilework looked familiar. It was mesmerizing, and as soon as she was through with her meal she crossed the street to get a closer look.

When she walked inside the station she knew she had been there before. She remembered how big everything seemed. The ceilings were four stories high. She remembered being enveloped by the stone floors and tall stained-glass windows. In the middle of the foyer was a huge wooden structure that must have been an old magazine stand from years gone by. To her right was a coffee shop and store, and to her left was a giant room filled with ticket windows. There were only a few trains using the station nowadays and at this hour it looked like a ghost town. The diminishing sunlight was casting shadows through the windows that made eerie patterns on the red-tile floor.

Nikki walked into the main waiting room. Rows of identical overstuffed brown leather chairs stretched all the way from the entrance to the area a hundred yards away where the tunnel began to lead you to the tracks. Two men were seated separately in each corner. Both looked like bums who came in to get a rest. She sat down in a chair in the middle of the room. It was so big that it made her feel like a child, which only intensified what was going on in her mind. She had sat here before and felt even smaller.

How old could she have been when she saw the train station for the first time? Four? Five? She closed her eyes and tried to remember. She suddenly felt the touch of her mother's hand holding hers and she jumped with a start. Her hand felt little and she was holding it almost above her head. She was walking with her mother toward the tunnel. The sweet, creamy smell of her mother came wafting back to her after all these years. She realized now that she couldn't think of her mother without remembering that smell. Every time Nikki had walked into her mother's dressing room, bathroom, or closet she was overcome with it.

She flashed again to a time when Lauren was out and she snuck down the hall. Nikki was lonely and wanted her mother. She spotted a royal blue jar with an opaque crystal bird on top. Climbing on the chair to reach the dressing table top, Nikki remembered how much she wanted to get into that jar. Her little hands turned the lid as best she could and the jar opened releasing that same delicious smell. The little girl sat there a long time, just breathing into the jar with her eyes closed. It was the closest she could get to her mother's love. Nikki opened her eyes in the train station and was stunned by the tears on her cheeks.

She stood up and went toward the tunnel, remembering that that was the direction she went with her mother. A couple of older uniformed men were at the entrance guarding the electric passenger carts like the kind they use at airports.

"May I help you?" asked the one on the left.

"I'm not sure," replied Nikki. "I'm sort of looking around."

"Are you from here?"

"Originally," answered Nikki.

"Oh we get a lot of people like you, coming back here. You were a baby, right?"

"I guess it's not so unusual." Nikki hesitated and then added, "Could I take one of those carts and just go look around?"

"Well, young lady, that's highly irregular. This tunnel leads to the tracks and back. That's it."

"Please, I just really feel the need to explore. I'll bring it right back."

The two men looked at each other. It was the quiet time. In fact, the place was virtually dead. This girl looked responsible.

With a promise to be back in fifteen minutes, Nikki pressed the accelerator and headed down the tunnel. There was a light every two hundred feet, which really wasn't enough, in her opinion. She felt a chill as she headed into more darkness, but then after another two minutes she found herself on the outside where spotlights illuminated the large trains just sitting on the tracks. She left the cart, her feet crunching against the tiny rocks that paved the way between the tracks.

Her hands went up to touch the gleaming silver train car. It was extremely cold—a jolt went through her. She felt the power and magnificence of the machine. She wanted to get into the engine car and start it up and go. Well, what could it hurt, she thought. I'll just sit in the seat if I can. She found the way in and in her excitement looking at the controls she did not hear the footsteps coming toward the train. She also did not hear them stop.

# Chapter 7

Hayden was having trouble concentrating. He programmed the computer correctly and the research was being spewed and printed. That wasn't the problem. He couldn't keep Nikki out of his mind any longer. There was something about that strawberry blond, apple-pie look that got him. Maybe it was because it was so American.

"American." That word again.

He was born in Los Angeles to a Chinese-American father and a French mother. Since the day he was born he heard how much his mother looked like France Nuyen, the gorgeous Eurasian actress who starred in *South Pacific*. His mother was tall and lanky with thick straight dark hair, big blue almond-shaped eyes, pouty lips, high cheekbones, and a peaches-and-cream complexion. His father was an average-looking Asian man, well-built, with a straight nose and exceptionally sweet personality.

Hayden was named for the movie star Sterling Hayden,

who was a favorite of his maternal grandmother. He realized he could have been named Sterling, which wasn't bad, but he liked Hayden better. Their neighborhood in Monterey Park, a suburb of Los Angeles, was unbelievably middle-class. It could have been in Iowa. Many Asians moved there as years went by, and his classmates were studious and well-behaved. He realized early on that having a French mother made him unique. Little girls were always teasing him and hitting him. His mother explained that they just wanted him to pay attention to them. When he was in art class in the fifth grade one girl threw her coin purse across the room and accidentally hit his cheek with it. He still had the slight scar under his left eye. By the time he was in his teens he allowed himself to see how handsome he was, but it never ruled him. When Mary Ellen Wong slipped him her panties under the desk in eleventh-grade English his fate was sealed. He could have any woman he wanted and did. He wore rubbers from age fifteen on, not wanting any "accidents" ruining his plans.

His father was a lawyer, and when Hayden showed signs of brilliance in English and social studies, he decided to follow in his father's footsteps. School was easy for him and he managed to balance his educational and social schedule. There were more Asians in his school than Caucasians, and even though his parents instilled pride in him, growing up in hip Los Angeles, seeing all the commercials, advertising, and films geared to whites made him feel slightly inferior deep down. He never talked about it, and his parents would have been shocked had they known. He certainly had as many white girls as he wanted, but when he did it was different than with an Asian. It was as if by touching her he became as privileged as she. It made him feel better about himself.

"Okay, so that's my childhood," said Hayden over lunch at the Hamburger Hamlet in Century City, which was the perfect place for a quick bite next to the office. "Now tell me about you. I don't know anything."

"Wait a second," said Nikki, "you left off at high school. You're not finished yet. It's still your turn."

"Are you sure I'm not boring you?" he asked.

"Not at all. I'm fascinated. Honest."

"Well, I went to Yale, and I really stood out," continued Hayden with some difficulty. "It was hard being different. On the one hand I had fun with the girls, if you'll excuse me, but people resented me for getting good grades. I felt like they thought I got them because I was different. There were hardly any Asians there, but it was even more confusing because my mom's white. It was weird for me. I felt alienated. That's why I spent the extra years going to grad school in criminal science. I didn't want to compete with everybody for the same jobs after law school. When I got the job offer from Mark's firm it was perfect. I didn't have to be stuck in that Eastern corporate nonsense. I thought the nonsense of Hollywood might be more fun."

"And is it?" asked Nikki.

"It is now," said Hayden, looking at Nikki intently.

Nikki just couldn't get over his resemblance to John Lone. He was gorgeous and it unnerved her.

Everything was working perfectly, as Hayden thought it would. He was happy in his work and satisfied in his non-committal but busy personal life. He was just speeding along joyfully, with no ties—until he met Nikki.

As they walked back to the office he glanced at her when she wasn't looking. She pushed that blond-American button in him, but she was different from the others. She was honorable, intelligent, and innocent all at the same time. Instead of feeling inferior, he felt like a friend, a helpmate, a soulmate. He could see how earnest she was, how dedicated and unjaded. And he also saw the unresolved issues about her mother. He decided to run Lauren Laverty through the computer. He wanted to know more about Nikki's past, feeling that might be the way to get her to really "see" him.

Roland stopped off and said hello to MCA President Ron Meyer, who was lunching with his former client Sylvester Stallone in the first booth to the right as you walked into The Grill in Beverly Hills. The booths were the best of course, but occasionally an actress might like to be seated at one of the smaller tables in the middle of the room. Those were hard to miss. The Grill was all dark wood with black and white tile floors, brass fixtures, and hunter green carpet on the stairs to the bathrooms on the second floor.

Roland's booth was the next one down and he took his place. It was cooler not to glance around the room. People could come to him. He didn't know why he picked up the menu because he had it memorized. He was either in a Cobb salad mood, a chicken hash mood, or a hamburger with a load of half French fries and half fried onions mood. He thought it would be better to eat salad with Sherry Lansing, the president of Paramount. If he ate beef he looked too carnivorous and insensitive. If he ate the chicken hash he looked too effeminate. Definitely the salad. He'd see what Sherry ordered.

Sherry Lansing, a five foot eleven former model who had risen to head two major studios, was a delight. She was warm as well as being a smart operator. She was definitely from the catch-more-flies-with-honey school. Roland enjoyed working with her because he always knew where he stood. Occasionally he would have to step in and work with an agent in a tough negotiation. His goal during lunch was to close a deal for a spec screenplay for a friend of his and Cruger's. It should be a simple deal. There was a mini bidding war on it, but he knew Sherry was the right buyer and Sherry knew he knew it. There wouldn't be much room for play. He really didn't care. It was the writer's first attempt at a script and whatever he got would be gravy. Roland was more interested in just furthering his friendship with Sherry. He also wished he could have sat on the other side of the table to overhear manager Joan Hyler lunching with Candy Bergen. He just knew that would be a dishy lunch, but whoever got to the booth first took the power seat facing the door. It was one of those unwritten Hollywood restaurant rules.

Sherry stopped to talk to Ronnie and Sly and then came over to Roland. They did a Hollywood air kiss.

"Darling," said Roland, "it's so good to see you. The merger looks terrific on you."

"I feel terrific," said Sherry, looking splendid in a tobacco-colored Calvin Klein suit with an Hermès scarf. "It all worked out well after so much turmoil. And how are you and Cruger?"

"Speaking of turmoil?" asked Roland. "Only kidding. Things are the same. We are a well-oiled machine living the good life."

"Shall we toast to all things good?" said Sherry, raising her iced tea to his.

"Absolutely," said Roland smiling.

The waiter came by to take their order. Sherry ordered a hamburger steak with fries.

So did Roland.

"All right, let's get it over with so we can play for the rest of the lunch," said Roland. "*Someone Like You* is cute and fresh and appeals to the young crowd. Please don't offer me scale. Fifty thousand isn't bad for a first screenplay but there are others interested."

"You're right, others are interested, but the deal isn't what's important. What's important is whether or not it gets made. I get movies made and you know it." Sherry paused to sip her tea. "It doesn't matter whether I give you fifty or Warner's does, or whether you get one or another of us to seventy-five. I'll bet that no studio has waived the fact that the advance would be deducted from the final fee. Am I right?"

"Keep talking," said Roland.

"Right. So if I pay you fifty against a hundred and twenty-five with a typical deduction, your client gets seventy-five in the end. If you sell to Warner's with a seventy-five against one hundred, your client gets twenty-five instead of fifty. Maybe he looks good in the trades because he got a larger advance, but in my deal he makes more in the end if the picture gets made."

"True," countered Roland. "He would get more if the picture got made, but how many of them do? You and I know these development deals are a dime a dozen."

"Well, I guess I'm asking you to bet on me and my ability to get things made. You'd bet on me, wouldn't you?"

Sherry was smooth. They both knew he was going to make a deal and they enjoyed this cat-and-mouse game. Sherry was great at it.

"I'd never bet against you. We have a deal."

Midway between the hamburger and a mouthful of onion rings, Roland saw Mark head for the men's room. "Would you excuse me for a moment?"

At the urinal he got the information he wanted. It was enough to stop his stream. He hoped Mark didn't notice.

For ten years the imposing sixteenth-century building proudly facing the Champs-Elysées had been the home of Franc International, one of the most powerful conglomerates in the world. When you entered from the street the reception area was solid marble, both floors and walls. The ceiling was two stories high. A mural of steel, glass, and brightly colored stones, almost a Greek mosaic, covered the ceiling, reflecting multicolored shimmers on the marble areas below. Four security guards were enclosed in the cen-

ter of a marble and glass cage in the middle of the area.
When one entered the building it was necessary to go to the
guards to get cleared through computers. Once cleared, a
guard would walk you to an elevator, unlocking it with a
special key. He would then program the elevator to stop only
at your floor.

Up on the penthouse floor, fifty-six-year-old Phillipe Gascon could survey all of Paris from his 360-degree view. He
was an extremely hefty man, weighing in at 250 pounds,
with very thick black hair and bushy eyebrows, who smoked
cigars constantly. His suits had to be made for him, and he
always wore a vest to match his suit. He wore the most expensive clothes, ties, shoes, jewelry he could find. When he
looked in the mirror he saw himself as Louis Jourdan in
*Gigi*, a suave, thin, handsome, thirty-year-old. When other
people looked at him they saw an aging crude peasant
dressed up like a would-be king. But he had so much money
and power people were afraid of him and treated him defer-
entially.

He liked to think of himself as someone who controlled
satellites of power all over the world. To him, power was in
communications, whether it was newspapers, radio stations,
television companies, movie theaters, or movie studios. He
owned them all over the world, but his most prized posses-
sion was Atlas Studios. It was his crown jewel. Having a
foothold in America was crucial for him.

Phillipe first saw America in the movies as a child. When
he saw James Dean in *Rebel Without a Cause* or Marlon
Brando in *The Wild One*, he pictured himself as those rebels,
the ones who would thumb their nose at everyone. He loved
their violent streak, and when he adopted that attitude on his
own streets in his poor section of Paris, it served him well.
He could scare off some of the men who were all over his
mother. Ever since his father had deserted them when he
was six, Phillipe felt he was responsible for her. She was

beautiful to him, and she was his. He greatly resented the other men and he tried to protect her, but as he matured he realized she didn't want protecting. He felt abandoned and angry, and he took that out onto the streets. It fit right in with Brando and Dean.

The older he became, however, the more he began to realize that there was something that people were more afraid of than violence, and that was the power of money. He noticed an air of confidence in a man who wore a beautiful suit. Suddenly as he watched his movies he saw that the men in the suits had control over the rebels in the streets. There was no more glamour to him in being an outsider. He wanted to be in control, he wanted to be in that suit. Money was the key to everything. He didn't want to be on the underbelly of life anymore.

Phillipe made sure that his official biography started with the story of his buying one radio station and then parlaying that into another, and then another, gradually spreading out into other ventures like television and newspapers. It never mentioned how he got the money, at age twenty-five, to buy that first station. And it never would. There were parts of Phillipe's life that he wanted to remain a mystery. He loved his high profile, but it was one that provoked questions and gave few answers, and that was perfect for him. Things were running very smoothly now, and he would keep it that way no matter what he had to do.

"This DNA thing is a bitch," said Nikki as she and Hayden were plotting their case. "The courts don't really like it. Only in Florida, New York, Pennsylvania, Oklahoma, Virginia, and Washington has it ever been admitted successfully, and that was a terrible struggle. Unless we can prove that our evidence meets the Kelly-Frye test we're doomed."

"What's that?"

"Well, California decided a while back to admit DNA but only if the evidence could be validated by an independent laboratory using criteria that the scientific community agreed upon. There are very few acceptable labs. The judge applies the Frye decision and overrules appeals if the definition of DNA is too broad. It's a ridiculously small window and easy for lawyers to lose because everyone is so nervous with the new technology. It's easier and safer to rule against it."

"Is there anything else I should know now that you've depressed me?" said Hayden.

"Yep. DNA is called 'novel scientific evidence,' and when it is offered in court the legal system faces competing concerns. There is a danger that if the evidence is accepted quickly it will be proven less reliable later by lawyers using statistics that can sway juries into believing it's not accurate enough. There's no question that we have to give it a shot and do the test and match it. If the results don't match we've got to go for it."

"We need to talk with Guy right away," said Hayden.

"Yes, and we've got to see Ana."

"I think we should obviously both go see Guy, he's our client," continued Hayden. "My instinct about Ana is that she would respond to you better. Once you make the call to set it up, a shoe drops and then we'll have to work fast. I'll set Marleaux up for Friday and here's Ana's number. Just introduce yourself. She'll know who you are. Trust me."

Joely thought, as she pasted on her gray beard and mustache, that this was her easiest job. She pulled back her hair, pinned it, and put on the skull cap. She next fit on the gray wig and put on the wire glasses. She dressed in a powder blue oxford cloth shirt, a striped tie, khaki slacks, loafers and then put on the apron. The white apron was crucial. It had to be the one that said "Frugal Gourmet" on it. Earlier in the day she drove to the Farmers Market to pick up the chicken that her client ordered, always from the same butcher. Joely knew that her client checked with the butcher to see if she indeed had gone to him, and she wanted everything to be perfect.

As she left her house she took the chicken, still in its wrapping, and put it in a paper bag. She put an overcoat on and walked out of her apartment. She hoped someone would be in the elevator because she loved to tease people. Sometimes they recognized her and sometimes they didn't. This time she was alone.

She rang his bell, chicken in hand. It was very important that she not break character, that she lower her voice and be the Frugal Gourmet from the moment the door was open.

"Hello, Mr. Gourmet," said her client, the president of the largest produce supply company on the West Coast. He was wearing the "usual," an apron and nothing else.

The house was formal English Tudor and Joely had a hard time keeping from laughing as this nude man marched around in his apron, addressing her as if she really were the Frugal Gourmet. His was no-nonsense kitchen talk and they headed to that room.

The kitchen was a lovely country English one with carved sideboards, a butcher block table in the center, a fireplace on the north side, and a long counter separating the kitchen from the family room. Her trick was seated on his side of the counter while she was on her kitchen side. She knew what to do and started.

"Tonight we are going to learn all about the chicken and how to stuff it," she said in her best gruff voice. It was coming by rote, but she always tried to make it sound as if it were the first time. "This chicken weighs six pounds and is a healthy hen. Look at how her legs move."

Joely sensuously started to move the legs, one at a time. "Up and down, up and down." She then turned on the water faucet. "It's important to make sure she is very clean. I'm using lukewarm water, spreading her legs and filling her cavity with it. I ease my hand in slowly, turning it from side to side making sure she's as clean as can be. Watch how I rinse the water in and out."

Joely could see the guy's hands go from the counter down to his apron and fumble with the material.

"Now we must oil her. Watch how I pour vegetable oil on my hands and softly rub her inside and out, over and over again. Let's turn her on her back and go deep inside to make sure she's oiled all over . . . in and out . . . in and out . . ."

She looked up and saw that hand going a mile a minute before she heard his big sigh. A smile came over his face.

"Thank you so much for the lesson, I'd like another one soon. Just pick up the envelope on the table by the door."

He walked away. Joely washed her hands, left the chicken spread-eagled, and went to the door. She had been there fifteen minutes and she made $1,000 and never was touched. Boy did she like this job!

"Sweet buns! Another big night I see," said Joely when Nikki opened the door that evening at seven-thirty in pajamas.

"What on earth are you doing in that outfit?" exclaimed Nikki. "Never mind. I don't want to know. Take off your beard and sit awhile."

Joely giggled as she dumped her costume.

The files Nikki were studying on Ana were open on the bed.

"You have some life," Joely teased. "When I'm in bed by seven-thirty I'm getting good money for it."

"And if I dress up like some guy on a cooking show you can bet it's Halloween," countered Nikki.

"C'mon, there has to be somebody who interests you, there just has to be. You have to have a life."

"I have a life."

"No you don't," said Joely.

"I do. I have my work, my aunt and uncle, I've made some new friends here. After all, what about you?"

"I am not your life. You haven't been out on one date since I've known you."

"That's just not for me," said Nikki, nervously shuffling her papers.

"And why is that?" said Joely, probing gently. "Everybody has to have something that gets them off."

"How delicately put," said Nikki.

"I'm being serious."

"So am I. I'm just not comfortable with it."

"Oh, I get it. If you don't get close, then you don't have to feel, and if you don't feel, then you won't get hurt."

"I've been hurt enough," said Nikki.

That was a tough argument for Joely because she knew Nikki's tragedy as a child could hardly be dismissed. She treaded gently.

"I know that you went through something horrible as a baby, and I'm not forgetting that. But you're lonely. You bury yourself in work, but don't think I haven't noticed how he looks at you."

"Him who?" asked Nikki defensively.

"Hayden."

"Oh, c'mon," said Nikki.

"Well you certainly aren't," joked Joely.

"Not coming on to him? What are you saying? Oh, you're just teasing me."

"No I'm not," said Joely. "I'm positive that you like him and I know he likes you."

Nikki was embarrassed and didn't say anything for a second. "Okay. I think he's bright, industrious, and very good-looking. But I've never given it a thought beyond that, and I don't intend to."

"Why don't I believe you?" asked Joely.

Nikki paused again. "You should. I'm just not good at things like that, not good at relationships. I'm better off if I stick to my work. I think this relationship business is just not for me, it's just too intimate."

"I think you're afraid of it so you just dismiss it. It's easier that way. Haven't you ever thought about a home and children, and loving, sharing commitment between two terrific people?"

"No offense, but look who these questions are coming from. I thought that you, of all people, would understand not wanting to commit," answered Nikki.

"You're right, but has it ever occurred to you that while you avoid out of fear, I go the other way and see tons of people getting paid for it so I make sure there's no chance of a real commitment? Maybe I'd love to stop what I'm doing, but I've been typed in this town and you can't escape. I may as well make the money, stash it, and then go to Iowa or Sweden and start over and have a real life . . . if I can ever quit."

In all the time they had known one another this was the first real conversation they had ever had. They had both exposed their fears to each other and were really forming a basis for a legitimate friendship.

Slightly uncomfortable with the revelations, and wanting to put Hayden out of her mind for the moment because the thought frightened her so, Nikki asked, "What about becoming a madam? You make more money and it seems easier."

"In the first place Ana had it sewn up for years. She didn't want any competitors and if one of the girls tried to set up a little fiefdom, the police came down on her fast," explained Joely. "Then when she made so much money in real estate that she wanted to go legit she turned her operation over to Cynthia Hammersmith. You see, Ana was a police informant and they looked the other way at her business because she gave them information. Now Cynthia has taken over and she has the same deal. The police know that Ana is her God-mother and they leave her alone. Ana takes a small cut off the top as an 'advisor' but Cynthia now has the risk and the major money. Ana is so rich nothing matters. She probably kept the advisor thing going just so she wouldn't get bored. She loves to know what goes on in this city, and her house on Friday nights is still the place to be."

"What happens there?"

"Some of her former clients, the biggest names in town, go for dinner, tell stories, drink whatever they want, smoke a little, and then they go out and party at Cynthia's with the girls. There are never any girls at Ana's, she's very cool now."

Nikki was dying to ask her about Greggie Alcott but it was just a little too soon. There would be time. First she had to have tea with Ana tomorrow. If Joely only knew . . .

"Hey, what's this?" said Joely excitedly, pointing to the new Mac Powerbook. "How cool. You got it."

"Yes, Hayden loaded the research files in it for me, and Beverly made other files. It's all organized. I'm not sure I understand it, but it's done."

"Did you get CompuServe and America Online?"

"Yep. The modem's ready to go. I am impressed with the research facilities they have. Why I can go right into the Library of Congress and the Smithsonian," said Nikki, showing her first snippet of enthusiasm for the new product.

"You can go into some hot stuff, too. Don't forget about that," said Joely, smiling.

"That's your kind of playing, and I certainly think you should enjoy yourself."

"Good idea. I don't feel like going out tonight. I've done my work. It's time to have Spago send up some food and go on an online fantasy trip. Have fun with the Smithsonian! Later!"

The computer frightened Nikki. It wasn't very big, and the colors were cute, she thought. But she didn't quite get the concept.

"Just practice," Hayden told her earlier. "Don't think about doing anything right, or serving a purpose. Just turn it on, wander around the files. Get used to how it works. Then go into an online service and just see what's available. You'll be comfortable in no time."

Okay, thought Nikki, I'll give it a shot. She placed the computer on her bed and settled in. She plugged it in, not wanting to use up the battery. There was an internal fax/modem so all she had to do was plug the phone line into a jack. She got all that straight and turned it on. It made a little sound and then a happy face clock icon came on. It made her feel less afraid.

Her files came up and she saw that between Hayden and Beverly, everything was set up properly. Each client had a folder and within that folder were documents labeled contracts, letters, faxes, notes, personal statistics, tax records, and wills coordinated with the mainframe computer in the office. It was actually quite magical. Beverly had installed Now Contact so all of Nikki's numbers that she would ever want were in the computer. There was an instruction file made up by Hayden telling her how to send a fax, how to work a modem, and how to get online.

She was ready now to go into America Online. She turned on the modem, clicked on the right things, and suddenly the departments were before her. She started to get excited when she realized she could get the latest news, the latest weather anywhere in the world, she could go into the Court TV file and see what was happening, she could get *Time*, the *New*

*York Times*, various other newspapers, and most importantly
find a forum or research library for any subject she wanted.

She decided to go into the Lifestyles Department and suddenly she saw clubs for cooking, bicycling, boating, French,
art. It was a real eye-opener. She loved cooking so she went
into that file and was faced with the happy dilemma of deciding whether she wanted to read recipes, look for a certain
book, or actually talk to people who were online at the very
moment. It was irresistible for her. She wanted to go into the
Cook's Forum to talk. She clicked in, saw her name go on
the board as Nickle. She then realized that Hayden must
have set things up that way to maintain her anonymity, and
she was grateful. She looked up in the corner and saw that
there were forty-four people in the forum right now. There
was a conversation going on between two women about the
best way to cook pot roast. They were deciding whether it
was important to braise first and then put in the vegetables
or just start everything altogether. Nikki believed in brais-
ing.

Her fingers went to the keyboard and she typed, *"Hi, I'm
new, but I love to cook. I braise my pot roast because it
keeps in the juices and makes it more moist."* She then
pressed "enter" and saw her words on the screen.

*"Welcome, Nickle,"* woman number one typed back.
*"How long have you been cooking and where are you
from?"*

Elated at the almost mystical form of communication,
Nikki replied. *"About six years, and I'm from Carmel, Cal-
ifornia."* She didn't want to say Hollywood or Los Angeles.
She felt it was better that way.

For the next twenty minutes she was engaged in "foodie"
heaven and having the time of her life. She forgot her ner-
vousness, and was eager to search other areas. She went into
Town Hall and got into a political discussion. She decided to
be really brave and go into Singles and Looking. She dis-

covered an electronic bulletin board of personal ads that she found intriguing, scandalous, and stupid all at the same time.

Then she found a list of "chat rooms," each with a different title. She checked into New York Babes.

*"So tell me what you like,"* asked Mr. Hunk.

*"Tall, wide, and handsome,"* answered LilyAnn.

*"I'm 6'2 and look like Tom Selleck."*

*"Love this. I look like Michelle Pfeiffer, maybe we should meet somewhere."*

Nikki couldn't believe what she was reading. There was no way either one of these people looked like what they were saying. She noticed that even though she was in the "room," she didn't have to speak. She could just "spy" by reading other people's conversation. She found this very intriguing and began to kind of get into it.

*"Hey Nickle!"*

Oh my God, thought Nikki. Of course they can talk to me here just like the cooking room or any of the rooms. I am on the board!

*"Hello,"* she typed.

*"What kind of music do you like?"* asked Jack.

*"I like Aretha Franklin,"* answered back Nikki, thinking that this conversation was okay. It couldn't get that personal. She wouldn't let it. All she had to do was click off.

Then three more people in the room all typed, *"Hi Nickle."*

She jumped in her seat. She wasn't ready to be this visible and she clicked out without saying goodbye.

She exited America Online and went into CompuServe. She recalled that on that service, you could just read conversations without your name going on the screen. It was more private and wouldn't scare her. She remembered that Joely typed "GO CB," and then when the CB directory appeared she clicked on Adult Band. She waited a second and up came a graph of little boxes with numbers in them. Each numbered box represented a "channel." Underneath the graph were four more boxes. The first one said "Tune," the second "Monitor," the third "Who," and the fourth, "Status." Nikki decided to work backwards. She sort of remembered that "Tune" was crucial and she wanted to stay away from it for the moment.

She clicked on "Status" and it was a graph showing you how many people were talking on each channel. She noted that channels one and thirty-three had the most people. Thirty-three was the Gay Channel. Thirty-four, she noticed, was the Lesbian Channel. She thought it might be interesting to read what they were saying sometime, but she continued her survey and clicked on "Who." "Who" was a list of what people were tuned in to each channel. It showed their screen names, which were obviously made-up "handles" like Kooch, Blue Axe, and Hunny Bunny.

Right now the channel one box was blinking and all she had to do was click on "Monitor" to read the conversation. If she did that, no one would know she was there. Only if you clicked on "Tune" did your handle go on the board and you could talk. She just wasn't ready to be noticed, so she clicked on "Monitor."

Suddenly her screen opened up and became full of dialogue.

Although they weren't using any four-letter words, she was shocked by what they were intimating. It was an electronic Sodom and Gomorrah. There was a part of her that was embarrassed by the intimacy, and another part that loved the voyeurism. They didn't even know she was there. She found it kind of amusing, but then as the minutes began to wear on she almost felt ashamed. She was wasting her time, she had more important things to do, and she turned off the machine.

Ana Sarstedt was a forty-three-year-old who looked like a twenty-three-year-old, thanks to "maintenance work" by

Steven Hoefflin, the top plastic surgeon in the business. She was a five foot seven rail-thin blonde from a poor side of Los Angeles. Her dream, from the time she was six years old, was to be a movie star. She was bright in school and could have done anything, but she was so desperate to get out of her blue-collar circumstances that she wanted instant stardom.

When she was twelve she saw the campaign of a woman named Raquel Welch, born Raquel Tejada, a former weather girl from San Diego with the same dream. Ana saw Raquel find a Svengali-type man, go to Europe, wear animal skins in B pictures, and turn that sexiness into a hot poster sold around the world. The marketing ability of Welch and her Svengali turned Welch into an international star and that's what Ana wanted to do.

At sixteen, Ana started hanging out at restaurants and movie theaters where the rich kids from Beverly Hills High School went. She was out to hook her backer, and by seventeen, a rich schnook named John Schwartz took the bait. Ana was really beautiful and really persuasive. Schwartz married her, and whisked her off to Italy. The poster of her in the tiger loincloth sold a little bit in Europe and did find its way to the States, but there already was one Raquel Welch. The world didn't need a copycat.

Dumping Schwartz, Ana had plenty of offers for a replacement in Europe, but they were offers of money. She realized she could literally sell her body, particularly in Paris, where the offers seemed to be greater. She was set up in an apartment on the Ile St. Louis, a charming island in the Seine between the Right and Left Banks. Ile St. Louis was like a little enclave in Paris. From a café at the tip, you had a magnificent view of Notre Dame. You never had to get off the island. Although it was minute, it boasted a few small hotels and many beautiful apartment buildings, burnished gold with age. Bakeries, boulangeries, salons du thé, antique stores—all boasted the best Paris had to offer.

Ana's keeper was a successful producer named Jacques-Yves Sologne. He gave her a few small parts in his movies, but nothing that would make her a star. She was a star in her bedroom and that's the way he wanted it. Ana was also given a substantial allowance and credit cards with no questions asked. She would spend her days going from St. Laurent to Dior, having her car and driver wait for her while she loaded up on merchandise. Sologne was married, so he frequently wasn't available, which suited Ana just fine. Occasionally he would call her and ask her to see one of his friends. At first she was incensed. After all, choosing to be with one man is a nice arrangement. Being available to others at his direction was something else entirely. Ana was not looking for love and a picket fence, but she was no tramp.

At first it was an actor whom Jacques-Yves wanted to encourage to take a part. Then maybe it was a friend of his who wanted a special birthday present. Occasionally the men would tip and she wouldn't tell Jacques-Yves. She viewed the extra money as one might view flowers before a prom. Ana was good at what she did and she set her mind a certain way to deal with all of it.

One day she got a call from Jacques-Yves asking for a special favor. A very wealthy man wanted to set him up with a long-term studio producing deal that would be worth millions. Jacques-Yves wanted the deal sealed: he would be eternally grateful. Millions, thought Ana, who had begun to resent being the icing on the cake without getting the really big money. She wondered who would give just one man millions. How much more money could this man have if he could spend that much just on one small deal? She dabbed on her favorite perfume and waited.

When she opened the door and saw Phillipe Gascon standing there she understood immediately. She knew it was a sign.

"My dear, you are lovely," he said.

She gazed at his girth. It did not please her. Nothing about him pleased her except his power. She was going to have to earn her Academy Award tonight.

"Please come in, I have your Dewar's and water all ready for you," she said with her best smile, turning, almost like the beginning of *The Loretta Young Show*, in an ice-blue floor-length hostess gown. Just a little bit of white lace was showing at the bodice.

She heard the couch squeak when he sat on it. If the couch squeaked what would she do?

She was an expert at light conversation, flattering to the man, and she soon had him talking about food and trips. He seemed to be perfectly happy.

"Would you like to go into the bedroom?" asked Ana.

"No."

"I see. Well, is there something else you would like?"

"Put this on," he said gruffly, reaching into his overcoat hanging over the side of the couch and pulling a leash and collar out from the pocket.

Ana played it cool as he placed the collar and snapped it around her neck. Suddenly he jumped off the couch on all fours and started barking. He motioned for her to do the same.

Disbelieving, Ana hit the floor like a prissy standard poodle while he growled and started to sniff her behind. He then grabbed the leash with his teeth and led her around the apartment. At this point Ana was praying he didn't find the potted palm. There was no telling what he would do and she was trying to keep a straight face.

He was pawing her, nudging her, growling all the while, and then he rolled over and waved his arms and legs in the air. His "paw" pulled the leash and she was on top of him, taffeta and all. He locked his paws around her and they rolled over and over as he licked her face. It was all playful and cute and she was getting into the spirit of things, starting to whimper and lick, too.

As soon as he felt she was having a good time he let out a ferocious growl, tossed her off him, and then using his huge arms and legs turned her over on all fours, narrowly missing the original Tiffany lamp on the side table. The growling was louder now and legitimately fierce. He pushed her dress up over her head and she felt his enormous weight on her back. It was difficult to hold him up. He took his teeth and pulled down her light blue silk panties. She heard his zipper go down and for some reason the absurdity of it all matched with his size and the power of his pocketbook made her very, very wet. She was imagining what kind of tool a character like this might have. She hoped it was just rear entry and not anal intercourse. She really hated that. She felt the searching head going up and down the liquid crack almost as if it were trying to decide which hole to enter. The indecision made her want it more. She started panting and she knew he loved it, she felt the expansion.

He started barking as loud as he could when he bypassed the rear end and made the entry she wanted. The faster he went the louder he barked.

She was moving her body back and forth opposite to him to feel him deeper. There was something about this man that was getting to her. She wanted more and more of him.

He let out a howl as he filled her up with his juice. He fell back in ecstasy.

But she wouldn't let it alone. She quickly turned over and massaged him to keep him hard. She knew it wouldn't last long and she jumped on it, pulling him into her with her thigh muscles and grabbing on to his head until her juice met his.

They were depleted in every way. Ana was shocked by the desire that he tapped into.

Ana didn't want to let him go so soon. They lingered over brandy as she asked intelligent business questions and drew him out.

"It's real estate, my dear. That's the key to everything. Owning property makes you autonomous. You can always get cash for it and your accounts look good," he said.

"Real estate has always fascinated me," said Ana sweetly. She planned to be so irresistible to him that she could dump Sologne and be Gascon's exclusively, for even more money. She knew he was intrigued by the fact that she was an American. She would play on that.

It took her only three weeks to make the switch. What could Sologne say? He was a married man who now had the multimillion-dollar deal arranged by Gascon. He worked for Gascon, in a sense, and had to just obey.

Ana was delighted. She of course took the "salary" increase from Phillipe, but instead of accepting his invitation to move to a larger place near the Ritz Hotel on the Right Bank, she asked him for the difference in money instead, telling him she wished to learn from him and invest in real estate, too. She also bought fewer clothes and kept more money. Phillipe admired her initiative and was bedazzled by her bedroom skills, so he was only too happy to set her up by phone with a broker in Los Angeles. She started off conservatively with a couple of duplexes. After a few months she sold one and bought an apartment building in West Hollywood. After five years with Phillipe her life was made. She had acquired a number of buildings and homes in profitable areas, not very high-end, because those properties could drop suddenly—but just middle-of-the-road dependable real estate.

And then there was the bonus she hadn't counted on. As the movers and shakers from Hollywood came to France to meet Gascon and align themselves with him, Phillipe would frequently send them to Ana. She was now intimately acquainted with a couple of studio heads, some Oscar-winning actors and directors, and agency magnates.

It was interesting, because her mind worked like Phillipe's. Without him even having to tell her she knew she should pass along information to him, but she underestimated his master plan.

"I think the time is right now, my darling," he said one morning over coffee and fresh croissants that Ana bought from the bakery down the street. She served them to him on a silver tray with a lace doily under the Limoges. They were filled with almond paste, his favorite.

She wanted to ask, "Right for what?" but she knew him well enough to know that he was being very serious and that she should just sit silently.

"You're going to go back to the United States."

Ana gasped, which was something she rarely did without getting paid for it.

"I adore you, and I will come see you there or fly you here from time to time, but I frankly view you more as a valuable business partner. Your information provides me with insight to make a killing on deals. If I place you right in the middle of Hollywood I think it would be even more valuable for both of us."

Ana's heart was pounding. She had actually been thinking about going home for some time and she certainly had the money to do it, but she never wanted to anger Phillipe. She couldn't believe her good luck.

"You no longer will be working, as it were. You are going to have a stable of the prettiest young girls in Los Angeles. Don't ask me how because it's already set up. You will be moving into a beautiful home on Nimes Road in Bel Air. It's a French Regency, which I chose because I wanted you to think of France and know that I'm not very far away. You'll have two secretaries who are extremely discreet. They have been interviewed, trained, and are poised to do your bidding. The phone lines are already in, the Rolodex is full. Take a few days to rest after you arrive and then start to meet your girls. The appointments are already set. You have a full house staff and a cook who is brilliant. I have arranged a special party on a Saturday night one month from now. The invitations are all in the mail. You will recognize many of the men, and there will be some new ones. One whole wing of the house is filled with bedrooms. That is safer than a hotel, although I have made contacts for you at the Bel Age and the Beverly Hills Hotel. Anyone using a code name can get a reservation there without questions asked if need be."

He was talking a mile a minute. Ana's mind was reeling. This was quite an operation that she was being given.

Phillipe continued. "People in the States are not as liberal as we are here about your business, so I have taken care of the police. They will not bother you. After one week there you will be visited by someone in the department to see if there is anything you need. Just make sure he has whatever he needs and answer any questions he has about people. Don't give him money and be sure and let me know if he asks for any. The money will be taken care of and it's better that you don't know how. I, of course, will take a very small percentage, 15 percent off the top, plus the information you give me. The house is paid for in full in your name, and I'll pay your credit card bills up to $10,000 a month. Anything over that you will assume. Charge $1,500 an hour for a girl, pro-rated if they want more than one girl, and you take 45 percent commission. If a client wants to take a girl on a trip it's $10,000 a week plus expenses. If he's a really wealthy guy who is hung up on a particular girl charge as much as $25,000 for a weekend if she goes overseas. The more you charge the more you'll get. You'll see. And just keep putting your profits into real estate. You'll be fine."

"When do you want me to leave?" she asked excitedly.

"Two weeks. That will put us right on schedule." And then he barked.

She knew it was time for the *chien* game one last time, and she was glad. It was time to make it on her own two feet instead of four.

# Chapter 8

Nikki felt uneasy picking out an outfit to meet a madam.
She knew that Ana was retired, of course, and now a proper
real estate magnate and charity lady, but she felt she was
going to be judged on some subtle scale that she had never
been subjected to before. She decided the more conservative
the better. She decided to wear a white silk blouse with a
DKNY navy blue suit, navy blue stockings, and navy blue
and white spectators. She wore pearl stud earrings and a
small pearl circle pin on her lapel. She did think it was funny
that those pearls symbolized virgins. She wondered if Ana
would get the joke. No doubt she would.

With Hayden wishing her good luck, she left the office
and slipped behind the wheel of her gray Buick Park Avenue. Mark had bought it for her with a tiny portion of her
inheritance money. It was very pretty, but she thought it
looked like an old lady's car. She wanted a BMW convertible, but had to pay attention when Mark explained about

carjacking in Los Angeles. He told her that it was not smart to drive a flashy car or a really expensive one like a Mercedes, particularly for young women. Someone might come up to the window, pull a gun, and even shoot her to get the car. A gray Buick was nondescript, just as luxurious inside as a top-of-the-line Cadillac or Lincoln, and it was safe. It attracted no attention. Nikki enjoyed driving the car because it just floated along in its padded leather luxury, but her heart was still with that hot convertible.

As the car turned in the east gate of Bel Air Nikki started to smile. She loved the trees and seclusion of Bel Air. It reminded her of the wooded areas of Carmel and Big Sur, even though the houses looked like Italian or French villas. She just concentrated on the green and loved it. She pulled up to a call box attached to an ornate copper gate. All she could see was a driveway up a hill beyond the gate—no house.

"May I help you?" asked the disembodied male voice coming from the speaker.

"Nikki Easterly to see Ana Sarstedt." She was pleased that she was there at exactly four P.M., the appointed time for tea.

"Drive up to the fountain area."

Nikki didn't know where that was, but the gate opened and she wound around up the hill. A house appeared in the distance that looked like it was out of one of those French historical movies where royalty lived. It was completely surrounded by a large veranda fenced in by carved cement poles. The front of the house was a large circular driveway around a fountain with enough parking for fifty cars. The stairs to the front door were really a graduated porch about twenty feet long, each stair getting you closer to the veranda. The door itself was glass reinforced with copper.

By the time she reached the front door it was opened and a butler in black tie was waiting for her.

"Miss Easterly? Ms. Sarstedt wants you to wait in the den. Please follow me."

Nikki glanced around quickly and noticed that the foyer by the front door was the size of her whole apartment. That foyer led to a grander hall that ran the length of the front of the house with doors all along the wall leading to various rooms. He walked her through the door straight ahead into the soft yellow living room with brocade sofas and inlaid end tables, and then turned left, through the gold and white dining room, into a den the size of a home basketball half-court. One wall was a big-screen TV, another was all stone with a fireplace you could walk into. The green leather fur-niture was placed on a Berber carpet. The effect was about as woodsy as one could get in a palace. Nikki thought that this had to be the largest house in all of Los Angeles.

"Please be seated." The butler motioned to the center couch.

Nikki sat down in front of copies of *Vanity Fair, Town and Country, Forbes*, and *Business Week*. She picked up *Business Week* and tried to engross herself in a story about the in-formation superhighway.

The distinctive sound of high heels on marble alerted Nikki that she was about to be graced with Madame Ana's presence. From her pictures, Nikki expected to see a beauti-ful, tasteful forty-three-year-old woman. Nikki had also studied the earlier pictures of Ana in her twenties, when she was flashy, but not cheap. The transformation could be seen by studying the pictures, but nothing was as good as seeing the real thing in person.

"Welcome, Miss Easterly," said the voice behind Nikki as she turned and rose to see the woman even more beautiful than Dina Merrill, the Post Cereal heiress turned actress. Ana was wearing a pink and black Chanel suit, black stock-ings, and black Chanel leather pumps with a black patent leather toe.

Nikki was fighting being struck dumb by the elegance of
Ana Sarstedt. It was impossible to believe that this woman
had been a hooker and a madam. She looked like the president of the Opera Guild.

"How do you do?" said Nikki. "Thank you for seeing
me."

"Please sit down."

Nikki sat on the green couch, Ana on the couch to her
right.

"I love having tea in the afternoon. It's such a civilized
ritual," continued Ana. "You would think I learned it in En-
gland, but I learned it in Paris when I was in my twenties."

Nikki was surprised Ana was even bringing up Paris.

"Have you ever been to Paris, Nikki?"

"No, I haven't, but I'd love to go."

"It's so beautiful. I have so many special places there that
bring back memories."

The butler came in holding a silver tray with little tea
sandwiches on it and an individual pot of tea, cup and
saucer, lemon, cream, a strainer over a bowl, and a silver
spoon. Another servant was right behind him with an identical tray. The butler served Ana, while the other one served
Nikki.

Nikki noted the linen doilies were trimmed in forest green
to match the couches. The china was old-fashioned Lenox
with gold trim.

"Please ring when you wish the scones, madam."

"My favorites are the tomato and cheese," said Ana.
"There's something so homey about them. I also love the
egg and cucumber, but try the watercress, too. Many people
think it's too bland, but I have them make it on pumpernickel with a special mayonnaise. Try it."

Nikki sampled the watercress first. "Yes, it's lovely."

They both fixed their tea in silence, Nikki feeling slightly
uncomfortable, even though Ana was being charming. The

madam thing didn't bother Nikki, the house didn't intimidate her . . . she couldn't figure out why she was so unsettled, yet she felt somehow safe with this woman as well, almost familiar. She just didn't get it, and she had to force herself to concentrate.

"I see no one, Nikki. Aren't you curious as to why you're allowed to be here?"

"Of course," answered Nikki, "but I didn't think it should be the first question out of my mouth."

"You're a wise young lady. I, on the other hand, dispense with things right away. I can do that now. I know it's distasteful to refer to one's own money, but since I never really had any growing up, I can say that now that I do have it I can do what I want. I do try to stay in the bounds of good taste, of course." She laughed, her eyes sparkling.

Nikki didn't know where this was going so she kept quiet, but she could certainly see how Ana's charm could move mountains.

"I am a little younger than what your mother would be now if she had lived," said Ana out of the blue.

That took Nikki aback.

"I was a huge fan of hers. She was extraordinarily beautiful and she actually could act. She didn't make it just because of her face. Are you aware of that?"

"I try not to think about my mother very much," said Nikki defensively, wondering how the whole focus of this interview had shifted to her before it even started. She wanted to ask questions about her mother, yet if she did she felt she would never get to what she really wanted to know about Ana. But Ana kept on talking, so Nikki's decision was made for her whether she liked it or not.

"Your mother was a handful. I remember the studios that she worked for had some real problems with her because she was such a free spirit, but I admire that in people."

Now Nikki wanted to defend her mother but she didn't quite know against what.

"She loved her men and she loved her work. She really lived life, you know. She had a fabulous time. It's like her star was snuffed out when it was shining at its brightest. The industry went crazy when it happened. I remember that you were taken away quickly to your aunt's. Meredith, I believe. She and Lauren really didn't get along. That's what the fan magazines said. I always thought that Meredith must have been jealous."

"My aunt hated Hollywood and never wanted to be a part of it," answered Nikki, immediately regretting that she added information and prolonged the topic.

"Do you hate Hollywood?"

"No. I mean, I don't know. I was too little when I left. I'm not from here."

"Well, you're here now," said Ana. "What do you think?"

"I think it's a planet unto itself with its own rules and values, or lack thereof. It's very peculiar."

"But a part of you wants to know about it, isn't there? I'll bet that in a way you blame Hollywood for killing your mother and you're here to investigate that."

"Why are we discussing this?" said Nikki, trying not to lose her composure. She had never experienced someone so direct, so personal, in such a short period of time. Ana seemed psychic. She was asking questions that Nikki didn't want to think about let alone know what the answers might be.

"I'm sorry, but you see I used to spend a lot of one-on-one time with people. You get to know them and size them up right away. I don't mean to make you uncomfortable, I wanted to meet you because I love Hollywood. The glamour still gets to me, and you are a child of Hollywood whether you like it or not. You are a part of Hollywood history."

"So are you," countered Nikki, "and that's why I'm here."

The sandwiches were no longer being touched, nor the tea

sipped by either woman. The meeting had taken on sharper edges.

"So you're interested in real estate?" challenged Ana.

"Absolutely not," Nikki retorted. "I'm interested in Greggie Alcott."

Ana didn't flinch. "Poor girl, that was a sad case. I guess she got mixed up with the wrong people."

"Who are the wrong people?" asked Nikki.

"Oh, that was just a figure of speech. Greggie liked hot sex and I guess she just invited the wrong man into her apartment. Why are we talking about this? The killer's in jail. It's all past history."

"Did you know Guy Marleaux? His mother says he's innocent."

"So does mine," Ana shot back.

"You do have a great sense of humor and style," said Nikki.

"Thank you, dear, you're sitting in the house that it bought me."

Nikki saw Ana's grin and couldn't help but laugh. She picked up an egg and cucumber sandwich.

"Why are you bringing all this up?" asked Ana.

"I'm sorry, but I can't discuss that."

"You expect me to answer your questions while you don't answer mine? That's no fun."

Nikki thought she'd plunge in one more time. "Marleaux was a messenger for Atlas Studios. I've read all your press clippings and you and your operation seem to be closely associated with them."

"Atlas, like all studios, has a revolving door for employees at that level. I wouldn't bother about that, I was close to every studio. I wouldn't bother about this case at all. It's in the past. I'd love to show you the gardens. Follow me."

Ana stood up and Nikki knew there would be no more conversation about Atlas. But she also knew she struck a nerve when she mentioned it, and it was a lead she planned to follow.

"I'm very proud of my flowers," said Ana, pointing to an English garden overgrown in the best sense of the word. "I love the wildness. They can grow free and I groom them myself. I have gardeners for the heavy work, and landscapers, too, but I like to do the detail work personally."

"The aroma coming from them is wonderful," said Nikki.

"Oh, you like scents?"

"Well, I never thought much about it until now. It's so magical here, the smell just overtakes you."

"Come, walk with me around to the front. I know you probably need to get back to the office and you're being polite about seeing my yard," said Ana.

"I'm enjoying myself, actually," said Nikki.

"What can you smell now, dear?" asked Ana when they were back at the circular driveway by Nikki's car.

"What do you mean?"

"Breathe in," Ana directed, leaning closer to Nikki.

Nikki did, and looked at her quizzically.

"It's Fresh Love, don't you remember? It's your mother's scent. She was my favorite star, as I told you, and you must know that she was the Fresh Love girl in all their ads and commercials."

Nikki's mouth dropped open only slightly, and she fought to catch herself so she wouldn't be vulnerable in front of Ana.

"Y-yes, I do remember," mumbled Nikki, turning to her car. She extended her hand quickly and said, "Thank you very much for tea."

Nikki drove the car down the driveway and stopped it when she got to the street. She pulled over, shutting her eyes, unable to forget that smell. It was her mother, her childhood, the love she had, the love she lost, the terror of death. She was shaking, and totally shocked that in one second the door had been opened to her deepest thoughts by a fragrance.

Without commenting on Fresh Love, Nikki recounted the Ana meeting to Hayden as they drove to the prison to see Guy Marleaux. Nikki had never been to a prison before and she was a little nervous.

"It's imposing gray cement, and frightening when you hear that door swing shut. They take your valuables away from you and put you in a room. It feels like you are in prison yourself. I'll be there with you so just try to relax. We need to hear Marleaux's story and see how he feels about the DNA in order to start the appeal petition."

"I need to ask you a question," said Nikki.

"Of course."

"I'm really in a time bind. All I want to do is work on this Marleaux case. It's all I think about. What do you do with your caseload when one case stands out in particular?"

"It's always a problem," said Hayden. "I certainly have been there. For me, I just keep telling myself that we're doing a job and we have a responsibility to all our clients. I just have to force myself to put a case down for a while and get to the next. I pretend that they're like math problems and you have to do all of them to finish your homework."

"But some of them are so boring, so routine. Mark is having me work on a little bit of everything. I have this stupid tax case where I'm working under George Livingston."

"He's one of our best tax specialists."

"I know, but our client is guilty and we should just make a deal with the IRS to pay them off. Then I've got a contract dispute over billing on a movie where the prints were already shipped and they violated this producer's contract and the credits are wrong. The producer wants the studio to get the prints back and redo the titles. The studio says they're sorry, they didn't mean to make a mistake and they'll fix the titles on the remaining unshipped prints. They say it's too expensive to do a recall. This is just nonsense. It doesn't mean anything compared to the Marleaux case."

"It's all important, Nikki, in certain ways. This all comes with the dinner, as we say in the Chinese food business," said Hayden laughing.

"Very funny," said Nikki in mock annoyance.

"Well, at least I got a laugh out of you. Just keep thinking it's a job and you're finishing your math problems. You'll get all the work done. You're too responsible not to."

The prison at Chino looked straight out of a movie. There were towers with guards and spotlights, an electrified fence, and a heavy guard gate which they passed through. Hayden saw to it that they had all the right credentials, but Nikki felt herself getting a little clammy while she was waiting in the office. They had to sit in an institutional green waiting room with scuffed chairs and no coffee table while they waited to be admitted to the prisoner visiting area. They only had to wait about fifteen minutes, but to Nikki it seemed like an hour.

"I can't believe they asked you to tell me not to wear halter tops or jeans. I'm a lawyer for God's sake," said Nikki.

"There are so many rules here, you just do them and don't even ask," said Hayden. "Actually, in the men's section of the prison they think if a woman wears a halter top she'll start a riot, and if you wear jeans they might think you're a prisoner who escaped from the women's section."

"Yeah, right," snapped Nikki.

There was a click and a door opened, revealing an armed guard.

"Marleaux party?"

Nikki and Hayden stood.

"Here are your locker keys. Please take off all jewelry. Ma'am, put your purse in there, and sir, your wallet. Take only a legal tablet and a pen with you."

They did as they were told.

"Now follow me to the shuttle bus."

Nikki looked at Hayden questioningly.

The bus drove through the main gate of the prison, past prisoners in jeans, T-shirts, and slip-on tennis shoes. Most of them were gardening.

"Do you know why they wear those kinds of shoes?" asked Hayden.

Nikki shook her head.

"They could strangle people with laces."

Nikki grimaced.

They got off the bus and went into another holding area where they had to take off their shoes and belts and walk through a metal detector and then through another electric gate. The echo of all those gates got to Nikki. It seemed so permanent and the constant clanging was something she would have a hard time forgetting.

The waiting area was filled with wives and family members sitting close together. The candy and coffee machines were in constant use.

"We had a one o'clock appointment and it's already one-thirty," said Nikki.

"Prison time is a whole other world. We'll be lucky if we see him soon. You never know what goes on. Maybe there's sudden lockup and he's detained. Who knows? We'll just have to wait."

An hour and a half later they were escorted into a six-by-six room with one glass wall with chicken wire inside the glass where they could be observed. Four folding chairs surrounded a metal table and one flat metal ashtray in the middle. The floors were concrete and the ceiling tiles had holes in them that you could count if you got bored.

A door, different from the one they used, opened, and in walked Guy Marleaux, a young man in his late twenties, pale and thin with soft brown hair. He wore wire glasses and had a shy smile.

The door closed and the three of them were alone except for the guard staring through the glass.

"I'm very glad to meet you," said Nikki, holding out her hand and smiling confidently. "This is Hayden Chou."

"I thank you for coming," said Guy softly, looking at the floor. "I'm so grateful. It is terrible here. I didn't do anything and my life is ruined. My family may not have much money, but we are proud people descended from the Huguenots. I am not supposed to be here. I hope you can help me."

Nikki's heart was touched immediately. Guy was so helpless. She felt immediately that he was innocent. It was not just the cries of a mother pulling at her heartstrings—she felt down to her toes that he had been railroaded.

"How is my mother?" he asked.

"She's fine and she believes in you totally," said Hayden. "We will arrange it for her to come on your next visitation day. It was important that we see you as soon as possible."

Hayden went on to discuss the DNA possibilities and that the first step was to get a sample of his DNA and get the results. If they didn't match the crime scene he was innocent and they had a case.

"We would then petition the court for a new trial based on new evidence," continued Hayden.

Guy was excited by the prospect and began asking questions. "My fingerprints are there, my hair is there, I was there. How can this help? I'll be convicted again."

Nikki was upset because Guy sounded so desperate.

"But if you didn't do it, then somebody else was there, too. He would have left DNA tracks. His could never match yours. This is new science but we have to go for it. The first thing we do is get a hair sample. Guy, just run your hands through your hair and hand us a couple. Don't let them drop on the table."

Guy's hand was shaking, but he did it.

"Good. Now we have a start. I think it would be best if you just took a deep breath and told us what happened from the beginning," said Nikki, placing her hand over his to calm him down.

He held his head in his hands. "I don't know where to begin."

"Tell us when you arrived in Los Angeles," said Hayden.

"I always loved movies as a child. In France, Hollywood is the end of the rainbow. I studied English all my life so I could come to the United States. I came to New Orleans first because we had relatives there. I worked as a busboy in a restaurant. Eventually I saved enough money for a bus ticket to L.A. I think that was in 1988," explained Guy slowly and carefully.

"I would have done anything to work on a soundstage. I went to all the studios to the personnel departments and applied for anything I could get. The first thing that came along was a messenger job for Atlas Studios. I loved doing it. I was all over the lot. I went to the soundstages, the editing rooms, the offices. I could go anywhere. Sometimes, if I had a few free minutes, I would wander on a stage and watch them shoot. I had an Atlas messenger uniform and nobody bothered me. I tried to be quiet, and I got to know some of the assistant directors and cameramen. They knew I was a fan and they wouldn't say anything if I watched. I was so happy," said Guy. He took a deep breath.

"I wish I had a glass of water."

"Do you want me to ask a guard?" asked Nikki.

"No, it's better that we just keep talking," said Guy nervously.

Nikki noticed how he folded his thumb inside his fingers, just like a baby.

"I lived in a one-room apartment near the studio so I could walk to work. After the first six months on the job they rented a little Dodge van for me—it was great. It was perfect for delivering packages, plus I could take it on the weekends, drive up the coast. It made me proud to be driving it because it said 'Atlas Studios' on the side. I couldn't believe how lucky I was. I also made friends with the girls in the publicity department and they would let me into some of the screenings. I was so lucky . . . But some weird things happened, too."

"Like what?" asked Hayden.

"I don't know . . ." he hesitated. "Like sometimes I didn't know what I was delivering. You can tell when it's a script or a book or costumes, but then I'd get calls at two A.M. from the head of the department asking me to rush up to a director's house or a famous star or even sometimes I'd go to David Solomon's or Joel Bronson's. Something told me not to ask questions."

"Did you know Solomon and Bronson?" asked Nikki.

"Not really. I knew their secretaries because of the deliveries."

"What kind of instructions did you get when you picked up the packages?" asked Hayden.

"Sometimes they would say nothing. Just hand me an address and that's it. Sometimes I would have to hand-deliver something and not ever leave it at the front door if someone wasn't home. On some rare occasions I was told if I ever got stopped by the police to throw the package outside the car so they wouldn't see it. There were never any labels on those packages. I got really nervous sometimes. I thought it was probably drugs."

Hayden and Nikki looked at each other.

"Did anything else ever happen that you found odd?" asked Hayden.

"Well, it wasn't odd, but it made me nervous." Guy looked at Nikki uncomfortably. "I feel funny talking about this."

"You mustn't feel funny. We need to know everything," said Nikki calmly. "It's all right."

"There were the girls. I mean not all the time, I never pursued any of them. But sometimes on a delivery somebody might like me. I was flattered, they were important people in Hollywood, very pretty. They would ask me in and look at me. I could tell they were more interested in me than the package. Forgive me, this is embarrassing, but I was amazed I was even in Hollywood. I couldn't believe it. Sometimes I would go to bed with them. I found the surprise of it all exciting because I never knew when it would happen. That's what happened with Greggie. She was so beautiful and sweet. She was lonely and wanted me to stay. It just happened."

"What just happened?" asked Hayden, who had been taking notes from the very beginning.

"The sex. We both wanted it. It was done and then I left."

"Let's go back," interrupted Nikki, who had already read the transcript of the original trial. "I know you delivered a package there at eleven P.M. Who called you?"

"Rob, the guy on duty at the studio that night. He told me to come to the guard gate and pick up a package and take it to the house on Hutton Drive. I don't know what was in it. It felt like a script. No big deal."

"And when you delivered it did you know who the girl was?" asked Hayden.

"I had seen her on the set of a couple of Alexis Panos's pictures. She wasn't in any of his movies, though. I just thought she was somebody's friend. Maybe his. I don't know. All I know is she asked me to come in and then we had sex. Please excuse me, Miss Easterly. This is hard for me. She was beautiful. It was just something to do."

Nikki nodded.

"I need more details," said Hayden. "What did she like?"

"Oh, I am sorry, this is too hard."

"I can handle it, Guy. I'm a grown-up," countered Nikki.

"I hate talking this way." He paused. "She liked it rough. She was scratching me and biting me. She wanted me to pull her hair and push her around. I am not used to this. It was exciting, but it didn't make me want to do it again."

"What happened when you were through?" asked Hayden.

Nikki was glad Hayden was taking over at this point; she thought it was better, and truthfully, she was embarrassed listening to this. There was a side of her that didn't really want to know what she was learning.

"She patted me on the cheek and said thanks, Guy, you're cute. I sort of felt used, dismissed. She turned over to go to sleep and I just let myself out."

"Was the door locked when you left?"

"I don't know. I just shut the door and didn't think about it."

"Then what did you do?"

"I went home and went to sleep. I didn't think anything until I heard the news later the next day. I almost fainted. Then I got very, very frightened. I thought I might lose my job if anybody knew I slept with a client or someone who worked with Atlas Studios. I was nervous for my job. I never dreamed I would be accused of murder. At first I wanted to go to the police to tell them I was there, but then I just kept my mouth shut to keep my job. I couldn't believe it when I was arrested. I can't believe I'm here now."

His voice started to break. "Please, help me. I don't understand how this could happen." He wiped the falling tears with his hands.

Nikki noticed they were very delicate.

"We'll do our very best to help you. Try to take it easy," said Hayden.

All three of them stood up.

Guy shook hands with both of them and just nodded. He couldn't speak anymore.

The next day when Guy's sample was sent off, Nikki started to hear a timer ticking. It was going to be an agonizing five days. She would have to do everything she could to keep herself moving. She knew she was getting too involved, and she remembered Meredith's words of caution about Nikki's working in that kind of law. Over and over Meredith had told her that she was too sensitive and too emotional. She was only now beginning to understand the warning.

She went home that night and looked at the computer. She had begun to use it regularly for her work, but more and more she would drift off into the online services. She would read *Time*, or check out the political bulletin board or whatever interested her at the moment, but more and more she began to find herself going into CB Adult. She would almost feel her fingers tingle on the keyboard as they were getting ready to go into it.

She started to think about it when she was reading the weather in Tanzania, pretending that she was really interested. She had to trick herself that she was really doing good work on the computer and reading interesting things, pursuing hobbies like cooking and travel, and that it was an accident when she'd check out the Adult Band for a little while. Almost like, well I'll just take a sip of that vodka, certainly not a whole drink.

She told no one about this little obsession, taking the position with Joely, Beverly, and Hayden that the computer was an excellent work tool. She gave no hint of the emotional involvement. Sometimes she even would refuse a dinner invitation in order to go home and get online. She knew that some nights were better than others. If you really wanted to read the weird stuff, tune in from ten to midnight West Coast time on a Saturday night.

The first time she decided to tune in rather than "Monitor," she chose her handle carefully. She didn't want it to be anything close to her real name. She chose Sweetie, which could be interpreted many ways.

*Hi Sweetie!*
*Hello. Do you taste sweet?*
*Ready for some fun, Sweetie?*

As soon as she clicked in and was on the screen, she was prepared for this, because she had been reading for weeks. But what she didn't know was that as soon as you clicked in, people would dial you up and a bell would ding in the computer signaling you had a special message. She was not aware of this, but after the first bell she saw a separate window come up from Swinging Papa.

*Wanna play in my room?*

Nikki thought for a moment, and then felt like an idiot. Of course that's what people meant by going to private rooms. They could talk to each other, say anything they wanted and the rest of the people on the channel couldn't read their conversation. She couldn't believe that she was suddenly alone with this guy. Gathering her nerve, she decided to play along for a while.

SWEETIE: I'd love to play. What did you have in mind?
SWINGING PAPA: I really am a Swinging Papa and I live in Nebraska. I'm 6'1 with sandy hair and a good physique. I work as a computer analyst. Tell me about you?
SWEETIE: I'm 5'5 and I look like Victoria Principal.

Nikki didn't know what to say, and that was the first thing that came into her mind. Men love Victoria Principal.

SP: Mmmmmm. What are you wearing right now?
S: Men's satin pajamas.
SP: Will you take off the bottoms?

Nikki felt herself shudder in her seat. She had never done anything like this. It was so bold, so scary. Yet, she told herself in that quick second, so risk-free. Shouldn't she finally try to go for it?

S: My bottoms are off.
SP: How sweet are you?
S: You'll have to investigate very slowly.
SP: Lie back, I'm tickling the inside of your thighs with my tongue.
S: It feels good.
SP: You're so soft. My lips are brushing against you, heading up to where you want me to be. I'm getting so close now. Can't you feel my breath in between your legs? Here comes my tongue.
S: Oh my God.
SP: I'm licking you now slow and fast, light and heavy, sucking, digging deep, you're begging for my cock but you get my fingers first. You're going to have to beg me for more.

Nikki's heart was beating and she couldn't catch her breath. This was nothing like she had ever felt before. She was shocked that she felt throbbing and wetness. It was too terrifying. She pressed "quit" and the screen went dark. Thank God, he can't ever find me, she thought.

It took Hayden and Nikki about a week to frame the petition. They went full-speed ahead with the test because they both had a strong feeling that Guy's DNA would not match the original samples found at Greggie's house. And indeed they were right. Nikki was so excited when the results came in that she wanted to shout it from the rooftops.

She ran to Mark's office.

"Calm down, Nikki," urged Mark. "I gave you this case because you love to work for the little guy, but we have to keep things quiet. I never dreamed this is the direction it would take. Let's not make a big deal of this. Let's just file our petition and wait. And don't discuss this with anyone. Get back to your regular cases now."

Nikki was disappointed with Mark's reaction. Did she only get to work on this a couple of weeks and then put it on the back burner to go to the money cases? It certainly appeared that way, but she didn't push it. He seemed to be on to other things already.

Instead of either Hayden or Nikki going down to the courthouse to file they sent a messenger who worked for the firm. It was important that someone unrecognizable do it. They also sent the runner to the filing place at four P.M., just at the end of the business day, so most or all of the reporters would miss it. And that's what happened. It was totally quiet the day the petition was filed. Normally it takes a court about thirty days to rule on a petition. By eleven A.M. the next morning, however, Nikki had received calls from a couple of reporters, which she didn't return, and she found out a police sergeant was waiting for Mark in his office. Things were beginning to ripple.

Mark thought it best if he spoke to the police, and he let Hayden handle the reporters. The reporters were angry that Hayden was the spokesman, they wanted Nikki. They remembered her from the divorce case and they would have loved to get a Lauren Laverty question in.

Mark simply told the police that they had new evidence that Guy Marleaux wasn't guilty, and he would wait for the court to rule on it. He wouldn't answer anything else.

\* \* \*

"There's a Douglas Collins here to see you. He doesn't have an appointment, but he insisted that I interrupt you. I'm sorry, sir."

Mark sat at his desk and smiled. He was not at all surprised by the visit. In fact he thought Collins would have been at his door sooner.

"Do send him in."

Mark rose as Collins entered. Mark was taller and wanted to show strength.

Douglas Collins was a lawyer in his early forties who had a thick head of white hair. He was dressed impeccably in a light gray suit, a pale pink shirt, and a subtle charcoal silk tie with pale, pale, pink polka dots. His shoes were black alligator. He was of counsel to Weisberg, Wilson, which meant in return for office space and a secretary and his occasional advice, Weisberg could use his name to get clients. It was a very valuable use for Weisberg because Collins had only one client—Phillipe Gascon.

"How are you, Mark?" said Collins charmingly.

Mark actually liked him. He thought he was bright and industrious, and didn't hold it against him that he was associated with Weisberg.

"I'm doing well. I haven't seen you out on the range lately."

"I've been going back and forth to Europe a lot," he answered.

"Good, then I'll challenge you to a game. How about a foursome Saturday at ten?"

"You're on," said Collins.

Mark deliberately paused to give Collins a second to start the real reason for the meeting. Just as Collins was about to speak, Mark said, "So what does Gascon want?"

Collins's rhythm was disturbed, but he recovered in a couple of seconds.

"Look, Mark, what's all this about the Greggie Alcott case? It's over and done with. Can't you leave well enough alone?"

"Who's asking?"

"C'mon, help me out here," said Collins.

"Maybe it's Guy Marleaux who needs the help," said Mark. "What if he's innocent?"

"He was proven guilty. Case closed."

"And Atlas is now scandal-free with a new regime of executives," countered Mark. "I always thought how convenient it was that Solomon and Bronson resigned and became independent producers with nonexclusive deals shortly after the murder. It was so pretty it almost had a bow tied around it."

"It's no secret that Gascon thought they were overspending. The resignations would have happened anyway," Collins responded.

Mark thought for a couple of seconds. He was well aware that if Gascon had been *forced* to fire Solomon and Bronson it would have cost him millions of dollars to push them out. He wondered what the connection was between the resignations and the Greggie Alcott case.

Mark continued. "So what's the big deal. They're out. The studio is fine, Gascon saved big bucks. Why would he care about Marleaux? It's not an important issue. I gave it to a junior associate. Big deal."

"I have delivered my message. Let it go. Things are fine the way they are, and that's the way we want them to stay," said Collins.

There was something in Collins's tone that Mark didn't like. It was almost imperceptible but it brought a chill to his spine. Gascon had very long arms.

Mark stood up. "Saturday at ten," he responded, extending his own very long arm.

\* \* \*

"Oh, darling, last night was incredible," said Ana, gazing at the taut body of her partner.

"I bet you say that to all the guys," he teased.

"That was a long time ago. You know you are special to me."

"Am I as special as the others?" he asked.

"More so. You are my favorite and you have been a good friend to me for many years," she answered, trailing the long sleeve of her pink lace nightgown over his chest. She could tell he was getting interested again, but she had another assignment.

"Darling, what's going on with this Marleaux thing?"

"Congratulations, you held the question till the morning. I'm proud of you," he said.

"Now don't be that way. You know I'm just curious."

"You can ask, but I'm not answering this one," he said. "And now, as gorgeous as you are, I'm getting up because I don't want to be late for my golf game."

Ana pouted, but inside she was worried. Phillipe wanted information, and she had just failed with her best source, a source she genuinely loved, which had made her position very difficult through the years. Ana never allowed herself to think about it for long because it was too painful. She turned over and shut her eyes so she wouldn't have to see Mark leave.

# Chapter 9

Within fifteen days the court sent a letter to Nikki responding to her writ of habeas corpus asking for a new trial based on new evidence. Without opening it she took it into Mark's office.

"It's here," she said solemnly.

"Now remember what I've told you. Most of the time you just get a letter saying your petition is summarily denied," cautioned Mark. "Half the time you never know whether the judge has even read it: maybe a clerk did and just told the judge to ignore it. There are so many of these petitions, practically every convicted criminal appeals."

Nikki took a deep breath and slit open the envelope. She let out a scream. "It's an order to show cause . . . we did it!"

Mark hugged her.

"This is incredible, my first criminal appeals case and we've pulled it off. I can't believe it."

"Well, I'm glad you're happy, but this is just a start. If for any reason you lose, just remember it's a long road."

"I know, I know," said Nikki. "First the State Court of Appeal, then God forbid, the State Supreme Court, the U.S. District, and I don't even want to think about the rest *or* the U.S. Supreme Court! Let me just enjoy this moment. We really did it!"

"And now is when our work is really cut out for us. We must consider things carefully because it could turn very ugly," said Mark. "We could go strictly by the law, research the DNA cases, file petitions, and return to our other cases."

"That's totally passive," said Nikki. "I don't want to do it."

"In order to confront things head-on, Nikki, you are exposed to some danger. I don't like that, it's something I never bargained for. I want you off the case. I'm sorry."

"What!" Nikki shouted. "This is everything I ever dreamed I wanted to do. This is why I became a lawyer. You can't do this to me. Just because I'm a woman you think of me as some frail thing. You're picturing me as a little girl because that's how long you've known me and that's not fair. If I were with another firm they wouldn't think of me that way."

"Nikki, please, I'm thinking of your safety. Maybe you're right. Maybe I am overprotective. But this is becoming serious business, and whether you were a man or a woman, at this point I would assign a team of lawyers to take on the case. You know very well that would be procedure."

"Uh huh," said Nikki cautiously.

"So, I will name you a member of the team. I will head it and you and Hayden are on it. We'll get more research people involved if you want. Also, if you need Alvin Marantz for anything, he'll be available. There's nobody better in high-finance issues than Alvin. By the way, if you and I were working for another firm, say Weisberg, Wilson, they'd never have taken the case in the first place. Moreover, as your boss there I would be telling you what was going to happen rather than discussing it with you as I am. So, shall we come to an agreement on this. We'll continue the case, but it will be our team?"

"Deal," said Nikki.

"Fine. In that case I want to confront things head-on. Nikki, I'm sending you and Hayden to Paris on the six o'clock plane tomorrow night. I want you to meet with Phillipe Gascon. I've already phoned Mrs. Marleaux at her home in France with the results. You can see her, too. I'll make all the arrangements, and I'll fill you in at lunch. We're eating in today and working straight through."

Nikki's excitement about going to France to see Phillipe Gascon almost overshadowed her delight at the petition results. She had forty-eight hours to get ready, and she knew just who to call.

Joely was at her door in seconds. "A million times, babe," answered Joely when Nikki asked her if she'd ever been to France. "And you should hear about some of the guys I went with."

"I'd rather hear about what the climate is, what to wear. We're staying at the Crillon. I'm sure Mark would book us somewhere nice."

"The Crillon? My God, it's a former palace. It's one of the most magnificent hotels in Paris. You'd better bring a lot of black. It's so beautiful. You'll stroll along the Seine, maybe go on a boat ride. It's perfect. Who knows what will happen . . ."

"Joely! This is a business trip."

"I know, but who says you can't get a little something going. I've never seen a person as disinterested as you. All you care about is your work."

"My work is about whether a man has a life or rots away in prison," said Nikki.

"That's noble and true," said Joely, "but what about your life? You should have one, too. Please, just try to relax a little. It's so beautiful there you can have time. You only have one business appointment, right?"

"Yes, but business is what this is about. A personal life's just not important to me now."

Joely paused, wondering for the umpteenth time what exactly was important for Nikki, but she let it go.

"All right, let's get to your closet. You're leaving tomorrow."

When word of the petition results filled the office gossip trough, Roland picked up the phone and called Douglas Collins. He knew Collins wouldn't be happy about the news but he'd better know as soon as possible. Collins would take it from there, and it was always good to keep Douglas happy. Roland had done his part, and so far as he was concerned he had more important things on his mind.

He had noticed lately that Cruger was becoming distant. Roland hadn't been as available lately because of his work. When he and Cruger first got together Roland doted on him and spent every waking hour trying to make him feel special. As his career escalated, his attention to Cruger waned. Roland was realizing that this was a serious mistake. Even though Roland now had money and prestige of his own, Cruger Delafield Grozbach Fowler IV was still the reason his career got started and would continue to flourish at the social and business level that it was. Cruger's power and money were awesome and Roland's association with it was crucial.

Roland left work early, something he never did anymore. He went home to plan an evening. He knew Cruger would be home at seven-thirty and saw that they had nothing scheduled for tonight. The first thing he did was send for the cook and butler.

"Tonight I'd like you to set the formal dining room table just for two, but use the best of everything. Make it as if we were having Prince Charles to dinner. You know what to do. I'd like the first course to be sautéed bay scallops, make sure they're really small. Place them in a dessert goblet with fresh tarragon on top. Then I'd like you to serve rack of lamb, medium rare, just the way Mr. Fowler likes it, with mashed potatoes and julienned zucchini. For dessert we'll have something light, just some fresh berries and cream, and would you have some caviar and champagne placed in our sitting room upstairs at seven-fifteen? Dinner will be at eight-thirty. Thank you, I know everything will be superb."

Roland went upstairs to their quarters, which took up the entire right half of the house. The door straight ahead of him led to their sitting room, a lovely beige affair with oversized cream chaises, thick oatmeal carpet, cashmere throws over each chaise, a big-screen TV, a fireplace, and a bar with a little kitchenette as well. To the left of the sitting room was Roland's home office. Cruger's was downstairs off the den. Roland could get to the bedroom either by going through the sitting room, or from the front hall entering through the door at the right angle from the sitting room.

He decided to go straight to the bedroom, an area that never failed to thrill him. It was at least forty by sixty feet, all done in shades of warm gray. Mirrors reflected the gray so it shimmered everywhere. The carpet was a light charcoal and the king-size bed was built on a carpeted lighter charcoal platform. The bedspread was dark gray—if one looked at the bed as art from a distance it looked like a modern sculpture. The drapes behind the bed had a slightly silver sheen and matched the drapes on the windows. There was a gray shadow plaid couch in a sitting area by the fireplace. Everything in the room was upholstered with soft edges, even the tables and chairs, so you had the effect of almost being in a gray cloud.

To the left and right of the bedroom were the bathroom and dressing room suites, his and his, with huge walk-in closets. Cruger's was on the left: it was all white and chrome. The ceiling was mirrored as was one wall. The separate shower and tub were enclosed in opaque glass blocks. The walls and floors were shiny white tile. Theatrical bulbs surrounded the mirror like the dressing room of a movie star. When the lights were on they bounced off everything in the room. The effect was dazzling.

As for Roland, his bathroom was the exact opposite. All the tile was black and the mirrors and lights reflected that darkness. It was like being in a private cave. The configuration of the rooms was the same, but in Roland's case he didn't use glass block for the shower and tub, he used clear glass so all you ever saw was black. His lights were on a rheostat so he could dim them. He loved to take a bath in near darkness.

He picked up the phone in the bathroom and dialed a number. "Hi, it's me. We need you tonight. Come here at ten. They'll let you in the back door."

With everything set, Roland walked to his closet and disrobed. He placed his suit on the valet to be steamed, threw his shirt, socks, and shorts in the hamper, and placed his tie in its position on the rack. Roland loved his ties. He had so many that he installed a motorized rack like the one in the cleaners for large clothes, only his was a small version just for ties. He loved to press the button and have the ties fly by.

He went into the bathroom and started the water running in the black tile tub, letting it get high enough for the Jacuzzi jets to be covered. He liked the water really hot, he wanted his body to be jolted by the temperature. As he reclined in the water he loved that touch of pain. It was a glorious wince. He lay back and put his head on the inflated black plastic swan, then reached back and got the remote control for the CD and put on his favorite disc, sounds of the jungle. He loved to lie in the darkness and hear the eerie sounds of danger. The CD started out nicely with birds and sounds of underbrush, an occasional drum. When the big cats began growling, he turned up the sound full-blast and put on the Jacuzzi, whose rumblings intensified the noises. This kind of tension and excitement got him ready for the night ahead. It was a crucial part of his regimen.

He heard Cruger come in the front door. He was ready. He was dressed in a black and burgundy satin smoking jacket with no shirt, the collar and cuffs of the jacket trimmed in black velvet matching his black velvet elastic waist slip-on trousers. He was barefoot.

"Up here," he called from the sitting room door.

Cruger didn't answer as he rushed up the stairs with an armload of scripts. He almost stumbled over Roland in his haste.

"For you," said Roland, holding out a dry martini with an onion in it. "Let me take your things. I think you should just sit down by the fire and get calm."

Cruger was stunned by this turn of events. "Well, well, you're focused again," he said. "And none too soon."

Roland saw the twinkle in Cruger's eyes despite the bitchy comment. He was glad he spent the afternoon organizing.

"Ahh," said Cruger when he landed on his chaise. "I really needed this. One of our actors just didn't show up today and it cost us three hours of shooting time until we could move scenes around. I'm going to kill him the next time I see him. We've written him out of this week's episode and we'll withhold his paycheck."

"Try not to think about that now. Why don't you have some caviar. I've done it just the way you like it—a tin and a spoon. Have some and I'll go get your bath ready."

Roland went into the bathroom and smiled to himself. It was working, he thought. I haven't lost it. Not wearing a shirt was just the right touch. Cruger liked his bath warm, not steaming hot, and Roland dropped some eucalyptus oil pellets in the water. He heard Cruger walk into his closet and get undressed.

He came into the bathroom holding the martini, still swallowing the caviar.

"Enjoy yourself. I'll meet you in the dining room at eight-thirty."

Roland took great pride in the fact that Cruger loved the dinner. He had been neglecting things and just letting the help make the choices. "You know, our social life is out of hand," said Roland. "I think we need to block out more time for ourselves. We need that."

"I appreciate that. I've missed you," said Cruger in a rare moment of sentimentality. "Some of our engagements are so important we can't miss them, but I think we should try to spend more weekends away."

"I agree, and I'll work with our secretaries to set that up, but for now, we'd better go upstairs for our after-dinner surprise."

Cruger laughed out loud, wondering what surprise it would be tonight.

When they walked into the bedroom it was darker than it was before. Cruger sat on the bed in anticipation. Suddenly a light went on in Cruger's dressing area and the door opened to reveal a back-lit hunk dressed in leather chaps, and leather vest and motorcycle boots. He was holding a whip and looking at Roland with danger in his eyes.

"Down boy," he said, cracking the whip.

A shiver went through Roland. He didn't move.

"Now!" he said.

Roland landed on all fours, nose to the gray carpet. He heard Cruger get up from the bed and felt him pull down his velvet trousers, leaving his rear torturously exposed.

"No . . ." said Roland.

"Yes," said Cruger, who sat back on the bed and nodded to the hunk.

The boots didn't make much of a sound on the carpet but Roland knew they were coming closer. He felt the whip almost tickle him as it lightly grazed his cheeks, teasing him. He felt himself getting excited. His fingers clutched the carpet . . . waiting.

*Crack!*

He felt the first sting, and he didn't move. The pain was sharp but he needed more to move through it.

Again he was struck, and then again.

"Ah . . . emm," he couldn't stop himself from making sounds. It was so glorious. His rear was moving now in anticipation, almost trying to "catch" the leather snake. He wanted more, so much more . . . he was tingling.

He heard Cruger get up and knew it was time for the hunk to disappear. His job had been done to perfection. It had made Cruger hot and ready. Roland felt Cruger's hand on his back grabbing at his shoulders, moving in behind him. Cruger started scratching his back with his nails making Roland cry out in pain, but Roland was concentrating on the largeness of Cruger. He wanted him inside so much that he was throbbing. There was no need for lubricant. Roland's ability to get so excited the natural way made it easy for his partners. He could remember Cruger going wild over that fact the first time they were together. It was as if Roland were born to be the master receptacle.

Suddenly Cruger filled him up and was riding him like a Harley. They were going up and down hills, over straightaways, cruising at 150 miles an hour. When Cruger exploded Roland was sure the whole neighborhood could hear. As he felt Cruger fade he grabbed ahold of himself with his hand and relieved himself. Cruger was never interested in truly mutual satisfaction. Roland just accepted it and spent more of Cruger's money as the years went by.

The lobby of the Crillon was more than Nikki could ever have imagined. It was like looking at one of her history books come to life. She wondered why it took her so long to come to Europe and then realized Meredith hadn't encouraged her to travel. Her life was one of nature and studying, and at the time it seemed perfectly all right, but now Nikki was wondering just how much she had missed. If France could have this kind of effect on her what did Egypt look like? Or China? She wanted to see everything.

Hayden was enchanted by her delight. He wanted to throw the whole case away and just show her Paris day and night. Her lawyerlike armor had almost melted away, and he was hoping to get through to her. But he wasn't quite sure what to do. He thought there was a possibility that she had "more than friends" feelings for him, but he wasn't certain. She was so hard to read, and he didn't want to cause problems in their working relationship. He had to walk a very fine line.

"Why don't we unpack and rest a little bit in our rooms, and then we'll go for a walk and have some dinner. We see Gascon tomorrow morning so I won't keep you out late, I promise," said Hayden.

Nikki thought he looked so sweet, but then put it out of her mind. "That would be wonderful, but we have to get back early. You know how important this appointment is."

"Yes, boss," said Hayden jokingly.

Nikki was entranced by her room. It was blue and gold with heavy drapes and antique furniture. The bed was canopied with the same material as the drapes, but it was the refrigerator, phones, and bathroom appliances that got her. She was fascinated by the goodies in the refrigerator, bottles with unfamiliar shapes, unfamiliar names but familiar liquids, little potato chip bags or candies that looked so *different*. The sound of the phone was strange, too. She felt as if she were in a foreign movie. She decided to unpack and take a bath before going out to dinner, almost giddy at the prospect.

After her bath she took out her computer. She could work off the battery if she were going to do office work, but she had brought along the electric cord as well as a phone cord. She thought she would try the internet and see what developed—she was curious about what she might find online in a foreign country. But her curiosity led to frustration when she realized that the phone systems were different and there was no way that a cord from the United States would work in the foreign jack. Her total lack of experience in traveling ruined her interlude, and then she got mad at herself for being so mad. It put her in a terrible mood to begin an evening.

She met Hayden at six in the lobby. He had on a lightweight beige gabardine suit with tan shoes, a white shirt, and a burgundy and camel striped tie. She took Joely's advice and was wearing a basic black dress with a shawl she borrowed from Joely.

"I thought we'd take a little walk first on the Left Bank. Shall we?" Hayden crooked his arm so she could slip hers into his and out they went. They got into a cab and took the short ride to the Left Bank, getting out in front of L'Hôtel, a charming hotel where Oscar Wilde used to stay. "Everybody tries to get his suite when they stay here," Hayden said. "It's incredible."

The night was just slightly crisp, but not cold enough for a coat. Nikki felt exhilarated as Hayden showed her the various pâtisseries, boulangeries, little shops, and bistros along the way. She marveled at the fountains, the music coming from the bistros and street musicians. "Oh, can we stop here and have a glass of wine before dinner?" she asked, pointing at a beautiful little café with outdoor tables across from a street bazaar.

"Of course," said Hayden getting a table. "Would you like red or white?"

"Red. I'm not in Hollywood so I don't have to order one of our stupid cover drinks."

"No, we're free, Nikki. I'll join you with red."

"Deux vins rouges, s'il vous plaît," said Hayden to the waiter.

"I didn't know you spoke French," said Nikki.

"I took it in school. I thought it was such a beautiful language." Hayden wanted to add, as beautiful as you, but he was afraid to.

"I'm sorry you haven't been to Europe before," he said instead. "It's so obvious how you would love it."

"I think that my aunt was just protecting me. My circumstances were so unusual." And then Nikki went silent.

"You don't like to talk about your mother, do you? I don't want to offend you in bringing it up," said Hayden gently.

"I tried not to think about it as a child. My aunt kept me so busy and showed me so many beautiful things. I always felt she didn't want to talk about it either. We never went to Los Angeles. The only trips we took were to national parks or San Francisco. I loved San Francisco. I think that's why I liked Boalt so much because it was near the city. My aunt and my mother were not close."

"Where did they grow up?"

"Orange County. My grandmother and grandfather were very strict. He was a mailman and she worked as the manager of a dry cleaners. They needed every penny: when Lauren and Meredith were born only a year and a half apart my grandfather had to take on another job. Aunt Meredith told me that she and Lauren started modeling as little girls and that brought in money. Lauren was always talking about going to Hollywood because it was so close, and when they were seventeen and eighteen they left. Meredith hated it and went to Northern California to study art, earning money working for a vet. Obviously Lauren stayed."

Hayden was dying to ask her more questions since she seemed to be receptive, but he didn't want to be too eager.

"I can't wait to show you where we're having dinner. It's only two blocks from here. Shall we?"

"I can't imagine it could be more perfect than where we are right now," said Nikki.

L'Ami Louis was one of the most famous bistros in all of France. It had been on the Left Bank for so many years people couldn't remember when it wasn't there. It was typical, with dark wood and mirrors, and the smells of roasted chicken on the spit, lamb and onions simmering.

"You must try the chicken, and in addition to the French fries you have to have the potato onion tart. It's amazing."

"Hey, French fries . . . that's very funny," said Nikki laughing a little. "You order everything for me. I'm in your hands." Nikki smiled.

She was feeling good now. She enjoyed the wine and loved where she was. The people around her looked so happy. It didn't bother her talking about her past to Hayden. It seemed to be okay because they weren't in Hollywood. The distance helped her to talk. She hadn't realized until she started talking, but she really had never spoken of any of these things to anyone. A burden lifted off her shoulders. She was happy to continue.

"I still cringe every time I hear my mother's name, but I'm not sure why," said Nikki tentatively.

Her continuing to talk about so personal a subject pleased and startled Hayden. He just nodded in response.

"I think maybe it's because I was so shielded and I don't know anything about her. Growing up it was like a mystery door that should never be opened, like something bad should be kept secret. Fan magazines were kept away from me; every time one of my mother's movies was on TV I wasn't allowed to watch. Of course as I got a little older I was curious, but still I avoid watching any of her movies. I've seen the Fresh Love ad in old magazines. I know she was one of the most famous women in the world at one point, but I don't know much about her real life. That fear is still with me. I've deliberately never driven by our home where she was killed. I haven't read up on the case. A crazed fan did it, he's in jail and that's that. But maybe that isn't that."

"What do you mean?"

"Well, maybe I think I need to go back a little bit to learn about myself. I think maybe a closed door is not a healthy thing. I have my own life now but I should know where I came from. I can't ask my grandparents. They died in a car crash. Meredith won't even discuss who my father was." And then she almost gasped.

Hayden covered her hand with his.

"I've never said that to anybody before. I can't believe I said it just now. I've heard the rumors, I'm not an idiot. She didn't want to get married . . . I don't know," she continued. "How could anybody expect me to not want to know these answers."

She was getting very agitated.

"Well you know I can help you find out anything," said Hayden sympathetically.

"You mean you and your computer?"

"Yes. Look at how easy it was between you in the library and me on the computer to find out all the information on the Marleaux case. There must be tons of information available on Lauren Laverty. If you want, we can make it our special project together. I don't want you to go through it alone. I will always be there if you need me."

He looked into her eyes and noticed they were starting to

tear up. He leaned across the table, touched her cheek and kissed her on the forehead, loving being that close to her.

She pulled back immediately.

He followed suit, concerned that he had moved too fast.

Nikki felt flushed and excited, but immediately pushed the unfamiliar feelings away.

"Hayden," she said very seriously, all business now. "There's something that I've been meaning to ask you, but the thought of it is terrifying after all these years."

"Please, go ahead," he said gently.

"With all the work we've been doing on DNA, do you think DNA could help me find out who my father is?"

Hayden saw the frightened look in Nikki's eyes, how hard it was for her to ask, how fragile she could be. He took a few seconds before he answered.

"Well, it certainly could be a possibility."

"Oh, my God," said Nikki aloud, realizing she was simply going to have to get over her fears to get to the truth.

"How do we do it?"

"I'm not sure, but let me look into it when we get back, and I'll let you know how real it may or may not be."

"Thank you," she said softly, fighting back tears.

Hayden resisted the impulse to take her hand. Instead he changed the subject and said, "I've got a surprise for you. Let's go!"

Nikki brightened and followed him out of the restaurant, where he led her to the Bateaux-mouches, boats that cruise along the Seine.

"Isn't it beautiful here?" asked Hayden, watching Nikki gaze at the City of Light.

"It's magical," answered Nikki, feeling his arm go around her shoulders. "I've never felt quite like this."

Their eyes met and lingered.

When Nikki closed her hotel room door behind her, her mind was filled with questions. Was something happening between her and Hayden, or was it her imagination? Her body was aglow. She was staring to feel safe with him in a way she had never felt before. As she started to get ready for bed, her old demons were beginning to talk to her. She was fighting to keep her wits about her now that he was out of sight. She was unnerved; she had let her guard down. Too many emotions. She couldn't lose her balance.

"Show them in," said Phillipe over the intercom. He couldn't wait to see what Lauren Laverty's daughter looked like. For a second he wondered to himself whether or not that was the reason he had agreed to this meeting in the first place. As she walked through the door he knew that, despite her being young enough to be his daughter or, worse, his granddaughter, he would have bedded her on the spot.

"Please sit down on the couch," said Phillipe, standing. "Are you enjoying Paris?"

"Yes, I've never been here before," answered Nikki.

And how I could show it to you, thought Phillipe before replying, "Well let me know if there is anything special you would like me to arrange."

"That's very kind of you to offer," said Hayden.

"Now what did you want to see me about?" asked Phillipe in his most cordial manner. There was no point in destroying them right from the top, he thought, sitting down on a chair facing the couch.

"We represent Guy Marleaux," said Hayden. "Do you know who he is?"

"Surely I'm not going on *Jeopardy!* this morning, why don't you just tell me?"

"He's the young man convicted of murdering Greggie Alcott a few years ago. Greggie was a hooker who worked for Madame Ana. We have reason to believe that the wrong man has been convicted, and in cases like this it's important to go back to the beginning. When Greggie was killed there were a lot of rumors of her and Madame Ana's connection to Atlas Studios employees. Marleaux also worked for Atlas. As you are the owner of Atlas's parent company we'd like to ask you a few questions."

Nikki was sitting straight up on the couch, her strawberry blond hair just grazing her powder blue suit collar. Phillipe smiled at her before turning his eyes to Hayden. "You may ask anything you like. I doubt if I have any answers."

"What was Madame Ana's connection to Atlas?"

"I don't have the slightest idea," answered Phillipe.

"You do know her, don't you?"

"Everyone has heard of her, young man."

"Did Bronson and Solomon know Greggie?"

"You'll have to ask them. They don't work for me," answered Phillipe, just beginning to let his annoyance show.

"Have you ever met Mr. Marleaux?"

"Never, and I think that our time is up. It was very gracious of me even to see you, and I can tell by your questions that you're simply on a fishing expedition. Atlas is merely one of the companies that I run, and it's from a very distant shore. You overestimate my involvement on a day-to-day basis. But I wouldn't want your trip here to be a waste. I've made eight o'clock reservations for you at Le Grand Véfour as my guests."

He stood up and gestured them to the door, still smiling, but not talking. As soon as they left the room he went to the phone. Both Douglas Collins and Ana were waiting.

"Well, that was ridiculous," said Nikki, steaming by the time they were out on the sidewalk.

"Let me tell you why it wasn't," said Hayden. "The fact that we flew all the way here told Gascon that we will stop at nothing. The fact that he saw us tells us that he is curious, interested, and very involved. It didn't matter really whether he answered our questions or not. It was a meeting about positioning for the battle ahead. Think of it this way. We've had our first round with him. It was over in fifteen minutes and now we have a free vacation until we leave tomorrow."

"What about the restaurant reservations?" asked Nikki.

"We cancel them and win the round."

"Good."

"How would you like to go see the *Mona Lisa* before we go back home?" asked Hayden, deciding to keep personal things light after having sensed Nikki's reticence to talk about the night before.

"That would be great, but first I'd like to go back to the hotel and regroup, check my messages," said Nikki.

When they got back to the Crillon Nikki went straight to her room. The message light was blinking. There was a message for her to call Mr. Phillipe Gascon immediately.

Without telling Hayden she returned the call. He asked if he could meet with her alone in the tea area of the Hotel Ritz at five P.M. She said that she would.

When she met Hayden in the lobby and told him about the arrangements he hit the roof.

"You can't meet with him alone!"

"Why not?" said Nikki defiantly. "Am I not old enough?"

"Don't be ridiculous. This is a formidable, possibly dangerous man. We don't know what he wants with you. I saw how he looked at you and I doubt that this is a business appointment for him," said Hayden.

"Look, I don't need you to behave like a jealous boyfriend here." Nikki was sorry the minute the words came out of her mouth.

"Nikki, I—"

"I'm so sorry, Hayden," said Nikki, softening. "I guess I'm a little anxious about things. An opportunity to be alone with Gascon is crucial to this case. I can take care of myself and I'm going."

"Where are you meeting him?"

"The Ritz."

"The hotel?"

"He didn't say a hotel room, I'm meeting him where they serve afternoon tea."

"Fine, but who knows where he'll take you from there. I'm going with you. You won't see me, but I'll be around."

"And you think that Gascon won't have men watching? They'll all see you."

"That's fine with me, then they'll know they're being watched, too. I think I should call Mark about this."

"No! Not yet. I'll handle it. We'll call him when I have something to report. Now just relax and let's go to the Louvre. I'd love to see it," said Nikki.

At five o'clock Nikki walked into the Ritz. She headed for the tea area on the left. A maître d' in white tie and tails met her and said, "Are you here for Monsieur Gascon?"

Nikki nodded and looked back. She wondered which Ficus tree Hayden was behind.

"Follow me."

Nikki followed him through the tea lobby and then turned right down the hall. She was becoming apprehensive now because she was no longer in a public area. The maître d' stopped and opened double doors revealing a gold, peach, and blue private dining room. It was gorgeous.

"Please be seated. Monsieur Gascon will be in momentarily."

Nikki sat on a far couch in a seating area beyond the dining room table. The room had a separate bar, crystal chandeliers, and was the most beautiful room she had ever seen.

"Ms. Easterly," said Gascon as he entered alone. "It was so kind of you to accept my invitation. I thank you. You needn't worry about Mr. Chou. My men have set him up with tea in the lobby. Is he your young man?"

"No, we're business associates."

"I see."

Nikki wanted to continue the questioning process that failed so miserably that morning, but she decided to let him take the lead.

A door opened and the waiter brought a full tea set on silver trays.

"I hope they have English Breakfast," Nikki said.

"If they don't have it, they'll get it," said Gascon.

"You know, I'll bet it's your attitude that nothing's unattainable that has made you so successful in business," said Nikki.

"You're right, there isn't anything I can't get," said Gascon, looking into her eyes.

"What exactly are you referring to, Mr. Gascon? Surely you can't be referring to me. Wouldn't that be silly."

"You misinterpret me, young lady. That's not a good mistake to make," he said coldly.

"We'll see who misinterprets whom, Mr. Gascon."

"I knew I'd like you," he said instantly, his mood changing. "I liked your mother, too."

Nikki put her teacup down.

"What exactly do you mean?" she asked, controlling her emotions.

"I'm sure you know that some of my holdings are television networks in many different countries. That was one of the first areas I got into. One of the things I did then was to bring famous American stars to Europe and pay them to do television specials. They would come over and I'd give them a crew and they'd go around the country visiting, talking to people, and then we'd do a concert in a theater. All edited together it made a lovely special. I brought your mother to Rome in the late 1960s, early 1970s. I can't quite remember the date. She was very beautiful."

God forbid, thought Nikki. I hope my mother didn't sleep with him.

"She was a great star and you look so much like her. My heart hurts a little bit. That's really why I wanted to see you. I was so much younger then. Being able to bring her to Europe meant so much to me. I apologize if I sound like a silly fan."

Nikki was beginning to see a slight charm in Gascon, but she made sure she caught herself.

"Mr. Gascon—"

"Please, call me Phillipe."

"I believe you that my mother was special to you. It's hard for me to talk about her, as you can imagine. But you would want her daughter to be successful because you know she would want that . . ." Nikki paused and couldn't believe the number she was doing . . .

"This case is my first big case. I didn't go to law school to become a fancy Hollywood lawyer. I work in Hollywood because Mark Ferguson was my guardian growing up. Your dream was owning conglomerates, my mother's was to be a star, mine is to help innocent people through the legal system. That's really all I want to do. I'm being totally honest with you now. When I'm in Hollywood I go to the restaurants I'm supposed to, I handle some stars, I wear nice clothes, but it isn't where my heart is. When I was given the Marleaux case I didn't even know what it was, and then I met Guy Marleaux. He had stars in his eyes about the business just like you. He loved to be on movie sets and around Hollywood. But he isn't a killer. He's just a young French boy who was in the wrong place at the wrong time. I know he's innocent because his DNA doesn't match. DNA's a new thing but I'm sure you've heard of it. There are probably many people in jail who wouldn't be there if DNA testing had been available. That's all this is about, personal freedom, the celebration of innocence, and me following my heart. I would be really grateful if you could help me in any way."

Nikki looked at Gascon's face carefully as she was talking. What started out as a bit of a con on her part turned into a heartfelt speech and she wasn't sorry she made it.

"I know about dreams, you are right. But it was a long time ago. Dreams are for children or fools. Reality is what I live with and I will never let anyone or anything destroy what I have built."

Gascon leaned in closer to her. "Don't you be a fool, Ms. Easterly," he said, his voice just threatening enough to get his point across.

She hated his breath on her, but he was moving even closer.

"Don't play in areas that are over your head, no matter how much it affects your heart. It's not healthy. I loved your mother, but she made that mistake, didn't she?"

Gascon then stood up, smiled with teeth and no eyes, and said, "Enjoy the rest of your stay, and I'll send you a cassette of your mother's special."

He left the room.

Nikki felt chilled by this man, and now had even more questions than before.

She knew he looked the other way where murder was concerned. His reputation as a dangerous, ruthless brute was well-earned. Yet she felt, for one second, there were no lies between them. A connection had been made, but perhaps it was unhealthy. She was afraid to wonder at that moment exactly where it might lead.

"I can't stand it!" screamed Ana into the phone. "My whole life is going down the toilet! There I was standing at Jimmy's after a nice lunch with Harold, you know my broker, and out from the bushes came a photographer snapping pictures of me like I was some criminal. You just know that in a few days those tabloids are going to have me plastered on the cover dredging up my past and the whole Greggie mess. This is getting out of hand. I thought you had everything under control."

"Please calm down, darling. We both knew that when Ferguson petitioned to have a new trial there were bound to be bumps in the road. You've done nothing wrong. It's unfortunate that this is all being brought up again, but I'll handle it. I suggest that you go on a vacation for the next month or so. I'll arrange for you to go to Africa. I have some terrific friends who can set you up on a wonderful safari way out into the jungle with guides and a butler and cook. You'll have a terrific time. I'll make all the arrangements, ask a friend to come along with you, and I'll have the tickets delivered to you tomorrow morning. Don't worry. Just have a good time."

Phillipe would take care of everything, just the way he always had.

Ana hung up the phone and for a second thought of asking Mark to go to Africa. Of course that would be impossible. Phillipe would find out, and she'd been so careful, she was sure no one knew. She always knew where the servants were when Mark was around, and she made sure that only the maid and the guard were kept on. She overpaid them enormously to keep their mouths shut, money that would supersede the money Phillipe was probably paying them on the side for information.

Ana hated being in between Mark and Phillipe. Phillipe wasn't a murderer, she thought, and why did Mark have to stir up a dead issue?

"This is all your fault," she said to Mark on the phone. "Don't be mad at me for having to go to Africa. I wanted to go to the Marie Antoinette Ball, and now I'm going to be looking at elephants' behinds. I have no choice now."

"You have such a way with words," said Mark.

"Don't try to tease me out of this. I hate being a target,

you know how I feel about my past. You've caused all of this. I should hate you. I wish I could hate you."

"Ana, how would you feel if you had a nice son who was innocent and sitting in jail for a murder he didn't commit? Wouldn't you want someone to stand up for him and fight?"

"I never wanted children. I don't like children."

"You aren't that tough. I know you, remember. I know your little secret that you actually have morals, regardless of certain choices you made in the past."

"Try not to spread it around. You'll ruin my reputation," said Ana teasingly, knowing once again he could make her feel better. "I wish you could come to Africa with me."

"You know I can't do that, but try to call me every Friday morning between nine and noon. I'll be waiting for the call. How long do you think you'll be gone?"

"Now that depends on you, doesn't it?" answered Ana.

Nikki needed to find exactly the right dress and she wasn't happy about it. She hated shopping for clothes.

"Your problems are solved," said Joely. "I've called Maxine Benston at Saks and she'll take care of you."

"How?" asked Nikki.

"She'll save your life from now on. All you do is go to the Fifth Avenue Club and ask for her. It's on the sixth floor. Tell her what kind of event you're going to and whether or not it's black tie. She'll then walk you through the store going to just the right department. You'll talk about what you like and don't like and she'll get your sizes. The next time you have to go anywhere or buy anything, all you have to do is call her up and tell her the occasion and you go directly to a private room in the Club and the clothes will all be ready for you to try on. She'll get everything from the shoes to the stockings, purse, whatever you need. You only ever really have to walk through the store once, unless you particularly enjoy it. And what's so great," added Joely excitedly, "is when stuff goes on sale that she thinks you'll like, she'll put it away so no one else can get it. You can build a wardrobe with her. Maybe you'll just get a black velvet skirt and a black chiffon blouse as staples and then she'll build around it as things come up. You can do the same thing with a basic beige suit for the day." Joely was almost breathless.

"You should be her press agent."

"You're going to love me for this," said Joely.

"I already do," answered Nikki.

Nikki was going with Mark Ferguson to the Marie Antoinette Ball, the most prestigious charity event in the city. It was held once a year and it combined people from the entertainment industry with corporate and medical giants. It had been started by the wife of a studio head long ago who died of breast cancer, and millions of dollars had been raised since, enough to establish a cancer clinic at USC. This year it was going to be particularly interesting because the underwriter for the ball was Atlas Studios, and the party was to be held on one of their biggest soundstages.

Nikki was not surprised when Mark first brought the ball up. She was well aware of his policy of making social appearances for the good of the firm. They had only three weeks before their motion for a new trial for Guy Marleaux would be heard, and Nikki and Hayden were spending all their waking hours working on it. But a smile came to Nikki's face when she heard the ball would be held at Atlas. She knew this would be a fun one.

The limo picked her up at six-thirty. Mark emitted a polite gasp when Nikki entered the car in a floor-length white Armani.

"You look stunning," he said.

Nikki could see the wistful look in his eye. She realized where his mind was: Lauren Laverty.

"Would you care for some champagne?" he asked.

Nikki saw the crystal goblets and the bottle of Cristall. "I'd love some, Uncle Mark."

She was sitting beside him, looking at the lights of the San Fernando Valley as they drove over the Sepulveda pass on the San Diego Freeway toward the studio. She felt Mark lean toward her and take a little sniff.

"That smell . . . it's wonderful. What is it, dear?"

"Fresh Love," said Nikki.

Mark stiffened slightly.

From the day that Nikki smelled her mother's fragrance at Ana's, she began to notice it more in Los Angeles. Whenever she was in a room with women over forty, like at a lunch in Beverly Hills, or a business cocktail party, she began to notice it. Women of that age, her mother's age, grew up with Fresh Love. She had actually asked Maxine at Saks about it and Maxine told her that Fresh Love was now considered equal with Chanel by the women who used it. The day she went to the store she stopped at the perfume counter as she was leaving with her clothes. It was all there . . . the Fresh Love body lotion, the Fresh Love face cream, bath soap, perfume, and what-have-you. In all the years that she had been in stores she never bothered to stop. That scent was her mother.

"May I help you?" asked the woman behind the counter.

"I'm not sure," said Nikki.

"Are you familiar with our line of products?"

"Sort of," answered Nikki hesitantly.

"Here, let me put some of our night cream on your hand. See how it feels."

"No!" said Nikki too abruptly. "I'm sorry. I'm in a hurry. Just give me a small bottle of the perfume and the body lotion. Thanks."

Nikki clutched the bag to her as she waited for her car.

When she walked into her apartment she hung up the

clothes and took the Fresh Love bottles out of their packages. The smell from the lotion bottle was already palpable. Nikki hesitated for about a minute and then she opened the lotion and sniffed it. She was hit in the stomach with memories, but she didn't stop. She put some on her hands, rubbing them together, and then she stroked her neck area gently, massaging the cream in. It was her mother's neck that she remembered, that nuzzling, burying herself in the warmth and love. Nikki couldn't stop the tears that sprang forth. It had been such a long time since she allowed them to surface. She wondered if she ever would be able to live without them.

"Nikki?" said Mark. "Are you all right?"

"Yes. I've never worn Fresh Love," answered Nikki, returning to the present and the effect she wanted it to have on Mark. "It reminds me of my mother so much that I couldn't bear to be around it. But I think I'm old enough now to start remembering things while I'm awake, instead of in nightmares. I thought if I forced myself to wear it I could start to recall some things. I want to remember more. Too much has been hidden from me. I want you to help me."

"Nikki, it was such a long time ago. Your life has turned out so well. Why dig up the past? I think it's much healthier to look toward the future."

"Do I take it that means you won't help me?" asked Nikki.

"I will always do what I can for you," said Mark, patting her hand.

But Nikki wasn't so sure.

Stage 13 of Atlas Studios was the size of a whole floor of a hotel. It was decorated like a French palace just before the revolution with gilt sconces, crystal chandeliers, fake Louis Quatorze furniture. It truly looked like a set out of a movie, and in fact Atlas had merely gone into its huge warehouse for the supplies. Each couple was announced by a "soldier of the Queen's Court," complete with four gentlemen doing live trumpet flourishes, followed by an entrance on a red carpet. The catering was by L'Orangerie, the finest French restaurant in Hollywood. Guests were directed to the cocktail area, a separate area to the left where there were displays of items for a silent auction to raise even more money. You could bid on Dodger game tickets, hockey tickets, trips, shopping sprees, rare autographed books, or you could walk up to a display of the St. Regis Hotel in New York and bid on a weekend for two complete with two tickets to *Phantom of the Opera*. The bidding for that prize started at $1,500. All you had to do was sign your name.

Nikki looked down and saw the name Kevin Costner and then $2,500 written beside it. It was followed by Norman Brokaw and $2,525. She kept going down the list, which looked like a Who's Who of Hollywood. Currently Michelle Pfeiffer had the high bid at $3,725.

"The bidding closes fifteen minutes before dinner and there is an announcement. If you really want something you wait until the last minute and stand by what you want with a pen ready to top the last bid. Sometimes it can get very nasty. A fistfight broke out last year over a basketball autographed by Magic Johnson. Some really obnoxious kid of a rich donor went around trying to overbid people at the last minute. This one vile child, son of a Beverly Hills judge or something, wrote his name after the deadline. The charity was furious because honorable people were cheated out of what they deserved. One was a member of the press who threatened to write about the incident. It was very ugly there for a while, because the charity didn't take the basketball away from the kid as they should have."

Mark went on to explain that the cocktail hour was all about mixing and doing deals, as well as bidding. In the dinner room he told her to notice how the tables were clustered, three for William Morris, four for the Creative Artists Agency, and two for ICM.

"Each studio has a table as do the important production companies. Most of the stars are guests of their agency or studio. The stars rarely pay for tickets, but occasionally if a wife of a star belongs to the group the star must then take an entire table and pick up the tab for the friends as well. It's all very political, but the money goes to a good cause. The thing that kills me though is that many people who are just interested in the cocktail hour stay politely for dinner but they try to duck out when the show starts. That is so rude to the headliners. A Bill Cosby or Peggy Lee will give of themselves for the evening and people walk out on them because they are tired, lazy, and disrespectful. Natalie Cole is singing tonight and she's incredible. You watch what happens and see who cuts out. It's usually the same people. Sometimes I wish the charity would just say, 'I'll take your money as a donation but please don't come.' Or they should sit those people in the back of the room, but then that wouldn't be power seating."

"Uncle Mark, you're getting yourself all worked up. Try to calm down," said Nikki. "This is my first Hollywood charity evening and already I hate it. You're destroying the glamour."

"I'm sorry, Nikki. Maybe it's just too many years of the same crap. There are a few people who actually do have pure souls and do good work, but tonight we're doing a little work of our own."

"I figured that."

"We've got to be careful because Weisberg, Wilson and Doug Collins also have their tables and they'll be watching us. We're making them more unhappy than we usually do these days," he said proudly.

"So what's the plan?" asked Nikki.

"I think it's time you met Solomon and Bronson," Mark said.

"But they don't work for Atlas anymore."

"That doesn't matter. They're still A players and would naturally be here. Their severance deal from Atlas was quite hefty and Atlas did have an exclusive one-year first-look deal, which means that Atlas had to see any of their scripts first. Now Atlas is nonexclusive with them and they can take their scripts anywhere."

"Do you think that Phillipe Gascon might be here tonight?" asked Nikki.

"I doubt it," said Mark.

"Oh."

It was time to move into the dining area and people were crowding around, making it difficult to maneuver.

"There's Solomon," said Mark.

Nikki noticed a guy who looked like a short, flashy ape with a tall redhead on his arm. "Good God," said Nikki.

"Yep. It's typical. He married a Miss Universe contestant from Venezuela. She was first runner-up. I'm sure that galls David. He probably tried for the winner and had to settle. But she is gorgeous."

The two couples bumped into each other at the door.

"David, how nice to see you and Sonja. I'd like you to meet my newest associate, Nikki Easterly."

Nikki extended her hand to David and then to Sonja. Sonja's red spangles nearly blinded her. "It's nice to meet you both."

"I've heard a lot about you, Nikki," said David. "You have some interesting cases," he added cryptically.

"I'm never bored, and from what I've heard about you, you aren't either."

Good girl, thought Mark as he watched David pause for a second to gather his thoughts.

"Well," said David. "We'll have to compare notes some-time." He put his arm around Sonja and said, "Shall we?"

"How about lunch on Monday, one o'clock at Le Dôme?" said Nikki.

David stopped in his tracks and looked at her. "You're on."

Mark laughed as he took her hand. "Too much, young lady, too much. You jumped right into the pool with the shark."

"I'm covered with oil," said Nikki with a sweet smile, try-ing to look as angelic as possible.

They were seated at Carly Singleton's table along with her date, Cruger Fowler, as well as Roland Bixby, Barbara Loring, a columnist for the *L.A. Times*, Michelle Pfeiffer and her husband, David Kelly, who was a producer client of Mark's, and Chevy and Jayni Chase.

Nikki was a little overwhelmed at the star power, so she kept quiet for the first few minutes. It was difficult to get a word in with Cruger and Carly at the same table. Chevy Chase wasn't particularly talkative in real life and Michelle Pfeiffer was quite shy, so Nikki joined them in letting the others carry the conversation.

"Now really, darlings," said Carly. "Don't you think that Natalie Cole has sung at enough of these things. In this year alone it's been St. Jude, the Peggy Lee Tribute, the AIDS benefit at Universal, and the $5,000-a-plate dinner for the President of the United States. How many times can we hear 'Unforgettable'?"

"Her father was great, she's great, but I agree, enough is enough," seconded Cruger.

"I think it's very nice that she donates her time," said Mark. "So many stars don't. It costs her thousands of dollars to do one of these benefits. It's just unfortunate that we all go to the same ones. However, I'm staying for the whole show, and I'm sure that the rest of you will, too, won't you."

It was not a question.

"I've never seen her before," said Nikki, "and I can't wait. I just love 'This Will Be.' "

"That's my favorite," piped up Michelle spontaneously. "I first saw her do it either at the Hollywood Bowl or the Amphitheater before it had a roof on it. I was waitressing then and I saved all my tips for months just to see her. It was a real thrill for me."

Nikki loved Michelle instantly.

After the dinner of grilled salmon, scalloped potato timbale, and fresh French-cut green beans, Nikki got up to go to the ladies' room.

Carly followed her.

After they finished washing their hands Nikki was transfixed watching Carly put on her lipstick in the mirror. Carly had beautiful, full lips and first she outlined them in a delicate peach/brown, and then she covered both lips in a taupe. She then applied a frosty creamy silver just in the front of the top and bottom lips where they parted, running her tongue just along the inside to catch any extra frost. Nikki thought if a close-up camera were just on those lips it would be shooting a porno movie.

"Did I ever thank you properly for that lovely annulment, darling?"

"You're very welcome, Carly. I'm glad it was successful."

"Your mother would have been proud of you."

Nikki was stunned. It was so unlike Carly to put a sensitive compliment together, but also it had never occurred to Nikki that they might have known each other, although it would make sense. Lauren would have been Carly's age had she lived.

Nikki thought she'd take a chance and ask a direct question. "What was my mother like?"

"Gorgeous, funny, smart, and she could act, too. She

loved people, she was very gregarious, and Mark was wildly in love with her. Hasn't he told you all of this?"

"He doesn't want to talk about it."

"I'm not surprised. He was engaged to her, and the circumstances of her ending were horrific for him."

Nikki's face darkened.

"I'm really sorry, there I go again running off at the mouth. You just handle everything the way Mark says. I'm sure he knows best."

Carly turned to leave.

"Wait, please!" said Nikki. "Tell me how you met my mother."

Carly laughed. "We were reading for a commercial, God, this was aeons ago. Neither one of us had made it yet. We were sitting in a waiting room somewhere, reading the script, just waiting our turn to audition. When you sit in a room like that you always check all the other girls out, so we caught each other's eye as we were looking around the room. I'll never forget what your mother said. 'You're going to get this job.' I replied, 'Why?' She answered, 'Because you're the only brunette in a roomful of blondes.' Well, everybody heard her and started to laugh. It's so rare that anybody speaks to anyone in a situation like that. But your mother was so friendly. I told her that I thought I wasn't going to get the job because obviously they wanted a blonde. I was probably there just for variety."

"So who got the job?"

"Your mother, of course. She was absolutely delicious-looking. We never really became friends. In those days after we both became successful, we were so wrapped up in our careers and our love lives that you just didn't maintain friendships with women. I hope that's changed now. I think we really missed out."

Carly stared intently at Nikki, focusing in on her for the very first time.

When Carly left, Nikki turned and looked in the mirror. She saw Lauren Laverty's face looking back at her.

Nikki was glad the show was over and she and Mark were back in the limo. She wanted to bring up her mother but she didn't want to be rebuffed again by him. She thought she'd proceed with doing her own research for a while and then confront him.

"Good night, dear," said Mark at the front door of the Shoreham Towers.

"I had a wonderful time, and just think, now David Solomon can worry about Monday all weekend," said Nikki cheerfully.

The doorman let her inside. As she was standing at the elevator she waved to the switchboard operator.

"Evening, Miss Easterly," he said as he got up from his position to go outside on a break.

Nikki was left alone in the lobby waiting for the elevator. It seemed to be taking quite a long time. Just as the doors opened, a figure burst out from the coatroom next to the switchboard area, jumping on Nikki, pulling her into the elevator, covering her hand with his mouth.

Buoyed with the strength of survival she bit his hand and screamed just before a slap silenced her. The elevator was moving up, away from any help, and she was terrified. She fell down against the wall and had the presence of mind to hit the alarm/emergency stop button. She had no way of knowing that the doorman had heard her screams, called the police, and was working with the switchboard man to bring the elevator back to the first floor.

The man came at her with hands going for her throat. Instead of pulling away from him she remembered from defense classes she had taken in college to go toward him and throw the full force of her arms up in the air, twisting her body and her arms over his, breaking his hold. At the next second when he was recovering from the shock of her actions she kneed him in the groin. When he went down she elbowed him on the back of his neck, pounding him to the ground. She never stopped screaming and was shocked that she could remember the moves and keep her presence of mind under such an attack.

The elevator started to move and she kept stomping and hitting. When the door opened, her attacker was on the floor and she was still fighting.

The two men on duty at the building ran toward her, one picking her up and carrying her away and the other jumping on the attacker. At that moment the police arrived.

"I'm all right," said Nikki, insisting on being let down. "Go let the police in." She rubbed her jaw and became aware of sting of the slap, and then she started to shake, only beginning to react to what had just happened. She didn't want to cry and it took everything she had to control herself.

She was surrounded by police.

"Let me see him! Let me see him!" she demanded, pushing her way to the elevator.

The guy was out cold.

"Turn him over."

She looked down at the forty-five-ish dark-haired man with a beard wearing a flannel shirt and dirty jeans and work boots.

"I don't have the slightest idea who he is. I've never seen him before in my life."

But Nikki had an idea, and it scared her to death. Was this some thug of Phillipe's? Would he really do whatever was necessary to stop any Atlas problems? She was now terrified. Could he really hurt her? The adrenaline that saved her during the attack was fast turning to stark terror.

"Let's check for ID," said the head cop, reaching in the guy's pants. "Hector Rodriguez it says, from Pico Rivera."

"What is that name again?" asked Nikki, her head still hurting.

"Hector Rodriguez."

"Unbelievable. It must be the kid's father," said Nikki.

"What are you talking about?" asked the cop. "Do you know him?"

"I defended his son as one of the few charity cases I took on as a summer intern in law school in San Francisco. His kid was guilty of assault and battery on three women. I remember he hated women and he hated me. There was no way my associate could win the case. The kid blamed me for going to prison, and I guess his father did, too."

"We have to take you down to the hospital to be checked out, it's procedure. I presume you'll press charges."

"Absolutely, and I'll go with you in a minute. I need to call someone. Where am I going?"

"Cedars emergency."

Nikki called Joely on the house phone. "There's a problem but don't worry, I'm okay. Don't ask any questions, just call Hayden and the two of you meet me at Cedars emergency right away."

Nikki hung up and walked to the ambulance. She took great pride in watching Hector limping and sniveling to the patrol car. Now that she was safe she realized that she originally thought the attack was related to the opening of the Marleaux case. There had been so many subtle threats. Maybe there really wasn't anything to worry about at all.

# Chapter 10

THE MASTER: So who is it tonight?

ROUGHMEUP: How about me, baby?

SILKY: I can beat her any day.

TM: Now girls, calm down. I just have a few questions.

HUNKY: Hey Master, give me a piece.

TM: Try it Hunk and you're dead.

HUNKY: No threats online. You know the rules.

TM: Try and make it, buddy. Now shove it.

RMU: Master, darling. Let's go to a private room.

TM: I'll set it up.

RMU: Well hello again. Where are you from?

TM: You're not going to start with all that computer-friendly stuff are you?

RMU: It's fun. I like to get a picture so I can fantasize.

TM: I'm from somewhere east of the Mississippi—And you?

RMU: Houston. I'm a dental hygienist here and I'm bored to tears. I live for these nights on my computer.

TM: How old are you really?

RMU: 24, and you?

TM: The Master never tells things like that. But if you want to know my measurements . . . it's 8 inches.

RMU: Mine are 37-23-36 and I love the sound of yours. What would you like to do with those 8 inches?

TM: You'll do exactly what I tell you when I tell you. Do you have a boyfriend?

RMU: Yes but he's really square. He only knows one position and gets embarrassed if I start to do anything to him.

TM: He's an idiot, but I'll take care of you. Take off all your clothes. Tell me where your computer is.

RMU: I have a laptop and it's sitting on my bed.

TM: Perfect.

RMU: I'm so glad you are pleased.

TM: You have no idea what pleasure is. You're about to find out. Are your clothes off?

RMU: Yes.

TM: Good. Now go to the freezer and get a tray of ice cubes. Run hot water over them for a few seconds.

RMU: WHAT??????

TM: I told you to do exactly as I say and if you don't I'll click you off and find someone who will.

RMU: Yes, sir. I'll be right back.

TM: That's much better, young lady.

RMU: OK, I'm back and I have the tray.

TM: Now lean back a little and spread your legs open wide.

RMU: OK, I'm set.

TM: Then take an ice cube and put it in your hand. Don't ask questions.

RMU: I'm doing it.

TM: Take the cube and run it along the inside of your crotch . . . slowly . . . feel it melt a little bit.

RMU: Ahhhhhhhhh.

TM: Has it melted completely?

RMU: It will in a second.

TM: Good. Now take a new cube and stick all its iciness inside you sharply. Startle yourself and let your fingers follow the cube.

RMU: On my God!!!

TM: Do it again and again, cube after cube, faster and faster, feel yourself start to grind with it. Shut your eyes and throw your head back . . . DO IT!!!!

RMU: Where are you?

Nikki hated it when the guys disappeared and left her dangling. As long as they were satisfied they just didn't give a damn. At least The Master was interesting. She'd developed a report-card-like system in her computer: when she found a guy who was out of the ordinary and held her attention, she would add his handle to a file so she could find him again. She also had a file set up for the creeps so she could stay away from them. The problem was that people could change their handles and she wouldn't know who they were.

Nikki found that using the name RoughMeUp got the best response. Her use of Sweetie was okay for a while, but the guys were boring. Crotch Queen brought out some really disgusting, classless ones. Nikki discovered that for some reason RoughMeUp attracted brighter, more inventive lovers. They would go into fantasies, be more creative. The Master was her favorite. She discovered him two months ago when she was Sweetie. She also had fun with Mr. Darkside and Jazzrider. She was getting so proficient at this now that sometimes she would go on with a completely new name and get three guys going at once. If someone was boring and uncreative she'd dump him after a few minutes and concentrate on the good ones. If someone really interested her she would check his profile in the computer. All she had to do was click on the "Who" and the list of people on the channel would appear. The names were just their handles, but then she could highlight a handle and click on "Profile" and immediately the city, or state, or sometimes city and state would appear below their name. Then a window would come up with more information such as date of birth, occupation, interests, and an ID number. It was impossible to tell whether or not people were lying on their profiles, so Nikki rarely bothered looking them up. Sometimes she noticed there would be no profile at all, just an ID number.

She was into CB again for round two and she couldn't find The Master. Her time on the computer now was about two hours a night. She told herself if she just stayed on between nine and eleven it wouldn't interfere with her job, she could get sleep, and it wasn't a problem. But on nights when she had to go out, she began to feel uneasy around nine. She was itching to go home, and it bothered her. But not so much that she was willing to make any changes.

The computer made a buzzing sound.

Nikki was receiving a call from a playmate.

ONE WISH: I'm tall, dark, and handsome, how about you?

ROUGHMEUP: I'm divine.

OW: Eat me?

RMU: Slow down, boy. Easy?

OW: Are you seated?

RMU: Yes. Should I be?

OW: Well, I didn't want you to fall over . . . and I want you real comfortable . . . and your legs spread slightly.

RMU: Legs spread. I'm sitting on a satin pillow.

OW: Yes!!

RMU: We're just getting started.

OW: And are you wearing little baby panties?

RMU: I am. They're lace, and honey-colored, with a big slit right where it should be.

OW: Wow! My favorite!

RMU: I knew that.

OW: That is really sexy. Crotchless? Really? Yummy . . . can I see? Show me.

RMU: Oh yes . . . take a peek at perfect dark pink.

OW: Yes, ma'am!!!

RMU: Yes.

OW: And moist and soft . . . mmm . . . spread a little more, I wanna see it all.

RMU: I've opened more . . . my panties are very wet . . . take it all! Tell me what you see.

OW: (big lump in my trousers at the thought of crotchless panties)

RMU: I'm got 'em in every color.

OW: You're so . . . wet . . . and pink, juicy lips . . .

RMU: But why are you still dressed? Good eyesight. What do you want to do with me?

OW: Hold on . . . lemme get with you.

RMU: I'm waiting and I'm beginning to throb.

OW: First I want to sit on the floor . . . right in front of you . . . on your satin pillow . . . me looking into your wet self. Can I stroke it? Just lightly run my finger along the edge of your lips . . .

RMU: Lovely. Please stroke. I love teasing.

OW: Maybe I'll dip my finger in and taste your honey . . . not too deep, just around the edge of your sweet wetness . . .

RMU: Oh, I love this!

OW: Maybe I'll draw along your thigh with my moist finger.

RMU: That makes me quiver.

OW: Your thighs are so soft . . . and warm.

RMU: They're a great pillow.

OW: OOOOO sweet . . . can I see your breasts?

RMU: I'm slowly unbuttoning my white satin pajama top.

OW: You . . . waiting . . . waiting . . . watching . . .

RMU: I'm peeling it off each shoulder.

OW: Lovely . . . slipping it off . . .

RMU: My breasts are at attention, smiling at you.

OW: Hello, babies!

RMU: Hello, handsome.

OW: Can I kiss them? . . . mmm . . . I'll be your guy.

RMU: They are dying for you.

OW: You be my hot little babies.

RMU: You got it. I'm on fire.

OW: Lemme lick them . . . suck your nipples lightly.

RMU: Yes . . .

OW: Me too. I'm so hard right now. I want your nipples in my mouth.

RMU: Both of them at once.

OW: Ooo . . . can I?

RMU: Just push me together with your big hands.

OW: You are big! Ooooooo . . . burying my head in between . . . licking away madly . . .

RMU: Great . . . I love to feel that . . .

OW: Sucking . . .

RMU: My hands are on your head, pushing . . .

OW: Covering your breasts with kisses.

RMU: Yes . . .

OW: Slowly getting lower . . .

RMU: Oh, boy.

OW: Across your tummy . . .

RMU: Down, down . . .

OW: Lower . . . at the top of your . . .

RMU: Please . . .

OW: Mmmmmm . . . licking slowly at your wetness.

RMU: My hips are rising.

OW: Just a little at first.

RMU: I want to swallow your face.

OW: Tasting . . . circling . . . sucking your juice out now . . .

RMU: More!

OW: Lapping . . . you're delicious.

RMU: So much juice we could both drown.

OW: Sucking . . . mmmm . . . face in it.

RMU: Yes!!!!

OW: Licking you everywhere . . . deep in with my tongue.

RMU: Deeper, deeper.

OW: Pushing my tongue in deeply, fucking you with my tongue . . . in and out.

RMU: My nails are in your scalp.

OW: Hold my head . . . push me in.

RMU: I'm smashing you into me.

OW: Can't get enough of you . . . sucking and licking . . .

RMU: I want all of you.

OW: I'm all here . . . and very hot.

RMU: Me too. Don't stop.

OW: Where can I touch you little girl? Everywhere?

RMU: Everywhere, every which way.

OW: How nasty do you wanna be, little hot one? Wanna bend over for me?

RMU: I thought you'd never ask.

OW: I'm gonna cum thinking about you . . .

RMU: Better wait for me!

OW: Oooooo. Show me everything baby!

RMU: I'm on all fours.

OW: Ohhhhhhhh . . . reach around and spread for me . . . I wanna see . . . I wanna see it all.

RMU: I'm sheer perfection, waiting for you.

OW: Ooooo what do you want from your guy?

RMU: I want you inside me BIG TIME!

OW: It is BIG! Where should I begin?

RMU: Go for it, I'm dying.

OW: My dick is throbbing now.

RMU: Begin where you want. I'm all yours.

OW: Should I tease you first to . . . get wet?

RMU: I'm soaking.

OW: So first I'm gonna dip into your hotness . . . just a few inches . . . in and out.

RMU: Yeah!!! You really make me want it.

OW: And try not to shoot my wad . . . and then . . .

RMU: Hold on . . . Don't come yet . . . I need you!!!! Do it to me!!!!

OW: I'm all yours, going deeper now, thrusting with all my might . . . over and over, we're rocking together . . . I can't take it . . . I'm exploding!!!!!!

Nikki was embarrassed by her real-life throbbing, but she loved it, too. She could get the feelings, all the excitement, and never have to get close to anybody. Not even Hayden, who scared her most of all because he was real. She loved doing it with words. Words were safe. They weren't people. People hurt you. She was totally protected in her private world.

# Chapter 11

Nikki had Beverly make a reservation at Le Dôme and she didn't even call Solomon's office to confirm. This was Nikki's test, to see exactly what he would do. If he didn't show, her time wouldn't be wasted. Le Dôme was only one minute from her condo and she could do some quiet work. If he showed, so much the better.

At one o'clock on the nose Nikki walked into Le Dôme.

"Ms. Easterly, how nice to see you today," said Eddie.

"I have a reservation—"

"Yes," Eddie broke in. "You're meeting Mr. Solomon. Let me show you to his table."

Nikki was annoyed. She had made the reservation and now all of a sudden it was *his* table?

It turned out to be the first table on the left in the front porch.

"Mr. Solomon eats here every Monday, Wednesday, and Friday," explained Eddie.

Well, at least he'll be here, Nikki thought.

Hot, crusty French bread was brought to the table. The smell was so appetizing that Nikki started buttering it immediately.

"It's really good here, isn't it?" said Solomon sitting down.

He was wearing bluejeans, a custom-made white dress shirt, a black leather jacket, black boots, and very expensive gold jewelry. His watch was gold and heavy, his chains even heavier.

Nikki found him absolutely disgusting. He looked like a street hustler with a $200 haircut who had come into money, and that's exactly what he was. He was also very smart.

"So why'd you want to have lunch with me?" asked Solomon. "You certainly don't want to pitch me a project."

"I want to talk to you about Atlas," answered Nikki. "Why did you accept my invitation?"

"I'm in love with Lauren Laverty."

Nikki walked right into that one.

"Ever since I was a little boy she was my dream girl. One of the first things I did at Atlas was go into the photo archives and look for some original shots of her. I took all of them and the negatives, too. There's one I have blown up on my office wall as we speak. It's a shot of her with one of the superheroes."

"I've seen it."

"You've been in my office?" he asked incredulously.

"Calm down, David. I haven't resorted to illegal searches yet to find out what I want to know."

"And what specifically is that?"

"May I take your order?" interrupted the waiter.

Nikki was not pleased.

"I'll have the chopped salad with chicken," said Nikki.

"And I'll have the steak with pommes frites," said

Solomon, only Nikki noticed he pronounced the "s" on pommes and frites.

"So, what do you want to know?" asked Solomon, almost brashly.

Nikki could see why this street kid had made it. He was in your face, with an attitude of such confidence and daring that you sat up and took notice. He had no manners, and even if he was wearing Armani jeans he still looked like a gang member, but none of that mattered when you were dealing with him face-to-face.

"Did you know Greggie Alcott?"

"Right to the point you are," he said. "Are you sure you weren't hanging out on the streets somewhere in New York and I missed you along the way?"

"Cute. Just an answer will do," said Nikki, assuming as bold an attitude as his.

"Sure I knew her. She was damn good at her job."

"And what job was that?"

"She was a hooker. You know that."

"Yes, but was she on Atlas's payroll?"

"Not directly. She was around for whoever wanted her, and it wasn't just people associated with Atlas. She was costly and brilliant. Well worth the money. Ana really knew how to pick them."

"Ana who?"

"You sound like an owl. There's no way you don't know about Ana Sarstedt. C'mon."

"Fine. So what about Ana's connection to Gascon?"

"He set her up in business originally as a favor for services rendered. I don't know if he got a cut or not. From what I hear he wasn't that interested."

"Really?"

Nikki let a few seconds go by and then she asked it. "Did you kill Greggie Alcott?"

She figured she was in a public place, what could he do?

"Boy do you have the balls of death. I like you, so I'm not going to go for your throat," he responded. "No, I didn't kill her. Some messenger did it."

"No he didn't. And you know that's why I've been asking all these questions."

"Well, if he didn't do it, I don't know who did. And if I knew something, I'd tell you, because I don't need Atlas, I don't need anything. I'm very rich, I don't blow my money anymore, and my independent deals are solid. I have no love for Gascon. He did a number on Joel and me. He can go fuck himself."

"What kind of number?"

"You don't let up, do you?"

"No. That's why I'm a good lawyer and I'm going to get Guy Marleaux off."

"How good are you?" he said.

"Knock it off. What kind of number?"

"Gascon is a control freak. He thought we were getting too powerful. He wanted his toy back so he aced us out."

"And how did he ace you out?"

"Rumors about the murder tainted the studio. The stock was slipping a little bit. Even though it got hushed up quickly, it was better for Gascon to have a new regime in. We were furious at the time, but the money did pacify us somewhat. However, *The Caper* and *Homebodies* put us on the map without him. He means nothing to us now. That's why I'm telling you this stuff. I just don't give a damn. We were caught up in something that we had nothing to do with. Now I've answered everything. It's your turn. Tell me about your mother."

Nikki almost died. She didn't expect the tables to turn so quickly.

"I don't know very much. I'm not playing games with you. I wasn't even raised here. I'm only just beginning to read clippings to start to learn about her," answered Nikki.

"I'll tell you one thing, if she were alive today I don't know where her career would be. Maybe she'd still be a huge star, maybe not, but I'd put her in one of my pictures no matter what. She'd be in her forties now. That's not a great age for leading ladies, and even though I do commercial movies that don't get very good reviews but make a lot of money, I'd buy one of those artsy scripts and give her a role that would get her an Oscar nomination for Best Supporting Actress. That's what I'd do."

"I can't tell you how sorry I am that you don't have that opportunity," said Nikki.

"Me, too."

It was interesting, thought Nikki as she was driving back to the office. Some sort of accord or mutual respect had been reached at the lunch. Nikki could never get by his brashness, but for some reason she liked him, which surprised her.

"Did you learn anything?" asked Hayden, who was waiting when she returned.

Nikki told him everything, which was the information they had suspected.

"Was he rude to you? He's a real pig."

"Let's just say we were nose-to-nose and no blood was shed. He's not as bad a guy as you think."

"I can't believe you're saying that."

"Truly don't give it another thought. Let's go on to more important things, like our brief," said Nikki.

"Well, we did such a thorough job the first time around, I really believe that's why we got our hearing. We should be getting the prosecution's briefs in two weeks and then we have ten days to respond, if we need to respond to anything."

"They'll just say that Marleaux had a fair trial, his evidence was heard, and he was convicted by a jury of his peers," said Nikki.

"Right, but they'll obviously dispute the DNA theory. They'll invoke the Kelly-Frye rule and try to say that we didn't have enough expert witnesses and that the scientific community didn't properly corroborate our results."

"True," said Nikki, "but we can combat that with the fact that we used the top laboratory in the country and that their results were allowed in two different trials. In *Andrews v. State* the Fifth District Court of Appeals upheld in Florida that DNA tests were admissible. Same thing with *Two Bulls* in South Dakota."

"You've really been doing your homework," said Hayden.

"This case is important to me. It's my first really big one, and besides, I can't wait to discuss in front of a male judge a case involving a man named Two Bulls involved in a rape. I just want to see his face."

"You do have quite a sense of humor . . ."

"I'm beginning to discover that you need it in this business."

"Do we want Marleaux in court?" asked Hayden, getting back to the subject at hand.

"I really do. He has such a sweet face. I want the judge to see that."

"Well, I have to go to Chino on another case so I'll see him. But I want you to be prepared that he might not want to come."

"What?"

"A lot of prisoners, once they are in the system, don't like to be shackled, thrown on a bus, put in the tank in the county with a lot of drunks, just to sit in a courtroom, especially when they can't testify."

"I still don't get it," said Nikki.

"There are work programs at the prison and Marleaux is a model prisoner. If he leaves he loses his place in seniority and has to go back to the beginning. My guess is that he'll stay there and just wait for us to give him the results."

"Amazing, just amazing," said Nikki. "I hope you're wrong."

"I cannot go," said Guy Marleaux as Hayden sat across from him in the visitors' room.

"But this could mean your life!"

"I am too frightened."

"Will you tell me what frightens you?"

Marleaux kept folding and unfolding a piece of paper he was holding.

"It's not that I wouldn't mind leaving here for a day or two," he said slowly. "But I'm afraid that if I get a taste of the outside, and for some reason we lose, I couldn't take having to come back. It would be too terrible for me. I cannot go through that again."

"But it would make a good impression on the judge if you were sitting there. It's so much harder to look you in the eye and rule against you. It might be just the thing that wins the case," implored Hayden.

"I'm sorry. Please understand. I don't want to hurt you, but I'm desperate. It's so hard in here, I know I couldn't take anything going wrong in the courtroom. If I ever get to leave, I want to know I'm never coming back."

Hayden had to accept it.

"What are my chances, do you think?"

"We are very hopeful. We have the DNA proof that you're innocent. The courts are gaining a better understanding of what that means. All we need is an acceptance of that evidence and then we can get you a new trial, which would be granted almost immediately. We won't lose that. Please try to stay hopeful. We'll do our very best for you."

"And Miss Easterly, what does she think? Why isn't she here?"

Hayden didn't expect those questions.

"I had to come here on another case as well so it was simpler for me to make the trip alone. Also, she's busy working on your case."

"But what does she think?" he asked again, somewhat pleadingly.

"She's ready to fight the rest of her life for you."

Hayden noticed a slight shy smile form just at the corners of Marleaux's mouth. For an instant he was jealous.

The hearing was in two weeks. The prosecution's briefs had run true to form and Nikki filed her appropriate responses. Hayden had lined up three witnesses. One, the doctor who did the DNA tests personally, and two experts to back him up. They were all due in town two days before the trial. Nikki was paying the bills for them, not only their airfares, hotels, and food, but their fees for testifying.

The morning after their arrival, Nikki and Hayden set up individual appointments for the witnesses so each could be prepared. They were on the forty-eight-hour countdown now. In a hearing—as opposed to a trial—only one lawyer is allowed to appear for each side. That meant that Nikki was going in alone on her first criminal case.

She spent hours with each witness, explaining the cases she was going to cite, what information she needed from them. These men were dry scientists and she hoped they wouldn't put the judge to sleep. It was her idea to keep it as short as possible with each one, get out the relevant information, and then get them off the stand. There was no point in drawing things out. Some lawyers droned on and on, repeating questions, frequently shooting themselves in the foot. Nikki was not going to be one of them.

Nikki went home that night with a heavy briefcase and a pounding heart. She was appearing before forty-five-year-old Judge Howard Molinsky, a man who preferred politics over law. Mark warned her he had other career ideas. Nikki was hoping that if that were true, and Molinsky was looking to make a name for himself, he would want to have a new trial with all this publicity. It might be the perfect entrée to become governor or go to the appellate bench.

Eating take-out dim sum from Chin Chin, Nikki spread her notes before her on the bed. She was in pajamas already, set her clock for six A.M., giving her time to shower and be calm. Court didn't start until ten, but she wanted to be there at nine. She needed to be asleep by ten so she would have eight hours.

Walking over to her closet, she opened the doors and stared. It boiled down to black, navy blue, camel, or gray. She chose the navy blue, deciding that black was too somber, gray humorless, and camel too cheery. Navy blue was it, with the white silk blouse and navy pumps. Very simple.

Her laptop was sitting on the bed where she had left it. She was home early and had plenty of time to play, but she knew tonight she couldn't do it. She didn't want to have her concentration disturbed, but it was killing her. It would be so easy to just go over and turn it on. Could she play for thirty minutes? Could she limit herself to that? Did she have the discipline? Tomorrow was the most important day in her career, she thought. How dare she bargain with herself? She must be strong. She would be strong, even if it killed her.

It didn't work. After about five minutes she made a deal with herself. She would stay on no more than twenty minutes. No matter what.

She was on the CB Adult Band in one minute. Tonight she was going to be EZ Lady. That should get callers fast.

Within seconds she had four different guys on the hook. After about five minutes she decided that Ride 'Em was the most creative.

EZ LADY: So you think you're a strong boy?
RIDE 'EM: As strong and big as they come. I really do have

a ranch and all I have to do is perform some riding tricks in a rodeo and those girls come right to me.

EZ: And what kind of tricks do you perform for them?

RE: Ever heard of a "penning"?

EZ: No, but I'd sure like to.

RE: Well, the calf runs around with me chasing her on my horse. I move her along and get her to go into the pen. It's like hockey with two teams going after calves instead of a puck. I finally get her in the pen, throw her on her side, and tie all four legs together. Women like that, too.

EZ: They like to watch the sport, or they want to be chased and tied?

RE: Never mind that watching stuff, I'm chasing you right now.

EZ: Run fast. I'm very clever.

RE: I'll get you.

At that moment Nikki's computer suddenly quit on her. It happened occasionally: the sign appeared on the screen saying, "The Host has failed to respond."

She was furious. This was just getting good and she had never been with a cowboy. What fertile territory.

She was faced with a choice now. She could quickly reconnect herself or she could go to bed. She had been online twenty-five minutes, five minutes over her allotted time.

She fretted and fumed, and then made the right decision. Guy Marleaux was more important. But she wasn't happy about her fixation for online play. The feelings it stirred up in her disturbed her. She was uncomfortable expressing herself with real people, but she was too bright not to realize that this obsession with anonymous sex was starting to reach an unhealthy level. But she couldn't solve that problem tonight. She needed to sleep and she needed to do it fast. There was only one thing to do.

She went to the bathroom, opened the medicine cabinet,

and took out the Valium bottle. She rarely used them. They were prescribed for her after the attack and she took them for a couple of days, but tonight she thought she'd have just a half of a yellow as she went to sleep. The Valium was the answer to everything tonight. It would calm her down, let her relax. It was important that she sleep well, six A.M. would come very quickly.

When the radio went off, the classical music station was playing a John Philip Sousa march. Nikki laughed and thought how appropriate. She didn't turn off the radio, letting the march fill her apartment. She marched to the refrigerator, got her orange juice and her vitamins, marched to the toaster to make a bagel, and then marched right into the bathroom and threw up.

It took all her willpower to fight the fear, take a shower, do her hair and makeup, get dressed, and get in the car. What's the matter with you, Easterly? she said to herself. You're good at what you do, you're prepared, your client is innocent. This is what you have wanted since you were a little girl. Now knock it off and get to work!

She parked underground at the courthouse and went in the elevator in the garage. She knew what floor the courtroom was on so she didn't have to go through the lobby. When the elevator doors opened on the fourth floor there were only two reporters standing there. As she was going through the metal detector she smiled at them and said, "I'm sorry, but I have nothing to say."

At nine-fifty-five the bailiff and court stenographer were seated and ready to go. The door opened and in walked the prosecutor assigned to the case by the district attorney. Hayden and Mark had told her about him as soon as they saw his name on the brief. Noah Edelman was an intellectual in his late thirties, with glasses and brown curly hair, of average height, wearing an off-the-rack gray suit and wing tips. Nikki immediately sized him up as a humorless, no-nonsense prosecutor to whom one case meant as much as the next. Efficiency was the key to him. She doubted that he had a passionate bone in his body.

"All rise, the Honorable Howard Molinsky presiding," said the bailiff. "Please be seated. Court is now in session."

Molinsky appeared, razor-thin, dark hair, and the tiniest nose Nikki had ever seen. It looked like it belonged on someone else's face. Molinsky looked at no one and sat down.

Nikki and Edelman sat down as well.

Molinsky looked up, first at Nikki, then at Edelman.

"The case *In re Marleaux*. Is the petitioner ready?"

"Yes, Your Honor."

"Respondent ready?"

"Yes, Your Honor."

"Call your first witness."

"Petitioner calls Dr. Cecil Conrad."

"State your name and spell it for the record," said the clerk.

Nikki could see that Conrad was a little nervous. He was at least fifty pounds overweight and she didn't want him to start sweating.

"Could you tell us, Doctor, where you work?" asked Nikki, still seated at the table.

"I work at the Maxwell Laboratory in New Jersey."

"What is your job there?"

"I am in charge of DNA research and testing."

"How long have you had this position?"

"Eight years."

"And what schools did you go to?"

"I went to Dartmouth for undergrad and Harvard Medical School."

"And where did you do your internship?"

"At Massachusetts General."

"And your residency?"

"Also Massachusetts General."

"What degrees do you hold?"

"I am a doctor of medicine, with specialties in pediatrics and forensic science."

"Are you on any boards or medical societies?"

"Yes, I'm a member of the American Society of Human Genetics, the American Board of Medical Genetics, the American College of Medical Genetics, and I'm board-certified."

Nikki rose from her seat and stood by the side of her table.

"And what is DNA?"

"It's deoxyribonucleic acid that is comprised of chains of letters or sequences. The letters are ATCG. The DNA is a genetic trail of codes. You can sequence the codes to construct an object. There are six billion letters to encode one human being. That would be two million pages of letters with three thousand letters per page for one human. The order of the letters is a gene. You break up the DNA into microbes and put it on a plate. Machines at the National Institute of Health in Washington, D.C., read the letters in fragments, and then a computer assembles the fragments into long strings that constitute our genes, or our genetic fingerprint. No two people can have the same DNA."

"Well, thank you, Doctor, that was quite comprehensive. What law enforcement agencies use DNA testing?"

"The FBI, CIA, and Interpol for sure, there may be more."

"How did you get a sample from Mr. Marleaux?"

"We obtained a sample of his hair and blood from your office."

"And did you also obtain samples from the original trial?"

"Yes we did, the police gave them to us."

"And what kind of tests did you do?"

"We took the pattern of Mr. Marleaux's DNA and also ran a test of a sample of hair that was on the body at the original crime scene."

"And what did you find?"

"The DNA did not match."

"So someone other than Mr. Marleaux had close contact with the victim."

"Objection," said Edelman. "Calls for a conclusion. This man is not a detective on the case. Also, leading the witness."

"Sustained," said Judge Molinsky.

"Dr. Conrad, did you run DNA tests on all the samples found at the trial—semen, skin, blood?"

"Yes, I did."

"And what did you find?"

"None of them matched Mr. Marleaux's DNA."

"No more questions."

"Your witness, Counselor."

Conrad took off his glasses and wiped them with his handkerchief.

Edelman rose and walked toward him.

"Are you aware that DNA results are not totally acceptable in the scientific community?"

"There is a minor controversy."

"And what might that be?"

"Well, sometimes it's easier to exclude a person with DNA than match them."

"What do you mean?"

"Well, we can get within one person in 1.25 million saying that it is a match, but if there is no match, there is an infinitesimal chance that the person could be within the 1.25 range."

"Is that good enough for you?"

"Yes."

"I see," said Edelman skeptically, and then he paused before asking the next question.

"Tell me, Doctor, did you have any other labs check your results?"

"No other labs ran the tests, but—"

"So only your lab did the work," interrupted Edelman.

Nikki knew where Edelman was going. Recently there was a case that relied on the Kelly-Frye rule in which the court ruled against DNA because a majority of scientific community opinions were not sought or did not gain acceptance in the scientific community. She was prepared for this, but it was agony to watch.

Edelman stepped in close to Conrad. "Did you ever think to give the results to anyone else?"

"I followed our normal procedure."

"Which means that you worked alone," said Edelman.

"Yes, I did."

Edelman walked away, shaking his head just slightly, and said, "No more questions."

Nikki knew that Edelman was aware through discovery that she was going to bring on two witnesses from the other two recognized expert DNA labs, but he was grandstanding. She also knew that he had his own experts to counteract hers.

It was fairly routine as her two experts verified the results of Dr. Conrad. Nikki made sure that the judge knew in each case that the labs had received the approval of the majority of the scientific community. In her research on DNA cases that failed, she learned that the lawyer lost because he sent the sample to an unrecognized lab and she didn't want that happening to her.

When Edelman declined to cross-examine her experts she was a little surprised. After the second one was finished, she concluded her case.

"Respondent calls Dr. Irving Landers."

Nikki knew that Landers worked with the National Research Council in Washington in the genetics area.

"Dr. Landers, what kind of work do you do for the National Research Council?"

"I'm a geneticist."

"Do you specialize in any particular area?"

"Yes, I wrote the report *DNA Technology in Forensic Science.*"

"And what was that about?"

"It acknowledges the controversy surrounding DNA evidence in criminal proceedings and provides recommendations designed to clear up the debate about DNA profiling."

"What exactly is the debate, sir?"

"Well, there is substantial disagreement over the validity of current population genetics with regard to the multiplication rule."

"Forgive me, but I need you to speak a little more simply," said Edelman. "What is the multiplication rule?"

"It is something used by laboratories to calculate the extremely low frequencies at which DNA patterns appear in different individuals."

"You mean that some people can have the same DNA pattern as others?"

"Yes, it is possible."

"Doctor, are you telling me that the DNA tests are not 100 percent foolproof?"

"Yes, I am, and the NRC concludes so."

"Do you know of any other organizations that believe DNA results are not foolproof?"

"Yes."

"What are they?"

"The FBI."

"Now that's surprising. How could it be that they have one of the largest DNA labs in the country?"

"There is a disagreement in the scientific community over the validity of assumption in the FBI approach to testing."

"What is that approach?"

"Their statistical methods for calculating probability have not been shown to be generally accepted under the Frye rule."

"Thank you, Doctor."

"Your witness."

Nikki was on her feet immediately.

"Doctor, did you or the FBI do the testing on my client?"

"No."

"By the way, does the age of the samples matter?"

"No, it doesn't, samples don't even need to be refrigerated."

Nikki knew that answer and had been waiting to get it in. She thought it would be more effective coming from a witness for the other side, plus she wanted to undercut Edelman if he tried that position himself.

Nikki continued.

"Doctor, what are the statistics about the frequency of the same DNA patterns? Is it one in five, one in ten, one in twenty people? What is it?"

"If the subcultures are matching in groupings it could be as low as one in ten thousand."

"And if the subcultures don't match?"

"It could be one in twenty million."

"Have you studied Mr. Marleaux's results?"

"Yes."

"What is your opinion on the subcultures?"

"There were no data on that."

"So you mean that Mr. Marleaux's chances of matching the murder samples would be one in twenty million."

"Yes, I guess so."

"Fine, I'll take those odds."

"Are you finished, Ms. Easterly?" asked Judge Molinsky.

"Yes, Your Honor."

"Redirect, Counselor?"

"Yes," said Edelman.

"Dr. Landers, if subculture tests had been done is it possible that the odds could be lowered?"

"Yes."

Edelman turned to sit down.

"Your Honor? One more question?"

"Go ahead, Ms. Easterly."

"Dr. Landers, if you had more data could you tell us if it would rain tomorrow?"

"Don't answer that, Doctor," said Judge Molinsky. "Mr. Easterly, don't try that again."

"Respondent rests."

"Petitioner rests."

In Edelman's closing argument he hammered away at the statistical problems of DNA tests and also repeatedly said that Marleaux had been tried fairly and was found guilty and that his hair, semen, and skin samples were at the murder scene.

Nikki confidently addressed the fact that the judge should read again Marleaux's testimony from the first trial and realize that science improves each week and that DNA has been a major advance. Since the DNA did not match, it was necessary to have a new trial. Clearly someone else had been there after Mr. Marleaux.

"I will take this under submission. You will have my decision sometime this afternoon," said Judge Molinsky. He left the room.

Nikki and Edelman packed up their notes and went in separate directions. Hayden drove down to the courthouse to have lunch with Nikki and keep her company. They went to the cafeteria, which made a hospital cafeteria look like a Beverly Hills restaurant. All the foods had been frozen or processed, with the exception of portions of the salad bar. She could barely eat, she just wanted to wait in the hall.

Edelman's office was on the ninth floor of the building, so when the call came in from the bailiff that the judge was ready to render a decision he could run right over.

They got the call at three-fifteen to be ready at three-thirty.

Nikki and Edelman were in their places when the judge came in. Nikki was sitting there with her hands folded, her heart in her mouth. She was pleased with her job and her witnesses. The tests didn't match. Her client was innocent.

"*In re Marleaux,* having considered the petition and the evidence today, the court denies the petition for writ of habeas corpus." He slammed down the gavel and left the court.

Nikki couldn't move.

Edelman nodded at her as if she were inanimate and walked out.

Hayden came in as Edelman left. He couldn't tell by looking at Edelman's face what happened, but when he saw Nikki he knew.

She turned to face him, trying not to cry. Her anger was coming out anyway.

"How could this happen? What kind of a moron is this judge? This is the 1990s. These tests are being approved all over the place. This is a travesty, I will not allow it to happen."

"I'm sorry, so sorry. I know you did everything right," said Hayden. "It really was a miracle the appeal got heard, as you know. As least you had a shot rather than getting a form letter saying cert denied."

"That's not good enough. I've got an innocent man in jail and I'm going to get him out. Who knows what agenda this judge had? Maybe the fact that he's politically ambitious backfired on us. Maybe he doesn't want this kind of tough case with the publicity. Well I've got news for him and everybody else. We're going to the State Court of Appeal, and if that doesn't work I'll just keep going. It will be terrible telling this to Guy and his mother, but I must give them hope. I'm not giving up, no matter what!"

"Do you want to go out the back way?" asked Hayden gently.

"Not on your life. It's the front door from now on and the press is going to hear all about it. Let's go!"

The minute Nikki walked out on the front steps of the courthouse she was surrounded by video cameras, reporters, and photographers.

"Is the Greggie Alcott scandal going to finally explode?" yelled one reporter Nikki could hear over the din.

"This isn't about Greggie Alcott. It's about an innocent man who should be released from jail. Guy Marleaux's DNA doesn't match other samples found at the scene. He said all along that Greggie was alive when he left. It may sound corny, but I'm fighting for justice. That's why I became a lawyer. The courts have to recognize new technology and keep up with the times."

"But you already lost," interjected another reporter.

"This is just one round. Don't you have a clue what's coming next?" Nikki asked defiantly.

"So tell us," said a reporter from KCBS in Los Angeles.

Nikki announced the appeal right on the steps of the courthouse. It was all Hayden could do to keep her from going right back to the office to start the paperwork.

"Okay," she said to Hayden. "I'll wait until tomorrow morning, but then the papers go out. It's essentially done. It's the same briefs, just a new cover letter requesting a hearing at a higher level. We'll get our answer in thirty days and I'm going to start counting as of tomorrow."

Back at the office the next day Mark agreed with Hayden about the reasons behind the judge's ruling. "You know, sometimes judges are just idiots," said Mark.

"That's comforting," said Nikki. "And by the way, this judge was a real pig. He kept referring to me as 'Ms. Easterly' and opposing counsel as 'Counselor.' Judges are supposed to refer to both lawyers, regardless of gender, as 'Counsel.' 'Counselor' is a male term that has gone by the wayside, and to use my name," she continued, her voice rising, "Well . . . maybe I will take a break later in the week and go to Carmel. I could stand looking at a tree for a while."

"Would you like some company?" asked Hayden, concealing his hopefulness. "I'd love to meet your aunt."

Nikki softened for a second. She simply didn't know what to do.

"Okay," she said tentatively, wondering whose voice she was speaking with. "We'll try it."

"Great," answered Hayden calmly.

"Is that your laptop?" asked Hayden, gesturing to the black soft leather carrying case in the back seat as they were driving up the Pacific Coast Highway to Carmel.

"Yes," answered Nikki, immediately regretting she hadn't packed it in with her other things in the suitcase.

"Well, it's nice that you like it enough to take it somewhere. That's a change for you, but I didn't think we were going to work in Carmel."

Nikki felt trapped. She couldn't let him know how she needed it. "Well, you never know. Something might come up. I just look at it as an electronic filing system anyway."

"How long has it been since you've seen your aunt?" asked Hayden.

Good. He's on a new subject, thought Nikki.

"About nine months," she answered. "We talk occasionally. She wasn't thrilled when I came to Los Angeles to practice. She's happy that I'm doing well, but she would have preferred it if I'd taken a job on the East Coast."

"Well I'm glad you didn't. How many times have you been up and down the coast this way?"

"Hardly ever," said Nikki. "Aunt Meredith didn't want me near Los Angeles. She didn't want me around anything to do with my mother. She was very protective. In fact, when we went to Disneyland when I was a little kid, we flew directly to Orange County rather than drive through L.A."

"Wow, you're kidding. That's really something. Is she still like that?"

"Yes, she never wants to talk about my mother, even now that I'm way old enough to understand things."

"I wonder what really happened between those two?" asked Hayden. "Was Meredith so jealous that Lauren had a career and she didn't?"

"Not according to Meredith. When you meet her you'll understand how happy she is. She's so non-Hollywood you won't believe it. She's an ethereal creature who is happier among animals, rocks, and trees. You'll see."

"Look, look over there," said Hayden excitedly. "Have you ever seen the Old Courthouse in Ventura?"

"No, of course not."

"You've got to."

Hayden pulled off the road and within two minutes they were in an area that looked like it was the late 1930s, early 1940s, filled with antique shops, thrift shops, diners, old hotels, a mission, storefront shops, little benches gathered around flower beds, and people smiling at each other in the street.

"This is amazing, it's like time stopped," exclaimed Nikki. "What a quaint little town. I'd love to walk around."

"We'll make a day of it soon," said Hayden. "Carmel is about five hours from here and we really should get there before dark. I'd like to take you to lunch in Santa Barbara and then make a beeline for Carmel."

"Where is Santa Barbara?" asked Nikki. "You know how much I love food."

Hayden laughed.

"Yes I certainly do. How about Julia Child's favorite restaurant?"

"Really? But I must not be dressed for it."

"Oh yes you are. It's called La Super Rica and it looks like a food stand in a trailer park but wow those tamales and pasilla chiles. I'm telling you . . ." he said, taking her hand.

Nikki felt herself jump a bit at his touch, but she didn't pull her hand away.

It was a long stretch from Santa Barbara to Carmel. Nikki's stomach was more than satisfied, but the length of the trip gave her almost too much time to think. She resented Meredith for not giving her information, yet she loved her as she would a mother and was very grateful for the wonderful childhood she had given her. But Nikki knew Meredith wouldn't be happy about the real reason for this visit.

Hayden sensed Nikki's apprehension, and he squeezed her hand from time to time, but he said nothing.

They reached the freeway exit and Nikki's stomach twinged.

"Get off here where it says Aguajito and keep going until you see Loma Alta," she directed.

"These trees are gorgeous," said Hayden, noting the huge Monterey pines lining the hills.

"This is called Jack's Peak. It's one of the highest mountains in the area. You can see all of Carmel and Monterey from our house," explained Nikki, getting excited at seeing her old haunts again.

"Incredible!" said Hayden, looking to the left. "Can I stop the car here for a second?"

"Yes, but hurry, the neighbors here hate tourists who stop no matter how beautiful the view is. It interferes with traffic.

Look to the right and you'll see Pebble Beach, see over there in that cove? To the right beyond it is the harbor of Monterey. C'mon now, we've got to get going."

Hayden started the car again. At the top of the hill was a wooden gate with animals carved in it.

"Pull in here," said Nikki. "I have to get out to unlock it."

She walked over to a large combination padlock and dialed 1-3-1-3.

"They don't go for electric gates up here," she said matter-of-factly.

They drove in on a dirt driveway surrounded by acres of land and trees. To the right there were animal pens and cabins. As they drove along there were chicken coops, a couple of barns, and more animal pens.

"That's the guest house where you'll stay right over there," said Nikki. "I'm going to stay in my old room. That's going to be a trip . . ."

"I really want to see your room, though," said Hayden.

"Don't worry, you'll see everything."

They had made their approach to the main area where the two-story-A-frame wooden ski-lodge-type house loomed before them. There were railings in front to tie up your horse, and a llama was resting in a small pen attached to the house.

"Pocahontas must have given birth recently," said Nikki, "that's what she's doing so close to the house. And you see these rocks? Meredith and I collected them from beaches and forests all over and then made them into this path leading to the front door. It really means a lot to me."

"Nikki! You're home!"

Meredith bolted from the front door, her long, straight blond hair flying. She was wearing jeans and cowboy boots, a black turtleneck, and a leather poncho.

Hayden was momentarily immobilized by the beauty of this woman, who was every bit as gorgeous as Lauren

Laverty. Their smile was the same, but Meredith's eyes seemed brighter, thought Hayden immediately.

Nikki and Meredith hugged a long time.

"Oh, sweetie, I've missed you, too. And you must be Hayden."

Meredith turned and smiled directly at him. He was almost blinded, her beauty was so ethereal. Standing there in her own forest, she was every bit the child of nature that Nikki had described.

"It's a pleasure to meet you."

"I can see why she had such a happy childhood here with you," said Hayden.

"Thank you, that's very kind. Why don't we all come in. I have some fresh lemonade I just made. Let's go out to the porch."

Hayden tried to take in the living room all at once. It was just as Nikki had described, with the stone fireplace in the middle. But Nikki had failed to mention the porch. It was an enormous veranda running the length of the house with carved wooden furniture made out of rough trees, a swing for two, a hot tub, bird feeders, and gorgeous flowers. But most of all, it looked down on the same view he saw when he asked to stop the car. It was overwhelming.

"We can ride our horses all the way along Carmel River right into town," said Meredith. "Just look over to the left and you can see the trail, even though we're very high up."

"This is truly one of the most beautiful spots I have ever seen," said Hayden.

"We love it here," said Meredith. "I'll be right back with the lemonade."

"Nikki, standing here I can understand now why Hollywood was so foreign to you. Even though you went to school in San Francisco, growing up in this peaceful place is what has made you the way you are. It makes you strong and quiet in the center so whirlwinds of craziness pass over you.

I'm amazed you didn't turn right around and come back here the minute you moved into the Shoreham Towers."

"You know why I didn't," said Nikki quietly. "I need to make my life whole again."

Meredith returned.

"You've arrived just before sunset," she said. "What would you rather do? Stay here and have a sip or two, or go to your rooms and unpack and meet me back here in an hour for cocktails? Oh, and Nikki, instead of going out tonight I made your favorite dinner. I thought you'd like to just stay home. Maybe tomorrow we'll show Hayden Point Lobos, have a little picnic, and then for dinner do one of our movable feasts up and down the coast."

Meredith turned to Hayden and continued. "When Nikki was a little girl we used to love to eat different courses in different restaurants. We'd start in either Big Sur or Carmel and just eat our way from one to the other."

"I think we'll go unpack and meet you back here. We'll take our lemonade with us," said Nikki.

Hayden drove with Nikki to the little house because Nikki thought it was better to park their car there in case they wanted to go for a drive and not disturb anybody. The little house was really a one-room log cabin with one wall contiguous to the horse ring on the left, and another wall on the right contiguous with the feeding room of the main barn.

"Look at that!" exclaimed Hayden, spotting a black horse looking in the window.

"That's Cosmos. He's Meredith's horse and he's adorable. He comes when I call him just like a dog. I'll show you later. He knows I'm in here and he's saying hello. I'd better go to him or his feelings will be hurt, I'll be right back."

Hayden looked around at his surroundings. There was a brass bed with a patchwork quilt and an old-fashioned pot-bellied stove that served as a fireplace. Next to that was a carved wooden rocking horse or rocking llama, to be specific, and an old oak table serving as a desk. A black and white TV with rabbit ears was in a wall unit that also housed a hot plate and refrigerator. A door led to the bathroom, again all log walls with two stained-glass windows. He felt as if he were standing in a cabin in a child's fairy tale. As he looked at Nikki through the window, he dared to dream for a second about her staying with him.

He walked to the window and watched Nikki nuzzling Cosmos. If that horse could jump up and hug her with his front legs he would have done so, he was so happy. Suddenly Nikki jumped on his back, no saddle, no reins, nothing. The two of them strutted around the ring like they were in a show. He loved seeing her this free, this happy. She was so intense in Los Angeles, but with good reason, he thought.

Nikki walked back to the main house. The door was unlocked as usual, and Meredith was waiting for her by the fireplace.

"He's certainly a nice young man," said Meredith.

"Yes, he is, but he's just a friend."

"Oh, Nikki, I can tell he likes you. And you like him, too. You can't fool me. Don't you want that in your life?"

"Aunt Meredith, I just got here. I haven't even unpacked. Please. I know you want good things for me, but I really don't want to get into this just now. I'm going upstairs to get organized and I'll see you in an hour, okay?" said Nikki, trying to keep things on an even keel because it was important that Meredith be comfortable and happy so Nikki could ask her questions later.

She bounded up the stairs and then stopped in her tracks when she stepped into her room. It was like a time warp. Nothing had changed. It was dusk, and the same shadows that chilled her every day of her young life were still around the top of the bookcases. She knew it was the trees brushing against the skylights, but for a second she almost had to fight an instinct to hide her head underneath the bedspread from the bad guys. Hating herself for so quickly falling back into grim childhood patterns, she forced herself to unpack. When she was through she lay on the bed, and debated shutting her eyes. It had been so long since she'd had a nightmare. She prayed these surroundings would be kinder to her as an adult tonight.

When Nikki went downstairs Meredith was already outside working at the grill. She looked at her through the window and thought of all the times she had seen her in that exact place. Her heart warmed at the fun memories she had, and she realized that Meredith was the one responsible for them. Nikki hated to question Meredith and possibly start some problems, but it was important for her to know certain things. The time had simply come.

After some brief pleasantries Nikki took a deep breath and asked Meredith why the two sisters differed on their view of Hollywood.

"Lauren loved it and I hated it. It's as simple as that," said Meredith, flipping over the grilled swordfish. "It's a good thing Bill isn't here this weekend. He hates seeing me upset, you know that. The past upsets me. Can't we just have a nice dinner?"

"I don't want to hurt you," said Nikki, "but I've been trying for so long to talk to you. You never wanted to say anything when I was younger and you used that as an excuse. Living in Los Angeles now I am constantly reminded of my mother. People are staring at me, reporters ask questions, I'm just not a person who can fit in. I need to know some things."

"Oh Nikki . . ."

"Please, Meredith. I'm not a kid anymore. Do you know what it's like to not know who your father is or anything much about your mother except what you read in old newspapers? I need you. I can't really know my whole self until I know about the past. Please," begged Nikki.

Meredith took the swordfish steaks off the grill. "Walk with me," she said.

They walked down to the garden spot where the statue of St. Francis was and sat down on the same bench where Nikki sat many times as a child when they had to talk.

"Nikki," said Meredith, "I honestly don't know who your father was. I don't know if he's alive or dead. I don't know anything about him."

"I read that my mother was on a concert tour for three months during the summer about a year before I was born. Do you know anything about that?"

"No. We weren't close then. I disapproved of her lifestyle. We fought about it every time we talked so we just stopped talking. It was easier for both of us."

Meredith paused and picked up a branch that was at her feet. She started twirling it.

"This is very hard to say," she hesitated. "Lauren died a horrible death, but people weren't that surprised, considering her behavior and who she hung around with. Your mother was a glamorous hippie who became a movie star. She believed in free love, free drugs. She went through money like water. If it hadn't been for Mark you'd have no inheritance."

"What about Mark and my mother? He won't talk about it either."

"He loved her very much and asked her repeatedly to set a wedding date. She loved him in her way, but she just couldn't be faithful to him. It was almost as if she felt she didn't deserve his goodness. She was very self-destructive, and she hated me because I never fell into the traps. She called me Goody. She was pathetic. I couldn't have saved her if I tried. No one could. I'm sorry, but the best thing that happened is that you got out of there when you did, regardless of the circumstances. Lauren just wasn't any good."

"How can you say that?" said Nikki, her voice rising. "She loved me! She told me every day. She held me and she felt good and she smelled sweet. Did you want her dead? Was I the prize?" yelled Nikki, suddenly standing up.

Meredith jumped up and faced her. Their noses were inches apart. "Yes, I wanted her away from you," said Meredith defiantly. "You were the only decent thing she ever did and I knew she'd destroy you. Connie was the one who took care of you. You were hugged for a minute and a half and then Lauren went out again with God-knows-who. She was either on location or in someone's bed. This is what I didn't want you to know. This is why I didn't want to get into this. I knew you'd never be able to hear it."

Nikki walked away from her and suddenly twirled around to face her again.

"You just didn't like her because she became a star and you didn't," snapped Nikki, instantly sorry that it slipped out.

"I've been waiting for you to accuse me of that. That's the easy way out. It looks so simple. The good sister and the bad sister. The pretty one and the ugly one, except I'm not ugly and you know it. We had the same modeling career. I had the same opportunities she did. I didn't need that validation. Lauren was much more insecure than I was. I wanted a life. Lauren didn't realize that Hollywood was an existence, not a life. They throw you out when you're forty. I didn't want that. She was so dependent on the love that you get from the adoration of fans and men, that she never could have survived what would have happened to her. In death she became young forever and a star forever. I don't think of it as a price she paid. It was her destiny and I think she knew it. I think she courted it. All she ever talked about was Marilyn Monroe and James Dean. Don't you get it?"

The two women stood staring at each other nose-to-nose again.

Then Meredith softened and started crying.

"It kills me that I couldn't save her. The pain of that is something I live with every day. By not talking about it I could try to forget it, and by not giving you information you could have a clear head and a happier life. Do you know how hard it was to look at you growing up and see her all over again?"

Nikki was crying, too, now. She put her arms around Meredith and cradled her head. "I love you," she said. "I know you did what you thought was right, but eventually we all have to deal with our pasts, you and I, and I have to find out everything in order to move forward."

Meredith lifted up her head. "What does that mean?" she asked softly.

"I'm not exactly sure," said Nikki, "but I'll know when enough is enough."

"Sweetie, I'm afraid for you. Let it go. I've told you all I know. There really isn't any more."

And Nikki knew that Meredith was telling the truth, but it was *her* truth as she knew it. Nikki would no longer bother her with questions, but she knew it wasn't over.

Three hours later and it was time for bed. Nikki, Hayden, and Meredith had finished their coffee and dessert around the center fireplace and Hayden excused himself. Meredith caught Nikki looking up the staircase toward her room.

"It's been a long time," said Meredith.

"I know. It feels a little strange up there," answered Nikki.

"Were you afraid at all when you first walked in?"

"A little. I've had too many bad nights up there."

"Would you rather stay in the den?" asked Meredith.

"Thanks, but I have to be a grown-up sometime and I guess this is it," said Nikki. "I'm sure everything will be fine. Good night."

Nikki walked upstairs the same way she had been doing since they had moved her up there. She fought the sense of déjà vu as she spotted the same wooden animals on the same little shelves in the staircase wall. When she was smaller she had named all of them and said good night to each one as she went to bed. It made her think she was surrounded by friends each night. Tonight she petted each one hello. She couldn't walk by without acknowledging them, that would be too sad, but she didn't want to say hello. She didn't want to be a little girl again.

Because nothing had changed, not even her bathroom wallpaper with the baby pigs on it, she realized she was going to have a bit of a battle on her hands. She washed her face and brushed her teeth and got out of the bathroom as fast as she could. She changed into her blue cotton men's Dior pajamas and jumped into bed. She propped up her pillows to read a novel she had brought with her, and opened it to where the bookmark was.

She loved reading Jane Austen novels, and she was in the middle of *Pride and Prejudice* for the third time. She started it just before coming up to Carmel in anticipation of just this moment. This kind of old-fashioned book went with her old-fashioned room.

Her laptop was nearby, but, at least for tonight, she didn't need it.

Reading always made her sleepy, and she was relieved to feel herself start to relax. The warmth of the electric blanket was very comforting. She looked down at the dial. It was set at four, and she remembered how she loved it at around seven when she was a child. She thought then that the heat would protect her from the bad people.

There was no wind. It was quiet and quite lovely. The same stars were shining through the skylights, and all was right with the world.

The hands were choking her so she couldn't cry out. Her feet were tied to the posts and she felt as if her head were going to slip down over the footboard. She fought back with her hands hitting against the strong body. She longed to cry out, but her throat was on fire. Please God, somebody help me!

She could feel him on top of her now, ripping her pajamas with one hand, and holding her arms over her head with the other. He slapped her face and told her to shut up. She didn't want to end up like Mommy, did she?

No! cried out Nikki into the night.

Her eyes snapped open and she jumped up in a sweat. No one had answered her cry.

Of course they didn't, you idiot, thought Nikki to herself. You never said anything! There wasn't anybody here.

Nikki was furious that she had had that nightmare again. She had been good for so long. Even though she realized that being in this room was an unusual circumstance that could trigger it, she was hard on herself, and wanted to go back to L.A. immediately.

Instead, she got up, put on a parka and boots, and decided to go visit Cosmos. He always made her feel better, and she wasn't afraid of being outside. She had named practically every tree on the property. She would be among friends.

Hayden woke to the soft murmurings. At first he couldn't make out what they were, he had been in such a sound sleep. They were coming from the horse ring. In a second he realized it could be Nikki. He looked at the clock: three-thirteen A.M.

Putting on his navy cashmere robe and slippers, he crept up to the window, where he saw Nikki with her arms around Cosmos's neck. He could see she was whispering to the horse, who seemed to be nodding in agreement. He observed how comfortable Nikki was with the animal, so connected and giving, no defenses. It was the first time he had seen that side of her. Her hair shone in the moonlight and

she looked so vulnerable. He studied her and thought she
was actually clinging strongly to the horse, as if to gather
strength. After a few seconds he turned his eyes away, not
wanting to invade her privacy.

He turned and walked to his front door, opened it and let
the air fill him up. It was a glorious night.

"Nikki," he called gently from the barn gate, not wanting
to scare her.

Nikki gasped.

"I'm so sorry, I didn't mean to scare you," said Hayden,
entering the ring and noticing Nikki didn't remove her arms
from Cosmos.

"I'm just a little jumpy."

"What's wrong?" asked Hayden, putting his hand on her
shoulder.

She turned to him. "I—I feel foolish. I had a nightmare. It
used to happen up here all the time. I hate that it happened
again. I thought I'd outgrown it, I thought I'd be better . . ."

Nikki's voice was increasing in intensity, her anxiety rising with it, tears beginning to fall.

Hayden held her and she let him.

"Nikki, I'm here. I won't let you go. You're safe now."

His arms felt good to her. She buried her face in his robe
and smelled his scent. He was rubbing her back now, and
she was calming down.

Nikki lifted her head and looked at him. She was going to
say thank you but the words wouldn't come out. She just
looked into his confident eyes and watched as his face came
toward hers. His lips were soft and full, not predatory. She
felt herself give back and forget all fears.

When Nikki came down to breakfast she had decided
that she really wanted to go back to Los Angeles. The re-
currence of the nightmare had disturbed her once it was
light, and she wanted to leave. But she realized it wouldn't

be polite to Hayden to ask him to run around right now and leave. She'd spend the day and see how she felt later. If she had to go, then she'd just tell him. She knew he'd understand.

"I have some fun places to show you," said Nikki, not mentioning her decision.

"Oh, really?" said Hayden.

"Absolutely, get a jacket and we'll be off. I'll take you someplace special for breakfast for starters."

Hayden noticed that Nikki was friendly, but back to being reserved. He would give her the space she wanted.

They crossed over the freeway and turned down Carpenter Avenue. It was the back way into the city of Carmel.

"Turn right on Ocean and then make a left on Dolores," said Nikki. "Park right here in front of this English country house."

Hayden looked up and saw the little hard-carved sign: THE TUCK BOX. "This is really charming."

They went inside and sat down at a table in the corner.

"Nikki! You're home," said a jolly woman coming toward them with a teapot.

"Barbara, I'd like you to meet my friend Hayden Chou. Hayden, this is Barbara Malmborg, the owner of the Tuck Box. She's known me since I was a little kid."

"She's my favorite, I just adore her," she said to Hayden.

"So what is it today, Nikki, Irish oatmeal or scones and eggs?"

"Both. I've been away too long and I have to have everything. Hayden, why don't you split the oatmeal with me and order eggs any way you like and scones, too."

"I guess that's it then," said Hayden.

"You won't believe the oatmeal, it's real and has raisins in it that plump up with heat, and you can put butter, brown sugar, maple syrup, or honey, and then add fresh cream."

"Where are we going from here?" asked Hayden.

"We're going to walk to the Mediterranean Market and get two of their picnic lunches to go. Then I'm taking you to my favorite spot in Carmel—Frank Lloyd Bench."

"Frank Lloyd Bench? I've heard of Frank Lloyd Wright," said Hayden. "But who's Frank Lloyd Bench?"

Nikki laughed, and went on to explain.

"When I was in high school, a bench was placed on a point overlooking Carmel Beach looking toward Pebble Beach. The bench is near where Frank Lloyd Wright's house is still standing. But the plaque on the bench says 'Frank Lloyd Bench' for some reason. I'd just like to sit on it the way I used to. It's a very special place to me, where I used to go to think things out. I'd like to share it with you."

"And then where are we going?"

"We're going hiking at Point Lobos. It's just amazing there and maybe we'll picnic. We're just going to be wandering around all day. I think we'll end up in Pacific Grove walking along the garden path overlooking the water at sunset. Then we'll dash down to the Post Ranch for dinner. It's the most beautiful place in all of Big Sur," said Nikki, feeling better.

"Well, I'm glad I have you along. I'd never know where to go without you. It sounds incredible."

"And then tomorrow morning the first thing we do is leave here and go back to L.A. I've got to get back. I think I can only contain myself for today showing you things. That gives me pleasure, but tomorrow I'm on the roller coaster again."

Hayden was disappointed that she wanted to leave so soon, but he knew he had to take it slow with Nikki. She had a purpose for coming here and he had to let her travel at her own speed.

"Wait a second, wait a second," said Nikki excitedly. "We have to stop here."

"Fine, but I don't think this is Point Lobos," answered Hayden, as they stopped in front of a charming little stone house in the middle of Carmel.

"I just have to see if Dr. Stanley is here," said Nikki. "I haven't seen her in so long. She's the one who really put me back together after . . . well, you know . . ."

"I'd love to meet her."

"She shouldn't be working on Saturday. Let's just ring the bell. Her office is in the back."

Nikki and Hayden walked up to the front door.

Nikki wondered if her sudden desire to see Dr. Stanley was instigated by that dream again. She hadn't visited her in the past few years. She had stopped going to her when she was fifteen. They had been together for nine years, through the most painful time of Nikki's life. As Nikki reflected, she believed that Dr. Carol Stanley was the person she had talked to the most in her whole life. She missed her. Coming back here was like visiting an old school. You walk in the halls and they don't seem as big, your locker wasn't as high, the benches weren't that low.

The door opened, Dr. Stanley yelled "Nikki!" and hugged her like the long-lost child that in a way she was.

"I hope you don't mind us barging in. This is Hayden Chou, a business associate of mine. We work at the same law firm."

"It's so nice to meet you, Hayden. Please come in."

Dr. Stanley's smile was just as bright, her eyes just as kind. There were wisps of gray in the curls, which only made her look more loving and understanding.

"I am so sorry that I haven't been by or spoken to you in so long. I feel terrible about that."

"Oh, Nikki, I've missed you. But you shouldn't feel bad. It's a hazard of my profession when the kids graduate. How've you been, what are you doing? Can I get you both some tea?"

"Oh, no thank you, we've just come from the Tuck Box."

"Scones?" asked Dr. Stanley.

Nikki laughed. "What else?"

"So tell me," Dr. Stanley said.

Nikki told her all about her current cases, focusing more on Marleaux, of course, then described her apartment, Mark, and the office.

"It all sounds so exciting. Are you happy? Are you enjoying yourself?" Dr. Stanley glanced over at Hayden.

Nikki turned to Hayden.

"I need to ask you a favor. I didn't really know I was going to come here today, and I need to talk to Dr. Stanley alone for just a few minutes. I hope you don't mind."

"Not at all," said Hayden. "I'll go for a walk."

"Thanks," said Nikki. "I really appreciate it. We'll go to Point Lobos right after this, I promise."

"Hayden," said Dr. Stanley, "if you walk to the end of the block and turn left, you'll be at the beach in about two minutes. It's a lovely walk. You can see all of Carmel Beach."

"Thanks, I'll do just that."

The minute the door shut Nikki looked at Dr. Stanley and started to sob.

Dr. Stanley's arms were instantly around her. "It's all right, dear Nikki. You haven't been here in a while. Memories are being stirred up. Do you have anyone to cry with in Los Angeles?"

"I never cry in L.A.," sniffed Nikki, trying to pull herself together.

"Maybe that's part of the problem. Do you feel alone there? Hayden is obviously very special to you, and I could see in his eyes that he cares. Isn't he someone you can turn to?"

"Yes, but I can't think about those things, there's so much going on inside me already. All I do is work and go home. But I really love my work. I love this case I'm working on.

As for Hayden, I'm scared. Just when I start to feel I get frozen inside."

"That will change in time, Nikki. All of these things are tied together. You won't let your emotions go because you feel you couldn't handle losing anybody ever again. That will work itself out."

"If you say so, but there are other problems in L.A."

"Such as?"

"This is really hard for me. I keep trying not to think about it."

"What, Nikki?"

"My mother."

"Remember what I told you almost every time we were together? I told you that you would never be able to forget, that you had to learn how to live with it, make peace with it. You know your mother loved you. We've talked about how nothing was your responsibility. You were doing well with that. That's one of the reasons why I thought it was okay for you to stop your sessions when you were a teenager. You were beginning to live life and I wanted you to experience some fun."

"But now there's a problem," said Nikki, finally able to articulate it.

"Please tell me."

"Everywhere I go in L.A. I'm reminded of my mother. Nobody lets me forget. I'm stopped by strangers because I look like her. I'm followed by the press because I'm her daughter. I find I can use it as an entrée in business, and I feel dirty because I do use it sometimes. I go into a department store and the Fresh Love counter smells like her. I can't get away from it."

"Are you sure you want to?"

"What do you mean?"

"You smell lovely today, Nikki. I don't ever recall you wearing perfume. What is it?" asked Dr. Stanley as gently as possible.

Nikki gulped and the tears started welling up again. "It's Fresh Love. My God, Dr. Stanley, I wasn't even aware that I put it on this morning. What's happening to me?"

"This is all to be expected, dear. The use of your mother's scent, where you live now, it all makes sense. By picking Los Angeles as a place to practice law you had to know what you were getting into. You're older now, Nikki, and I don't need to treat you like a child. I can talk to you directly. When I heard that you were going to Hollywood, even though I knew part of the motivation was to be protected by Mark Ferguson, I also knew you were on the final quest to confront your mother. Meredith tended to bury it, and you needed to feel safe before you could confront it. You're going through the cycle, Nikki, and that's healthy. This last part of the journey isn't going to be easy, but I think it's necessary. You were always going to make this journey. You'll come full circle and be a happy human being. I think what's going on is good and I encourage you to keep going with it, no matter how painful it is."

Nikki was crying again. "Her pictures are everywhere. I'm mad at her for leaving me, and I miss her so much. I need to know her. I need to know everything about her. I need to know who my father was. Can you understand?"

"Of course, darling. This is normal; in fact, this is a breakthrough for you. And it's something that needs to be done carefully. You shouldn't do this alone. It's going to bring up so many issues for you. I want you to call me, or come up and see me whenever you want. This is a crucial time in your life, and I'm here for you. Please know that you are not alone. You can't be alone."

"I had a nightmare last night," revealed Nikki. "I didn't scream or anything. I woke up and handled it myself. I guess it was because I was back in my room. I haven't had one since I moved to L.A."

"Don't worry about it. If I can use a sort of silly analogy, you're like a pot of soup that is boiling. You were on simmer for so many years just so you could cope. The boiling could result in nightmares, fears, disturbances, but boiling over in the end is good because you get rid of the bad and there's tremendous calm. After all this is over you'll have control of the burner."

Nikki laughed. "You always do have a way of making an important point and having me end up in a smile. You really have saved my life so many times. I'll really pay attention to your advice. I'll do my best to try to not deal with all this by myself."

Just then there was a knock at the front door.

Dr. Stanley opened it for Hayden.

"That beach is gorgeous. How are things in here?" asked Hayden.

"We're doing just fine," said Dr. Stanley confidently.

"I just love that lady," said Nikki when she and Hayden were in the car. "She really understands me. I can't wait to get back to L.A."

"What?"

"I wish we could fly back right now," said Nikki.

"What do you mean?" asked Hayden.

"It's time to hit the computers and the libraries about Lauren."

"You mean in our spare time?" teased Hayden.

"I'm serious."

"I know, and we'll do it. Why don't we just skip the rest of what we were going to do, go back to the house, pack, and take off early."

"Oh, Hayden, thank you. You really understand. If we can do that, I promise I'll show you Point Lobos and Big Sur as we drive back. How's that?"

"Deal. Now what are you going to say to Meredith about our leaving early?"

"Good question," said Nikki. "I'm just going to tell her the truth. That we have more work in L.A. than we thought, and we're going to go down the coast the long way and look at things as we go back. She'll be okay."

Nikki wished she hadn't agreed to go the long way. If they'd taken the freeway and not the coast route they would have been back in six hours. This way it would take eight. But she felt she had to show Hayden a few things. She knew he could tell she had something else on her mind, and for a long time Nikki was quiet in the car.

"Okay, Nikki. Please tell me. You've been too quiet."

"All right. When we get to L.A., which will be in about two hours, I'd like to drive straight to my mother's house."

"You mean where she was murdered?" asked Hayden incredulously.

"It's the only house I know of hers, naturally that's the one I mean."

"Have you not been by there since you moved to L.A.?"

"I've never had the nerve. But I think I can handle it today."

"Are you sure this is something you want to do?" asked Hayden.

"Totally. It's time. I'll be fine," she said determinedly.

Precisely at six-fifteen P.M. Nikki and Hayden pulled up to 718 N. Linden Drive in the flats of Beverly Hills. Many homes in this area had been leveled and new, larger homes built on existing lots, but not 718 N. Linden. It was exactly as it was, preserved as some sort of shrine. Even tour buses called Graveline Tours would come by in a hearse as part of a tour of the death sites of Hollywood stars. It was a two-story Spanish house, white, with a red-tile roof. There was a nice size lawn in front with a path from the driveway to the front door. The elm tree that Nikki played under was still to the right of the front door.

"The house was built in the 1930s. Everything inside is dark wood with beamed ceilings. My favorite part of the house was a little nook just to the inside of the front door that was a telephone area. It's arched with a little shelf and stool and a phone sitting on it. I used to love to hide underneath the shelf," said Nikki, her voice catching.

"I have to ask you again. Are you sure you want to do this?"

"Yes, but I don't want to sneak around. If people are home they'll call the police. I'd better just go up to the front door and tell them who I am and ask to come in."

"If that's what you want . . ."

The doorbell rang and it seemed like aeons before someone answered. It was a man in bermuda shorts and a knit polo shirt, barefoot, wearing glasses. He looked like he was in his early fifties.

"Hi, please excuse the intrusion. My name is Nikki Easterly and I used to live here as a child. It would mean a great deal to me if I could come in and look around. I know this is unusual, but I'm not a weirdo. This really is legit. It would mean so much to me."

The man looked at Hayden.

"This is Hayden Chou. We're both lawyers and he's my friend."

"When did you live here?" asked the man, not moving from the door.

"The early 1970s," answered Nikki, waiting for the recognition to come.

"You're her daughter, aren't you?" he asked slowly.

Nikki nodded and waited.

"I'm Dr. Nathan. Please come in. I realize what's happening now. Come meet my wife."

He turned and motioned them in. Nikki took a deep breath, entered, and immediately looked to the right. The nook was still there. There was no phone in it, a beautiful vase with flowers was on the shelf. She wished she could have hidden under it again right then and there. She tried to look around and see everything at once as she followed the doctor. It was overwhelming. There were no big changes architecturally. The paint was all new, some of the colors were different, a new carpet here and there, but it was her house, and it practically paralyzed her.

"Dear, this is Nikki Easterly, Lauren Laverty's daughter, and her friend Hayden Chou. They wanted to walk around the house and I thought it was okay."

"Oh, my, this is quite an event," said Mrs. Nathan. "We knew of the history of the house, of course. Your mother was so gorgeous. It was a thrill when we bought the house."

"When did you buy it?" asked Nikki.

"About five years ago," answered Mrs. Nathan. "I don't know if we could have been the first people to live in it after the—" She caught herself and looked at Nikki. "I'm so sorry. This is a little awkward. Why don't you just look around. Take your time. Gregory and I will be right here in the den watching TV."

"Let's go out in the backyard first," said Nikki.

Hayden followed her as she stopped in the kitchen.

"The appliances are new, but the layout is the same, so's the maroon and white tile. I used to sit on that counter right over there and watch Connie cook my lunch. Look at that service porch. I saw kittens being born there. My Kimmy lived until he was seventeen. He went to Carmel with me. I stayed home from nursery school that day because I was sick and I had no idea Katy would be giving birth, but I saw it all right there." Nikki felt a heaviness settle in. It was as if she had never left. All the sights, smells, and sounds came back to her. Time had stopped.

"This door will take us to the backyard."

And what a backyard it was, with a twenty-by-forty-foot ice blue pool with two diving boards, a white pool house with green palm trees, and a tennis court off to the side. "My sandbox used to be over there where that tree is now. I guess somebody removed it and planted a tree. I remember my mother lounging around near the shallow end. There was a guy, very tan, who kept putting oil on her. Who was that? My God, who was that?" she said, grabbing Hayden.

"Take it easy. We have time. It could have been Mark," said Hayden.

"Yes, it could have, but it could also have been anyone, according to Meredith."

Nikki walked to the patio area.

"I remember clowns here. White faces, red noses, cake, songs. I was happy."

"How are you doing now?" asked Hayden.

"It's weird. It's really weird. Have you been back to the home where you grew up?" she asked.

"My parents still live there. It looks smaller to me each time I go back, and yes, it's very weird. I don't know what's harder, seeing your parents still in the same house with no progress, or going back like this to a house with no one left inside."

"I think this is, I assure you," answered Nikki. "Let's go back in the house."

She walked back in the kitchen and stopped.

"I don't know whether to go up the servants' stairs in the back by the main staircase to get to the second floor. Either way it will be awful. I ran down the big stairs when I saw my mother's body."

"I'll do whatever you want. Would you like to go upstairs the back way and go to your room first?" asked Hayden gently.

"No, I'm going to go for it. My room is irrelevant," said Nikki, suddenly braver than ever before.

She walked back into the main hall and looked at the stairs. They were unusually wide, five feet across, with the same faux gold railings.

"The brocade wall covering is still here. That's interesting. Let's go."

Together they went up the stairs, up to the top.

"Turn right," she said, and they walked to the end of the hall. The door to the master bedroom was closed.

"I know it will be different, the furniture is new, maybe it will all be new," she said hopefully. But her eyes caught a glimpse of the gold sconces and she let out a little gasp.

She pushed open the door slowly. A four-poster bed was in the same place. It wasn't the same bed, but close enough. Night was beginning to come and shadows played on the walls. It was too much to take. Nikki could feel blackness enveloping her body. She was losing touch with reality. Nikki dropped to her knees sobbing. "The cords, the cords, I can still see them. Look! There they are." She crawled to the bed, grabbing one of the posts screaming, "Mommy, no . . ."

# Chapter 12

By the time Hayden reached her, Nikki was screaming and writhing out of control.

"Nikki, Nikki, it'll be all right," said Hayden, trying to soothe her. He was holding her and rocking her. "You've got to try to get hold of yourself. We don't want these people to see you like this."

Nikki was moaning now, not screaming. As Hayden continued to stroke her, speak softly to her, the moaning changed to whimpering. Nikki was becoming the child she was when she last was in this bedroom.

"I've got you, Nikki. Shhh. Everything's okay. I want you to try to stand up now, if you can. I'll hold on to you."

"Is everything okay in there?" called Dr. Nathan from downstairs.

"We'll be fine, thanks," answered Hayden, struggling to keep Nikki upright.

Nikki was unsteady on her feet. Her eyes were glassy, but she was able to move. Hayden guided her along the hall and down the stairs, whispering encouragement with every step. When he saw Dr. Nathan he just gave him a look that said, it's fine, just let us go, I'll take care of her. Hayden knew that the doctor understood what had happened.

The ride home to the Shoreham Towers was only six minutes. Nikki never said a word and kept staring straight ahead. Occasionally she would twitch a little bit. Hayden saw to it that she got into her apartment, and pulled out the couch for her while she put on a robe. He was worried when she stayed in the bathroom too long.

"Would you like me to call Dr. Stanley for you, Nikki?" he called into the bathroom.

Opening the door, Nikki shook her head no as she got into bed.

"I don't want to leave you alone," said Hayden.

Nikki stared at him for several seconds and then she weakly said, "Sleep. I must sleep. I took a Valium. I don't want to talk, I want to be by myself. Please understand. I need you to go."

"Oh, Nikki, I hate leaving you," said Hayden kneeling by the bed.

"Please, it's the only way I'll get through this. I'll be all right, it was just such a shock."

Hayden wanted to stay with her with every fiber of his being, but he let her have her way. He knew he would be by the phone all night, and for a second thought of sleeping in his car just to be near her.

Sitting at her desk the next morning, she was overwhelmed by how strong the childhood images still were. She was totally thrown by her reaction, thinking she was much stronger. But she knew she had to face the demons. She had hidden from them long enough and no matter how awful she felt at the moment, she had to go forward. She needed answers.

There was a knock at the door and Beverly came in.

"Nothing from the state court," announced Beverly right away, "but I think you should open this letter first. There's something strange about it."

"What do you mean?" said Nikki, still slightly dazed.

"I don't know. It just looks peculiar."

Nikki took the letter. There was no return address and her name was printed in small capital letters that were perfectly formed.

"That's interesting," she said. "It says Nikki L. Easterly. I never use my middle initial. Not even on school records. It was Meredith's idea. It stands for Laverty, of course, and she wanted to keep that away from me. How odd . . ."

Nikki took a letter opener and slit the side rather than the top, slipping out a single, unfolded piece of paper.

From down the hall Hayden heard her terror-stricken scream and he came running. Beverly was comforting the sobbing Nikki by the time he got there.

"Read this," said Beverly, thrusting the note in his face.

*You don't know when to stop, do you? I'm watching you, and your actions will have consequences. It won't have been the first time that tragedy has stricken you. Maybe you're even used to your destiny by now.*

"I'm calling the police," said Beverly.

"Don't," said Hayden, just as quickly. "Let's talk to Mark."

"Wait," said Nikki, lifting up her head, trying to compose herself. "Please, everybody, just wait, please, this is too much. Too much is going on. I'm trying so hard to deal with it. Hayden, would you stay with me, and Beverly, will you ask Mark to come down here, please?"

"I will," said Beverly, "but I still think we should call the police. I'm with Hayden on this."

Mark was there in a minute or two, looking very concerned.

"Let me see it. Beverly told me a little bit."

He read the note. "This is just too dangerous. It's exactly what I was afraid of for you, Nikki. Nobody can intimidate me, but your safety is another matter. Would you consider letting me put someone else on the Marleaux case?"

"No!" Nikki shouted.

"This is all too hard on you, the implications are too far-reaching. You've already been attacked once."

"That was totally unrelated," said Nikki. "And I took care of him rather well," she snapped.

"You're not Wonder Woman. This isn't a cartoon. Meredith would never forgive me if anything happened to you. I'd never forgive myself, Lauren would never forgive me."

Nikki looked up at him in shock. It was the first time her name had slipped from his lips in an honest, revealing way.

"Uncle Mark, I can't quit now. And I mean that in every area. You've been trying to protect me my whole life. We couldn't stop the Marleaux case even if it went to another firm. It has taken on a life of its own. If I walked away now I couldn't live with myself. It's why I became a lawyer. If I quit this case I would have to quit the profession." Nikki rose from her desk, resuming control of the situation.

"I cracked for a minute. That won't happen again. I don't want the police called. I've had it with being everybody's baby."

"But Nikki," said Hayden, "this is too dangerous." He was debating telling Mark about the night before but the look he saw on Nikki's face shut him up fast.

"This is only one note," said Nikki. "Apparently there are many people who don't want Marleaux to go forward for lots of reasons. Maybe this came from Gascon, maybe it came from someone we don't even know about. Who knows? What if this is just a scare tactic and they have no intention of hurting me? I can't let that innocent man stay in jail. My career is on the line here."

"All right, all right, kids," said Mark, sounding very fatherly. "Let's just all calm down."

Mark continued. "Hayden, I want you to take this letter and envelope to a lab and get it tested for fingerprints and run a check. And Nikki, you can stay on the case, but whether you like it or not I will have a security man following you at all times."

"Oh for God's sake," said Nikki.

"No, for *your* sake," said Mark. "When you leave the office today he'll be behind you. Don't even bother to spot him, he'll be there."

"Okay, fine. He's going to be in for an interesting time. He's going to be a busy boy."

"What do you mean by that?" asked Mark. "There's no more legwork on Marleaux. We either get a letter from the appeal court in a couple of days saying they grant us a hearing or not. If they grant us a review you're ready. If we're denied, it's just another written petition to the California Supreme Court, and knowing you, you already have it ready just in case."

"You're right, I do. But I have other cases to work on."

"Well I'm glad you're finally understanding that you have to give equal time to all the cases you're involved with at the firm. I'm glad you're not fighting me on that anymore."

"Not exactly," said Nikki.

"What does that mean? Aren't you working on the other cases? What about that tax problem?"

"Relax, I'm on it, Uncle Mark. It's just that I want to work on a special case that has been plaguing me for years."

"What case?" asked Mark.

"The Lauren Laverty murder."

"Oh God," said Mark. "Nikki, leave it alone. It's over and done with."

"Maybe for you but not for me. I have to complete the circle. I have to know who I am."

"You know who you are," said Mark strongly. "Meredith and I have done everything to see that you had a good childhood and are happy now. Please don't do this, please let it go," begged Mark.

"I just can't," said Nikki defiantly. "I'm not being ungrateful, but there are things I have to know. You've pampered me, sheltered me, and I know you thought you were doing the right thing. I went to work here rather than on the East Coast because I knew I'd feel safe. But I'm beginning to realize another reason brought me here. Somehow I knew I had to go to the place where everything started to really figure out what my life's all about. I'm being guided by a strong force, Uncle Mark. I don't even know what it is sometimes, but I feel it so deeply. I just have to follow through."

"Well you're going to follow through with that bodyguard by your side," said Mark as he kissed her and walked away.

Beverly also knew to keep quiet, which was a rarity for her. She left them alone.

When Hayden and Nikki left about an hour later to go to his computer office downtown, Mark's security man was right behind them. She spotted him and smiled. He was irrelevant. She was on a mission.

"I can't believe all this!" said Nikki as the printer finished spewing forth over sixty pages of material on Lauren.

"This is nothing," said Hayden. "These are just the records about the murder. I haven't gone into the general clipping file. That must be thousands of pages of publicity."

"It doesn't matter. There has to be something in there. I need to read everything. I'm not quite sure what I'm looking for but I'll know it when I see it," said Nikki. "Is there also a way you can just print out publicity concerning the years from 1968 to 1970?"

"Yes, I can do that."

"That's crucial to me. I know there's some clue to my father in there, I just know it. I also want to know if there's any news footage or interviews on her. There must be. I want to see all of it. I'm going to take all these pages home to read. If you don't mind, keep printing out everything. You have me convinced now that I don't need to go to the library for everything, but I have a feeling that the film stuff or TV interviews will be there or at the UCLA television archives. We'll go over there after I finish reading. Would you mind bringing the rest of the pages to the apartment? I'm going to read until I can't see anymore."

"You're going to exhaust yourself."

"So be it," said Nikki.

She stood up to leave when it hit her.

"I haven't heard from you about my father and DNA," said Nikki.

Hayden paused before he spoke. "As I said before, there certainly is a possibility. Obviously we can't test the entire male population of this planet, and we don't even know if your father is still alive. We need to narrow things down a bit, but my guess is that it would be totally accurate. I'll give more thought to it, I promise."

"Oh my God," said Nikki, fathoming it on all levels, realizing the implications, and gathering the strength to face them.

"Nikki, are you sure you want to go through with all of this? You're going on all fronts. You just won't be able to handle all this emotionally," said Hayden.

"Excuse me? Who appointed you my knight in shining armor? You're supposed to be helping me. I thought we were going to work together on this," snapped Nikki.

"See what I mean. You just took my head off, and I didn't deserve it."

"You're right. I'm sorry. I know you're totally there for me. I'll get some rest tonight and I'll be fine."

"Nikki, please . . ." said Hayden, extending his arms to her.

Nikki looked at his beautiful, warm eyes and let herself be engulfed in his kindness.

"I care about you so much," Hayden whispered in her ear.

She felt his breath and raised her mouth to his, and that moment in the moonlight in Carmel came rushing back to her.

"You look a little stressed this morning, Nikki," said Roland as they met in the elevator.

Nikki really detested him now but tried not to show it.

"Just some heavy homework."

"Any news from the appeal court yet?"

Why did Nikki get the feeling Roland wanted her to lose? There was something in his voice. For a second she wondered exactly how much he hated her and what he might do about it, but she shook off that feeling. Maybe she was getting a little paranoid.

"Should be today or tomorrow. I have high hopes," answered Nikki.

Roland went into his office and called Doug Collins. "It should be any minute," he reported. "Now, is the other meeting set?"

"All done," said Collins. "You, Weisberg, Wilson, and myself, Thursday night."

"Good. I hope you picked someplace private. We don't want all hell to break loose. I need to handle my clients carefully and move them at the appropriate time," said Roland.

"Don't worry. We'll meet you in the private room at the

Mandarin, and see what kind of deal we can strike. Then you worry about your clients."

Tough cookie, thought Roland, but I'll handle it. I'm the one with the million-dollar billings.

When Thursday night came he was ready for them. The Mandarin on Camden Drive was one of the most beautiful restaurants in Beverly Hills. It was all green tile and dark wood with Chinese carvings. The back room was covered with screens, and many an important meeting went on in there.

Roland was dressed conservatively for him. Not Brooks Brothers, of course, but muted Hugo Boss. He knew Cruger liked it and thought it would be effective.

"Gentlemen," said Roland. "It's nice to see you this evening." He smiled at Dexter Wilson when he said it, not giving a hint of their forays to Weisberg or Collins.

"Good to see you, Roland," said Herbert Weisberg. "As you can see I've ordered some champagne, and I thought you might enjoy some potstickers and shrimp toast to start with."

"Thank you. I am a little hungry."

Roland sat down and mixed a special sauce while everyone watched him. He first put a dollop of white vinegar on the small plate, then placed the same-size dollop of soy sauce right next to it. In the middle he put just a dash of hot chili oil and then mixed it together with a chopstick.

"It's my favorite way to eat Chinese hors d'oeuvres," he continued. "Let me make a dish for each of you."

"That would be very nice," said Collins.

Weisberg wanted to get on with it. He was not there for gourmet dining instructions.

"Do you have the sheets?" he asked.

"Of course," said Roland. "No one outside my firm has ever seen this. It is highly confidential."

"Yes, yes, I understand," continued Weisberg, "but you understand that we have to see what we are buying."

Roland understood and took out a portfolio of spreadsheets showing every client he had, their current and projected billings for the next five years.

While Weisberg, Collins, and Wilson studied them, Roland ate. The papers spoke for themselves and he knew they were impressive. He didn't need to add anything. He was sure that they would be starving after they were through reading them.

Weisberg helped himself to a potsticker.

Roland knew he had him, no matter how he postured.

"So how many of these can you really bring with you," said Wilson, speaking for the first time.

As Roland framed his answer he pictured Wilson the way he was at lunch two weeks ago at the gym where he pulled down Roland's zipper in the men's room.

Smiling, he said, "Many of them will come. I've spoken to all of them. Some may be loyal to Mark just out of tradition, but others said they were ready to come. I estimate at the worst, with not all clients coming, my new billings should be three million the first year."

"Waiter!" shouted Weisberg. "We'd like an order of Peking duck, lemon chicken, Kung Pao scallops, Yang Chow fried rice, Buddha's Feast, and vegetable lo-mein."

You've got it! thought Roland. He could have the whole deal sewn up in a few days—he hoped.

Nikki went into her office only an hour before the mail was delivered. Sure enough, the letter arrived and Nikki anxiously took it to Hayden's office to open. How she was praying to see the words, "Court issues order to show cause why this petition should not be granted."

Unfortunately it said, "Summarily Denied."

"I can't stand this!" Nikki fumed. "What kind of system is this? My guy is innocent and no one wants to hear it."

"Calm down, please. This is typical," counseled Hayden. "As Mark told you, each justice is given the brief to read, but his clerk gets it first. In many cases the justice never even reads the brief. The clerk can just tell him he thinks it isn't interesting, and then the justice takes a pass. It's a crazy system because we never know whether or not the brief even makes it to the meeting of all the justices. We don't even know if it came to a vote. It's maddening."

"I really don't believe this. How can anyone be heard?"

"Well, sometimes publicity does it, or sometimes publicity can scare them away from hearing something. Sometimes there's an interesting issue and it piques a justice's curiosity. This quiet little case is becoming a hot potato."

"Well, hot or not, the petition goes today to the California Supreme Court."

"Okay, round three it is," said Hayden. "But this isn't one where you hear in ten days like the court of appeal. The State Supreme Court can hold us up for six months, or they can rule on it in thirty days. You never know. The average is ninety days."

"I think they'll rule on it quickly. If it's so hot, they'll want to dump it fast. That's my inclination. Or, of course, they could let time go by and hope that it gets buried and that people will forget in six months. We'll just have to see. Right now there's something I want to do."

"What's that?" asked Hayden, never sure where Nikki was headed.

"I've read everything about my mother so far. I know her favorite restaurants, her favorite color—none of that helps me. I have compiled a list of the people around her, her agent, her hairdresser, makeup man, friends, her press agent from the studio. I want to talk to all of them. But there's something I need you to do for me. I want to talk to Rafael Sanchez."

"Oh, Nikki," said Hayden, who had been hoping this moment would never come. "Are you sure you can handle it?"

"Yes, I want to talk to the man who murdered her. He says he's innocent, you know. I've read all the records."

"They all say that, remember," cautioned Hayden.

"Right, like Guy Marleaux."

Nikki had made her point.

Hayden just stared at her, waiting for the next question.

"Hayden, Sanchez never had the chance back then for a DNA test, did he?"

"Oh, Nikki . . ."

"Hayden, I need you to do this. It's so important for me. I have to know everything. My whole life I've felt like there was something wrong with me because my mother was murdered. It's almost as if I murdered her. You know little kids always blame themselves for everything. I have to lay this to rest. Please set up the Sanchez meeting and arrange to get the original samples. I want this to happen as fast as it can. I'm going to start questioning the people on this list. I think I'll start with Norman Brokaw at William Morris. He's chairman of the board now."

William Morris was located one block south of Wilshire Boulevard in Beverly Hills. They were a hugely successful corporation both in agency revenue and real estate. Not only did they own their building, but they owned the one across the street and the one behind it, as well as other holdings the public didn't know about. There was no problem in Brokaw seeing Nikki. Beverly told her how eager his secretary sounded when she made the call. He would see Nikki right away.

Nikki had just sunk down in the huge black leather couch in the waiting room and was about to pick up a copy of *Va-*

*riety* when Mary, one of Mr. Brokaw's secretaries, appeared in the doorway and called to her.

"Please follow me, it's just around the corner."

Nikki noticed office after office on either side of the wood-paneled hall, with more wood-paneled secretaries' areas in front of each office. They turned the corner and went into a separate reception area where she was introduced to Linda, Mr. Brokaw's other secretary.

She sat on a chair in their outer office and within seconds after she heard a buzz, an impeccably dressed man with a broad smile approached her.

"Nikki, it's an honor to have you at William Morris. I adored your mother," said this giant in the industry who was only a couple of inches taller than she was. He had on a navy blue pin-striped suit, a powder blue shirt with a white collar, and a paisley tie. His shoes were the finest Italian loafers.

The office was the size of a mens' club smoking room with dark green carpet, leather couches and chairs, more wood paneling and shutters. It was so quiet that it almost seemed that no business went on there. It was a gentlemen's den with silver-framed pictures of every President of the United States since Eisenhower autographed to Brokaw, a picture of Brokaw with Henry Kissinger, one with Bill Cosby, a client who had generated millions for the agency, to say nothing of Brokaw's personal commission and stock in the company, and one of Marilyn Monroe with a man Nikki didn't recognize.

Brokaw saw her look at it and said, "That's my uncle Johnny Hyde with his discovery. I started in the mail room here fifty years ago and I think it is a privilege to have been a part of such history. I can remember taking twenty-five scripts at a time to Kim Novak with firm offers and just shaking because she was so beautiful. I have a picture of me with your mother, too, but I took it down years ago because it made me sad. I always keep it around, though. Would you like to see it?"

"Of course," said Nikki.

Brokaw went to a cabinet under the left bookcase. He opened the door and pulled out a drawer, reaching inside to get yet another silver picture frame. He handed it to Nikki.

It was a picture of the two of them taken right where she was sitting with him now. Lauren was holding a pen and signing a contract. Brokaw, with dark brown hair instead of the gray, was seated next to her holding the papers.

"You both really look like you're celebrating a very happy occasion," said Nikki, wondering now if their celebrating went on after hours as well. "What's happening here?"

"She was signing the contract for the Fresh Love deal. At that time it was the most lucrative contract ever done for a star and a product. She got a million dollars cash up front, plus a cut of the sales for as long as she was the spokesperson."

"Really?" said Nikki, quite surprised at the terms. "And how long did the deal last?"

"There's no other way to put this," said Brokaw, hesitating. "It died when she did."

"Oh."

There was a moment of silence, which Brokaw filled by saying, "She was the most beautiful client I ever had. She was an angel."

"How close were you to her?" asked Nikki straight out.

"I learned early on from my Uncle Johnny never to get involved with clients. He learned the hard way. I loved your mother but it was just from afar."

"Where did you meet her?"

"One of our agent-trainees met her at a party and was so excited by her beauty that he brought her to us. In those days we could take a chance on an unknown. The business wasn't as brutal as it is now. I was the head of the motion picture department then and I took her under my wing."

"Did you ever meet my Aunt Meredith?"

"I knew of her, but she had left by the time I got involved. I know that Lauren never discussed her family."

"Did she discuss her private life at all? From what I've read she was, uh, active, shall I say."

"This is very awkward talking to you like this. I feel a little funny," said Brokaw.

"But you had to deal with it. After all, wasn't she pregnant and unmarried when she had me? Surely the cosmetics people weren't thrilled about that."

Linda appeared with two iced teas on a silver tray.

"Actually what they did was keep her spots off the air for the six months after the pregnancy, and they asked her not to show herself in public or be photographed pregnant, or with you for a year after your birth. She was so sweet, so loved by the public, that it didn't really matter about her having a baby. She was selling so much product they were afraid to drop her. It all worked out rather well."

"Do you remember where she was or what she was doing the year before I was born . . . around 1968, 1969?"

"I happen to remember that because we got her a spot singing a nominated song on the Oscar show that brought the house down in March of 1968. No one really knew that she could sing that well, she was young, it was the first time a sexy rock and roll number was done on that show, and it opened up a whole new career for her. We put together a concert tour, a couple of engagements a month for about six months, and then she went into shooting, let me see, I think it was *The Best Love*. Actually as I think back, she came to me shortly before the shoot was over to say she was pregnant. She was worried about what to do."

"You mean she was considering having an abortion?" said Nikki anxiously, the thought never having occurred to her before.

"No, no, no, my God. I never thought I would ever be having this conversation," said a rattled Brokaw. "She wanted you. She loved kids."

"I certainly don't remember seeing her a lot for someone who loved kids that much," Nikki commented bitterly.

"Please don't think that. You can't imagine the pressure she was under. She was a huge star. People were after her to sing, act, endorse things, do talk shows. It was a zoo."

"You haven't answered my question about her private life. I know she was engaged to Mark Ferguson. But was there anyone else?"

"In all deference to your mother's memory, I'd rather not get into that."

"Please, I need you to. Do you know what it's like growing up and not knowing who your father is? It is torture. It's bad enough to have a parent murdered, but to not even know the existence of the other one is too much to live with. I need your help. For all I know, you could be my father and just be handing me a line about never sleeping with clients," said Nikki, slightly raising her voice.

"Nikki, please!" said Brokaw jumping up. "It's not true. You have to understand the times. It was the late 1960s. There was a sexual revolution going on, and frankly I wasn't a part of it. That was for the kids in their twenties, like your mother. It was a time of experimentation, pushing limits, having fun, and your mother did that. In all honesty, I don't know how many or who she saw. It was a crazy time. She always had Mark at her side at industry functions."

Nikki just looked at him.

Brokaw spoke up. "All I know is that your mother, for all her sweetness, did have a busy love life, if you want to call it that, but she wasn't a tramp, you must believe that."

"Why? She died like one."

"Nikki! You're wrong, listen to me. I knew her. She was

kind and loving. She didn't do anything that others of her generation weren't doing. Don't condemn her. She loved you."

Nikki's eyes started to tear up and Brokaw went to her.

"I was devastated by her death," continued Brokaw. "She didn't want to leave you. I've had enough therapy to know that the little kid inside you still blames her for abandoning you. You mustn't do that. She loved you," he paused. "Just a second, I've got an idea. I'm going to get you a copy of a Merv Griffin show she did when you were two. Watch that. You'll see what I mean. I'm going to set up a private screening for you. I promise you it will help you understand her."

"Thank you, I really appreciate that. Do you happen to have any of her commercials, or that Oscar show? It would save me time going to the UCLA archives to get copies."

"We don't publicize it, Nikki, but William Morris has a vault of tapes and films the size of any school library. You won't need to go to UCLA. I have everything your mother ever did."

"Not necessarily the movies, I'm looking for the interviews, the live stuff, more things that are clues to her life and who she was."

"I understand, and I'll get you what you want. You'll hear from Mary or Linda as soon as I can gather everything and set up the screening room. I'll be happy to help you, and please call me Norman."

"Thank you so much, I can't tell you how much this means to me," said Nikki.

"You already have. There isn't anything I wouldn't do for Lauren's little girl," he said, taking her hand.

"May I ask you one more thing before I leave?" said Nikki.

"Of course."

"Here's a list of people I've compiled who I want to talk to. Will you look it over and tell me who is really valuable?"

Brokaw scanned the list and said, "You've got the inner circle, but the most important one on the list is Red Wagner, her makeup man. I don't know if he's still around or even if he's alive. He was an old-timer then, but he was her very best friend. There isn't anything he wouldn't know about Lauren Laverty. It's fine to talk to the others, you never know what you might find out, but I suspect that Red is the key. I may even have an old number on him. I'll check my Rolodex."

Nikki was extraordinarily grateful to Norman. She was glad she started with him and hoped he'd call quickly. She didn't feel like going back to the office. She could go into some of the Beverly Hills stores, but she hated shopping. And then it hit her. She was within walking distance of the brand-new Beverly Hills Library. Surely they would have records of local Beverly Hills newspapers from twenty-five to thirty years ago. That was a new angle. Lauren lived in Beverly Hills. She might find something.

She turned the computer on as soon as she got home. It had been an exhausting day at the library, but very fruitful. Her mind was filled with information and images of her mother. Nikki put on sweats, clicked into CB on Compu-Serve and waited for the connection. It had been a while since she found The Master. Not that she hadn't been having a good time, but she missed his cleverness and creativity. Nikki had taken to asking guys to go on fantasy trips and some of them were real duds, but every once in a while there was a winner, with an imagination and some writing ability. They'd go to a cafe or an igloo or one guy even took her on a safari. It was fun, but she really wanted to play with The Master. She checked the member directory: no one was listed under that handle.

She was in! The Channel Selector was up and she was ready to go. This time, instead of going to a channel she decided to go directly to Who's Here to see if The Master was online. She clicked on and scrolled through all the names and there he was! She now had a choice. She could find out what room he was in and enter the room, begin to chat and then see if he called her to a private room, or she could send him an IM, or instant message.

The hell with it, thought Nikki, as she sent him the IM.

"Ding," went her computer. Up came a screen saying "The Master."

THE MASTER: So here you are, RoughMeUp. We seem to keep missing each other.

ROUGHMEUP: Not anymore. Where've you been? Did you get bored and find a new hobby?

TM: Certainly not, young lady. I treasure these moments. I just have a very busy schedule.

RMU: Exactly how young do you think I am? And how old are you?

TM: Now, now, we exist on another plane.

RMU: I know we do, but I have a real life and so do you. I wonder what you really do. You must wonder about me.

TM: That's for me to know and you to find out—or not. So what's your mood tonight?

RMU: I want to play with you.

TM: What do you want to play?

RMU: MY game, this time, not yours.

TM: Really? Do you think that I would ever relinquish control? Silly, silly.

RMU: So here's the deal. I'm going to give you a character and a setting, and you supply the rest. Indulge your fantasies. I'll do anything you want . . . I want you to dream . . . what would you like to do to me . . . where would you like to do it. Just let your mind wander . . .

TM: Your profile says you live in Los Angeles.

RMU: Oh . . . you've been checking on me?

TM: Well, it's not very hard to get the city.

Nikki immediately clicked on his profile while The Master was online. Maybe then she would find him. She needed to do it fast. It came up in about forty seconds, forty long seconds. There it was: "User #158, Frederickson, Maryland."

TM: Too much time. So you know about Frederickson. Bully for you.

RMU: So I'm curious. I've never heard of Frederickson.

TM: Neither have I.

RMU: OK fine. I give up. Are you ready to play?

TM: Ready.

RMU: Fine. The setting is Hollywood and the character I'm playing is a movie star.

Nikki was sorry the minute she said it. It's just that that's all she could think about, considering what she'd been doing. Who knows, this might be fun, she thought, making the best of it. She couldn't change the fantasy now.

TM: It's 8 p.m. and I'm in a bungalow at the Beverly Hills Hotel. My Rolls-Royce has picked you up and delivered you to my door. I'm a producer who's in town from New York and you're my girl for the evening. There's a part in my movie you really want. You may be a big star, but your acting isn't taken seriously. My part might get you an Oscar. You are wearing a black silk sheath with spaghetti straps, sheer black stockings, and black satin heels. You have on a single strand of pearls with matching earrings.

RMU: How tasteful.

TM: Knock it off—it's my fantasy and you asked for it.

RMU: Yes, sir.

TM: I've made you a Manhattan complete with the cherry. Save that cherry. Room service has just knocked on the door. It's a silver tray with caviar on it. After all, we're in Hollywood. You should be treated like a movie star. You don't really want to go to that premiere do you? Wouldn't you rather stay in my bungalow?

RMU: Absolutely.

TM: The floor is shiny linoleum made up of black and white squares. There is a stone fireplace with a mantel, and two plush green love seats facing each other on each side of the fireplace. A low butler's table serves as the coffee table. Next to the front door, in the corner, is a walnut desk and chair. In the other corner is a chaise with a standing floor lamp. To the right of the fireplace is a small kitchen, but fully equipped.

RMU: What does the bedroom look like?

TM: Not yet. You do as I say when I say. Now take off your dress, but leave on those pearls and earrings. Take off your stockings but wear your shoes. I love those heels. Here, sit on the couch and finish your drink. I'm going to put on some music. Sinatra will do.

RMU: This couch tickles.

TM: Too bad. That's what you get when you parade around naked. Finish your drink.

RMU: It's delicious.

TM: Let's dance. I want you to feel the studs on my tuxedo shirt next to your body. There, that's great. I love your naked body in my arms. I'm pushing your shoulders down now. As you slip to the floor on your knees you are running your red lips on my shirt, leaving a trail. Now undo my pants.

RMU: I'm doing it with my teeth.

TM: Good girl. Now try to do the zipper.

RMU: I've got it. I'm pulling your pants down now.

TM: Wait! Pull my shorts down with your teeth. Tease me.

RMU: My mouth is on top of you now. I can feel you swelling. I'm kissing you on your shorts . . . Now I'm pulling them down, down. You're huge!

TM: Your lips are around me. I'm grabbing your head and

rolling it around. I want to feel your tongue, your teeth. Eat me . . . I want you to be starving.

RMU: Mmmmmmmm.

TM: I don't want to come yet. Tease me gently. Let me breathe. That's good. I'm pulling you up now, smothering your mouth with mine, leading you into the bedroom. I've ordered a special bed for tonight. The hotel sent in a four-poster. I love nakedness against color. Let me see you on top of the green comforter. Do you want to play the caviar game?

RMU: Absolutely.

TM: Lie down, I'll go get the caviar . . . I'm back. You look gorgeous.

RMU: What color is my hair?

TM: Why silky blond, of course. It's so divine against the green.

Nikki gasped. Blond against green. Why had he picked blond? Wasn't her mother's body lying on an emerald green comforter? Jesus Christ! Now calm down, she told herself. All this research is getting to me. Everybody knows the Beverly Hills Hotel's colors are green. Maybe it's a fluke. Most guys would fantasize blond. But . . .

TM: Where have you gone? Hello?

Nikki snapped to. She needed more information. She was so high from the rush she didn't know what to do.

RMU: I'm here. I love emerald green, too. Is that your favorite color?

TM: It is. I love it so much that I had Montblanc make a special pen for me in that color. It's the only one in existence and I'm never without it. But I don't want to talk about color. I'm not through with you. Before the caviar game there's one more thing I want you to do. Now lie very still while I use some soft black cord to tie you up. I wouldn't want you to go anywhere before I was through with you.

Flash again. Nikki was sure the cords around her mother were black. Stop it, she said to herself. Black is the most common color in bondage. Just stop it. But it was very hard for her to calm down. She was perspiring now—and she was so hot from him she was beginning to be embarrassed by the feeling between her legs.

TM: I'm taking a spoonful of caviar and putting it on your breasts. I think I'll even add some lemon. Can't you feel it running down you? I'm licking it off you now. No time for the sour cream yet. God that tastes great. My hand feels you getting wet. Let me dip my hardness into the caviar now, lick it off me, keep swallowing. Lick it clean. There, there. That's it. Now I'll put sour cream on it. I'm smearing it on your thighs, inside you with my fingers. You want me, don't you? Tell me how much you want me!

RMU: I've got to have you!

TM: Why????

RMU: Because I want you.

TM: You don't want me, you whore, you just want my movie. I know you and all the men you've had. You can't turn me into filth. Well you're gonna stay open and take me . . . hour after hour. I'm shoving it in you. That's what you're good for. You're twisted upside down. Just plant those heels into the headboard and take it! Yes. Yes . . . harder, again . . . outside and then all the way in. You can't scream, you can't stop me . . .

The raw passion she felt was quickly being replaced by abject fear. What kind of psycho was this, anyway? She had to keep him talking.

RMU: More, more.

But there was no more. He had left the screen. He had come, he had used her, played with her mind and body, and now he was gone. But this time wasn't like all the others. She never cared if they left her as long as she was amused. But not now. A horrendous feeling of dread came over her. This guy was so sick it was scary.

Trying to gather her wits she quickly went into Who's Here. He had disappeared. She went into the Members' Directory but of course found nothing. She just sat there in shock, not knowing what to do. What happened couldn't have been a coincidence. She was the one who started the game and set it up as a movie star in Hollywood. But the hair color, the comforter, his anger at all the other men the movie star had—what could it be? What if it was the murderer? Did she just have sex with her mother's killer? Could it be that bizarre? Nikki was beside herself, terrified at her reaction to this man, her addiction to him, and totally stunned at the possible connection to her mother. She didn't know how much longer she could handle this alone. Maybe she was losing it and needed to see a doctor. Maybe she had found a killer. She couldn't think anymore. She was going to need help on this.

She stood up and started pacing. I should call the police, but how on earth can I tell them that I'm a computer sex junkie? It's mortifying. No, I can't go to them. I could go to Hayden! He'd help me. Oh, no. How can I tell him about myself? Joely won't know what to do, but she'd be the one who could handle my addiction confession. Damn. I have to talk to Hayden. He's the next best thing to the police.

Summoning all her courage she called Hayden and asked that he come to the apartment right away. Nikki was physically ill at the thought of revealing her hobby to Hayden. She had let him in a little bit, made herself vulnerable, and now she cared about how he felt. She knew he would be shocked and possibly even hurt by her confession, but she was so shocked by The Master that she had no other choice.

He was there in twenty minutes.

"Are you all right? Is everything okay? You sounded terrible on the phone. Did you have another nightmare? Did someone try to hurt you?"

"I'm not all right, no one hurt me, but we have to talk. Come sit by the kitchen."

Hayden sat down and waited.

"Do you want some coffee?" asked Nikki.

"No, I want you to tell me what's going on."

"This is very difficult for me because it is personal and it's embarrassing," Nikki began, still pacing. She couldn't sit down, and she couldn't face him.

She started talking slowly. "One night a while back Joely showed me how to play around with those computer sex rooms. I laughed at her at first, but I found I was drawn to it."

Nikki stopped moving and looked at him.

"This is truly humiliating for me. I just can't stand it," she said, beginning to fidget. "Never mind. I'm sorry I called you. Please just go. I'll figure out another way."

"I'm not going," said Hayden emphatically. "Whatever it is, we'll deal with it. Please just try to take a breath, sit here next to me, and let's talk."

Hayden reached for Nikki's hand and she took it. She sat down on the couch and just looked at him.

"It's okay, just go on," said Hayden in an even voice.

"At night I come home and I play. I use different names, and I've made some friends—I mean, men that I play with. Of course we don't know who we really are."

"You do what?" said Hayden, unable to restrain his incredulity.

Nikki jumped up. "See! That's why I didn't want to tell

anyone, but I don't know who else to turn to. This is so difficult for me."

"You're right," said Hayden. "How stupid can I be? I told you whatever you said I could handle and I blew it. I'm so sorry. Please give me another chance."

"I wouldn't be telling you this at all if I had any other choice. It's you or the police," she said, calming down slightly. "Something happened tonight. Something terrible, weird, and maybe just a coincidence."

Nikki paused and then spoke. "I think I was talking to the man who murdered my mother."

"What! How do you know?"

"He knew too much. There were details only the murderer would know. I need you to help me find him. Do you know anyone at CompuServe's headquarters?"

"All that is confidential. They could have their license taken away."

"You've got to try it. The only thing I know is his code, his handle, and the city he says he's from."

"Well, give it all to me and I'll see what I can do, but in the meantime, Nikki, I think you'd better start getting more rest. I think you should stay off the computer. I think this craziness is getting to you. I will try to help you, but for now I think you should go to sleep. I'll see you at the office in the morning."

Hayden had made his exit as gently as he could, trying not to sound devastated. Nikki was in genuine trouble, but so was he. He had fallen hard, and now he wasn't sure who she was.

Nikki didn't feel a great deal better about anything at this point, especially herself, and she noticed that Hayden left with a hug and not a kiss.

Rafael Sanchez didn't want to see Nikki Easterly. The warden at Folsom was a friend of Hayden's and had called Sanchez in to discuss Nikki's request personally. Hayden was told that Sanchez was a very angry man, furious at being locked up for twenty years for a murder he claimed he didn't commit. Hayden asked him to go back and ask Sanchez to see him because Hayden might have a way to get him out. That worked, and although Nikki was unhappy she couldn't go along, Hayden was on his way to Folsom.

It was the same routine of searches, clearances, and locked doors, but eventually he came face-to-face with Sanchez, a thin, wiry guy with lots of hair all over his body and a thick scar along his left cheek. Hayden didn't want to meet *him* in a dark alley.

"What do you want?" snarled Sanchez.

"To talk to you," said Hayden calmly.

"What about?"

"You know what about," said Hayden.

"Yes, the bitches."

"What did you say?"

"Bitches, all of them. That movie star broad got me in here. I hate her, she ruined my life. And seeing her kid is just a reminder of the Big Screw."

"The Big Screw?"

"Got any cigarettes?"

Hayden knew to bring some. He pushed an unopened pack toward Sanchez.

"The Big Screw is what happened to me. I didn't do that dame. Did I have a bad record, yeah. If I got back out might I hurt somebody? You'd better believe it. These places breed hate. My old man always told me I'd end up like this."

"What about your mother?"

"Don't you ever mention her!" screamed Sanchez.

The guards opened the door to see if everything was okay and Hayden waved them back.

"Do you hate all women?" asked Hayden bravely.

"As a matter of fact I do. That's why I hurt them, but I didn't hurt Miss Movie Star. I was framed," said Sanchez.

"This sounds like dialogue out of a prison movie," said Hayden.

"Well you called the meeting, if you don't want to hear it you can leave."

"What if I told you there might be a way to get you out?"

"Yeah, I've heard that one before."

"I'm serious. There's a new test. I've done this before. It's a genetic blueprint called DNA. Give me a hair sample and we'll see if it matches samples from the murder. It might not, you know, *if* you're innocent."

Hayden challenged Sanchez with a look.

"What the hell? What do I got to lose. Take all the hair you want. God knows I've got enough."

Sanchez ripped some right off his chest without flinching.

Hayden tried to conceal his wince.

"That enough for ya? Can I go back now? I'll probably never hear from you again. This is just a scam. My fingerprints weren't even at the scene. My alibi didn't stick and I had a bad record. That was it."

"You'll hear from me, I promise."

"Uh huh."

Sanchez got up and asked for the guard to take him away as Hayden slipped the hair into an envelope.

It took only seventy-two hours for Norman to get the footage Nikki wanted. Nikki had thought it over and decided to watch by herself. It was more important for Hayden to continue his work on Sanchez and The Master, and she felt that she wanted this moment to be between her mother and herself.

"Are you ready, Ms. Easterly?" asked the disembodied voice over the speaker. "Just press the intercom button to answer."

"Yes, thank you," she replied.

"Raise or lower the volume as you wish. The knob is located on the console next to you."

The lights dimmed gradually and the room was pitch black. Nikki was very apprehensive.

"When I want to feel my very best," said the gorgeous face that suddenly illuminated the room, "I use Fresh Love all over my skin. It makes it feel so smooth to the touch . . . mine or anybody else's," the face said suggestively—the body was covered in only a towel with her voluminous blond curls framing her face. "Watch," she said as the camera zoomed in on her thigh covered with rivulets of cream running down slowly, tauntingly, from her thigh to her knee, then down her calf.

A big cut to a close-up of Lauren's face saying, "Fresh Love . . . Don't you want it?"

Nikki hit the intercom instantly.

"Will you run that again, please?"

As she was watching it for the second time she began to come out of shock. She had seen beautiful girls advertising products all her life, but to see her mother, in her twenties, melting the camera lens, stunned her. She was more beautiful than I ever imagined, thought Nikki.

"May I continue with the rest now?" asked the voice.

"Yes," answered Nikki.

Up came a tape of the Academy Awards. It was cued up to Lauren's number. The announcer was saying, "Ladies and gentlemen, tonight we have a real surprise for you. I bet you didn't know that our beautiful Lauren Laverty could sing. She's had three box office hits and now this. She's going to knock you out. Here she is singing the third nominated song of the evening, 'Show Me Your Way,' from *Live for Life*. Lauren Laverty!"

The camera cut to a shimmering silver curtain that parted on Lauren in a silver strapless bodysuit and matching silver boots. She had sixteen backup dancers in black bodysuits with silver trim. Her voice was a cross between the sexiness of Ann-Margret and the power of Whitney Houston.

Nikki rose up just a little bit out of her seat. Again she was mesmerized by what she was seeing. She had had no clue as to her mother's talent. She had never seen any of this footage. No wonder people had gone nuts over her—she was sweet and sexy at the same time. She never appeared to be a slut. She was an innocent tease, thought Nikki. It came across on both the commercials she had just seen and now this.

She sat through some news footage of openings with her mother and Mark Ferguson, Warren Beaty, Jack Nicholson, a group of girls including Ali MacGraw and Candy Bergen, and then some B roll footage started. Nikki realized that this footage of her two-year-old birthday party was very rare. It was on the reel just before the Merv Griffin interview. Norman had told her to look out for it. Apparently Griffin sent a crew to the house to shoot a whole story that he aired with her mother's guest shot.

Nikki was mesmerized seeing herself being held lovingly by Lauren, surrounded by some other young children and their mothers. The backyard was decorated with flowers that must have been tied on trees; a small children's carousel complete with wooden horses for riding stood in the middle of the yard. Her mother was wearing a yellow cotton sundress with short sleeves and a ruffled hem. She looked like an angel holding and loving a littler angel in a soft white blanket.

"Nikki, can you say hello to Merv?" she heard her mother's voice say. Her eyes started to fill with tears as she saw her mother take her hand and wave to the camera.

"Nikki's a little shy today, Merv, but she watches you all the time, don't you, little darlin'?" said Lauren, kissing Nikki's forehead.

Nikki was sobbing now, the pain of what she had lost

coming from so deep a place that she didn't know it existed. The vein in her forehead was throbbing with the pain of the loss. Her mother really did love her, her mother was real, and warm, and alive. She would have given anything at that moment to feel those arms around her, and Nikki knew down into the depths of her soul that she could never rest until she found out what really happened. She had fallen under the spell of her mother's love all over again, and this time she knew it was real and deserved. She had to find out no matter what.

# Chapter 13

She was eye-to-eye with the rhinoceros. It looked so much like Phillipe that she had to fight the urge to kill it, and she was grateful that a camera was in her hand instead of a gun.

Ana was in the back of the jeep, dressed in khaki pants, matching khaki shirt, a white gauze kerchief tied around her forehead to keep the sweat off, and hiking boots. She was out in the middle of nowhere, on one of her daily trips to nowhere. The guide, sixteen-year-old Jumoba, was beginning to look good to her. She knew she was in serious trouble.

"Look, Joan, doesn't that rhino look like Phillipe?"

"How quaint, they must have the same diet doctor," said Joan, a bleached-blond real estate agent who made most of her sales by sleeping with clients in the houses that were for sale.

"Look, honey," said Joan. "I've done my two weeks' duty here. I can't take it anymore. My nails need doing, I'm missing my facial with Aida. I've got to go."

"You can't. I'll die."

"You will not, and you know it."

"Yes, I will. Without you I'll have no one."

"Can't you fly someone else in?" asked Joan. "I'll go back and tell a select few. I know nobody's supposed to know where you are, but I'll tell Judy and Sandy. One of them will come. I'll tell them about the catered lunches under the trees, the gorgeous white hunters, they'll love it. I'll lie. It'll work."

It was two and a half months ago that Joan promised to send a replacement. Since then, the only two-legged companions Ana had were the guides and any guests who checked into Tigertops, the elegant gaming club where she was staying. She was near nothing that interested her. Ethiopia was to the north, and the isle of Madagascar just off the coast. If she hopped a plane, Egypt wasn't *that* far away, and she wouldn't have minded a cruise down the Nile, but she knew Phillipe wouldn't allow that.

Her accommodations were magnificent. Tigertops was a combination of British and African, so you had beamed ceilings and four-poster beds with huge swaths of white netting. All the furnishings were white, setting off the natural wood walls, ceiling, and floors. Even the art was carved. There were very large picture windows on both sides of her cabin with views of mountains and jungles. The windows slid all the way into the wall and created the feeling that you were almost always outdoors. At night the breeze was delightful, but Ana was too nervous to sleep with the windows open. She'd had enough warnings from Phillipe to know early on in their relationship that being too close to him could be dangerous. At night she slept with the ceiling fan on and felt safer.

Most nights, during the cocktail hour, she would go to the lounge where they had CNN on a satellite dish. That was her only connection to the world. She never heard anything about the Marleaux case. The occasional phone calls from Phillipe hadn't seemed alarming, and she wanted to go home. Last night's call was typical.

"Phillipe, I know that I begged you to get me away, but this is enough. It's been ages. Surely I can come home."

"No, you can't. If you don't like Africa I'll charter a boat for you to go around the fjords."

"I'm so lonely here. It would be worse on a boat, then I'd see no one and I'd freeze. Here I sweat, there I'd be nuts. You know how I hate the cold. Maybe I could come to Paris, perhaps get a little house in Menton, something. I'm going nuts."

"I'm sorry, things are not cleared up here. You'll still be hounded. I'm just doing this to protect you," said Phillipe.

"And what are you doing about protecting yourself?"

"Ana, you know better than to ask me what I'm doing, and you also should remember that I never lose," said Phillipe, who was now annoyed. "This isn't like you. What are you asking these questions for?"

"I was just concerned about you, that's all."

Phillipe didn't answer.

"Well, how much longer do I have to be away?" asked Ana, changing the subject.

"I really don't know."

"Please, I need some sort of timetable. I'm going crazy."

"Right, on $1,500 a day. You poor thing," said Phillipe. "Try and cope."

One of the things Ana hated the most was not being able to see Mark. Phone calls were difficult at this distance and she was never certain if they were private. Surely, since she had not heard anything on the news, and Phillipe's calls were infrequent, it would be all right if she left. She could bribe the people at the hotel to say she was still here if Phillipe called. Who would know she was back in L.A. if she didn't leave the house for a while. She really didn't see why that couldn't work.

After a short visit with the concierge her plans were set. In forty-eight hours she would fly back to the United States, stopping in New York to change planes. Normally, with a mandatory stopover in New York Ana would stay for a few days and play, but she missed her home, and she missed Mark more than she thought she would.

The months away taught her something. She had tried her whole life not to have real feelings because it made her job easier. But now that she was legitimately in "real estate and portfolio management" (her own), she felt she could really have a life. She actually longed for the day when maybe she and Mark could be a legitimate couple. But then she was getting ahead of herself. She and Mark had never discussed feelings. What if he didn't think of her in the same way?

Time in Africa allowed her to reflect, and she had noticed that since she'd been a madam, and had that reputation, anytime she started to see a man and anything serious might develop, he shied away eventually. One man actually told her that he thought she was great, but that he was afraid of how her reputation would affect his business partners and his family. She realized that this was the penance that she was stuck with possibly forever, for the choice she made early in her life. But without that early choice she wouldn't have the comforts that she had now. So which was worse? She had never stopped to analyze her life. She was too busy at charity functions, gossiping on the phone, shopping, buying stocks, to ever think about anything else. She learned in Africa that when you stop moving you start thinking. She had never made it as a movie star, and she thought that the money would make up for it, but it never had. She didn't allow herself to dwell on it when it was happening, but to this day each time she went to a movie theater and the lights went down, she wished her face were on the screen. In

Africa she faced those hurts and she thought about what kind of life she could have if she were free.

She really cared for Mark. Dare she hope that there might be a legitimate relationship there? Could it be possible? What if he would run away, too? What if she'd never get over her past?

The trip home felt like it took a week. Her body was killing her. She was never so happy to see the back seat of a limo in her life. When her driver, Henry, met her at the airport she almost hugged him, she was so happy to be back in civilization.

"Now remember, Henry, no one is to know that you picked me up tonight, understand?" she said as she slipped him $500.

"Welcome home, Miss Ana," said Alistair, the butler. "Everything is ready for you."

"Don't even bring my luggage to my room. Everything should just be sent out and cleaned and burned if you ask me. I never want to see Africa or wear those clothes again. I'm going to lock myself in my room and take a bath for at least two hours."

Ana raced upstairs and into her room. Soft lights had been turned on, her bed was turned down, music was coming very gently from the speakers in all four corners of the ceiling.

She stripped off her clothes in the dressing area and walked into the bathroom, smiling when she saw how Alistair had anticipated her. Her bath was drawn, candles were lit. She eased herself into the seven-foot-long marble Jacuzzi tub and felt the warm water soothe her soul. She didn't even want to turn the Jacuzzi on because it would make too much noise and disturb this moment of peace. Home at last, the moment she had been waiting for.

"Happy now?" snarled the voice in the doorway.

Ana jumped.

"Phillipe? What a surprise," she said, trying to remain cool.

"No, the so-called surprise is that you're in Los Angeles instead of where you're supposed to be. You're the one who begged me for help when you were afraid your 'good name' would be smeared by all the Greggie Alcott stuff coming out again. I told you I'd help you and I did. I'm the one who knows when it's best to come back. I told you to stay there. You don't have a clue about what's going on here. Since when have you started disobeying my orders? What happened to your manners?" he continued. And then louder, "Who in the hell do you think you are?"

"But Phillipe . . ."

"Get out of that tub!"

Ana emerged dripping and soapy, reaching for a towel.

Phillipe got there first. He grabbed the towel, hurled it in the water, and wrung it out in all of three seconds. He struck at her with the wet towel as if it were a whip.

Normally Ana might think that this was a new sexual game and go along with it, but she was genuinely frightened.

"Ow, that hurts!"

"Doesn't it?" Phillipe said as he swung again, hitting her thigh.

Ana was beginning to cower in the corner. She had always heard Phillipe had this side but she had never seen it. This was a far cry from "doggie." She wondered whether her barking right now might snap him out of this rage. She decided against it.

Phillipe had the tie from her robe in his hands. He grabbed her roughly and tied her hands to the towel bar, her whole backside exposed to him.

"No!" she cried.

Too late. The towel kept lashing out at her over and over again, her backside stinging, aching.

"Stop, please stop," she begged. "I'm sorry. I'll never disobey you again, never. I was just so lonely there and—"

"Shut up!"

The next smack she felt was his hand, and it hurt much worse than the towel. Her knees buckled with the pain.

"Have you had enough?" he asked.

"Yes," she murmured through tears.

He untied her and she fell to the floor. He made no sexual advances toward her. That told her that her worst fears had come true. What she had just experienced was not teasingly violent foreplay, it was just plain violence, and she never wanted it to happen to her again. She didn't deserve to be treated like that. No one did. She had to make sure it would never happen again. He didn't control her money anymore. She was taking care of herself. The call girl business ended years ago. Why was she still letting him into her life? Why did she spy for him? Her debt had been paid. But if she quit he'd probably have her killed. Deep down she knew why she could never leave.

"Get up and follow me," he said.

She did as she was told and put on her robe.

He didn't stop her.

She followed him into the sitting area in the bedroom. She just sat there and waited for him to speak.

"Let's talk about Mark Ferguson," he said.

Her heart almost stopped beating.

"Don't think for a second that I don't know about your relationship. Someone being a source is one thing. I endorse that. But he is more than that. Once you fall in love with someone you're useless to me. It's not good for someone to become useless."

Ana was terrified now, trying to control her shaking without him seeing it.

"But there is a way to keep yourself from becoming useless. I want Mark to stop this Marleaux case. This is not news to you, but you have failed so far. I don't want you to fail any longer. I'm giving you a chance here. You see, I really don't need you. There are other people close to Mark, someone in particular he's devoted to, and I could go right to that area and take care of the problem, but that would be too easy. It would let you off the hook, and I don't want to do that right now. I want you on it—swinging."

It was all Ana could do to muster up a comeback, but she had to look strong. "Couldn't you handle it in the courts? I know you have friends everywhere at all levels. What's the big deal?"

"You ignorant food. You let me take care of my friends and worry about the other avenues. Have you ever known me to just follow one plan?"

"No."

"Then shut up and do your job."

He got up and walked toward the door. "I'm going back to Paris immediately. I won't need you to let me know your progress."

Alone, shivering, Ana started to cry. She was scared to death.


Hayden had had a difficult time recovering from Nikki's news. It was a lot for him to absorb, but his professional side took over. She needed his help, and that was what he had to focus on and put his emotions aside.

Trying to find The Master was virtually impossible. The Frederickson, Maryland, location was a phony. No such town existed. There was a Frederick, Maryland. Hayden thought he might check all the users in that city, but it was a long shot. He had to tell Nikki.

"Without a real ID number or a real name, there's nothing my friend at CompuServe can do. We need you to get him on the line again and then call me. We only need him on for about two minutes to trace something. But remember, if he has a laptop, he could be anywhere and everywhere. How do we know that he's been in the same location each time he's talked to you? We don't. You know the hours he's usually on. I need you to keep trying to get him. He could fool you, you know, and be on using a different name. It's pretty impossible. If he doesn't want to be found, we won't be able to get him." explained Hayden.

The first time Nikki turned on the computer to find him she realized the joy had gone. Her addiction to the chat rooms had vanished. This time when she clicked into CB she went right to Who's Here. If The Master wasn't listed she would wait, constantly watching the top of the screen for newcomers. It was tedious and nerve-racking. He was nowhere to be found. Once again she tried the Main Directory but there was still no listing under The Master. She tried leaving an e-mail under that name but the computer told her there was no one by that name. She was flipping out. She tried looking up people by city, and discovered on her own that there was no Frederickson. She looked up Frederick, as Hayden suggested, and found 180 names, which she gave to him to check out. She was feeling completely hopeless. Four weeks had gone by, but she was not giving up.

She was once again glued to the screen, watching to see if his name would come up, and then her little bell rang. It was The Master! She quickly picked up her cellular phone that she kept by her computer just for this purpose and called Hayden to tell him to start the trace. She could feel her voice tightening, fighting back that damn stammer.

ROUGHMEUP: Where have you been? I've missed you.
THE MASTER: I'm always around. You should know that.

Nikki looked at the clock: they had been connected for forty-eight seconds.

RMU: I can't wait to play with you. I love your fantasies.

TM: Do you my dear? Last time you picked the setting and the character. It's my turn.

RMU: Go for it.

One minute and twenty-three seconds said the clock. God, don't let him disappear, prayed Nikki.

TM: OK. The setting is Carmel and the character is a lawyer.

Nikki thought she was going to throw up. Who was this guy? Oh my God. Please let Hayden get an ID and a location. Hurry. Where was he coming from?

RMU: I like it. Have you ever been to Carmel?

TM: How do you know I'm not there right now?

RMU: I don't. So where are you?

TM: Silly girl. You don't think you'll ever find out, do you?

It was way over two minutes. There was no way Hayden didn't have a location. With a guy as smart as The Master he would have to know he could be traced. Why would he stay on so long? This is just too close, too sick, thought Nikki.

RMU: So what's the game? What do lawyers mean to you?

TM: What do movie stars mean to you, little girl?

RMU: This is your turn. What do you like to do with lawyers?

TM: Maybe the same thing I like to do to movie stars . . .

RMU: Tell me . . .

RMU: Hello?

Damn, thought Nikki as The Master's name faded from the screen. She rushed to call Hayden. "Did you get him? Oh, Hayden, he's crazy. I think he knows who I am. I think he's trying to kill me or taunt me or something. I don't know. This is insane. He has to be the one who killed my mother. God."

"Charlottesville, Virginia. I have the phone company working on it now. My guy at the computer company traced the number. We'll know in the morning. Do you think you can sleep? Would you like to go for a drive?"

"Thanks, but I need to just be here and deal with things," said Nikki, hoping she sounded believable.

Nikki hung up the phone and started shaking uncontrollably. She could feel the sweat pouring off her body. That was *it*. This was her nightmare come true. She had known it in her soul since she was a child. The man who killed her mother was going to kill her, too. She was sobbing now, curled up in a fetal position, irrational. Flashes of Dr. Stanley went through her mind. That soft soothing voice of healing and logic. Sure, doctor. I believed you, thought Nikki angrily. Smiling faces of Meredith, Mark, everything's okay, darling, phrases . . . sounds . . . the cords . . . Nikki couldn't move her wrists. She was literally paralyzed with fear. Where was Meredith to tickle her foot? That's a lot of crap. It's happening . . . I'm going to die like Mommy.

She blacked out.

How Nikki got herself to the office the next morning, she never knew. She somehow pulled it together, remembering that she did have a bodyguard twenty-four hours a day. She fought hard to get back her composure and that fighting strength she knew she had. She was reasonably presentable when Hayden appeared in her office.

"The Master was using a laptop in a motel along Route 20. The room was paid for with cash and the description from the desk clerk was negligible. Something about a mustache and glasses."

"So what you're saying is that we basically have nothing."

"At least we know he's on the East Coast."

"Well, at least that's where he was last night," said Nikki caustically.

"I'm not going to give up, but I'm not so sure you should try to contact him anymore. I think it's too dangerous," said Hayden.

"Maybe yes, and maybe no," answered Nikki, not really having an opinion at that moment.

What Nikki didn't know was that Mark had a meeting every morning with her bodyguard. He wanted to make sure she was safe at all times. But the bodyguard had no way of knowing what had happened to Nikki the night before. He wasn't in the room. His report consisted of telling Mark that she spent a quiet evening at home.

Having a bodyguard around a firm was not something that Mark liked, but the only people aware of it were Nikki, Hayden, and Beverly. The bodyguard, Andy Frank, worked for Gavin De Becker, a specialist in security matters in Hollywood. Frank was well-trained and this morning he had a bonus for Mark.

"That fellow Roland Bixby."

"Yes?" said Mark.

"You'd better watch your back."

"Really?" said Mark, not surprised.

"The other day I was in the men's room at Jimmy's and I heard a conversation between Roland and somebody named Collins, like they were going into business or something."

"Well, my good man, you shall receive extra pay for that bit of information," said a pleased Mark. "Now forget that you told it to me."

Mark closed his door and went to his computer, pulling up a list of Roland's clients and their billings. It was impressive. Roland would be very attractive to another firm, that kind of client raid or defection being front-page news. Mark never liked Roland, and it would only be natural that he would try to go to the one firm Mark despised. Mark wondered who made the approach, whether it was Roland calling Weisberg, or the reverse. Maybe Doug Collins is doing this to get back at me for not cooperating in the Gascon matter. That would be hardball, thought Mark.

Of course, if Roland left, so would Cruger Fowler, and that would be a loss. Cruger had been an original client of the office. Mark did have the option of taking Cruger to lunch and putting his cards on the table, but he also knew there was a domestic loyalty question in that situation. As to the other clients, there were eight. Five were ones Mark turned over to Roland and three were Roland's alone. Although Roland was a good lawyer who brought in big money, he wouldn't miss him, and if he could save some of his clients from switching, the loss of Roland wouldn't be so bad.

Mark had to be careful. Chances were Roland had told the clients he was leaving or had at least begun some sort of wooing process. Mark didn't want to tip his hand by calling and asking for a meeting. This was the part of the law business that he didn't like. He liked his work, he wanted to be paid well, and he thought he earned his money and reputation. This nastiness displeased him. Clients of law offices were not under contract to the firm, so they could leave whenever they wished. If they were on percentage deals, they would continue to pay the firm on a job that was worked on prior to their leaving. Mark checked each of the five and saw that even if they left, the firm would continue to make hundreds of thousands of dollars for at least two more years. So any new law firm could only bill the new business and not collect on the older, very rich deals. That would be a hindrance to Roland, thought Mark, but Weisberg, Wilson wouldn't care. They'd look to the future for the long run about the billings, and eat it at the beginning just to get back at Mark.

After thinking about this for an hour he decided to be bold. He placed calls to all five clients and called for a meeting tomorrow morning at eight in his conference room. He told each of them that it was confidential. If they told Roland, so be it. Mark just wanted to get them in a room.

Mark arrived at seven-thirty A.M. along with the caterer from Nate 'n' Al's deli. There were platters of smoked salmon, whitefish, cod, freshly cut onions, and tubs of cream cheese along with bagels of every kind as well as bialys and onion rolls. The office chef arrived early and was brewing fresh coffee and tea. A service area and complete kitchen for the chef was located in between the conference room and the private dining room so he could be available for all occasions. Mark felt it would be too much to offer eggs and pancakes. He wanted this meeting short and sweet. The food was available for whoever wished to eat, or who could swallow after what Mark had to say.

At eight A.M. the five clients walked in, not all of them surprised to see each other. There was Lewis Delano, president of Delano Productions; the talk show host James Clifford, who also was a large stockholder in the company that distributed his show; Dana Schwartz, the home shopping manufacturer of more goods than any other supplier; Leonard Mossberg, chairman and CEO of Global Studios; and Jones Wagner, producer-writer of three top ten comedy series. All told, the clients in that room represented $20 million in billings over the next five years.

"Thank you so much for coming," said Mark. "Please help yourself to anything you like." He sat as they joined him at the table.

"Well I'm going right for a pumpernickel with lox," said Wagner.

"How can you just go for food, you know something's up?" said Schwartz.

"Nothing stops my appetite," continued Wagner. "Obviously we're in some sort of war council meeting."

Wagner's comments made people uncomfortable, sensed Mark. He thought he'd better jump in.

"Okay, everyone, now look. What I'm doing this morning is highly unusual. Some or all of you are aware that Roland Bixby, a lawyer whom I have trained to be excellent, might be planning a little coup. He's had meetings with another firm, you all probably know about that, and for all I know you've had meetings with them, too."

Mossberg looked down.

"People move around in this business. They change agents, publicists, husbands, studio heads. It's just a fact of life. They sometimes change lawyers, too. I accept that. But what I don't accept is a lack of loyalty and respect when someone has done a good job. Each and every one of you came to this firm because of me. I am the senior partner working directly with Roland on your accounts, but, as happens sometimes, you do grow closer to the everyday point man. I could have taken each and every one of you out to dinner, bought you expensive wine, given you rounds of golf at your favorite clubs. But that's just not who I am. I consider myself a partner, a friend, someone who has not failed you in any way. I like to believe that my firm is above shark level."

Mark looked around. No one was eating.

"Roland is going to be leaving this firm whether he has made that decision or not. Those gathered here at this table are only some of his clients. He has others who will follow him out the door. Perhaps one or two of you will do the same. I hope not. You're here because I consider you family. I want to get this out in the open and let you make a choice. I don't sneak around in restaurants' private rooms. I'm not interested in those kinds of games. If anyone wants a private meeting with me to discuss something they feel should be corrected or adjusted, I'm available. This is the only time we're going to discuss this like this. Just make your decision. I don't need to pitch you. You know who I am and the kind of work I do. Now, Leonard, would you please pass the whitefish?"

The meeting was over by eighty-forty-five and Mark returned to his office. At nine A.M. Roland walked in unannounced.

"Roland," said Mark coldly.

"Don't think I didn't know ahead of time about your little meeting this morning. The only reason I didn't come is because I thought I'd let you hang yourself."

"My dear, dear Roland. I'm sure Weisberg, Wilson will be delighted to have you even sooner than they expected. In fact, I hope they have an office for you available this morning because I had yours packed up last night and the boxes messengered to them at eight. You'll find your secretary waiting in the lobby for you over there and everything you'll need."

"I'm going to sue you from here to kingdom come," screamed Roland.

"On what grounds?"

"I'll think of some, don't you worry," snarled Roland.

"I don't worry at all. You're the one who's in violation of the partnership agreement and I'm sure the bar association would be interested. You be sure and let me know if you want me to contact them. In the meantime, turn around, say hello to the guard, and enjoy the walk to your car. Good morning."

Ana had been tortured about what to do with Mark ever since she had come back. Her encounter with Phillipe in the bathroom scared her sufficiently to stay away from letting anyone know she was back in town. It was difficult for her not to see Mark, since he represented a possible real future for her. At some point she'd have to see him because Phillipe was pressing her for information. The situation had become so complicated. Dare she take Mark into her confidence, or should she just continue to spy, sleep with him, and keep Phillipe happy? She had never trusted anyone in her life before except herself. If she was wrong about Mark and gave him damaging information there was no telling what Phillipe would do. She had better make the right choice. But if she chose helping Phillipe and Mark ever found out, he would never marry her. She was in a horrendous position, still terrified of Phillipe, yet longing for a free life with someone to love.

She picked up the phone and called Mark, who seemed to be overjoyed to hear her voice.

"I want to come spend a whole evening with you. It can't be tonight because there's a meeting I just can't get out of. I'm so sorry," said Mark.

"How about tomorrow night?"

"Perfect. I'll see you at the house at eight," said Mark.

Ana hung up the phone and knew she had twenty-four hours to make a decision.

Mark sat back and assessed the situation. He had been distracted by the Roland problem, but he felt now that it was under control. He initially thought he would only be in danger of losing Leonard Mossberg. It would be unfortunate, but the hard truth was that Mossberg was older, and in the twilight of his career. His earnings, while enormous, were at a peak. There was no future. If he had to lose somebody, Mark would rather it be this kind of situation. The other clients had been calling him, almost courting him, to assure him of their loyalty. It pleased Mark that they responded so well. He had worked hard for his reputation.

Ana was another matter. He had been very careful through the years not to let on that he knew that she was still in contact with Phillipe. Most people thought that when she went legit the connection was broken, but Mark knew differently. It also didn't matter to him because he never gave any information he didn't want Phillipe to have. In fact, he used Ana in reverse, and she never knew it. It really had been quite convenient for him.

When the doorbell rang, Ana was ready. She had given Alistair the night off so she and Mark could be totally alone. She was wearing a black velvet dressing gown trimmed in gold. The dinner was in the oven warming drawer waiting to be served.

"You look beautiful," said Mark.

"Thank you, darling. I missed you terribly." Ana embraced him.

"Was it really as bad as you told me on the phone?"

"Well, it's not Africa's fault. It's an interesting place to visit for a week or so, but not to be trapped there. Come in. Let's go to the den."

The fire was burning, the lights were adjusted perfectly. Mark's martini was ready, and Ana joined him.

They sat down on the couch.

It was a little awkward, which surprised Ana.

"So how's the Roland thing going?" she asked. "Everybody's talking about your master stroke."

Mark debated responding with "you tell me." He wasn't angry in any way, but something happened while she was gone. He was tired of the games. But he was positive that Phillipe was mixed up in the Marleaux case and therefore might be a threat to Nikki. Uncertain yet about what to do with Ana, he knew he still needed her for Nikki's sake. He was not so sure he needed her for anything else. It was time for him to cut the crap, and he hoped she'd follow suit.

"Ana, I'm sure you know Roland tried to raid my firm because Doug Collins was behind it. It's okay. Let's stop talking around things."

"Mark, I don't know what to do. I'm suddenly very scared. I have feelings for you. I'm in a terrible position."

He took her hands.

"Has Phillipe threatened you?"

There it was. Out in the open. Ana started to cry, something Mark had never seen.

"His very presence scares me. I don't know what he might do to me. He feels as though he owns me because he gave me my start, and he really is responsible for the good things I have, but I paid a price . . . and I can't get him out of my life. The pressure goes away for periods at a time, when he's not interested in anything going on here. But Mark, this Marleaux appeal is something he won't let go of. I've tried not to look too carefully at his business tactics through the years, and I don't want to look at this, but I'm afraid he's going to hurt someone."

Mark's heart went out to her but he kept his head.

"Marleaux is innocent. We have the proof. All my firm wants to do is get an innocent man out of jail. We're not looking for the real killer. It's not our job, and frankly, even if we finally get a new trial for Marleaux and the conviction is overturned, and the police decided to reopen the case, which is a big *if*, I doubt that they will put any effort into finding the killer. If they reopen the case it's a public relations number. Why don't you try to reassure Phillipe that this is merely about freeing an innocent man? I don't think the other shoe will ever drop. And the other shoe is the only thing he cares about. If he did have anything to do with Greggie's death, I doubt that it will ever be solved. You and I both know that a hit man probably did it. End of story. Tell him that. You know how to deliver the information. In fact it will be easier on me if you do that."

"Of course I will. I know just what to say to him. Oh,

Mark, this is the first time that you and I have spoken to each other really openly. I was so frightened to be open with you because I don't want to lose you, yet I thought Phillipe would hurt me. Can it be true that you and I might be building some trust? I want that more than anything."

"Time will tell that. I would like it to be that way," said Mark. "In fact, I'd like us to talk a little more."

"What about?"

"Do you know how Phillipe has been spending his time lately or what projects he's interested in?" Mark could see Ana hesitate. This was the first time he'd been so bold and to the point.

"He's been very close-mouthed with me over the past few months, but I do know he's been going to Japan a lot."

Mark's brain clicked into gear, but he didn't let her see it.

"Thanks. You are very special to me," said Mark, moving closer.

"I love you, Mark," said Ana, bringing her face close to his and kissing him.

Mark returned the kiss and didn't pull back.

Ana was too caught up in the moment to notice that he didn't say he loved her.

The next morning she reported to Phillipe by phone. He had flown back to Paris on his private plane so she knew he'd be in his office.

"Hello, it's me," said Ana.

"Yes. How is Mark?"

"I saw him last night."

"Tell me something I don't know," said Phillipe nastily.

"He said he doesn't care who murdered Greggie. He just wants to get Marleaux out."

"Uh huh. Well the police care, and they'll be all over it if this case gets any bigger."

"Mark said that didn't matter because they couldn't find

anything. He said a hit man did it and it wouldn't be traceable. He said the police would give up quickly."

"Do you think that Mark is capable of telling you just what he thinks you want to hear so he can get into your pants?"

Ana was so disgusted by Phillipe that she wanted to hang up and have him disappear from her life forever, but she knew that would never happen. At least for now she didn't have an idea of what to do unless Mark married her. Maybe that would do it. Maybe Mark would protect her. She had served her purpose for Phillipe.

"Are you there? You're too quiet," said Phillipe.

"I'm here. I can only tell you what he said. He was quite convinced that Marleaux was the only issue, not Greggie Alcott, and I believe him," Ana said firmly. It was easier to do when he was six thousand miles away.

"Oh you do? Well that's such a comfort to me," responded Phillipe sarcastically. "Now I don't have to worry about anything anymore."

Instead of biting back, Ana answered, "Good, then I won't either. Goodbye, Phillipe."

"I always say goodbye first, Ana," she heard him say just before she clicked down the receiver.

She called Mark and told him of the conversation. He seemed pleased, but cautioned her against believing that Phillipe was pacified. She was disappointed that he didn't ask to see her, and a feeling of sadness came over her.

She was going to fight it, though. She'd wait two days and if she hadn't heard from him she'd call. Since she wasn't supposed to be in town, no one was expecting her permanent Friday soiree of an all-male dinner with special women guests for dessert. She was free on Friday. Maybe he was free, too.

*    *    *

Mark was on the phone to Alvin Marantz at his office in San Francisco the next morning. "Are you about done with that portfolio study?"

"Yes. Franc International has more legs that a centipede. No wonder you needed help on this one," said Alvin.

"Well, that's what I have you for, Mr. Corporate Finance. Now I need you to come down here just for the day to explain all of this to Nikki and me. You've been wanting to meet her anyway. You two will be great together."

"I know how much she means to you, Mark. Is everything going well?" asked Alvin.

"She's top-notch, but she's about to be in over her corporate head. We can't let that happen. I just know there's something else behind this Phillipe Gascon stuff besides Greggie, and I just bet the answer's somewhere in your charts. By the way, call your contacts in Japan. He's up to something."

"Will do," said Alvin. "How about if I come down Wednesday. I'll meet you in your office at ten. That'll give me a full day up here to work on everything."

"Good, see you then."


"Nikki, here's that case you requested on the Glasser matter," said Beverly, "and you have Mr. Marantz at ten."

"You, too? That meeting is all Mark has been reminding me about. He's wild about this Alvin."

"They're like brothers. They love each other but don't get to see each other very much. Alvin and Sarah are wonderful people. I'm sure you'll meet her one day, too."

"You know I need one more case looked up before I can finish my work on this report for the litigation department. Mark's trying to teach me there are no small cases. This one's about a man who wants to sue an airline because he claims their being late caused him to be late to an appointment and lose an account. Sounds a little petty to me, but I'll keep doing my work like a good little soldier."

"If Mark were here he'd remind you that the petty cases are the ones that pay the bills," said Beverly. "But of course, I'm not Mark, and it wouldn't be my place to say something like that . . ."

"Okay, okay," laughed Nikki. "I'll be good. Maybe Alvin can distract me."

When Nikki entered Mark's office, charts of Franc International covered two walls.

"Nikki, I'd like you to meet Alvin Marantz," said Mark.

"Hello, I've heard so much about you," said Nikki to the portly man, who came up to her shoulder. She thought he had the warmest eyes and furriest mustache she had ever seen. It was thick, curly, and jet black.

"This is a great moment for me," said Alvin. "I know how much happiness you bring to Mark."

"Thank you." She liked this man instantly.

"Nikki, sit down. As you can see, Alvin has produced a guide map to Phillipe Gascon's businesses, but I'm going to let Alvin take over from here."

"This is one of the smartest men I've ever come across. If you think about it, Nikki, there are three sure ways of making money. People must eat, get sick, and die. Those are fundamental parts of life. Gascon owns, if you look at the red dots, supermarket chains in many countries. Check it out."

Nikki was looking at a sea of red, green, and blue dots. "Amazing. What are the blue and green ones?"

"Blue means health and green means death."

"What?"

"Gascon owns hospitals and health care centers and insurance companies. That's blue. The green dots, which I've noticed have been decreasing in my study, are funeral homes and cemeteries. He seems to be selling off part of that area. I guess he realized that insurance and medicine are more profitable. Cremation just doesn't cut it, you know, financially speaking."

"So what does this have to do with the entertainment business and the newspapers?" asked Nikki.

"It provides the secure financing. Owning insurance companies and hospitals is better than owning banks. He's a genius. Now that the electronic age is opening up you'll see him buying phone companies, software companies, the works."

"What about Atlas?"

"Atlas is not his most profitable company, but it represents his ego. He has a thing about Hollywood and the United States. It's crazy. He's crazy, a megalomaniac of the worst kind."

"Would he kill?"

"There'd be no blood on his hands, but he'd order murder like he'd order a ham sandwich."

"Swell," said Nikki.

"What about Japan?" asked Mark.

"How did we get from murder to Japan?" asked Nikki.

"Calm down, you two," teased Alvin. "Gascon has made several trips to Japan recently because he realizes that the Japanese are tiring of investments in America. They haven't seen a very good return. He's trying to get them involved in some of his new communications projects, but he's having a problem. The Japanese want control if they spend their money. Gascon never lets control out of his hands. It's another thing that makes him crazy."

"Well, thank God he didn't ask me for another lunch date," cracked Nikki.

"Is she always like this?" asked Alvin.

"Yes," said Mark.

"Then I'd better come down here more often," said Alvin, as he and Mark looked at Nikki like amused uncles.

# Chapter 14

The denial of the appeal from the Ninth Circuit made Nikki absolutely irate. She was pacing in front of Mark, her beige Blahnik heels making marks in the carpet, holding the four letters and waving them around the room.

"We have spent the last nine months on this ridiculous paper trail that they call the justice system. 'Summarily denied' from the California State Court of Appeal, 'Summarily denied' from the California State Supreme Court, 'Summarily denied' from the U.S. District Court, and now 'Summarily denied' from the U.S. Ninth Circuit Court. What's wrong with these people? Don't they read? I've got an innocent man here. Does Franc International have that much power? I can't believe that. There aren't that many crooked judges. That can't have fixed this completely. What's wrong with this country? Do I have to go to the U.S. Supreme Court now?"

"Yes, you do," answered Mark soberly.

Nikki paused in amazement.

"My God, I never thought it would come to this. This is insane."

"Welcome to the legal profession, my dear. You were the one who wanted to defend the less fortunate."

"That's right and I will do it all the way."

"I know that," said Mark, "but now we're into a whole different ball game. Do you realize that if they grant the petition you'll be the youngest lawyer ever to try a case before the U.S. Supreme Court?"

"Me?"

"Yes, you."

"I never thought that would happen. I guess in the back of my mind I always thought that if, God forbid, we had to go this far, you'd take over. You've got to be kidding."

"No, I'm not. And furthermore, only one attorney is allowed to speak or be in the courtroom. It's simply one-on-one with the Court."

"I remember that from law school," said Nikki gulping, "but I never thought I'd be living it myself. You mean I would have to go to Washington alone?"

"No, of course not. Dear Nikki, don't worry. This is Uncle Mark, remember? I have a plan. Why don't we go to the conference room. Hayden is already waiting for us."

"Great," said Nikki.

The conference room overlooked all of Century City and had a view through to downtown Los Angeles. There was a layer of brown air hovering over the city under a blue sky.

"Good morning," said Hayden, sitting in front of a series of yellow legal pads.

"I can't believe we breathe that air," said Nikki. "Look at that."

"I can see you're in a fine mood today. Why don't you have some iced tea? I've ordered some for all of us," continued Hayden.

"How can you be so calm?"

"Let's get started," said Mark. "In anticipation of this situation I asked Hayden in advance to gather material on the U.S. Supreme Court Justices. Remember, the U.S. Supreme Court in the Daubert case ruled that an expert opinion, based on scientific technique, is admissible if it is generally accepted as a reliable technique among the scientific community, which makes the Frye rule a little more liberal. That's the good news. The bad news is that in another new case, *Herrera v. Collins*, the U.S. Supreme Court just ruled that on a petition for habeas corpus, the claim of actual innocence, based on newly discovered evidence, is not grounds for federal habeas relief."

"What? That's nuts," said Nikki.

"I agree, but nevertheless, it will affect our case, which I need not remind you is an exact combination of the two I just cited, getting DNA accepted and getting a new trial based on new evidence. Nikki, you need to be prepared, it will be a miracle if the Court agrees to hear this. You must be aware of that."

"I want nothing except truth, justice, and the American way," said Nikki with a deliberately arrogant smile.

"Great, you've gone from Wonder Woman to Lois Lane."

"Fine, Clark, let's get started."

"Good. At least there's a little laughter here," said Hayden.

"So why are we doing this now, if only a miracle will get this case heard?"

"Don't you believe in miracles?" asked Mark in mock innocence.

Nikki thought about him for a second. He was very quiet in his power, but when he wanted to exercise it, it came from nowhere. She wondered just what kind of political influence he had in Washington that might have this case raised from the mass of appeals sent in. He wouldn't be working on Justices' profiles at this moment if it were a waste of time. Mark never wasted time.

"All right, let's get to know our cast of characters. Of the nine Justices, three are swing votes. We should know who they are, what they're like, and what arguments appeal to them. Let's talk about the Chief Justice, Charles Wiseman. This is an emotional liberal but a tight interpreter of the law. That makes him very difficult to figure out."

"Wiseman, Charles," read Hayden, "age sixty-three, undergraduate Berkeley, law school Yale, on a scholarship. Couldn't decide whether to be a doctor or lawyer in grammar school, but in junior high law won out. He married a psychology student named Barbara right after college and they have three sons and five grandchildren. The Wisemans live in Potomac, Maryland. She gave up her practice early on to raise the kids, and she's very active in children's charities. He doesn't play golf or like any sports. He's a real bookworm, a serious guy, total academic."

"Didn't he write a couple of books?" asked Nikki.

"Very good," Hayden replied. "I've ordered them for us and they'll be here tomorrow. I have copies for each of us. We certainly can learn how his reasoning goes by reading them."

"Tell us about Alonzo Cunningham III," said Mark. "He's also a swing vote."

"Yuck," said Nikki. "I can't stand him. Don't look at me like that, Hayden, he's a pompous hypocrite who thinks women are second-class citizens. I loathe him and so does everyone else. He doesn't deserve to be there. I'd like to personally impeach him."

"Are you through?" asked Hayden.

"I might just be starting."

"And what if he votes our way?" asked Mark calmly.

"I'd be delighted, but I wouldn't change my opinion of him."

"Okay, Alonzo Cunningham III," continued Hayden impassively, "born in Georgia, got scholarships all through school, graduated from University of Pennsylvania, Georgetown Law, married a schoolteacher named Virginia, he's forty-eight and they have no children."

"Forty-eight! Think of how long he has to live," lamented Nikki.

Both men shot her a look.

"He has voted conservatively on most issues but he can throw in a wild card. He has a soft spot for the disenfranchised or the railroaded. That might be how we can get to him," continued Hayden.

"The last swing vote is Eric Burgess," said Mark. "That's the good-looking one."

"I've never noticed," said Nikki.

"Continue please, Hayden."

"Eric Burgess is the lone bachelor on the court. He's very quiet, you never know what he's thinking. But he has a brilliant mind. He's quite a character, taking a high school equivalency test and getting into Northwestern and studying for law school. He was an orphan and there's not much about him. He became friendly with the right people in Washington through his school connections and got himself appointed to the Ninth Circuit."

"Okay, Hayden, I'm going to assign you to Cunningham. Nikki, I'm sparing you that and giving you Burgess. I'll take Wiseman. We each will try to learn as much as we can to be as prepared as possible. This is a first-class battle. Send the petition today. We'll be ready just in case."

Nikki and Hayden decided to go out to lunch. This was a rare treat since they both had been so busy.

"What do you feel like?" asked Hayden.

"A wreck," answered Nikki.

"No, I meant what did you want to eat? Food always makes you happy. Mexican, Greek, Italian?"

"Mexican. I'm craving a breakfast burrito from Gloria's."

They went west along Olympic Boulevard until they came to Stoner Avenue and the purple shack that served some of the best Mexican food in the city. Parked alongside were police cars and fire trucks, and in under the awning they were surrounded by uniforms.

"You know if the men in uniform are here how good the food is," said Nikki. "If you don't want a breakfast burrito, Gloria makes special tamales and pupusas from El Salvador, homemade lemonade, and just about any Mexican dish you can think of."

"What's a breakfast burrito?"

"Scrambled eggs, bacon, and hash browns stuffed in a flour tortilla with refried beans, cheese, and rice," recounted Nikki cheerfully.

"That sounds amazing," said Hayden.

"Oh, yes, I don't care what time of day it is, I always have to have one."

They ordered at the counter and then found a corner table under the awning. It was only seconds before Nikki started in again.

"I'm going nuts," said Nikki. "It's all too much. We found out months ago that Sanchez's DNA didn't match the murder scene. It's bad enough I have to worry about Marleaux, but now I don't even know who killed my mother, or maybe I do. And what about The Master? That could be crucial, you know."

"Yes, and I told you, I think we should tell the police about him," said Hayden.

"Not yet," said Nikki. "I don't want any publicity. I need to resolve things between my mother and myself without any spotlight. I'll let you know when."

Nikki reached for a tortilla chip the same time Hayden did. Their hands grazed for just a second.

"You first," said Hayden sweetly, the business tone totally gone from his voice.

"No, you," said Nikki, picking up the dish and handing it to him, holding his eyes with her gaze. She couldn't deny the sparks, but she just didn't want to handle it head-on yet.

"Is there anything that you can remember, any personal detail that The Master may have revealed to you in the conversations?" asked Hayden, taking the chips and crunching teasingly as he spoke.

"I have gone over and over in my mind and I can't think of anything. God, how I wish I had printed them out while he was online," said Nikki.

"This really is a brutal time. We know very well that Franc International had to be responsible for Greggie's death. We know that Marleaux didn't do it, there was no known motive for Bronson or Solomon. The connection between Ana and Phillipe is very clear, as is the connection between Ana and Greggie. There's just no evidence around to make anything stick. They had to have hired a hit man. We'll never find who really did it," said Hayden.

"What if Greggie was insignificant? What if she was just a small part of a larger scheme?" asked Nikki. "Murder is a pretty drastic thing to do just to get rid of a regime at a studio."

"Yes, but when removal of that regime means more control for Gascon and rising stock prices into the millions, it's not so trivial," said Hayden.

"Good point."

"Now what else is bothering you? I can tell there's something," said Hayden.

"Remember how I wanted to talk to people who knew my mother?" asked Nikki. "Well, I've had lovely meetings with some of the people around Lauren, but I can't find Red Wagner. Norman Brokaw's number for him wasn't good, the makeup union gets his mail back from the post office marked 'addressee unknown,' and he's the only one she took with her on the concert tour. I've just got to find him."

"What about his relatives, have you checked on that? Find out who he put as beneficiary on his medical insurance through the union. They have to have a record of that."

"Good idea, I'll do it," said Nikki. "And thanks. I know I've been a little bit insane lately. I really appreciate your helping me."

Nikki welcomed being alone in her apartment for a couple of hours. She just wanted to lie down and try not to think. She debated putting on the TV, but decided to try and just shut her eyes. It had all been a bit much. Suddenly she was dealing with a real mother, a hoped-for trail to her father, and a possible U.S. Supreme Court case. She couldn't get the pictures of her mother out of her mind. Her emotions were so mixed up. She hated her mother for leaving her, hated her for sleeping around, and yet she almost fell in love with an image that millions of people did love. She didn't know what to make of it, and she didn't want to discuss it with Meredith. She just had to go through it on her own.

She didn't know how much time had passed, but when she woke up the light was blinking on the answering machine. Hayden had called to leave a number for Red Wagner's sister. Just as Nikki wrote it down there was a knock on her door.

"It's too quiet in there! What's going on?"

It was Joely.

Nikki got up and let her friend in.

"How do you like it?" asked Joely, dressed in a black Azzedine Alaia bodysuit.

"What?"

"My belt."

"It's gorgeous," said Nikki, admiring the heavy silver buckle snake ornament.

"It should be, it cost $3,500."

"For a belt buckle?" asked Nikki incredulously.

"Of course," said Joely. "It's a Barry Keiselstein-Cord."

"Well, naturally, I should have known," said Nikki, not knowing at all.

"I bought it for myself," said Joely proudly. "I didn't get it from some guy. I like that. I should do this more often."

"That's fine, as long as you have enough money put away in a safe place for your retirement."

"What are you, E. F. Hutton?" said Joely. "You're so conservative. Get with it, girl."

Joely went to the refrigerator, got out a Diet Coke and sat on the bed.

"Guess what the rumor on the street is?"

"I don't know, but I'm sure you'll tell me."

"I think it will interest you," said Joely. "Phillipe Gascon is supposedly coming to the States on a visit. It's his first in five years."

"Really," said Nikki, giving her full attention. "Do you know why he's coming or where he's going or who he's seeing?"

"My God, give me a break. I come in with a hot scoop and now you want everything. I'll get on it, and you will, too."

"Do you mind if I make a fast call?"

"I was expecting it," said Joely.

Nikki wondered to herself if Gascon's visit had something to do with the increased activity on the Marleaux case. She also wondered if he was going to stop in Washington first. She called Mark immediately.

Mark hung up after speaking to Nikki and then dialed another number.

"Ana, how are you?"

"Oh, Mark. Good. Are we set for Thursday?"

"You may be busier Thursday than you expected."

"What do you mean?"

"Gascon's coming to town. There's a big board meeting at Atlas," explained Mark.

"I truly haven't heard from him yet and I don't know whether he would see me. Our relationship is not as pleasant as it used to be. We talk on the phone, he gets his information, but the last time I saw him it was ugly. I hope he never comes by again."

"What happened? What did he do to you?" said Mark agitatedly.

"He was unhappy over the Marleaux situation. It was just when I came back from Africa before I saw you."

"You mean he has been in Los Angeles fairly recently?" asked Mark.

"Yes, and I don't want to go into what happened."

"Did he hurt you? Because if he did I'll see to it that—"

"Let it go," said Ana. "I'm fine. I don't want any more trouble."

Mark let it go.

"Do you know if he went anywhere else in the U.S. on that last visit?"

"No. He had his own plane and could have flown anywhere. I do know that he was back in Paris within seventy-two hours of his visit with me. What are you trying to figure out?"

"Whether or not he went to D.C. Do you know if he has any contacts there?"

"Of course he does. I met a number of his friends in Paris. He referred to them as his 'government buddies.' It was years ago and I don't remember any of the names," Ana said.

"If I showed you some pictures would you remember a face?"

"I could try. But it was years ago."

"Good. I'll bring some Thursday night."

Red Wagner's sister had been very helpful to Nikki as soon as she realized it was Lauren's daughter. She told Nikki that she wrote to Red at a post office box in Palm Desert and gave her the number. She also asked Nikki to notify her if she found her brother because she wanted to see him.

It took Hayden only a few minutes to find out which post office in Palm Desert was the right one, and then he sent an investigator to discover what he could and report back. The investigator reported that Red was a handyman who lived in a secluded trailer park way out in the desert. He came in regularly once every two weeks to get his mail.

Nikki received this information two days before Red was to go to the post office again. She also got a description of him and she left the night before, driving through the desert in the cool hours before checking into the Marriott Desert Spring Resort in Palm Desert. Even though her mission was serious, Nikki stood in the middle of the lobby and laughed out loud. Never had she seen a sight like this.

There was a waterfall flowing down the center of the lobby to the ground floor below where it emptied out into a fountain area. She couldn't resist going down there, and once again could not believe what she saw. Next to the fountain area was a giant man-made lake with gondolas on it. If you wanted to go to one of the hotel's restaurants, you had to go by boat! They even had pseudo-gondoliers in costume ready to take you. The boats were motorized, though, no rowing. Nikki immediately jumped on board. It was too much.

"Just take me anywhere, I'm not hungry."

"But which restaurant do you want to go to?"

"It doesn't matter, I won't eat anyway."

As people began to gather on board they looked at her as if she were a troublemaker, so she kept quiet.

"How many for La Strada? La Strada coming up on the left," the gondolier announced.

Three people got off.

"Next stop La Cantina."

Six people got off.

Nikki was now the only one on the boat.

He looked at her and said, "Next stop Tokyo Kaikan."

Nikki thought about it and suddenly a bit of sake and some sushi at the bar sounded pretty good to her.

He appeared to be relieved that she got off.

Nikki went to her room after a delicious meal, called Hayden, and then went to sleep. She wanted to be at the post office by seven A.M.

Precisely at six-fifty-five A.M. she pulled into the lot. The post office was located at the end of Main Street, a newly developed part of Palm Desert constructed to look like an old desert town where all the buildings looked like light brown abode huts. Everything about it was manicured and cute. She parked her car in the shade and hoped that Red would come soon. She really didn't want to be stuck out there for hours in ninety-plus temperatures.

Eight o'clock came.

Nine o'clock came.

Ten o'clock. Nikki was thirsty and hot, the temperature rising quickly in the desert. Rolling her windows down, Nikki grabbed some cold water she had packed in a cooler, and decided to step out for a little break. She went into the post office and looked around. It was quite small, only two windows for business, and the boxes were along the east wall. She walked over to them almost hoping that she could magically pick his out and use X-ray vision to see what was inside. She was standing there when she heard some steps behind her.

She turned around and knew instantly it was Red. The description of the full head of white hair and the bushy white beard was unmistakable. He looked to be about seventy, wearing bluejean shorts and a tank top with desert boots, even in the heat. Her heartbeat quickened. She didn't want to scare him so she had to contain her excitement and went over to the stamp machine to put in some change while he opened his box. She took her stamps, and when he left she followed him outside.

Using her friendliest voice she said, "Excuse me, sir. My name is Nikki Easterly. Are you Red Wagner?"

"What did you say your name was?" he said, stopping short.

Nikki thought he seemed okay and not too wary.

"It's Nikki Easterly. I'm Lauren Laverty's daughter."

She saw his chest cave in almost to the point of a sob. He grabbed her hands in his and said, "My child, my child."

My child? thought Nikki. My God. She forced herself to remain composed.

"Then you're Red."

"Oh, yes, how I loved your mother," he said, recovering himself a little bit. "I'm so happy to see you. I've wanted to know what has happened to you."

"Can we go somewhere and talk?" asked Nikki.

"Sure, let's go up the street to the café and get a back booth. No one will bother us."

Nikki followed him up the street. A couple of times he looked at her and said, "I can't believe it, I just can't believe it."

They walked into the restaurant, a nicely decorated coffee shop in yellow and white, and found a booth. No one was around yet to speak of. Nikki ordered a Coke and he had iced coffee.

"I don't know where to begin," said Nikki.

"Just tell me everything. I haven't seen you since you were six."

"Six, that means you were around in that last year," said Nikki, trying not to show her excitement.

"I was always around, honey."

"Were you there the day she was murdered?"

"That's still hard for me. Do we have to talk about it right away?"

"No, of course not," said Nikki, not wanting to lose him.

She told him about Meredith, her childhood, her schooling, and her legal career, without discussing any case she was on.

"This is hard for me, too. I'm trying to learn about my mother through film clips and talking to people. I wish it didn't have to be like this. She was very beautiful. I never realized how much until recently."

"She was the most beautiful woman I ever knew, both inside and out. She was kind, sweet, she was always helping people, giving money away to causes, and she loved life. She loved to have fun. She loved people. She was one of God's chosen ones. The specialness just radiated from her," said Red, his eyes shining.

"How did you two meet?"

"It was right when she came to Hollywood. I was a makeup man on a photo shoot for some modeling she was doing. We hit it off right away. She wasn't famous yet, both of us were starting out and we just spent time together."

Nikki was dying to ask him if they had been lovers, but again, she didn't want to scare him off. She sensed that he knew she was skirting the issue.

"You know what I'd like to do?" asked Red. "I'd like to leave here and have you follow me to my trailer. I'd feel more comfortable talking there and I have some photographs I'd like to show you. Would that be all right?"

"Sure, that would be great. How far out is it? Do I need to get gas?"

"It's about thirty minutes outside of here, it's kind of deserted."

Nikki had a full tank, she was just trying to get an estimate of how far they might be going. When she got to her car she called Beverly and told her approximately where she was going. Nikki knew her guard wouldn't be far behind, but she hoped Red wouldn't see him and be scared. Although Red seemed sweet enough, she couldn't be too careful. He might not be what he seemed.

They turned left out of town, past shopping centers and housing developments, and within fifteen minutes they were on a remote highway. She couldn't imagine anyone wanting to live this far out. She would ask him about that.

Within another fifteen minutes or so a cluster of large palm trees appeared on the right, with a gathering of six or seven trailers camped beneath them. There were two big generators for electricity, and a crude water hookup to an old well.

He parked his truck and she pulled in beside him.

He walked to a large Winnebago, one of the older models.

"Come on in," he said.

Nikki followed and walked into a very neat setup—everything was beige and brown, worn but neat. To the right was the driver's area with a steering wheel, console, radio. Above it was a platform with a bed on it. In the middle of the Winnebago was a dining booth and behind it a kitchen area complete with TV and microwave. On the other side was a little bathroom with a toilet and sink in it, and the whole rear section was a bedroom with a double bed and a bathtub. It was old, but luxurious in its day.

"Do you know what this is?" Red asked, gesturing with his arms around the trailer.

"No."

"This was your mother's portable dressing room. She had it with her on every picture. I used to do her makeup right there where you're standing."

"You're kidding!"

"No, I'm not. Mr. Ferguson gave it to me. She was given it by the studio and he knew she would want me to have it. We spent some of our happiest moments in this thing. It went everywhere. Every personal appearance, every movie, just everywhere."

"You really knew her better than anyone, didn't you?" asked Nikki gently.

"Yes, I did," he said, getting quiet.

"You loved her very much."

He paused a second, looked at her and said, "Better than anyone."

A look passed between the two of them. Nikki did not need to ask if they had been lovers, but she did need to ask about her father.

"Did you go with her on that singing tour in 1968?"

"Sure did, it was crazy. We did about twenty dates and we flew while the Winnebago was shipped. We did a section of the country at a time."

"Which section did you do first?"

"We went to the Northwest, spent a lot of time there."

"Was my mother surrounded by a lot of guys?"

He shot her a look.

"Yes," he said with slightly clenched teeth.

Nikki felt a slight chill, and brushed it away.

"Were any of them decent in your opinion?"

"I try not to have an opinion about them," he said.

"But I have a feeling you didn't like them very much."

"They weren't good enough for her."

"Not as good as you?" she asked as sweetly as she could. Fortunately he didn't get upset.

"That's true," he said calmly. "It was very difficult on me. She, uh, we had different ideas about relationships."

"Did you like Mark Ferguson?"

"Yes, he was a good guy."

"Do you think she would have married him?"

"It's hard to tell. I'm sorry, but she wasn't faithful to him. He just looked the other way because he loved her so much. When she died I heard he left town for a while. I had to do the same. When I came back I tried to go on doing makeup but I just didn't want to touch anybody else. This place is good for me. It's been fine out here. I don't have to think, I can just be with nature, feel her presence among the stars, do odd jobs. Mark just buried himself in his work. He never loved anybody again."

Nikki looked around again at her surroundings. She saw that there were no pictures of Lauren.

"Did you have some pictures you wanted to show me?"

"Hang on, I'll be right back."

He excused himself and went to the bedroom. Nikki heard some shuffling around and then he came back with a scrapbook.

"I shot pictures everywhere we went. Here you can see how happy we were, what fun we had."

Nikki opened the album and saw pictures of them in her backyard, on sets, in dressing rooms, on a Ferris wheel, at a hot dog stand.

"Where were these taken?" Nikki asked, referring to the Ferris wheel and the hot dog stand.

"Oh, that was fun. There was a county fair in Sacramento. We were up there doing a singing gig. Things were great, we were having a ball but then it became a disaster."

"What do you mean?"

"There was this kid, our roadie got sick and we needed to hire a replacement just for the night. That's when she met Rocky."

"Who's Rocky?"

"I just called him that. I couldn't stand him. He put on such airs, told stories about himself, pretending to be some rich kid . . . you know, Rockefeller. That's why I called him that. Lauren was wild about him. She took him with us for six weeks of the tour. They would lock themselves up in hotel rooms for hours. He'd almost make her late for her shows. Everybody despised him, but she couldn't see it. Whatever he wanted, he got, presents, her attention. It made me nuts."

"Then what happened?"

"Well it's the weirdest thing, one day he was just gone. I couldn't bring his name up to her, it was as if he never existed. She never talked about it again."

"When was this exactly?"

"The spring of 1968."

Nikki felt that chill again, and that wasn't easy in the desert heat. Her whole body told her she was onto something.

"Red, I need to ask you a very difficult question. And I really need you to take time and answer it for me. Please."

"All right."

She took a deep breath. "Do you know who my father was?"

Red looked down at his boots. He placed his hands on his knees and raised his head up to look her square in the eye.

"Nikki, I kinda thought that's where this was going. I can tell you one thing, I sure wish I was your father. I asked your mother and she said no and I believed her. The timing wasn't right."

"The timing was right for Rocky, wasn't it? I was born February 13, 1969."

"Good God," said Red.

"Please tell me everything you know about him," she urged.

"I don't know any more than what I told you. He was

hanging out at concerts in Sacramento in 1968. He was part of the music scene back then. I don't know any more."

"You can tell me what he looked like back then."

"He was tall, long dark hair, way past his shoulders, wire glasses, mustache. He looked like any other hippie guy. I'm sorry. He didn't talk to anybody once he got close to Lauren. We never learned anything about him."

"Well who hired him that night?"

"I suppose our road manager who got sick."

"What's his name and where might he be?"

"I'm sorry. He never returned to the tour. He overdosed and died."

Nikki looked dejected.

"Don't feel that bad, honey. Your mother wanted you all to herself. She didn't want to share you with a man. You meant a lot to her. Just let it go."

"I can't. It's important to me to know who I am. And you don't know that my mother wouldn't have told me who my father was when I got older. We never had a chance."

Red took her hand in his and gently said, "I'm so glad you found me. You're like Lauren come back to life. I'll do anything I can for you, just come back and visit me from time to time?"

He looked so wistful, Nikki's heart went out to him.

"I have a better idea. I'd like you to have dinner with me tonight. Would you?"

"Sure I would."

"Great. Do you get seasick?"

"What?"

"Oh, never mind. You'll see. I'm at the Marriott Desert Springs."

Hayden was on the Phillipe Gascon situation as soon as Mark told him. He found out that it was very unusual for

Gascon to come to the yearly meeting, that he did it only every few years.

He tailed Gascon personally and found that he checked into the Four Seasons, had dinner with Ana alone at Eclipse, dropped her off, and then went back to the hotel. There was no way Hayden could tell if there were any other visitors from where he was stationed in the lobby. He later talked to the floor concierge and after giving him $50 he was told that there had been two male visitors to Gascon's room after ten P.M., but he was unable to find out who they were. Gascon had gone to the board meeting the next day and then gone right to the airport from the studio to return to France.

Mark was waiting for Ana when she was dropped off. He himself was driven to her house so his car wouldn't be on the street or anywhere Gascon could see it. He had been assured by Ana that Gascon wouldn't be coming in.

Ana explained that once she knew he was going to take her to Eclipse, his use of her this trip was strictly public, which was exactly what she wanted.

"So what did he talk about?" asked Mark when Ana met him in the den.

"He never mentioned the Marleaux case. I was shocked. It was as if it had never happened."

"What did he talk about then?" insisted Mark. "Everything he says to you is a message of some sort."

"I know that's usually true, but not in this case. He talked about some different stocks that he thought I should buy, what properties he thought were good in Los Angeles that were coming up. He said the old ICM building on Beverly Boulevard was coming up for sale and that I shouldn't buy it, it would be a bad investment. Just things like that. He was like the old Phillipe, advising me thoughtfully on building a portfolio. He wasn't behaving like a monster at all. I actually had a very nice dinner with him."

"Did anyone come over to the table to say hello to him?" asked Mark.

"Yes. Roland Bixby and Cruger Fowler, and Sally Field."

"They all weren't together were they?"

"Of course not. Sally was with some man I didn't recognize who stayed at her table, and Roland and Cruger, of course, were together."

"What did Roland say?"

"He was effusive about the new Atlas product for the fall. I really don't like him. He's oily."

"And Cruger?"

"Just polite Hollywood things. Nothing earth-shattering. I'm telling you, it was just a typical power-filled evening at Eclipse."

"When Phillipe is around nothing is typical. You're missing something."

"I really don't think so, Mark," said Ana, getting a little annoyed. "I've been reading this man for twenty years. I know him like a book."

Ana was sorry she said it, because it made her out to be the kind of woman she didn't want to be for Mark. But he had hurt her.

Mark saw the look on Ana's face and realized he had been a bit hard on her. Changing his attitude he said, "You know, I think the fact that Phillipe behaved calmly and normally is what's interesting. I bet that he did that in order to not give any hint about what he's really doing. I was probably looking for hidden messages, when the actual message was that the normalcy was a performance."

"Maybe."

Mark took out the pictures.

"I'm sorry to add more questions here but this case is very important to me."

He showed her pictures of Chief Justice Wiseman and all the Supreme Court Justices.

"Well of course I recognize everyone. It's the Supreme Court, silly," said Ana.

"Yes, but do you remember any of them from years back? Have you ever seen any one of them personally?"

"No, I haven't."

"How about President Allingham?"

"No, not him either. How much longer are we going to continue with this?"

"We're through," said Mark.

Ana was feeling very used again. Mark considered the possibility that Phillipe was just having her be a dinner decoration. Then she came home to an inquisition. She was beginning to wonder exactly how much Mark cared for her. Maybe she was just someone whose company he enjoyed both in and out of bed, who was useful to him, too. She was beginning to feel ill.

"I'm sorry, Mark. I just don't feel well. Maybe it was something I ate. I'm going to have to lie down."

"Is there anything I can do? Can I get you a doctor?"

"No, thank you. Just call a cab for yourself. I'm going upstairs now. Please excuse me. Good night."

Ana felt her mood blacken with each step farther away from Mark. By the time she got to her room she collapsed on the bed. In a few moments she heard the front door close, and she took a deep breath. She wasn't physically ill, but she was sick about what had become of her life. Suddenly now it was all in front of her. The depression that had been coming on in Africa was in full force. She had always been afraid to spend too much time thinking because she knew she wouldn't be able to disregard the conclusion.

As she lay there she realized that she had never made it as an actress, she became a hooker. She wasn't a socialite, she was passably accepted by people because she was rich, but she knew that people probably laughed at her behind her back, because she got her seed money by being on her back.

No good man would ever have her. She knew that now. She could give all the dinners that she wanted, sit through all the operas and concerts, be given awards by charities because she would give so much money that they would have to honor her eventually, but she was what she was. She took the low road, and it was time for her to get out of the fantasy she was living in. She didn't want to live with herself anymore.

She felt heavy as she walked to the bathroom, opened the medicine cabinet, and looked at all the pills. She had enough in there to kill the front line of the Dallas Cowboys.

She took out Valium, Dilaudid, and Seconal. The Valium would keep her from throwing up the other pills. She had read that in a book somewhere.

She went back into the little pantry area of the bedroom and took out a bottle of vodka to take the pills with, and brought everything back to her nightstand.

Going to the closet, she took out her peach silk peignoir set with the beige alençon lace and put it on.

She got back into bed, poured herself a large glass of the vodka, and placed three Dilaudid and three Valium in her hand. She had no problem swallowing pills and thought that three handfuls should do it.

Tears were streaming down her face now. She had never felt so worthless and so sad. She looked down at the pills. It was easy. In about ten minutes she'd never know a thing. The next morning Alistair would find her.

And then what? Would he call a doctor? Would he call 911? No. He would call Phillipe. She had surmised years ago that Alistair was on Phillipe's payroll. Phillipe would be directing what would happen to her even in death. He would be sitting in that office in Paris dictating everything, screwing her over again just like he always did, even after her last dying breath.

What if he told Alistair to call no one? What if he sent his jet to pick up the body that Alistair carefully shoved into a garment bag, and she was flown to an unknown destination? Word could just be put out that "Ms. Sarstedt is on an extended trip around the world." No one would even know she had died. If she left a note it would be destroyed. She could write to Joan or Mark and mail it, but then she'd have to get up now, write it, and drive to a mailbox.

She was getting angry now, and the anger revived her. She would be damned if she gave Phillipe that last say over what happened to her. If she was going to die, she would plan everything. It would be foolproof and perfect. Fuck Phillipe, Ana thought. Fuck all of you. I'll die when I'm good and ready.

Ana put all the pills back in the cabinet and poured the vodka down the sink. She stayed in her peach peignoir set and had a lovely night's sleep.

During a frantic call from Nikki in Palm Desert, Hayden was asked to find out anything about Sacramento underground newspapers, music clubs that might have been around for over twenty-five years. She wanted all the information by the end of the day, naturally. She told him she planned to go to Sacramento herself the following day.

"So what'd you find out?" were the first words out of Nikki's mouth when she walked into the office.

"And good morning to you," said Hayden.

She waited for a response.

"Okay. I talked to a buddy of mine at the *Sacramento Bee*. There's a guy he knows who used to be a rock critic, quit a couple of months ago. He supposedly is familiar with the music scene up there. There's also a paper called the *Weekly Reader*. It's only ten years old, but it's along the lines of our *Free Press*. There may be somebody there who was around twenty-five years ago. It's a shot. My friend's name is David

Stern and he's waiting for your call. He'll set you up with the critic."

"Beverly, will you get me a seat on the one P.M. flight to Sacramento please?" said Nikki over the intercom.

"Do you want a hotel?" asked the voice.

"Yes."

"Fine, the only place up there that isn't a toilet is the Hyatt. You're not going to the garden spot of the world," said Beverly.

Nikki had brought a suitcase to the office in order to be ready at a moment's notice. She caught her plane and checked into the Hyatt at four o'clock. She hadn't had time to change her clothes, so she met the critic in what she traveled in—jeans, a white shirt, and a navy blazer. Stern had set up the meeting with Orson Foyt in the Hyatt bar at five o'clock. She spotted him immediately. Stern told her to look for someone who looked like Jerry Garcia of the Grateful Dead. When she walked into the bar there was no way she could miss this look-alike. He looked like he was a band member, rather than a critic.

"Hi, I'm Nikki Easterly. Thanks for meeting me."

"No problem, David's a friend of mine."

"I need to get right to this because I don't have a lot of time, I'm sorry."

"Cool. Just shoot."

"My mother was Lauren Laverty and I've been told she did a concert tour in 1968 and one of the stops was Sacramento."

"Right, I saw the concert."

"You did? That's great."

"No, she was great. She was really somethin'," he said a little lasciviously for Nikki's taste.

"The night she was here her road manager got sick and

she hired a temporary one. His nickname was Rocky. Would you know anything about that?"

"Sorry. I've never heard of him."

"Well his name wasn't Rocky. Some people on the tour just called him that."

"Do you have a picture or anything? What does he look like?"

"I don't have any picture. He was described to me as tall, with long dark hair, thin, and wire glasses."

"Lady, you just described a whole generation."

Nikki was beginning to feel helpless.

"I know this is crazy, but I've got to find him. Was there any nightclub that was popular then where someone like that might hang out?"

"Sure. It was called Daddy's but it closed seven years ago," said Orson. "Nothing around now except some coffeehouses with an occasional acoustic player. That's why I quit the paper. It's a real drag here now. I'm thinking of moving to Mendocino."

"What about a paper here called the *Weekly Reader*. I know it wasn't around twenty-five years ago, but is there anybody working there who was?"

"Wow, let's see . . . I think you want Dave Thompson. He knew a lot of people. He usually has dinner at a vegetarian restaurant next to the paper. They work late there. It's on 15th Street at Washington. It's called the Flaming Carrot, try that."

Nikki thanked him for his time and ended the conversation before he started asking questions that she didn't want to answer.

The Flaming Carrot was not in the best part of town, and Nikki was slightly uneasy as she got out of the cab.

"Are you sure this is where you want to go, lady?" asked the driver.

"Yes, but could you come back for me in thirty minutes. I'd appreciate it."

"You got it."

Nikki walked into the restaurant. It was a threadbare kind of place, just bare wood, oilcloth-covered tables, mismatched chairs. It was clean, though, and it smelled good. Nikki actually loved fresh vegetable soup, although she was not in a place that would be her first choice to partake. She stood at the door and a waitress walked over to her.

"One or two?"

"Is the manager here?" asked Nikki.

"No. Is there something I can help you with?"

"Maybe. Do you know a writer named Dave Thompson?"

"You mean D.T.?"

"If that's what he calls himself."

"Sure. He's in that back booth with those guys. He's the one in the leather vest."

"Thank you very much."

Nikki headed in that direction, checking out D.T. He looked like a biker, not one of her more comfortable images. But she couldn't afford to be picky.

"Mr. Thompson?"

"Who wants him?"

"I do. I flew in from Los Angeles to ask him a couple of questions. I'm trying to find somebody."

"Well sit right down here, sweetie, I'm somebody," he said laughingly.

Nikki disliked him instantly, and for a second was taken aback by his calling her sweetie, a name she had used on the computer board.

"Thanks, I'll just get a chair. Are you Mr. Thompson?"

"Hell, yes he is," said one of the other men.

Nikki thought about it for a second and decided to go for it.

"Anybody here remember Lauren Laverty?"

There was instant recognition and comments from the guys.

"Well I'm her daughter."

The same guy let out a low whistle.

She ignored it.

"Mr. Thompson, I'm looking for someone who was around my mother during the 1968 concert tour . . ."

"And who might that be?"

"His nickname was Rocky." She then continued to explain whatever information she had. Thompson had a blank look on his face and she was feeling discouraged even as she spoke.

"I don't know anyone named Rocky."

"Oh," she said dejectedly.

"Wait a second, did you say he was always around her like some groupie?"

"Yes."

"There was this one guy, now that I think of it. He was kind of creepy. Named Eddie . . . Eddie Brinkley. I remember the Brinkley because it reminded me of the newscaster. He was obsessed with her, carried her pictures around. Seems to me he followed her to the next town, got some kind of low-level job. He may be who you're looking for."

"That's great!" said Nikki. "Do you have any idea where he would be now?"

"You've got to be kidding. I hardly knew where he was then. But I do remember that he was born in Sacramento."

"Thank you, you've been a tremendous help."

She walked outside. The cab hadn't returned. Standing at the curb in an unfamiliar run-down area in the dark wasn't her idea of a good time. Was that a shadow she saw behind the dumpster in the alley? She wrapped her arms around herself and looked at her watch. If that cab didn't show up in five minutes she was going to go back in the restaurant, call another, and wait inside. She looked back at the restaurant door and saw D.T.'s face peering out at her quizzically. Then the cab arrived.

Nikki's first call, as usual, was to Hayden when she got back to the hotel. "I need anything you can get on an Eddie Brinkley, born in Sacramento about fifty years ago. Check the DMV, Hall of Records, local high schools . . . I don't know why I'm telling you this. You know what to do."

"Nikki," she heard him say. "Something important has happened. You need to come back here right away. The U.S. Supreme Court has ruled and they're going to hear the case."

"Oh my God!" screamed Nikki.

# Chapter 15

*I* find this extremely insulting," said Justice Eric Burgess. "Since when are we investigated like common criminals?"

"Now really, Eric, that's hardly the case," said Chief Justice Wiseman, wiping his horn-rimmed glasses.

"Ah yes, our Chief Voice of Reason," said Burgess with unveiled sarcasm.

It was a typical eight A.M. Wednesday morning weekly meeting. The Justices, and occasionally their clerks included, got together to decide which cases they would or would not hear, and to discuss general business of interest to the Court. They were seated in street clothes in the conference room located directly behind the court. It was a room full of tradition, with pictures of every Justice who had gone before them, and Presidents of the United States. Each Justice had a specific seat at the table according to seniority. At his or her place was a white note tablet with the crest of the Supreme Court and the name of the Justice, a water glass, and a gold-engraved pen. Sometimes for a joke a Justice would use one of the souvenir pens sold at the gift shop for two dollars, a thin, gray pen with "U.S. Supreme Court" stamped on it in fake gold.

The walls were off-white with matching crown molding, which beautifully set off the maroon carpet. The furniture was mahogany and the chairs were covered in brown leather.

"Eric, I thought you were the one pushing for this case," said Wiseman. "It could have gone right by the wayside as far as I'm concerned. We've already ruled on new evidence in habeas cases."

"Yes, but this one is different, it has the DNA challenge, too, which is particularly difficult in California. For all its progressiveness, that state lags behind in accepting scientific evidence based on newer testing," said Burgess. "However, to have this Ferguson firm do special checks on us is ridiculous. We all, for the most part, have impeccable records."

Cunningham saw that Burgess directed that crack to him, and rather than respond he just ran his thumb alongside the legal tablet.

Wiseman stepped in right away to avoid the normal dissension that went on between the two of them.

"Frankly, I am impressed. It's been a long time since a firm was so dedicated and thorough. I think you should be flattered," said Wiseman.

"Well, I agree with Eric," said Georgina Carlson, the third woman ever appointed to the court. "I don't want anyone trying to second-guess me or play to me. I'll rule the way I rule and that's it."

Wiseman liked her a lot. He respected her forthrightness and consistency, and she also dressed so elegantly in silk blouses and tailored suits. "I'm sure you will, Georgina; in fact I base my life on it," he said.

Then Cunningham spoke up. "How do we know for sure

that it is the Marleaux case that is causing all this investigation? It could be anything."

Burgess had an answer ready before Wiseman could get
in. "Alonzo, we tied the inquiries to a Hayden Chou who
works at that firm. What else do you need?"

"I need to get back to my office," he replied. "Is there
anything else, Charles?"

"No, that should wrap it up. It was at the tail end of my
list for this morning. See you all in court."

Eric Burgess was having a difficult morning. He hated
those meetings where he was questioned about things. He
didn't believe that Justices should be investigated and that
was that.

"Miss Harwick, could you come in here please?" he
asked as he walked through his reception area on the way
to his office.

He didn't break stride as he spoke, and she followed him
in with her pad. Slamming his papers down a little harder
than usual before he took a seat, he said, "Miss Harwick,
here is a copy of the Marleaux petition. The lawyer assigned
to the case is a Miss Nikki Easterly. I want you to call the
proper people in Washington and get a dossier on her and I
want you to make sure that someone from here deliberately
leaks our investigation to a Hayden Chou at the Ferguson
firm in Century City. Understood?"

"Yes, sir."

"It's top priority. Please get back to me within forty-eight
hours on this."

He shooed her out and picked up his private line.

All of the Justices' private offices were in a row to the right
of the conference room. Their front doors faced the main hall,
but it was not common knowledge among the public that
there was a back hall and that each Justice could come and

go without anyone knowing. What was also interesting was that they could go into each other's offices that way, although it was rarely used for that purpose.

When Charles Wiseman heard the knock at his back door he was surprised.

"Come in."

"I need to see you," said Alonzo.

"Is there something wrong?" said Charles, looking over his glasses and putting down his pen.

"Yes. Eric Burgess is what's wrong."

Charles sighed. He was beginning to feel more like a junior high school boys' vice principal than a Chief Justice.

"I can't take it anymore, you've got to speak to him," said Alonzo.

"Can't take what?"

"You know very well, the slurs, the cracks. That prejudiced bastard has been after me since the day I got here."

"Alonzo, this is a delicate subject that you can't seem to let go of. I'm sorry to remind you that you were a very unpopular choice for this position. Many people feel you were not qualified and they resent the fact that you are here. That's just the way it is. It's something you have to live with."

"You don't pull any punches, do you?"

"Not behind doors I don't. I'm not a camp counselor. This is a situation we all have to live with for life. I've made my bed, you've made yours, and Eric has made his. I've said this to you before, you must talk to him directly. But if I see either you or him counteracting each other's votes out of spite, if I ever suspect that the proper wheels of justice are not turning, I will report you both to the President. And I think you are aware that President Allingwood's attorney general was Burgess's roommate in college. Now I believe we should just calm down, and proceed with the day. What do you think?"

Cunningham got up and walked out the back door as quietly as he entered.

Nikki was on edge about everything, and the last thing she wanted to do tonight was have dinner with a prospective client, although she was delighted to spend an evening with Mark. The dinner was early, at a restaurant called Jimmy's, a beautiful spot on the edge of Century City that was one of Los Angeles's finest restaurants. She had dressed in a suit that would also be appropriate at dinner, and she was looking forward to the chocolate soufflé for dessert. That should get her through. But it was rare that Mark had to entertain to get a client. Usually they came to him without the courting.

"Do I really have to do this?" asked Nikki as she and Mark were walking to Jimmy's.

"Would you ask a question like that if I were just your boss and not your 'uncle.' "

"Probably not, but you know there are parts about lawyering that I just don't care for."

"I do know that, Nikki, and I also have spent time with you and shown you the importance of all sides of what we do. Encouraging new business is just as important as doing a good job for the clients we already represent. Need I remind you that the money we are losing over doing the Marleaux case pro bono is in the hundreds of thousands of dollars. Perhaps that will help you to see Mr. Nakashiwa in a new light. Without accounts like his, we couldn't afford to indulge your Marleaux case."

"I'm sorry, Mark. Sometimes I behave like a brat."

"This is true," he said good-naturedly. "Actually I'm sorry I haven't had a chance to get you up to speed about this meeting. I know you've heard of Mr. Nakashiwa. He'll be with an interpreter, and another executive from his company. The microchip they've invented has made them a $3 billion company in the past five years. They want a foothold in Hollywood. We can arrange for them to buy a studio, or they can finance two or three top independent producers as partners in a new company, sort of like the old United Artists. Whatever they want, our commission would be enormous."

"I certainly see the financial implications here, but I just hate the foreign intervention in our American studios. I think Hollywood should own the studios and make the pictures."

"Spoken like a true Laverty," said Mark. "Your mother would have said the same thing. But it's the 1990s now. Everyone can use money. We can't afford to be nationalistic, but I don't disagree with you, Nikki, you should know that."

"I have a great idea," said Nikki. "Remember when we talked about Phillipe wooing the Japanese to invest in Europe? Well, wouldn't it just drive him nuts if we brokered a deal for them to try to buy his precious Atlas?"

"That would make him crazy," Mark agreed.

"Delightfully so," said Nikki with a smirk. "But if the bottom line is money, that's Phillipe's, too, isn't it? Maybe we should rattle his cage a little whether the Japanese buy Atlas or not . . ."

"I do love you and your very special mind," said Mark.

Nikki and Mark arrived first, just the way Mark wanted. Jimmy gave them the number one booth just to the right of the door when you entered the main dining room. They were only in their seats for seconds when Mr. Nakashiwa arrived along with his interpreter, Mr. Hideko, and a business associate, Mr. Kyokota.

Nikki thought Mr. Nakashiwa looked like one of those actors who played the bad Japanese enemies in the war movies from the 1940s that she saw on TV from time to time. She chastised herself for thinking that, and made a conscious effort to behave. Mr. Kyokota was younger, studious, a little gray at the temples and wore glasses. As for the interpreter, he was charming and well-schooled in Western ways.

Jimmy sent hot sake to the table as a gesture of welcome. Nikki knew that it was bad luck for any Japanese person to pour his or her own sake, so, being next to Mr. Nakashiwa anyway, she nodded her head a little and reached over to pour his sake for him. She didn't feel she was compromising her feminist beliefs. She was bowing to custom and simply doing business.

Nakashiwa spoke quickly to the interpreter.

"Mr. Nakashiwa wants you to know how pleased he is that you understand our customs. Have you been to Japan?"

"No, I haven't, but I grew up near a community called Seaside where there are many Asians. I love studying different cultures, their food, art, music, literature."

Each time Nikki spoke, the interpreter would translate and then do the same for her when Mr. Nakashiwa spoke. It was slow going, but it was working.

"Where did you go to law school?"

"I went to Boalt. It's a law school connected to UC Berkeley."

"And this Seaside, where is that?"

"It's right next door to the Carmel-Monterey area."

"Carmel-Monterey," said Mr. Nakashiwa in broken English, getting very excited. He then spoke in a torrent to the interpreter.

After what seemed like minutes, Mr. Hideko said, "Mr. Nakashiwa is an avid golfer. He wants to buy the Pacific Grove Golf Course and the Lodge. He wants to know what you think."

Mark kicked her under the table. She knew she was in a spot. She personally did not want the Japanese to buy her landmark and Mark knew it.

Nikki thought carefully before answering. "Pacific Grove is very special to me and special to everyone in the area. It is one of the most beautiful golf courses in the world. As for an investment, I think you would do very well. But I caution you to be careful about raising the greens fees too high to get a quick return on your investment. Golfers there have been members for many years and think of the club as their home. If they perceive that they are not welcome, they will take their business elsewhere and your investment will not work out."

Mark and Nikki watched Nakashiwa's face as Nikki's answer was being related to him. He was nodding, nodding, and then he said something short back to Mr. Hideko.

"Smart girl," said Mr. Hideko.

Mark laughed first, joined by everyone.

"I'm glad you respect honesty, Mr. Nakashiwa. That's the way our firm works," said Nikki.

By the time the dessert arrived Mr. Nakashiwa would have done anything Nikki asked. His trust for her was sealed by the time they got to entertainment industry topics, and Nikki was sure she piqued his interest about Atlas. By coffee he was a client of Mark and Nikki's, and within thirty days they would have a prospectus to him on buying suggestions.

"Nikki, you are masterful," said Mark, taking her hand as they walked back to the office. "It's not that terrible, being the soliciting side occasionally, is it?"

"They seemed to be all right. They're very rich, and I pray they don't buy my club," said Nikki.

"You realize that by mentioning Atlas by name that they will immediately begin their own investigation of the studio. That's how the Japanese work," said Mark.

Nikki smiled at him in fake innocence and said, "Gee, really? Why, I never knew that. Just think, Mr. Gascon might be a little upset."

The flowers on Nikki's desk the next morning were gigantic.

"So . . . what's this?" asked Beverly conspiratorially.

"I guess I made quite an impression on Mr. Nakashiwa," said Nikki. "The dinner went really well, and his company is going to be a fabulous client."

"Boy are you sounding like a lawyer," teased Beverly.

Nikki took the card, opened it, and screamed.

### *I told you to stop. You're going to be next.*

The guard was at her side in two seconds. Beverly was bringing her water.

Mark ran in, followed by Hayden.

"What is it? Nikki? Are you okay?"

Beverly showed them the card.

"I want everyone out except Nikki and Hayden."

"Find out everything you can about those flowers, where they came from, how they were delivered—everything. From now on nothing is to be put into this office," said Mark adamantly to the guard.

Nikki was shaking. "This is getting ridiculous. I'm tired of people trying to scare me. Who knows who it is now. Maybe it's my mother's real killer."

"What are you talking about?" asked Mark. "Your mother's killer is in jail."

Nikki shot Hayden a look. Mark didn't know about Sanchez, The Master, or Rocky.

"I'm just crazy right now," said Nikki, covering slightly. "This must be Phillipe's doing."

"I'm not so sure, there's a possibility he's been neutralized . . . or maybe not, maybe he already found out about our dinner . . ." said Mark, his voice trailing off.

"Hayden, watch over her. I've got some calls to make," said Mark, leaving.

"Are you sure you want to go through with this?" said

Hayden. "Things are getting out of hand. I'm really frightened for your life."

"Don't you get it? My life depends on all of this. What's
wrong with you? Why can't you see that?"

"I can see it, I just don't want you hurt. Can't you see
that?" said Hayden.

"Yes, but it doesn't matter," said Nikki. "This issue is
larger than Marleaux or Atlas. If I don't win this case then it
doesn't matter whether Sanchez's DNA doesn't match. No
DNA will be admissible in this retrial situation. I won't be
able to do anything about it and then nothing will be solved.
I have to do this for my mother and me. This cycle has to
end. I'm playing hardball. We're going at this from all sides.
I want the sales prospectus on the Atlas figures put into high
gear for Nakashiwa, and I won't give up trying to find The
Master. Now what about the Sacramento investigation? Has
that guy you assigned come up with anything on Brinkley?"

Hayden knew when he was up against Nikki's brick wall,
but he also held out every hope that if all of this could be resolved she'd be able to deal with her personal life, and he
was determined that it would include him. He vowed to keep
the guards on her and to watch her himself as well.

"Not yet, but he's working on it," said Hayden, finally answering Nikki's question.

"What's taking so long, this is crucial," said Nikki.

"It's coming, I promise you. Now why don't we spend the
day reviewing the recent Supreme Court cases on crime and
read everybody's opinions and dissents. I think that would
be a good idea. We have files now on everyone and we
should review Burgess, Wiseman, and Cunningham. And
while we're on them, there's something you should know."

"It sounds serious."

"Well, while we've been investigating them, they've been
investigating you," said Hayden.

"You're kidding!"

"No, my sources have told me that a file's been created on you in Washington and that someone on the Court ordered it."

"That's extremely unusual," said Nikki. "Isn't it?"

"Very," said Hayden. "Suddenly everything we're involved in is unusual. I don't like it."

"I don't either, but it isn't boring," said Nikki, breaking out into a smile for the first time today. "Let's have Beverly order in from Nate 'n' Al's and we'll get to work."

They had one month to get ready for Washington.

Nikki and Hayden's life became a full rehearsal for arguments in front of the court. Mark would play Chief Justice Wiseman, and Nikki would argue. Hayden questioned her as if he were Burgess, Cunningham, Carlson, or any of the others. The trial in Washington would be similar to the trial Nikki lost in Superior Court in Los Angeles, one lawyer for each side talking to a panel of judges, instead of just one. But this time there would be no witnesses, no experts. It was all up to Nikki and how she could speak in behalf of her brief. The U.S. Supreme Court was one-on-one. Lawyer-to-lawyer, and Nikki had only thirty minutes to make her case. So did Edelman—that was the law.

It was very unusual for a lawyer as inexperienced as Nikki, no matter how talented, to wind up in front of the U.S. Supreme Court. She had heard of one young lawyer, Linda De Metrick, who worked for five years on her very first murder case trying to overturn a conviction. She ended up in front of the California Supreme Court and won, all by herself, at the age of twenty-eight. Nikki was twenty-five.

"All right, Nikki, we're set," said Mark during a break in their work. "I've made arrangements to accompany you to Washington on the twenty-seventh. We'll stay at the Willard, and I'll introduce you to some very special people so you'll feel comfortable after I leave. I'll stay several days to show you around and let you get the feel of everything. I've arranged to give you a tour of the Supreme Court while they're not in session so you'll know what it's like to stand in the room. I'll take you to the Library of Congress and show you how to use it. By the time I'm through with you, you'll feel like a native. I'm really looking forward to this."

"Mark, that's so wonderful of you, I really appreciate it. It'll be really nice spending that kind of time together, even though the circumstances are positively terrifying."

He laughed. "Don't you worry about a thing. I've got it all under control. As a matter of fact, I'm going to leave early today and go to the gym. You two are beautifully organized and this body needs a workout. My brain can rest."

Nikki and Hayden immediately huddled over a dossier on their third corroborating scientific expert and waved Mark out the door.

"It may be five o'clock for him," said Hayden, "but it's the middle of our work time."

"Okay, let's hit it."

By the time Nikki got home it was nine-thirty and she was exhausted. Too tired to cook, she popped a frozen pasta dinner in the microwave. Tossing her dirty clothes in the hamper, she brushed her teeth, washed her face, and put on cotton boxer shorts and a T-shirt. In ten minutes she was ready and so was her dinner. She pulled out her bed, got a tray, and brought the dinner to bed with her. When she sat in bed and rested against the pillow it was as if she collapsed from the world.

She looked at the computer and wondered if he was there. Tonight she was going to fight the urge to find him. She turned on the TV, not wanting to watch anything relevant, so she punched in AMC in time to catch the beginning of *An American in Paris*. Perfect, she thought, and placed the first bit of pasta primavera into her mouth. She knew she had one of the most important moments in her life coming up and she wanted to rest as much as she could.

The limo came to pick her up at six-forty-five A.M. Joely had helped her pack, and Nikki felt ready, except for the pending business in Sacramento. Hayden assured her that he would personally go up there if need be and that he'd stay on it. They planned to talk every night and every morning.

Mark had told Nikki that he wanted them to arrive two weeks before the trial was to start, which was fine with Nikki. She had never been to Washington and hoped she could concentrate on the sights as much as the case.

Mark knew her number one priority, of course, was the case, but he wanted her to see the city he loved. He had also never gone away with her, and for him it would be a real treat, almost a generational sharing. They hadn't spent time together like this since the early years in Carmel.

The car picked Mark up in Beverly Hills on the way to the airport and then deposited them at American Airlines, where they went right to the Admiral's Club and Nikki had some orange juice and a bagel. Mark just had black coffee. He knew that Nikki had never flown first-class across the country and he was happy to make that available to her. He was the King of the Frequent Flier Miles, but he would have paid for her ticket out of his own pocket if need be.

They were picked up at Dulles Airport in Virginia and driven to D.C.

Nikki thought it was amazing that there were so many states right there, touching each other. She thrilled at the sight of the Potomac River, and on the way into the city Mark pointed out the Kennedy Center sitting regally on the water, and the Watergate Apartments and Hotel nearby. Nikki was charmed going through the Georgetown area, and couldn't believe it when they stopped on Pennsylvania Avenue.

"Walk with me, Nikki," he said. "I want to show you the White House."

"It looks like a postcard sitting there. It's beautiful, but it's smaller than I had imagined," said Nikki.

"We could have stayed at the Hay-Adams Hotel across the street over there," pointed out Mark, "but we'll go there for breakfast and you can see it. I thought you'd like the Willard. It's another great old hotel with a window on the world, plus you're going to love the Occidental Grill at lunch next door. Absolutely everybody goes there."

"I trust you. I'm sure you picked everything out perfectly."

They checked into the Willard. Nikki was shown to her blue room, which adjoined the living room of Mark's suite.

"This is so incredible. I feel like I'm sleeping in the Lincoln Bedroom," said Nikki.

"This hotel has been restored to what it was when it was first built in the early 1900s. The antiques are real. Only the fax machines, refrigerators, phones, and TVs make it modern," he explained. "Why don't you unpack and rest a little bit. It's six o'clock now. I'll knock on your door at seven-thirty for dinner. We're going to a casual place, no jeans, but pants and a jacket are just fine. I'm not wearing a tie."

At eight o'clock he walked her into the Prime Rib and eyes turned.

Nikki immediately realized that he had taken her to some very in male watering hole. Right away she spotted Senator Ted Kennedy having dinner with Barbara Walters. In the left corner booth were Lynda Carter and her husband, Robert Altman; Larry King was at the first booth with Senator Dianne Feinstein and her husband, Richard Blum.

"Mark, I didn't know you were in town," said Larry, introducing everyone.

"Nikki, that's quite a case you're going to try," continued Larry. "I have my eye on it. Regardless of the outcome I want you on my show to discuss it. It's a big deal here for someone of your age to appear before the Court. You'll be big news after this."

Nikki knew that Larry thought he was complimenting her, but the last thing she wanted was more attention drawn to herself. It was bad enough in Hollywood, but once the Laverty connection got out in Washington, coupled with her work, it wouldn't be easy.

"I'm just here for about ten days, showing her around," said Mark, "but I'd love to see you for lunch, Larry. I'm at the Willard. And by the way, Senator, I'm so pleased with the good work you do for California. You are a great leader. I wish you could be President one day."

"Why, thank you, Mr. Ferguson, I'm overwhelmed."

"I had no idea you knew so many people in Washington," said Nikki when they were in the limo after dinner.

"Well, I do."

"I'm sorry, I didn't mean to say that you only knew people in Hollywood or New York; I guess my mind just didn't go beyond those two cities. I guess I thought the entertainment industry didn't reach back here."

"Almost all important cases are related to something in Washington. You'll find that out as you continue to practice. You may find yourself back here a lot if you win your case. You have no idea what's in store for you," said Mark.

Nikki noticed they weren't taking the same route back.

"Where are we going?" she said excitedly.

"I have a tradition," Mark explained. "The first night I arrive in Washington, I always go to the Lincoln Memorial and look out over everything. Even if there's a storm, I still go there. It's my favorite spot in all of Washington."

Nikki's jaw dropped when the limo let them off and she got her first glimpse of the Memorial. It rose up like a huge building silhouetted against the sky by the magnificent lights placed at all the right spots.

"I can't believe this," said Nikki. "I could never imagine anything like this."

"Let's go up the steps and say hello to Abe," said Mark.

Nikki climbed the multitude of steps, placing her hand in Mark's. When they got to the top she couldn't stop staring at Lincoln.

"Listen, I think I can hear him breathe. I think he's about to say something," she said.

"That was my reaction, too, when I saw him for the first time," said Mark.

"When was that?"

"I came the summer of my senior year in high school and I knew I would be back again and again," answered Mark. "I want you to walk all around in here, read what the walls say, but first you must turn around."

Nikki did as she was asked and couldn't believe what she saw. All of Washington stretched out before her with the reflecting pond extending as far as her eyes could see.

"Look to the right, you'll see the Jefferson Memorial. I'll show you that tomorrow as well as the Washington Monument. To the left is the Vietnam Memorial, which you will also see. But right now I want you to come sit down with me."

He walked her to the top of the stairs and they sat, facing out.

"Look straight ahead and picture a million people standing there listening to Martin Luther King's 'I Have a Dream' speech. Just sit here and feel it."

Mark was filled to capacity with the majesty of the moment. She let herself get carried away with the night air, almost hearing the voices of former leaders in the wind.

"You know, you see pictures on the evening news, you study history at school, but this makes it all real. I'll never again look at a picture or watch a news show without realizing the significance of it. I can't thank you enough."

"You're so welcome, Nikki. There's a lot I can show you all around the world. I'm sorry we haven't had more time together, but we'll just make time," said Mark, taking her hand. "I had to show you this place first, I want it to be your place of strength and refuge. Even when you are not in Washington I want you to think of this moment, close your eyes, see Lincoln and this grand edifice, and take a deep breath, and know everything will be all right."

"I promise you I will, Uncle Mark."

The next morning a car and driver showed up at the Willard at ten A.M. and the front desk rang the room.

"Our car is ready," said Mark.

"Where are we going?"

"You'll see," he answered.

The car only traveled for about five minutes up to Capitol Hill. Nikki recognized it from pictures.

The car stopped.

"Okay. Let's get out here."

Nikki got out and looked up.

"Well, there it is, Nikki, the U.S. Supreme Court."

Standing before Nikki was a huge square marble building with about a hundred steps rising up to the columns that crossed the front.

"This is the most imposing structure I've ever seen. Even the White House looks friendlier than this. I think I'm going to die," said Nikki.

"No you're not, you're going to come with me."

They bounded up the steps. Inside they passed through a metal detector.

"This looks like a museum," said Nikki, viewing the wide corridor hung with paintings of past and present Justices.

"To the right is the gift shop and the left is the court. Why don't we go directly to the court?"

"I can't handle it yet. Let's go the gift shop, please?"

"All right, Nikki, anything for you."

They walked down a long white marble corridor to a small gift shop filled with people.

"This reminds me of Disneyland, only instead of a mouse logo on everything here you have the U.S. Supreme Court. Look, there are pens, key rings, notepads, T-shirts, ashtrays, belts, coin purses, mugs. This is hysterical. I wonder who gets all this money," remarked Nikki as she watched people lining up clutching their souvenirs.

"Uncle Sam, of course. They have these shops in most of the government buildings."

"Well, I think I have to have something from here, don't you?"

"Hopefully you'll bring home a victory," said Mark.

"I hope so, too, but right now I'll settle for a pen and a notepad. Look at that. They have plastic covers over the notepaper as if it were a luxurious leather-covered pad. The seal is embossed in the plastic covers. I think I'll get a dark green one. Is there anything you want, Uncle Mark?"

"I'm fine, Nikki." He smiled. Maybe it was better for her to come in here first. She could see a humorous side to the Court now and it might be less imposing.

"Are you ready now to go into the courtroom?"

"Yes, but how can we get in?"

"They aren't in session today. I've made some calls. Don't worry."

There was a guard standing at the carved wooden doors that opened onto the court.

"Mark Ferguson."

The guard checked his list.

"Go on in, sir."

Mark opened the door for Nikki and she found herself

standing in a very cold, elegant room. The gallery was not very large. The walls and ceiling were white, including the molding. All the rows of seats were brown wood. A large United States flag was hanging from one wall. A blue velvet curtain was hanging behind the Justices' table, which was on a raised stage. A lectern was in the middle of the floor in front of the stage.

"Go stand there."

Nikki looked at Mark hesitantly.

"Go ahead, it belongs to you. You're a citizen of the United States. You have the right to speak your mind. In fact, you're one of the lucky few who ever get to this position. Stand up there and take that right."

Nikki breathed a sigh and walked over to it. She just looked at it, walked around it, and stared at it, almost paralyzed.

"Now stand there behind it. Put your hands on the sides."

She did as she was told.

"Very good, Nikki."

She looked back at him.

"No. Look at the Justices. See them there. Look them right in the eye. Now feel your feet on the ground. Feel them planted. Feel the strength in your feet and hands."

Nikki was concentrating. She felt a little less scared. She could feel her feet. She liked the feel of the wood in her hands.

"Now speak out. I want to hear you say, 'Mr. Chief Justice, Justices, I am Nikki Easterly.' C'mon, say it."

Nikki whispered it.

"I can't hear you! Say it again. Let Guy Marleaux hear you. Let your voice be his. Represent his freedom!"

"Mr. Chief Justice, Justices, I am Nikki Easterly!"

"That's it! That was terrific. Now do it again and yell it. No one will hear you. This is a soundproof room. Just scream it! Now!"

Nikki screamed it. It felt great.

"Now let that be the first thing you think of when you stand here for real next week. Promise me you won't let anything else into your head during that first second."

"I promise."

"Then you're ready."

Nikki's days from that moment on were filled with constant awe as Mark took her to see the House and Senate, have lunch in the Senate Dining Room with Dianne Feinstein, visit the National Archives and the Library of Congress.

Their mornings and late afternoons were always filled with going over the case. He had seen to it that she met a couple of Washingtonians she felt comfortable with, who could be of some assistance after he left. One was a woman named Theo Hayes, who was married to the great-great-grandson of Rutherford B. Hayes, a no-nonsense insider whom Nikki liked instantly, and the other was Gayle Lewis, wife of the CEO of National Public Radio, Phill Lewis. Both women knew the city and its politics and they promised Mark they'd keep a good watch on Nikki.

The night before Mark was leaving for Los Angeles, he arranged a dinner at the private Georgetown Club, a big power meeting place. It was on a side street, and you wouldn't even know from the front that it was a club. It looked like a three-story brick home with brick steps leading up to the front door.

Mark rang the bell and a butler answered and took their coats. They were shown into a bar/reception area that, to Nikki, now that she had been in Washington for over ten days, had the traditional Washington look: dark wood, crown molding, leather furniture, either green, navy, or burgundy carpet, antique lamps with green shades, and a fireplace. The pictures were either oil landscapes of the U.S., old photographs, or architectural line drawings. She had it down now. The carpet in the Georgetown Club was green.

She took the martini that was handed to her and let Mark show her around. First there was a little library behind the main bar. Then there was a "garden room," consisting of a gazebo, plantlike wallpaper, and white wood accents. Downstairs was a small private banquet room that looked like an English den, and above the main floor were four dining rooms, a large wood-paneled main one, a very tiny private wine cellar with a table and chairs for four, and two other private rooms of varying sizes. It was an elegant club, with captains in black tie and waiters in short white jackets.

They were shown to one of two booths in a dark corner, each one walled in with dark wood sides. The seats were damask-covered floral banquettes, extremely comfortable.

"What do you feel like tonight?" asked Mark.

"I feel like getting you to stay longer."

"Oh, Nikki, you're in great shape. You've memorized every DNA case that's come down the pike. We've rehearsed your statement over and over again. You're perfect."

The captain interrupted with the specials of the evening. "Tonight we have fresh salmon en croûte accompanied by dilled new potatoes and fresh young asparagus. We have rack of lamb with a ragout of vegetables and soufflé potatoes, or venison in a burgundy marrow reduction with fried julienne of leeks and potatoes. All entrées come with Kentucky limestone lettuce vinaigrette or our own Caesar salad made right at the table."

"Nikki?"

"I'll have the salmon, I don't eat Bambi."

"Neither do I, I'll have the salmon as well," said Mark.

"And to start," asked the captain.

"Caesar salad," replied Nikki.

"That's good for me," answered Mark, "and I'd like to see the wine list."

When the chardonnay was poured Mark raised his glass. "To you, Nikki, to a winning case, and a successful life."

"And to you, for being my guide."

Halfway through the salad Nikki told Mark how worried she really was.

"You mean about the case?"

"Yes."

"I know it's the most important thing you've ever done, but you have right on your side. Remember what I told you. You must talk directly to Wiseman, Burgess, and Cunningham on crucial points. Make sure you have eye contact with everyone at least three times, and don't make it too obvious how you're playing it, but I promise you that those men are the key. Wiseman is a square, so don't smile at him. You don't want him to think you're flirting with him. Just be sincere when you talk to him. There have been lots of stories about Cunningham. He'll probably try to see up your skirt. Just be ladylike. Burgess is a tough call. He's never been married and his life is very private. He's wedded to his work and has never had a blemish on his record. He's a lot like Souter."

"I think I've brought the right clothes, but frankly I resent that because I'm a woman I have to discuss what I'm wearing like I'm going on an audition to be one of *Charlie's Angels*."

"I'm not going to take that personally."

"Oh, I didn't mean you," she said quickly, "but I don't sit and discuss what you wear and whether or not the judge you're appearing before is male or female, gay or straight, or likes prints!"

"Very funny," Mark chuckled.

Nikki joined him in laughter for a second and then suddenly she saw him throw his fork down, grab his throat, and gasp.

"Mark, you're choking! Drink some water, here," she said anxiously.

He tried to drink, but was standing now, his napkin having fallen to the floor. He was unable to get any air and he was losing color.

"Help!" screamed Nikki as she rushed behind him and tried to do the Heimlich maneuver.

In seconds the captain was at her side. "I can do this, please move!"

He crunched Mark's diaphragm in with his forearms and a crouton popped out.

"Oh, thank God," said Nikki running to hug him. "Here, sit down, have some water."

He sat back in his chair and wiped his brow. "Boy, that was awful. I think I'll just rest here a minute and catch my breath."

"Is there anything I can get you, sir?" asked the captain.

"Oh my God, thank you so much for what you did."

"Yes, thank you, I wasn't strong enough to do it," said Nikki.

Nikki sat beside Mark on the outside of the booth. She was stroking his hand to help him relax. She was as shaken up as he was. "Would you like to go back to the hotel? It's fine with me."

"No, no, I'll be fine in a minute, I just feel clammy and I wish the pain would go away."

"What pain?" asked a very concerned Nikki.

"Where the guy pushed my chest. I guess he's really strong. Ahhhhh!" Mark grabbed his chest and fell to the floor.

Nikki knew at once that this was not a normal reaction to choking, it looked more like a heart attack to her. She screamed for help a second time in ten minutes.

"Call an ambulance, I think he's having a heart attack, hurry," she yelled, tears covering her cheeks.

She rushed back to Mark and cradled his head in her lap. He didn't look like he was breathing. She whispered in his ear, "Hang on, I'm here, you're going to be okay, the paramedics are coming. Stay with me, stay with me." Her heart was pounding so hard out of fear that she thought they might have to examine her, too.

She rode in the ambulance with him, an oxygen mask covering his face. The paramedics had administered an IV.

"Is he going to be all right? He has to be all right."

"We're doing all we can, ma'am," answered the paramedic, who looked to be about twenty-three. "We'll be at the hospital in three more minutes."

Nikki tried to put her arm around Mark's head.

"Ma'am, you can't do that. You're interfering with our work."

"I'm sorry, I'm sorry. How's he doing now?"

"Ma'am, please. He's the same."

"But what does that mean? You've got to tell me something."

"His breathing is shallow. I just don't know anything yet."

Nikki felt as if an anvil had just fallen on her chest.

An emergency crew was ready for them when they arrived. They put Mark on a stretcher and rushed him into a treatment room. The doctors were barking orders at each other.

"I'm going in!" said Nikki, trying to follow the doctors. "I have to be with him. This just can't be the end. There's so much more . . ."

Nikki felt someone's hands and a kind voice in her ear.

"I'm taking you to the waiting room now, dear, and someone will come out and talk to you as soon as we know anything."

Nikki couldn't see or hear. Once again she knew the true meaning of fear, only this time the cause was Mark, not her mother.

# Chapter 16

Hayden felt it was time to go to Sacramento himself. He was getting impatient with his sources and wanted to confront people face-to-face. He knew the information in Sacramento was crucial for Nikki. If it panned out it would give her everything she needed to put things at rest. He was worried about her, but knew she was in good hands with Mark.

When Hayden checked into the Hyatt, all he had was the name of Eddie Brinkley's parents, which was not easy to obtain. Hayden's investigator found out that Brinkley had dropped out of school in junior high, had never obtained a driver's license or a Social Security number, and practically never existed. Since Sacramento was not that big a town, when the high school records failed to yield a Brinkley, Hayden instructed his man to go down to the junior high level. There he located Mr. and Mrs. Ralph Brinkley at 103 Cherry Plain Avenue.

That was the house Hayden found himself standing in front of at six-thirty P.M. on that Thursday night. The house was definitely in the wrong part of town. It was yellow stucco, with holes in the plaster, a porch that listed to one side, cement chipped off the steps, and a withered lawn. Faded curtains hung in the windows, and lights were on in the living room.

Hayden walked up the steps, trying to hear if there were any sounds coming from the house. He thought he heard a TV in the back. He rang the bell and waited. There was no answer. He rang again. Finally he heard footsteps coming toward the door.

"Who's there?"

It was hard for Hayden to understand the words.

"My name is Hayden Chou and I'm looking for Mr. and Mrs. Brinkley."

A few seconds passed and he heard a latch being opened, then the door, and then a Japanese man in his sixties appeared.

Hayden could see that the man was pleased that Hayden wasn't Occidental.

"What do you want, please?" said the man.

"I'm looking for the Brinkleys. This was their last known address. Are you Mr. Brinkley?" he asked, trying to not be too shocked.

"No, I'm Mr. Hakata. I bought this house from them about eight years ago."

"Do you have any idea where they moved to?"

"No, sorry."

"So you don't even know if they are still in Sacramento?"

"No."

"Can you remember anything about them, like where he worked?"

"Let me see . . . I think he was a bricklayer or something like that, but I can't be positive."

"Is there anything else that you can tell me about them? Did you know if they had a son?"

"Sorry, no."

Hayden could see that any more conversation was useless.

"Well, thank you very much for talking to me."

Hayden was very disappointed as he drove back to the hotel. He just couldn't let it end there, though. He thought for a second and realized that possibly Brinkley was in a craft union, a mason association, a construction union, something. He remembered a Teamster friend in San Francisco who might be able to call somebody in Sacramento to run checks of those unions. It was a real long shot, but it was his only hope at the moment. He also thought of trying military records; if Eddie Brinkley or Ralph Brinkley had enlisted, there would at least be a record. He then decided to call Nikki and let her know what he was up to. He didn't want to give her too detailed a report because she was under so much pressure in Washington.

The next morning he made his calls right away. He then went over to a friend in the secretary of state's office to see if Eddie or Ralph had a voting address, and to have his buddy call the military departments in California.

By the afternoon he had come up with nothing—no voting record, nothing from the military, and the first three unions had nothing. There was only one more to go and all he could do was wait in frustration. Sacramento was not exactly a thrilling place. He decided to stay in his room, have room service, and watch a movie. There was no point in calling Nikki with an update yet.

His phone rang at eight A.M. with the news that a Ralph Brinkley was a member of the masonry union with an address at 607 Guthrie, on the outskirts of the city. Hayden didn't even order breakfast. He got on the phone with the concierge, got directions to Guthrie and off he went.

This neighborhood was worse than the first one. These apartments almost looked like projects in Detroit or New York. Babies were crying, laundry was hanging out windows, it was very depressing.

The Brinkleys were on the fourth floor. One look at the elevator and he decided to walk up.

The smells in the hall ranged from fresh-cooked bacon to last week's garbage. The walls were peeling green paint and the floors brown linoleum.

He reached 412 and knocked.

"Yes?" said a woman's voice.

"Mrs. Brinkley?"

"Yes, who's there?"

"I'm looking for Eddie, I'm a friend."

The door opened and he saw a sweet-looking woman in her seventies who looked as if she'd had a hard life. He could tell at once that she had been a proud woman. Her eyes were gentle, and she took off her apron and straightened her sweater when she saw him.

"Who are you?"

"My name is Hayden Chou and I'm looking for your husband."

"Why?"

"It's about your son. May I come in?"

She opened the door for him and he walked into a living room made up of unmatched, used furniture, but it was polished. There were faded doilies on the coffee table, remnants of a better life. Mrs. Brinkley tried to make the best of what she had. He thought he'd start with Ralph first.

"Is Mr. Brinkley at home?"

"He's dead."

"I'm very sorry," said Hayden.

"How do you know Eddie?" she asked cautiously.

"I don't really know him, I just want to talk to him."

"Are you a policeman?"

"No."

She perked up.

"I'm trying to locate Eddie for a friend of mine. She thinks he knew her mother a long time ago. Her mother died and she's just trying to get some family information."

"I wish I could help you, but I haven't seen him since he was thirteen years old," explained Mrs. Brinkley, relaxing just a bit. "He was a difficult boy, a real loner. I couldn't keep him in school, he kept running away. I never could figure it out because he was a bright boy. I don't know what his problem was, but it broke my heart. I'm all alone now, I could use him."

"So you don't have any idea what city he'd be in, what kind of work he might be doing?"

"I really know nothing. Ever since Ralph and I got him he was a strange kid."

"Got him?"

"We adopted him when he was a year old."

"Really," said Hayden, his interest soaring. "Did he know he was adopted?"

"Oh, yes."

"Did he ever ask who his real parents were?"

"No, he didn't."

"Did he know which adoption agency he came from?"

She paused to think.

"I'm trying to remember the name of it, let alone if I ever told him. I might have told him, I just don't know. I think it was called the Cecilia Boyd Home, now that you've asked me. Gosh, I haven't thought of them in years."

"Do you know if they exist today?" asked Hayden.

"Don't know. But they were right downtown. What's the family problem you're looking into?"

"Well, I'm not quite sure yet, but it's sort of similar about reuniting a child and a parent."

"Are Eddie's birth parents looking for him?" she asked, her concern growing.

"No, no," answered Hayden. "I'm going to try to find Eddie, Mrs. Brinkley. And when I do, I'll call you and tell you where he is. That's a promise. I will get back to you." Hayden felt sorry for this lonely woman and wanted to help.

"Thank you, you're very nice."

While the pieces of the puzzle weren't exactly coming together, at least Hayden had some pieces to work on, he thought, as he went to his car to find a phone book and the Cecilia Boyd Home.

Nikki's first call had been to Beverly when she finally got her senses back in the waiting room. Beverly was giving Nikki the names of Mark's doctors in Beverly Hills when a nurse came in.

"Hang on, Beverly. Are you looking for me? I'm with Mark Ferguson," she said, her voice rising. "Is he okay? What's happening?"

"Are you Nikki?"

"Yes. Has he said my name? You mean he's alive?"

"Yes, but we have a critical situation here. The doctor wanted me to tell you we are transferring him to cardiac surgery. There's been tremendous damage to the heart. An emergency bypass is imperative. Dr. Harry Adler is the hospital's chief cardiologist. He's taking over the case. He wants you to go to the waiting room on the fifth floor."

"What do you think his chances are?" asked Nikki tearfully.

"I never answer those questions. But we have our best team on it. I suggest you pray, if that is comfortable for you."

Then she was gone and Nikki was left in the waiting room holding the phone.

"Nikki, Nikki," Beverly was yelling.

Nikki finally heard the voice from the receiver in her hand.

"Oh, Beverly," cried Nikki. "What are we going to do?"

"You're going to call me once an hour right at the top and that's how we're going to get through this. Let's just do it an hour at a time."

"Fine. I'm switching to another floor and I'll call you with the number of that phone. Can you call Hayden for me and give him that number when I give it to you?"

The first hour was terrifying for Nikki. She just sat in the waiting room and didn't move. She didn't read, drink tea, nothing. It was the longest hour of her life.

When her watch said eleven P.M. she called Beverly on the dot.

"No news."

"Of course not, and this early no news is good news. I think you should try to get out of there. Would you be more comfortable back at the hotel?"

"No. I don't know what to do. I'm sorry. I keep repeating myself. Did you get Hayden?"

"I left an urgent message. I'm sure he'll call you soon," said Beverly.

"That's okay. One hour at a time. You call me at midnight."

Nikki went back to the couch. She loved Mark and was scared to death for him. She also was angry that someone might be leaving her, particularly someone she thought of as family, and that bothered her terribly. What if he really was her family and he died on the table without ever telling her? That was something she couldn't bear. Last on her list of worries was the court case. While it did concern her, nothing compared to Mark's life at this moment.

"Oh, Hayden, thank God," said Nikki, picking up the phone on the first ring. "Can you believe this? I'm tortured here. I can't take it. We can't lose Mark."

"I can get on a plane right now," said Hayden. "Nothing is more important to me than being with you."

Nikki was crying. "I can't take you away from what you're doing. As much as I need you here, I need the information you might find out even more. But hurry, Hayden, hurry, I'm truly freaking out here."

"Why don't you go for a walk around the hospital?" suggested Hayden. "Anything to get you moving. It's too late for you to go outside."

"Maybe I'll do that. It looks like it's still going to be hours."

"I'll stay in constant touch, Nikki. Try and feel me next to you at all times."

"That's so sweet . . . thank you."

Nikki hung up and started to walk. She didn't want to look into the rooms and see more sickness, so she kept her eyes straight ahead. She was going to go into the main lobby and look in the gift shop windows.

When she got there she automatically turned toward the front door rather than the gift shop, walking outside to get some air. Despite what was going on inside, Washington at night was peaceful and beautiful.

"Taxi?"

Nikki looked up and saw the yellow cab. She got in.

"Where to, Miss?"

"I don't know, could you just drive a little bit?"

"Sure. You must be having a bad night," said the cabby, an older man with a Russian accent.

"I'll take you by the White House. That's always nice and it's just a couple of blocks."

The car headed off in that direction and Nikki said, "No, wait. Would you take me to the Lincoln Memorial?"

"Sure, but I'm not going to leave you there, not at this hour. I'll wait for you. Will you be wanting to go back to the hospital?"

"Yes, thank you."

When the cab stopped and Nikki looked out her window she saw that the lights were still on around the Memorial. It didn't seem scary at all. There were even some people around.

"I'll be back shortly," said Nikki.

"I'll be here."

Nikki climbed the steps for the second time in her life, and this time she was alone. As she got closer to the top, Lincoln was becoming more and more of a presence. He looked so dignified and strong sitting in that chair. Nikki thought he looked like he was guarding not only the whole city and its people, but democracy for the whole world. He may even be guarding Mark and me, she thought.

She didn't want to turn around and sit on the steps as she had with Mark. She wanted to look at Lincoln, to get comfort from him. What was it Mark said when he took her here so recently? Wasn't it that he came here when he needed strength? He wanted to share that with Nikki. Nikki thought how ironic it was that his special place was now going to give her strength for him. She had never dreamed that she would need it so soon, and for Mark himself.

Don't let us down, Mr. Lincoln, thought Nikki. You've inspired people for generations both by word and deed. I'm begging you now not for myself, but for Mark. Give him the strength to fight this, to come out alive and be okay. He has put his faith in you time and again and I'm going to do the same right now. There's a reason why Mark introduced us, and it's in front of us this very moment. I have faith in you, too.

Nikki took her last look before turning around and it was almost as if she saw Lincoln breathe.

Maybe it was Nikki who finally took a breath and felt stronger.

Back at the hospital Nikki called Beverly at the top of the

hour. Two had passed and it would probably last two hours more, but she felt a little better.

"I'm going to call Meredith. I think I can do that now."

"I'll be here," said Beverly.

Nikki hated to make this kind of phone call, but Meredith had to be told. She knew Meredith and Mark had kind of a love/hate relationship, but so be it.

"Hi Meri, it's Nikki. Don't worry, I'm fine. Yes, I'm still in Washington. There's a problem with Mark. He's had a bad heart attack. They're doing emergency bypass surgery now. It'll be a few hours before we know anything."

"Nikki, I'm so sorry. I know how you love him."

"Thanks, this is very hard."

"I'm going down to St. Francis right now and say a prayer for him. Would you like that?"

"Yes, very much."

"Just know that I'm here for you, you can come home at any time, and I want you to call me as soon as you know anything," said Meredith.

"I'll call you as soon as I know anything. Bye-bye."

After what seemed an eternity, two doctors came out and told Nikki that they had done a quadruple bypass and that Mark was stable.

"Is he going to be all right?" asked Nikki.

"The next twenty-four hours are critical—there was a lot of damage. The surgery went well, but we are always cautious in these matters. Let's all just hope for a good result."

"May I see him?"

"No, he's in recovery and then he has to be in intensive care for several days. You can visit him there tomorrow if he's stabilized. I think you should go home and rest."

Nikki was still distressed.

"This isn't bad news. He survived, now go take care of yourself, please."

It was four in the morning and pitch black outside. Nikki walked out of the hospital door in a daze. When she got to the curb a cab was there.

"Ride, lady?"

It was her Russian friend.

"You are a gift," she said.

"Is everything okay?"

"It's a little better. Will you take me to the Willard?"

"With pleasure."

When Nikki got back to the Willard she deliberately used the door directly to her bedroom. She didn't want to go through the living room and see some of Mark's things. The light was blinking on her phone and the message said to call Hayden no matter what time it was.

She tossed her purse down and dialed immediately. When she heard him say "Hello," she tried to say his name but just broke down sobbing.

After a few minutes she regained her composure and told Hayden everything.

"Don't lose faith. Mark isn't going anywhere so fast. He has too much to do. I promise you. Just hold on."

"I'm trying."

"Are you up to discussing what's happening in Sacramento?"

"What's happening in Sacramento?"

"I found Eddie Brinkley's mother, and he's adopted."

"That's good news/bad news. Did she tell you where he is?"

"She doesn't have a clue."

"Terrific," she said with dismay. "What about the adoption agency?"

"I went there today, of course they won't say anything. As you know, they can't by law."

"Of course, Hayden, but you and I know there are ways to get information, whether it's a call from someone on high in Washington, and I may just have someone, or, frankly, some money can change hands."

"I know you're anxious, Nikki. I have a lot of friends, too. It's more important for you to be with Mark and try to rest. Your case starts so soon."

"Don't I know it. I can't believe the timing of all this."

"Exactly. That's why I want you to leave the adoption thing to me. I have my ways. I'll get the information. It may take a little while, but I'll get it. I don't want you to concern yourself with it. Right now Eddie Brinkley is a needle in a haystack. Even if I find him we don't have the slightest idea if he's related to you. The whole thing is a long shot."

"Yes, but at the moment, it's the only shot we have. I have to take it," said Nikki determinedly.

"And I will, I'll give it my all, I'll get him. You just worry about the Supreme Court and Mark, I think that's more than enough. Now try to get some sleep. I'll keep you posted. Say good night."

"Okay, good night, okay okay," Nikki laughed a little and hung up.

She needed to make one more call before going to sleep. Joely had really wanted her to stay in touch and Nikki hadn't. No matter how tired she was, tonight she wanted to touch base.

"Well, my God, girl, I thought you were being held hostage in the White House basement!" Joely bubbled.

Nikki filled her in on Mark immediately and Joely's mood changed.

"Wow, what a mess on your shoulders, Nikki. I won't go into anything that's happening with me. My life's totally fine compared to yours. Is there anything I can do?"

"Yes," said Nikki. "Just keep having a good time. One of us should."

"At least you haven't totally lost your spirit."

"I'm hanging in . . . and hanging up. Bye, Joely."

\* \* \*

She slept until ten and called the hospital. Mark was holding his own, but she wanted to get there as fast as she could.

She had never been in an intensive care unit. It was one large room with the patients' beds arranged like spokes in a wheel around the center desk where nurses and doctors monitored them. There were beeps of machines, the hissing of air pressure of oxygen being pumped, and the whooshing of liquids going through tubes in each patient. The quiet ringing of phones meshed with the beeps of heart monitors. Surrounding these sounds were the lights from more machines, nurses' station monitors, and automatic doors. They were sights and sounds she'd never forget as long as she lived.

Mark was in one of the beds with tubes coming out his chest, a tube down his nose, catheters by his feet, and IVs in his hands. It was startling and heartbreaking. He wasn't conscious, but the nurse told her she could go over and hold his hand. Mark was shielded from other patients by screens.

There was a chair next to the bed. She sat down and took his hand. He was still so handsome, Nikki thought, even in this condition. He was pale and weak, but his inner strength came through. She thought about all the things they had done together in the past week and a half. He shared so much with her, showed her things that meant a lot to him, gave of himself. She couldn't help but wonder if there was any other motivation to his attention and kindness on this trip. It was almost as if he had given her a present, the kind of time that, yes, a father and daughter would share together. Was he going to tell me something during dinner at the Georgetown Club? she wondered. Was this why he spent so much time here? Nikki analyzed the situation and realized that he didn't have any separate business while he was in Washington, and most of their business concerning the trial could have been condensed into a four-day trip for him rather than being broken up into work mornings, and afternoon sightseeing excursions. He obviously wanted to spend time with her.

Mark was beginning to wake up. He stared at Nikki and winked. She squeezed his hand and leaned over to kiss him on the cheek.

"Don't try to talk too much," she said. "I thank God you're all right. Boy, when you choke on a crouton, you choke on a crouton!"

He smiled as best he could.

"What day is it?" he whispered.

"It's Thursday."

"Oh, no," he said. "Your case starts next Thursday and look what I've caused."

"Don't be ridiculous, I won't hear that kind of nonsense. The important thing is that you get well. We both know I'm prepared. You should stop talking anyway. It's too hard for you. Be good, now."

"I will, but I'm worried about you. The pressure you're under is horrendous."

"I'm fine, I'm fine," she insisted.

"You know you're not alone here."

"What do you mean?" she asked.

"The guard has been with us the whole time and will continue to watch you."

"I forgot all about that guard. I thought you were talking about the new guard you introduced me to."

"Who?" he asked weakly.

"Abe Lincoln. I saw him while you were in surgery. He didn't let us down," said Nikki, placing her hand over his.

A tear fell from Mark's eye.

Nikki stopped herself and said, "Will you listen to us? You don't want me to worry about you, I don't want you to worry about me, we sound like family."

"That's what we are, Nikki."

She froze in her seat and cautiously asked, "What exactly

do you mean by that?" Did she dare think that the moment had finally come?

"I love you like a daughter, you know that," said Mark.

Again Nikki didn't know what he meant. What was he trying to tell her?

"Mark—"

"I know what you want, Nikki. I know what you've been trying to ask me. I wish to God it were true. I wish you were my daughter, but you're not. The truth is, your mother was pregnant with our child a couple of years before you were born. She lost it in the first five weeks. I was devastated, and it affected our relationship. When she became pregnant with you, she was engaged to me, but it was in name only by that time. I'm so sorry, but there is no way that I'm your father, at least biologically, but I hope you'll consider me to be in every other way. I look upon you as our child."

His voice was getting weaker and weaker and it was a strain for him to talk, but Nikki could see that this was something he needed to tell her. He drifted back to sleep, the medication taking over.

This was not the news Nikki wanted to hear. She loved Mark, and she was angry with him for not being her father. She felt terrible that she was angry, but she couldn't help it. And what was that about his being devastated at the loss of a baby, she asked herself. He didn't mention that Lauren was upset. Did he just forget, or did Lauren not care? Maybe she wanted to be through with Mark. Nikki would never know, and that upset her, too. She was getting so tired of not knowing, and she felt great disappointment at Mark's revelation, because deep down she had always wished he'd been her father.

But there was another emotion creeping up on her. As she sat there looking at Mark, she knew he loved her. Her feelings for him were very strong. It was confusing, because for so long she wanted him to be her father. But he was family, and she could feel herself letting the fear and anger drift away. In its place was a softening, a love for him. It was the first time she really allowed herself to feel love. She was so protective, so guarded because of her childhood trauma, that she buried everything. Maybe it was time she started opening up. At least this was a beginning.

Hayden's experience at the Boyd adoption agency was exactly what he thought it would. be. The records were sealed, they wouldn't open them, he could go to court, all the usual interferences. He was prepared for it, but he just wanted to at least try to go through official channels. What he needed now was someone very high up in state or federal government in the children's services area, who simply through friendship, not pressure, could get the records opened.

He decided to return to Los Angeles and make the phone calls. There was no telling how long it would take, and there was no need to wait in Sacramento. He could always get on a plane again and come back.

When he walked into the office utter chaos reigned. He rushed to Beverly's area.

"Relax, relax, everything's fine," she said to him before he even asked anything.

"What about Mark?"

"Intensive care, still hanging in, looks pretty good. That's where Nikki is now. We can't call in there, but she'll be calling me in about forty minutes. I'll put you right on, don't worry."

Hayden went down the hall to his office to try to concentrate. He was in a state of shock about Mark, nervous for Nikki because the timing couldn't be worse. He badly wanted to get on a plane to Washington, but Nikki wanted him to continue on the Brinkley matter, so he placed five phone calls to friends in various state and federal government offices. He was determined to move forward on this as quickly as possible.

By the end of the day, all five had returned his calls and were on the case. He felt confident that within a few hours he would have the name of Brinkley's parents and, hopefully, be able to see them or at least talk to them by phone.

"Well now, look who's sitting up," said Nikki when she went to Mark's room on Sunday.

"Yes, I'm a little better. I wish I were stronger. I want to be there for you outside the courtroom."

"Nonsense. You just got out of intensive care. How do you like your top-priority floor? You have hot and cold running nurses."

"But I'm worried about you. I feel so bad that I've placed this burden on you. You have enough to worry about," said Mark.

"Now just stop it. I'm going to be fine and so are you. The firm is fine. Don't even ask anything. I just want you to relax. I'll take care of the war."

"Is tomorrow your first day? I'm sorry. I've lost track of time."

"You're excused. You were a little busy," said Nikki trying to get a smile out of him. He looked so weak and helpless. "And, no, the case won't be heard until later in the week. Don't worry, you, Abe, and I will do our best. Now you just rest. I'll be back tomorrow."

"I love you, Nikki," said Mark.

"I love you, too," she said, and felt good saying it.

She hadn't been quite sure what to do about the hotel. When Mark was hospitalized there was no reason for her to be in a two-bedroom suite all by herself. The office was paying for it originally because Mark was there. Ordinarily, the client would pay for the lawyer's expenses, but in this case Marleaux had no money. Nikki decided that the prudent thing to do would be to pack Mark's things and move them to the closet in the living room, and give up Mark's bedroom. Nikki could have moved everything to her room and given up the living room as well, but she decided that she could benefit from the use of the living room as a place to just get away. The pressure was unspeakably awful, and when she arrived back after the visit with Mark, she just collapsed on the bed.

Hayden was in the office early Friday morning because he knew that Federal Express deliveries were at ten o'clock. It was nine-thirty A.M. now and he kept looking at his watch. He had a funny feeling in his stomach and couldn't quite figure out why. His source in Washington pulled the right strings and had the Brinkley adoption records photocopied by late afternoon. No one wanted the copies faxed. It was better to get them through FedEx, and Hayden was more than ready. He only hoped that they would lead him somewhere. He could tell in his phone conversation with Nikki that she was becoming obsessed with it and he wanted to just rule Brinkley out or in and get on with it.

"The envelope you wanted is here, sir," said the voice on the intercom.

"I'll be right out."

Hayden walked quickly to the receptionist area and took the envelope. He checked the address and knew this was what he was waiting for. He turned and went back into his office, opening the envelope on the way.

Sitting back in his desk he read, "Cecilia Boyd Adoption Home, Brinkley adoption, November 13, 1944. A one-year-old white male, adopted by Mr. and Mrs. Ralph Brinkley, 103 Cherry Plain Avenue, Sacramento. Child has no living relatives, placed in foster home at six months upon the death of parents in an automobile crash. Parents' name: Daniel and

Louise Burgess. Baby's Given Name: Daniel Reichert Burgess."

Swell, thought Hayden, another dead end, literally. With no living relatives there was nowhere to turn. He put the report down on his desk and turned his chair toward the wall. He put his head against the chair and sighed, worrying about how he could break this news to Nikki.

He continued to think, trying to find another route to search out Brinkley. Of all the luck, he thought to himself, dead parents, no relatives. But what if Eddie had gone back to his real name? Hayden thought it might be worth checking it out, so through his office computer he hooked up to the main terminal in his secret computer lab and ran Daniel Burgess through every possible area. He came up with nothing.

He turned his chair around again and faced the report, thrumming his fingers on it. His eyes looked down at his thumb because he inadvertently slammed it a little hard on the desk. Just then his eyes caught the name once more and locked on it: Burgess. Burgess? he thought. It couldn't be. How funny, it was a name one didn't hear that much, and yet here it was again, surfacing after Nikki had spent so much time gathering information on Justice Burgess. What a funny coincidence, he thought, as he put the report in his center drawer and called his secretary in to start returning phone calls left over from yesterday.

As the day wore on, he found his concentration slipping away from the work at hand, and back to the Burgess coincidence. Who was it who said, "There are no coincidences," he thought.

He picked up the phone.

"Beverly, would you go in Nikki's files and bring me the one on Eric Burgess, please? Thank you."

A few minutes later Beverly brought it to him and he shut his door.

It was a very complete, straightforward file on Burgess's speeches, his cases, pictures of him being nominated and sworn in, and his official biography. It seemed that Burgess started college at Northwestern at a later age than usual, twenty-two. There was no mention of his high school or hometown, or birthplace, which Hayden found odd. Was it just another coincidence that it was left out?

That night he went into his computer and hooked up with Northwestern's database. He could do that with any school or institution because his equipment was so powerful. Most schools now had very large databases and certainly articles about a famous alumnus like Burgess would be found in the college newspaper.

It wasn't easy to get to the information, as he had to code in a lot of inquiries, which took about an hour. Finally he was connected and began to search. He found the same bio that was in the folder he had, he downloaded some pictures taken when Burgess went back to be honored, obtained copies of speeches given by Burgess, and then he began to scan the college newspaper. Way down at the bottom of a story on one of Burgess's visits in the mid-1980s, there was the following sentence: "Burgess's rise as a jurist and his success in college was a very unusual occurrence considering he never graduated from high school and took an equivalency exam."

Hayden could have sworn that Mrs. Brinkley commented that her son quit school in junior high.

Fortunately he had brought his notes home with him and he checked. He was right! Now the coincidences were beginning to concern him. He had to decide whether or not to tell Nikki of his suspicions. She was right there in Washington about to start arguing in front of Burgess! The implications were mind-boggling. And wasn't Burgess the one who was investigating Nikki?

He was now in a desperate hurry. He needed the Northwestern records, and they would have to be accessed by a secret code known only to the university. He had to get that code to see what Burgess wrote on his application to get in. He had a feeling that Burgess would have no traceable past before the high school equivalency exam.

Hayden was filled with a sense of dread. His body went cold as he tried to chase the thought out of his mind. What if Burgess really was Brinkley, and his obsession with Lauren was out of control years ago? What if Burgess's prints matched those at Lauren's murder scene?

By noon the next day he had enough information to book himself to Washington. All the pieces were coming together and it was unfair to keep Nikki in the dark any longer.

He took the red-eye and met Nikki at her hotel at eight A.M. Sunday morning.

"I know there's something up. I could tell in your voice. It's Brinkley, isn't it?" said Nikki, as she opened the door in her robe.

Hayden had placed his luggage in the corner and sat on the living room couch.

Nikki was seated with her orange juice and bagel.

"Hayden, you're scaring me, there's something wrong. You're like steel. I can't stand it, you've got to tell me. Is Eddie my father? Did you find him?" she said anxiously.

"We'll know if Eddie's your father when we take blood tests, but it's certainly possible that he is."

"Then you've spoken to him. Will he take the tests? Where is he? Can I meet him?"

Nikki's words came tumbling out. Hayden could see how excited and hopeful she was getting.

"Come sit closer to me, I'm just going to tell you from the beginning everything I've found out and the conclusions I've drawn. It isn't what you expected and it will have an impact on you concerning the Marleaux case."

"What! I don't understand. What's going on? This is killing me."

"As you know, Eddie Brinkley was adopted, so Brinkley isn't his real last name. I also found out that Eddie didn't graduate from high school and seemed to disappear off the map. You know I was pulling strings to get the original adoption records."

"Yes, yes," said Nikki impatiently.

"Well, his real name isn't Eddie, it's Daniel."

"Right."

"And his real last name is Burgess."

"Yes."

Hayden waited for it to sink in.

"No . . . wait . . . You can't mean that—I mean there must be lots of Burgesses. What are you saying? Have you investigated further? What are we into here?"

"Just bear with me a second. I couldn't find any information on Daniel Burgess, but, like you, I just thought I'd take a shot at Burgess. Actually, it's not that common a name. I knew that Justice Burgess went to Northwestern and I got into their computer. It seems their famous alum, Eric Burgess, took a high school equivalency exam to get in, and has no known past before college."

"Good God, are you sure?"

"Yes I am, so far, but we've got to get more, Nikki, and that's going to be up to you."

Nikki grabbed his hand when she grasped the enormity of what was happening. She didn't feel cold, she didn't feel anger, she was numb. She was speechless for about thirty seconds.

She slowly began to speak. "What do you mean up to me? I'm going to have to face that man on Thursday. This is unbelievable, I don't know what to feel. If he is Brinkley, then he's probably known all along who I am, and he knows he's my father."

"We don't know for sure yet, Nikki, that he's your father. We need to do tests."

Nikki was too far gone theorizing for Hayden to get her attention.

"If he's the one who killed Lauren it must have been because she wouldn't acknowledge him. We've read the police and autopsy reports on her murder. We have the other samples. What if his match there, too? If he did it, Burgess is an insane, vicious pervert. Oh my God, Hayden, how on earth do I deal with this?"

"That's why I didn't want to come here until I was positive you needed to know this information."

"And how am I going to concentrate? I can't let Marleaux down!"

Hayden put his hands on her shoulders. "I know you've been under the most horrible pressure. Not only are you arguing in front of the U.S. Supreme Court, but you've had to handle Mark all alone. To now have to tell you about the possible Brinkley-Burgess connection is torture for me. I've just added yet another unspeakable layer of pressure."

"This is beyond belief."

"Nikki, you are a professional and you'll do your job, but there's something else you need to do."

"What?"

"We need to get hair and nail samples from Burgess."

"Oh sure, I'll just call him up, tell him I'm moonlighting as a barber/manicurist. It'll work great," said Nikki sarcastically.

Hayden just looked at her. "Think clearly, Nikki."

"Okay . . . maybe I can call up Theo and Gayle. They know everything. Surely one of them could find out where Burgess gets his hair cut."

"Good, call them right now."

Nikki disappeared into the bedroom for ten minutes, and

then returned saying, "They'll find out. We should know in thirty minutes."

"Great. Now, assuming we'll get that information, we'd better pray that Burgess has scheduled an appointment or we'll have to just pay off his guy to go to his office, do his work, and get the samples."

"Then what's next?" asked Nikki.

"I have a fingerprint for Brinkley, and my sources at the FBI are getting one for Burgess. As soon as we get the samples we'll set a session in the FBI lab and we'll learn everything."

"That's a good scenario, but we only have three days to pull this off."

The phone rang and Nikki picked it up.

"You're kidding? Are you sure? Unbelievable. Do you know him? Truly God is watching over us. Can your husband make the call? That's great. We have to go along, though. I know we'll have to hide. This is too much. If it weren't so serious I might be amused by what we're about to do. Call me back as soon as it's set up."

"What is it? From your end of the conversation it sounded like we've been blessed with the luck of the gods," said Hayden.

"We have. Theo's husband goes to Burgess's barber. He called the shop and the son answered the phone. It seems that his father is using Sundays to show the kid how to cut hair. The barber is apparently very savvy in Washington high jinks and he didn't bat an eye when Hayes asked when Burgess was coming in and asked for an appointment at the same time. I swear to you that Burgess is going in there at five o'clock tomorrow."

"Amazing, it's too pat," said Hayden.

"Not when you have Abe Lincoln on your side," said Nikki.

"Would you care to explain that?"

"Too much time, just trust me. Anyway, Theo is going to go in with her husband, Tommy. You and I will be sitting in a car on a side street. While Tommy gets his hair cut, he and Theo will distract Burgess and Theo will grab some hair. The manicurist is a cousin of Theo's manicurist. They all came over from Vietnam. She'll insist that she give Burgess a free manicure and slip Theo the nail samples."

"This sounds like an old episode of *Moonlighting*," said Hayden.

"Let's hope Theo and Tommy are as clever as Cybill and Bruce. There are no retakes."

"Why Nikki, how Hollywood of you," teased Hayden.

"I know you're trying to keep this light at the moment," said Nikki, "but if I focus on all this I'll barely be able to breathe."

Nikki paused and looked at him. "Thank you, thank you for all this work, for everything it means to me."

"I'd do anything for you, Nikki," said Hayden, taking her hands in his. He leaned over and kissed her lovingly.

Nikki was glad he was with her.

It seemed like an eternity until Nikki and Hayden found themselves in the car on M Street. Nikki ducked as she saw Burgess go into the ground-floor shop in the small office building.

"I'm a nervous wreck," said Nikki.

"Let's just hope that Theo and Tommy aren't. It shouldn't take them very long. Did you say she was coming out with the hair samples first just in case anything went wrong in the nail area?"

"Yes. She wanted to be sure that we at least had something," said Nikki.

In fifteen minutes Theo Hayes rounded the corner in a pale pink Escada suit, pink wide-brimmed hat, and matching heels.

"This is so much fun. I'm having the best time," she said giggling.

"Did you get anything?" asked Nikki.

"Of course," Theo said, opening her bag to reveal a Kleenex filled with hair. "Isn't this divine? I'm going back for round two. He doesn't want to stay because he didn't schedule the time for it. When I left, the manicurist was telling him she'd just buff his nails in five minutes. I think he was buying it. She knows what to do."

In about forty-five minutes they were in front of the FBI.

"Are you sure they won't leak any of this stuff?" asked Nikki.

"They've got the best lab in town. It's fine, they're expecting us. We'll be locked away with a friend of a friend. He can be trusted."

"Okay," said Nikki.

The guard cleared them and they took the elevator down. Hayden didn't talk in the elevator, and Nikki noticed there was a camera in there.

When they got out he whispered, "I can't tell you what a fantasy this is for a computer freak. To be able to touch the keyboards of the FBI computer . . . well, that's really something. I just wish the circumstances were better."

They knocked on the door marked "C" and an older man in a lab coat answered.

"Name please?"

"Hayden Chou and Nikki Easterly."

"Come in. I'm Dr. Schwab. Do you have the samples?"

Nikki gave him the hair and nail samples, still in the tissue.

He walked into another room and came back without the tissue. "It's being worked on now. We can only do preliminary findings because of the time problem. No RFLP testing at all, just regular tests for matches and then PCR."

"What about that print I asked you to get?" asked Hayden.

"We have it. Do you have the print from your end?"

"Yes, it's right here."

"Let me take it and we'll code them both into the computer. As soon as it's coded in from the next room, I'll connect in here," explained the doctor. "This should take no time at all. Why don't you have a seat behind me and just watch the screen. I'll be right back."

Nikki was fascinated to watch the images start to come up on the screen, little lines that eventually made a print.

"There it is," said Hayden.

"Now let's check and see if the new one is ready." The doctor pressed some keys and waited. A split screen came up with Hayden's copy of the print at Lauren's crime scene on the left side.

Nikki's eyes were glued to the right side of the screen where Burgess's print would come up. She saw the beginning of the lines, but it was not an instant process. It was a line at a time.

The more lines that appeared, the more it seemed to match the other print. A sickening feeling was overtaking her as it became obvious there was a match.

"Well, there you have it, a perfect match," said the doctor. "I hope that helps you," he asked pleasantly, not knowing the import of this.

"Yes, thank you very much," said Hayden. "I appreciate your doing this and keeping our confidence. Would you please keep these records confidential and in a safe place. We will be needing them. Now how long will it be before we can have the DNA results on the hair and nails?"

"That will take us all night. I suggest you go back to your hotel and wait for our call in the morning."

Hayden knew to get Nikki out of there as fast as he could. Once they were out the door she was running as fast as she could toward the park. He chased after her at top speed, listening to her fight back screams. He caught up to her as she was holding on to a tree and gagging.

"I want to call President Allingham," Nikki said when she could talk.

"We have many choices here and need to think it through. It's a California case," said Hayden. "We have jurisdiction."

"Yes, but it's a national figure. If not Allingham, then we go to the FBI right now," said Nikki.

"And what are you going to say? All we know is that Burgess is Brinkley. That isn't a crime. We need to compare the DNA results."

"But you can take my blood and its DNA and compare it to his hair to see if he's my father?" said Nikki wildly.

"Yes, but let's take this one step at a time. There's too much going on. It's too easy to make mistakes or jump to conclusions," cautioned Hayden.

Nikki looked at him and spoke as forcefully as she was able.

"There isn't a doubt in my mind that this man is my father, and probably a murderer. I don't know how I'm going to prove it, but I'm going to talk to him alone somehow. I just have to, if it's the last thing I do. Everything's at stake."

"And the Marleaux case? Are you going to blow the whistle now on Burgess, dismantle the court, and then go back again to hear it later? Or are you going to wait, sit on the Burgess evidence, and try the case appropriately? You know darn well if you do anything you'll blow everything."

Nikki was calmer now. "Okay. You're right, we'll wait but then we nail him. I'm going to get to him, I tell you."

By Wednesday afternoon, the day before Nikki was to go to court, she and Hayden had the results of the test. Everything was a match. Not only was Eric Burgess Eddie Brinkley, but his DNA matched that at Lauren's murder scene.

"I don't even know what to say," said Nikki, "except I've got to know now definitely if he's my father."

"That can be done in half a day. Now we have a decision to make. We have the results and it's time to go to the police."

"I can't believe how calmly we're discussing this. The murderer of my mother is sitting on the Supreme Court! My God, this is incredible, but we can't go to the police yet. I've waited my whole adult life to do something important in law. I have a chance to save a man's life and get a ruling that can save other people's lives. If I can just get up the courage to go into that courtroom, in front of Burgess, I know I can win it. I must make that my first priority."

"What if, God forbid, Burgess has been following you? His sources are also very high up. What if he knows you know? You could be putting yourself in a very dangerous position going into that court."

"Hayden, I don't think he's going to go for me in front of the court. We don't know what he knows. He would never risk anything like that. I think what I'd like to do now is go see Mark. Maybe he can give me some help, but I can't tell him anything. His heart's too fragile."

"Sure, let's go visit him," said Hayden.

Mark's color was much better, many of the tubes had been removed, and he was sitting up a bit.

"Nikki, darling, and Hayden, how good to see you. Well, tomorrow's the big day."

"Don't I know it!" said Nikki.

"How nervous are you?"

"More than you could ever know."

"Here, sit down on the bed next to me, Nikki. You remember what I told you about planting your feet and speaking up? Well, that's just technique and you'll do it right away. What isn't technique is heart. You have the case law, you know what to say, but it's important to project how you feel. Your mother would be so proud if she knew what you were doing."

Nikki felt strongly at that moment that somehow Lauren knew that her own daughter had found her killer. She wished she could share it with Mark, and it broke her heart. But in time he would know.

"You just go in there and be yourself, Nikki," Mark was continuing as she tuned back in. "This is a performance, and you inherited that gift from your mother, too. Go out there in the spotlight and use it."

It was so dark she could only feel his form. As he lay on top of her she heard her breathing change. He was heavy. His hands forced hers above her head and he growled, "You do everything I say." "Yes, Master," she heard herself saying. His other hand held her head to the side so she couldn't see his face no matter how hard she struggled. She felt the silk cord go around her hands, but instead of tying them to the bedpost she felt herself being twisted around so suddenly her head was at the footboard. "No," she tried to scream, pictures of her mother's death flashing in her mind. Did she catch a look at his face? It seemed to be hazy, just a black hole, she couldn't make it out. "One foot, you get only one foot," he said as her right foot was tied down. "You've been very bad. You have to be punished." She heard him unzip himself, and she was totally helpless. He could do anything.

"Oh, you're panting now, are you, you whore. That's how bad you want it. Well, you can't feel me yet and I'm so big."

Nikki was struggling against the cords, desperately fighting for freedom. "Help!" she tried to scream but he thrust upward with his body, knees on either side of her head now, threatening to fill her mouth up down to her throat. Her cries were stifled by his taut dangerous body.

"Master, I'll do anything," she said, trying a different approach.

The Master knew she meant it. He knew she wanted him, no matter how afraid she was, and he was going for it . . . going to make her crazy, plunging in and out of whatever he wanted until she screamed she could take it no more. And then he'd kill her.

"Stop!"

The lights were on and Nikki felt Hayden's arms shaking her awake. "Are you all right? Are you having one of those nightmares?"

Nikki looked at him, still in a dreamlike state. He was holding her, speaking to her, stroking her, calming her down. She barely heard him say something about court in four hours. All she remembered before she went back to sleep was Hayden sitting by her bed, holding her hand. She didn't want to think anymore.

The wake-up call came at seven A.M. Nikki's eyes shot open like rockets. Hayden was just waking up in the chair next to her bed.

"How are you doing? That must have been a very bad dream," said Hayden.

"Yes. I want to forget about it, please."

"All right. Why don't I order some breakfast while you shower. We have ninety minutes to get to court."

"There's something I want you to do for me," said Nikki. Hayden nodded.

"When we walk into court I want you to give this note to the clerk and tell him to put it in Justice Burgess's office as the session starts. That way I know he won't have read it before he sees me."

"What's in it? I'm worried about you."

"I'm a big girl, Hayden."

"Okay, I give up. I'll do anything," said Hayden.

Nikki remembered those words from her dream but said nothing.

Nikki didn't care. She had more important things to think about. Putting on her light beige Donna Karan with the cream silk blouse and the camel and white Chanels, she thought the outfit was nondescript tasteful, not sexy, but pretty. It was businesslike but not barracuda-ish. She thought it was perfect. All her papers were ready in her briefcase the way she had placed them the night before.

They walked through the lobby at eight o'clock, got into the first cab they saw, and she said, "U.S. Supreme Court."

God bless Mark for taking me to this building earlier, she thought to herself as she got out in front of the hugely imposing structure. Because she had seen it before, the color paintings of each Justice that lined the foyer didn't intimidate her. Hi, guys, she thought to herself, trying to force bravado so she wouldn't be too scared.

Hayden just walked alongside, realizing she needed silence.

"Counselor," said Noah Edelman when he saw Nikki approach the waiting area outside the courtroom.

"Mr. Edelman, how nice to see you again," said Nikki extending her hand.

A few photographers were watching and she liked the idea of the videotape news cameras getting the shot of her reaching out. Nikki was pleased that it was not a circus atmosphere, just a reasonable amount of press covering a trial.

At eight-fifty-five A.M. the courtroom doors opened. She had no idea whether Edelman had ever been inside.

She took her place at the petitioner's table and laid out her notes, and saw Hayden deliver the note. At exactly nine A.M. the nine black-robed Justices filed out and took their places in front of the blue curtain, each seated at the same long solid wood table. As they sat there, they looked to Nikki like a painting come to life, she was so familiar with each of their faces.

Nikki couldn't take her eyes off Burgess. He appeared to be staring at her. Nikki thought it was a glare, actually, more than a stare. She knew that Cunningham, Burgess, and Wiseman knew that she had checked up on them. Could Burgess have found out about Hayden's investigation? She was getting extremely nervous.

She focused on Burgess's eyebrows. Hers were always a slightly different shape from Lauren's. It was a subtle difference, because the two looked so much alike. Nikki's eyebrows were less curved and they went up at the ends. Was it her imagination or did Burgess's go up, too? She was fighting hard for concentration and got it back just in time.

Wiseman sat in the center and spoke first.

"Good morning."

"Good morning, Mr. Chief Justice," Nikki and Edelman said together.

"Is the petitioner ready?"

"Yes, Your Honor."

"Respondent?"

"Yes, Your Honor."

"You may begin, then."

Nikki stood up, took a deep breath, and approached the lectern. The wood felt familiar as she placed her hands on it. It felt like a friend. In one second she felt her feet planted, and in a booming voice, and in honor of Mark she said, "Mr. Chief Justice, Justices, I'm Nikki Easterly." Her voice was strong, proud, and clear. She felt that Mark could hear her.

"Your Honor, I call the court's attention to the findings by Barry Scheck and Peter Neufield, respected experts on DNA, who have repeatedly and successfully argued that exculpatory results are totally accurate and should be admitted. I again refer to the Kotler case, on which they worked eleven years to get the evidence admitted and accepted by the courts. They finally got DNA admitted in that crucial case, which proves my point of exculpatory acceptance conclusively. They have even started something called the Innocence Project, specifically designed to use DNA to free innocent people."

Nikki was not looking at Burgess now. She simply couldn't. After she was through, during Edelman's thirty minutes, she could stare all she wanted.

"These are tricky times now. Technology and the law are learning to live with each other. New rulings are being made every day. But this country stands for freedom, not wrongful incarceration. We are not proud of the innocent people burned at the stake. If we could bring them back to life we would. Well, here's a chance to do just that. You can rule to admit accurate scientific evidence that proves that Guy Marleaux was wrongfully imprisoned. On behalf of Guy Marleaux, and all the Guy Marleaux wrongfully in prison, I implore you to give him back his freedom, and move us into the next century."

Nikki paused and gathered her strength. She looked right at Burgess.

"Murderers are despicable people who should be caught and given the most severe punishment possible. Guy Marleaux is an innocent man, and you have the proof before you. I thank you for listening to me, and I pray for Guy Marleaux and your wisdom. Thank you."

"The Court recognizes the respondent."

Noah Edelman walked confidently to the podium.

"Mr. Chief Justice, Justices. You have my brief before you and I know you've studied it carefully. You are aware that in only fifteen states out of fifty is DNA admitted on a regular basis. My cases cited proved beyond a reasonable doubt that DNA is still too new to have a universal ruling. It should be left to the states . . ."

Nikki wanted to shout out, I know that, you moron. I'm not asking for a universal ruling. Don't confuse the issue. This is only one case that we're dealing with. She hated that there was no rebuttal. She knew Edelman was going to go by the book and claim that "the case was prosecuted diligently and carefully" and there was no need to change a thing. Diffusing it with the states' rights issue was always a convenient cover for the more conservative Justices to hide under. She hated Edelman for using it.

But she was happy with her whole argument and her performance.

As Edelman droned on she allowed herself to look at Burgess again. He was listening carefully to Edelman, taking some notes. She wondered what he was really thinking and she decided to not take her eyes off of him for a second. She just wanted to see if he would sneak a look at her. He did. Nikki and Burgess were glaring at each other. Maybe it was Burgess, she thought who urged that this case come to court, just so he could see her.

It seemed to Nikki that Edelman took forever to complete his argument, but in fact, it was of course only the allotted thirty minutes.

Wiseman banged his gavel and said, "Thank you both. We will get back to you with our ruling." Wiseman got up to leave and Burgess was right with him.

Nikki watched them disappear behind the curtain. Only her desire to get a verdict for Marleaux kept her from following them.

"Let's get to it now," said Burgess, walking along with the others.

"Can't we even get a lunch break?" asked Cunningham.

"Why don't we just go in and start. I'll have lunch brought in," said Wiseman.

"That's great. I believe this is an easy one. The guy deserves a new trial. DNA should be admitted, don't you all agree?" said Burgess.

"Could we get to the room first?" asked Cunningham. "I'd like to at least sit down. And I'd like to consider the Constitution, if you don't mind. Why are you pushing this, Burgess, do you have somewhere to go? You seem like you're in a big hurry."

"Burgess is right," said Wiseman. "The truth is it's about time for the Supreme Court to issue a universal ruling on DNA. We all know that, and this case fits all the requirements. It'll be a quick vote for the petitioner. I'm sure it will take us a lot longer to write our opinions, God knows."

"Fine then. Let's take a fifteen-minute break and convene back in the conference room, and get it over with," said Burgess.

There were more photographers and video cameras than usual outside the building and also in the hall. They knew when news was coming.

"How do you think it's going to go, Miss Easterly?"

"I'm very hopeful."

"What are you going to do if you win? You'll be the youngest person ever to have done such a thing."

"I'm not going to think about that now. We'll find out at the end of the year. I'm just going to do my job," replied Nikki.

After they had passed the reporters Nikki said, "Hayden, you stay here, please. There's something I have to do," and she turned and went back into the courtroom.

Hayden didn't like the sound of that at all: he was determined to follow her.

The courtroom was empty now and she knew what she had to do. She just had to get to Burgess. She couldn't let it go. In one second she shot behind the bench where the Justices sat and found herself in the hall. She was alone and assumed the Justices were in another meeting.

She was determined to get to Burgess's office. Thanks to Mark and the tour, she knew about the back hall, so she could avoid the secretaries. Her heart in her throat, she slipped around the corridor and found herself in the much narrower hall. She started walking past doors and names, and then she saw "Burgess."

Inside, Eric Burgess was holding Nikki's note:

*I need to speak to you about Lauren Laverty and extenuating circumstances.*

# Chapter 17

A strange smile broke out on his face. When Burgess saw her in court he couldn't believe how much she looked like Lauren up close. Christ, she even smelled like her. It was that damn Fresh Love. Did she wear it just to make him crazy or was it a coincidence? There was no way she could know his secret. It would be impossible . . . But this note?

Nikki stopped for a second before putting her hand on the doorknob. What would she find? Did she really want him to be there? What would she say to him? Was he really her father? She had never felt the anxiety in her life that she was feeling now. But she was also filled with a strange bravado. There were so many emotions and thoughts that her mind felt as if a buzz saw was running through it.

She thought for a second and realized that if she froze up at his presence she could always just thank him for hearing her case and try to get out. Taking a deep breath, she opened the door.

Their eyes met.

"Hello, Ms. Easterly, I've been expecting you."

His attitude was arrogant and she didn't like it. She was beginning to fill with rage toward him but held it in check.

"You'd better come in and shut the door," he said. "Now what's this all about? This is highly irregular. You are not supposed to make contact with a Justice while you have a case pending. That's first-year law school stuff. You should be brighter than that. I should call security and have you reported immediately."

Now that he was face-to-face with her, only inches separating them, he was dizzy because it was Lauren come back to life.

"That really wouldn't be a good idea," said Nikki, trying not to let him bully her. "We have a lot to talk about."

"I don't think so. I think you'd better leave," said Burgess, taking a step forward to usher her toward the door.

Nikki sidestepped him and walked farther into the room. She was at the front of his desk.

"You don't have any pictures up, Justice Burgess. Don't you have any family?" asked Nikki, noticing how expectionally neat the brown and green office was.

"No I don't. There's no room in my life for that. Now you're being impertinent and you're going to have to leave."

"But, sir, we have so much in common: for instance, our connection to movie stars."

"Stop playing games, you already mentioned Lauren Laverty in your note. We all know she was a star. It's no secret you're her daughter. Congratulations and goodbye." Burgess picked up the phone and started to dial.

"I wouldn't do that . . . Mr. Brinkley," said Nikki coldly.

Burgess put down the phone, sat at his desk and opened his front draw slightly. Nikki could see his eyes change color almost to black. But she couldn't stop now, she just couldn't.

"We have proof that you murdered Lauren Laverty. You fell in love with her while she was on the road, she dumped you and you couldn't handle it. You were the ultimate groupie, Mr. Brinkley. Rafael Sanchez was framed and you know it."

"Your naïveté amazes me, Nikki. You couldn't have proof. Now back off or I'll have you disbarred."

"Well, for your information the DNA shows that—"

"Hold it right there," shouted Burgess. "What are you trying to do, get me to vote your way by barging in my office and discussing DNA behind the court's back? Now get out of here or I'll see to it that Marleaux spends the rest of his life behind bars."

"Nonsense. Stop trying to divert attention," Nikki retorted. "Maybe I should have you disbarred. You don't stand a chance here. The FBI has it all, your hair, your nails, we can get your blood but we don't need it. The DNA samples from Lauren's murder scene match you, you bastard. And while I'm at it, you son of a bitch, you are my father. I just know it. The DNA will prove that, too."

"Young lady, you are insane. I have no idea what you are talking about, and this time I'm not going to put down the phone."

"Go ahead, call everyone, because if you don't I will. How do you think this story is going to look in tomorrow's *Washington Post*? Don't think I haven't already spoken to them or to the police," said Nikki.

Burgess got up and wandered over to a credenza with a complete computer system, CD-ROM, scanner, laser printer, speakers, and a laptop.

No wonder there are no papers around, everything is in the computer, he's into technology, thought Nikki. That interest might help his belief in DNA, she thought, letting her mind go back to the Marleaux case for a second.

The Justice picked up a pen from the laptop and began to finger it gently. Nikki couldn't help but notice his actions. There was something so eerie about him. Then it hit her! In that second she knew it was the one missing link that she had been searching for, the one thing that tied it all together. It was the emerald green Mont Blanc pen! The Master! Only The Master had a special pen like this. It all made sense. He loved computers. Burgess The Master? Oh my God . . . my mother!

This was the moment Burgess was waiting for. He knew she'd figure it out and become so thrown that he could make his move. From his pocket he took the gun that he had slipped in when he went to the credenza.

Nikki was face-to-face with the barrel.

At that moment they both knew everything. No more mysteries.

Was this the way she was going to die? thought Nikki. Did all those childhood nightmares come down to this moment? Why did I have to take matters into my own hands?

She tried to talk to him but that choking in her throat started, the fidgeting started, as if she were six.

Fight it! C'mon girl. Fight! Nikki told herself.

Burgess's eyes were now ablaze and the smile on his face was pure evil.

"Go ahead, ask me," he growled.

Nikki opened her mouth. Nothing came out.

"It's Daddy's little girl trying to speak. The Master knows you. You're a whore just like your mommy."

She knew then and there that he was her father, and she was gagging at the thought of their computer sex games. But she knew she had to be tough.

"You killed her, didn't you?" asked Nikki with a sudden bravery, taking a chance he might admit everything. She spat out the words.

"She was a whore, I told you that," snapped Burgess. "She didn't want me anymore, but she wanted everybody else. She had to die."

Nikki didn't have a clue as to what he would do next.

"But there's only your word; there's no evidence."

"No, my partner knows, and the FBI and the media."

He was moving closer to her.

She was getting more and more terrified and decided to try another tack. "But I'm your daughter. You wouldn't shoot your own daughter . . . you'd fuck her, but you wouldn't shoot her, would you? What would the other Justices have to say about that?"

He lunged toward her, his body smashing up against the computers. His teeth were so close to her ear that she thought he was going to bite it.

Instead he grabbed her and violently threw her toward the back door, the gun pressed against her throat.

Nikki was twisting and turning, doing everything she could to get away from the barrel of that gun. She grabbed at it with all her might, trying to throw him off balance, the two of them struggling to the floor. His sweat was leaving stains all over her, his grunting disgusting. He jumped, trying to put his full weight on her as Nikki felt the gun getting closer to her temple.

"Hold it right there!" the voice screamed from the doorway. "Drop it!"

Nikki looked up to see Hayden and three policemen rushing through the door. She could feel the indecision in Burgess's body. Her eyes met his. For an instant she thought he was going to kill himself, but in seconds he had crumpled on top of her, releasing the gun and wailing like a hunted animal. It was a sound she would never forget.

The rest of the early evening was a blur for Nikki. She had a vague recollection of Burgess covering his face with his coat as he was cuffed and carried away. She could remember the ice-cold white of the toilet bowl pressed against her forehead when she could throw up no longer. She remembered Hayden's arms holding her for the longest time while she cried. She heard bells ringing and realized that the phone in the living room was ringing every minute and a half with questions from reporters.

When she woke up for sure, she walked into the living room and saw Hayden turn off the TV set.

"No, don't. I want to see it," said Nikki.

"Are you sure? It isn't pretty."

"It wasn't pretty living it."

It was on every channel. They tuned in to CNN. It was being heralded as the biggest scandal in Washington since Watergate. She saw President Allingham give a statement saying that even though he had appointed Burgess, he certainly wasn't responsible for his past. Allingham said that he had always been satisfied with the research job his associates had done on Burgess, that he had faith in his staff, but perhaps that faith was not well-placed. He had not been well-served and he would replace his entire judicial advisory group immediately. He would endeavor to announce a new nominee for the court as soon as his new staff was in order.

"The implications of this are so wide-reaching," said Nikki. "Look, now the presidency is in danger."

"Wait, here comes Charles Wiseman. It gets better," said Hayden.

"On behalf of the United States Supreme Court, the Justices and I want to extend our sympathy to Nikki Easterly and her family. We are horrified by the actions that took place at our offices today. At no time did we ever receive any information detrimental to the character of Eric Burgess. It is not our job to appoint or advise. We accept the recommendations of the President and Congress. We assume they have done their jobs. Your Court will continue to work faithfully to uphold the laws of the land."

"Unbelievable," said Nikki.

"Yes, and you have calls from Allingham and Wiseman, as well as half the Western world," said Hayden.

"Is Mark okay?" asked a concerned Nikki.

"He's fine. He's just worried about you. I told him you were handling it."

"He'll be my only call for now."

"You also have calls from Larry King, who said he met you at the Prime Rib with Mark, Diane Sawyer, Jane Pauley, Dan Rather, and Barbara Walters. And more importantly, Dr. Stanley called."

Nikki shook her head and reached for Hayden.

"Just hold me," she said, and she started to cry again.

After the gentle crying subsided, she asked Hayden, "So where is he? What's happening?"

"You mean Burgess of course?"

"Right."

"Well, he isn't making any statements, they have him in the prison hospital on a suicide watch. He's been charged with murder, conspiracy to defraud the government, attempted murder on you, carrying an unregistered, concealed firearm, just about everything you can think of. Lawyers are swarming around him like vultures to represent him. The word on the street is that it's between F. Lee Bailey and Johnnie Cochran."

"Perfect. They all deserve each other," said Nikki.

"He'll plead temporary insanity to all of it," said Hayden.

"I can't bear the thought of having to face him at a trial. I want this to end, and it's only beginning. I'll never be left alone now."

Their attention went back to the TV.

"We interrupt this newscast to bring you a special live feed from the office of Senator Robert Dollinger."

Nikki and Hayden watched as the face of Dollinger, an opportunistic politician par excellence, came on the screen.

"I have called an emergency meeting of the heads of all the Senate committees, and we have voted to call for the appointment of a special prosecutor to investigate the President, his judicial advisers, and all the members of the U.S. Supreme Court. Never in the history of our country have we been so badly embarrassed around the world. From the top down, the White House has made a shambles of our American ethics and it makes me sick. Starting tomorrow morning we will open the Senate to a full vote and I am confident a special prosecutor will be appointed. I assure you, ladies and gentlemen of the United States, we will get to the bottom of this and fix it. Thank you for your time."

"I'm surprised he didn't announce his candidacy at the end," said Nikki. "But frankly, how could something like this happen? What's the matter with Allingham? It was clear that Burgess was his boy."

"I'm sure it was just some political greasing of the wheel. Nothing out of the ordinary. But maybe some good can come out of this and perhaps people will pay closer attention to research and background in the future," said Hayden. "Right now I just care about you and how you feel."

Three thousand miles away Joely sat wide-eyed in front of CNN. She dialed Nikki at the Willard as fast as her fingers could fly.

"Is this Hayden?" asked Joely when a male voice answered the phone.

"This is Hayden Chou. May I help you?" he said, not recognizing her voice.

"For heaven's sake—it's Joely."

"I'm sorry, but if you knew the people who've been calling here unannounced," said Hayden.

"Ooo, tell me, I bet it's been amazing."

"I'll let Nikki tell you, here she is."

"Joely, hi. I'm sort of in a daze. This is all too much for me."

"But I'm sure Hayden is helping," teased Joely. "Are you two staying in the same room?"

"You're unbelievable. Is that all you can think about?"

"Well, you've got to have some good news in all of this, now haven't you? I only have your best interest at heart," explained Joely.

The ringing of the phone woke Mark up. He had thought he told the hospital to hold his calls.

"Hello," he answered weakly.

"It's Ana. I had to get through to you. Are you all right?"

"I've had better times, but they tell me I'm going to make it."

"I'm so happy for you, Mark. I'm going to make it, too," said Ana.

"What do you mean?"

"I've told Phillipe he can never see me, call me, or ever be in my life again. He knows if he tries anything, I'll go to the police. I have enough on him."

"Aren't you afraid for your safety?"

"No. We both know I'm really of no use to him anymore. I'm sure he has others who are more valuable. I want a different life. I'm putting my house up for sale and moving somewhere, I'm not sure where yet. He knows I want a new life. I have enough money to live well. I feel good about what I'm doing and I just wanted to find out that you were going to be all right and tell you goodbye."

"But where will you go? Do you have any idea?"

"Maybe Aspen, maybe Hawaii, who knows?"

"I'd like you to let me know where you are, Ana. Would you do that please?" asked Mark.

Ana paused, thinking that this was not the response she

expected—what a pleasant surprise. "Yes, Mark. I'll call you. Stay well."

Eric Burgess looked up at the ceiling of his high-security cell. For the first forty-eight hours of his confinement he was on a suicide watch with no privacy. He couldn't bear to be embarrassed further by breaking down in front of people. As soon as he was placed in the police car, his cover personality took over. He was haughty, imperious, disdainful of the officers, but most of all he never let anything show. For forty-eight hours he successfully blocked out what had happened. He was Eric Burgess, a Justice of the Supreme Court of the United States. Who was this Eddie Brinkley anyway? Someone who died a long time ago. Eric Burgess was a star, in many ways a bigger one that Lauren, he thought. He had real power. His word could change laws and dictate how Americans behaved.

He had been transferred to this new cell just two hours ago. He liked it better because he was alone. In fact, he soon realized that he was the only one on the cell block. Must be some sort of special privilege, he thought. Good. They were treating him right. He didn't deserve to be in here. What he had done to Lauren was justified. She had asked for it. What else did she expect?

"Burgess?" said the guard walking down the corridor.

"What?" he answered testily.

"I've got a present for you. Here, take a look at this, Mr. High and Mighty."

The guard pushed a TV set in front of the cell. It was too far away for Burgess to get to any of the controls.

"I'll just leave it on CNN for you."

"Why thank you, cable in prison, how nice," he answered sarcastically.

"My pleasure, you animal."

Burgess focused his attention on the screen. It was a story about foreign aid, a subject he always considered boring. *Oh, well, I haven't anything else to do,* he thought.

"Stay tuned for tonight's thirty-minute special, 'Downfall of a Judicial Pervert,' our continuing coverage of the case of Eric Burgess, arrested for the sex murder of movie star Lauren Laverty."

Burgess's eyes bugged out in his head as the program opened with shots of newspaper headlines: "The Murdering Justice," "Justice of Death," "From Justice to Star-Killer," with the voice-over of the announcer saying that this could be the scandal of all scandals.

"Turn this off!" screamed Burgess. "Guard!"

No one came. He couldn't tune out anything. He saw Allingham, he saw Wiseman, he saw clips of Lauren, Fresh Love commercials, clips of his speeches. The press had even found his adoptive mother.

"No! Stop!" he shouted, pounding his head into the wall to make it all go away. His head felt like it was going to burst, but he wanted the pain . . . anything to keep from experiencing what was happening to him. He couldn't stop looking at the set and his face splashed across it.

His head jerked back involuntarily and he raised his hands to his temples. This was a different kind of pain. He felt himself losing consciousness. He never knew when he hit the floor.

Nikki was seated in the living room of the suite, the police having just left.

"When can we go home, Hayden?" asked Nikki, sipping from her fourth cup of English Breakfast tea.

"Your meeting with the police went well and they should have everything they need by now. You won't be needed back here until the trial. As far as Mark is concerned, he has given you his blessing to go. He'll be home in three weeks anyway."

Hayden got up from his chair and sat next to her on the couch. "I think we should disappear for a while. How'd you like to drive across the country, just stopping wherever we want. Let's get a big change of scenery, away from sophisticated cities. The bad things are over. Isn't it time for us, now? There can be an us, can't there, Nikki? That's what I want so much. Tell me how you feel. I need to know."

"Feelings are all I've been dealing with the past three days. Everything's been bubbling up inside me. I think I've been closed up for so long, I'm afraid. Now I know what it's like to have your nightmares come true."

"But you've only had one nightmare, isn't that right?" said Hayden.

"Right," answered Nikki. "So supposedly my problems are behind me."

"That's how I see it. Blue skies ahead."

"It's going to take some time, you know."

"I know that. I have all the time in the world for you," he said.

"I'm still going to get scared from time to time."

"I'll be there. Oh, Nikki, I'm so happy." He reached to kiss her.

The phone rang.

"Hello," said Hayden, quite annoyed. "What is it now? What! How bad? Interesting. Thanks for letting us know."

"What is it?" asked Nikki, alarmed. "Is it Mark?"

"No, no. It's Burgess. He's just had a massive stroke. He's almost totally paralyzed."

"His mind is clear?" asked Nikki.

"Yes, apparently he's conscious and he's not terminal."

"You mean he could go on like that indefinitely?" asked Nikki.

"Probably," answered Hayden, thinking exactly what Nikki was.

"God does work his little miracles, doesn't he?" said Nikki.

Standing up immediately, Nikki said, "Hayden, there's something I have to do before we leave."

"Okay."

"I've got to see Burgess one last time."

"Oh, Nikki, no. Let it go."

"No, I won't. I can't. I'm going to call the police myself. I have to do this, Hayden. Please understand."

Nikki approached the door of Room 112 of the prison hospital alone. There was a guard stationed at either end of the floor, but no one directly in front of Burgess's door. She supposed it wasn't necessary to have a guard directly at his door, since he was paralyzed and could move only his right eyelid, or so she was told. Still, she was nervous when she went to open the door. What if this were just another game? What if he was going to leap up with that horrendous grin on his face when she entered the room?

Gathering her strength, she pushed the door open, slowly putting one foot in front of the other. The first thing she saw was the end of the bed with a chart hanging from it. As the door opened further, it revealed a large lump of a body in bed, with tubes coming out of it. The sound of a respirator filled the room.

Walking closer to the bed she saw those eyes staring at her. They were as bright and cold as she remembered them. They were jerking around in excitement, sending out so much energy that for one second her fear overtook her again. Then she focused on the fact that one side of his face was listing. The left eyelid was sagging a bit, and there was some drool on his chin.

What were those eyes trying to say to her? Did he want

her to kill him? Did he still want to kill her? To save him from this horrible prison he was trapped in for the rest of his life? Did he want to apologize to her?

"Hello, Eric," said Nikki, matter-of-factly, standing close to him at the side of the bed. How easily she could have touched him. "I just had to see for myself. You don't mind, do you? I wanted to see what happens to a murderer, an emotional rapist, and a pathological liar."

Eric's eyes went to steel and were very, very still.

"I wonder which one of your qualities I inherited? Certainly I couldn't have gotten anything from experience or environment. You saw to that. You took both parents away from me. You tried to destroy my childhood, and then you tried to destroy me."

Nikki paused a second and then leaned in. Not only did she want him to hear every word, to feel her anger and intensity, but she wanted him to smell Fresh Love one more time.

"Well, I did get something from you, whether you like it or not. I got your determination and your strength. That strength won't save you now. It will save me, but that strength inside of your body will drive you crazy. You have no more outlets for it. It is your punishment and it is my savior."

She pulled back and let her words sink in, buoyed by how good it made her feel to finally express herself after all these years. There were no more lies now.

"You really hurt me. You made me an orphan. You can't imagine the pain and the fear that I've had to live with. You made me feel like there was something wrong with me. And now I have to live with the knowledge that my father murdered my mother and played sick games with me. But I'm not going to play victim anymore. I'll deal with these things and go on. You know, Mother would have been proud of me at this moment, and if you had channeled your passion earlier in beneficial areas, who knows, maybe she would have loved being married to a Supreme Court Justice. You could have had it all. You could have had a wife who loved you, and a daughter who idolized you . . . What's that? A little tear on your face? No, it couldn't be. The Master is always in control. Well this time, I am. In a strange way you've given me back my life and I promise you, Daddy, I'm going to finally start living it."

Nikki just stood there, hands on hips, and looked at him. She saw all her past tragedies lying there in that bed. She turned away and walked toward her future.

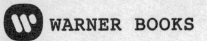